DIE OF
SHAME

Also by Mark Billingham

The DI Tom Thorne series
Sleepyhead
Scaredy Cat
Lazybones
The Burning Girl
Lifeless
Buried
Death Message
Bloodline
From the Dead
The Demands (*published as* Good as Dead
in the United Kingdom)
The Dying Hours
The Bones Beneath
Time of Death

Other fiction
In the Dark
Rush of Blood

MARK BILLINGHAM

DIE OF SHAME

Atlantic Monthly Press
New York

First published in Great Britain in 2016 by Little, Brown

First published by Grove Atlantic, June 2016

Printed in the United States of America

ISBN 978-0-8021-2525-5
eISBN 978-0-8021-9036-9

Atlantic Monthly Press
an imprint of Grove Atlantic
154 West 14th Street
New York, NY 10011

Distributed by Publishers Group West

groveatlantic.com

16 17 18 19   10 9 8 7 6 5 4 3 2 1

To my friend, Michael.
For showing me, every day, what recovery really means.

If a way to the Better there be, it exacts a full look at the Worst.

THOMAS HARDY

PROLOGUE

THE VISITOR

THE FINAL VISIT

'I didn't think you were coming back,' the prisoner says. He had begun to roll a cigarette as soon as he'd sat down and now he licks the edge of the paper, his eyes fixed on the person in the chair opposite.

'I had a lot of running around to do.'

'Yeah?'

'A bit of detective work, after what you said last time.'

He is trying hard not to look nervous, or even particularly interested, struggling to remember exactly what he said all those weeks before. What he might have given away. He says, 'It's rubbish, isn't it? Everything you put in that first letter. The reason you've been coming.'

'Sorry about that.'

He slaps his hand on the table, but not in anger. He's just pleased to have been proved right. 'I knew it.'

'What do you care? You'll be out soon enough.'

'Yeah, I knew it first time I saw you.'

'Really?'

'You don't look like a student.'

'What do I look like?'

He shrugs, roll-up complete. 'Well, you're obviously some kind of nutter.'

The visitor nods. 'I can't really argue with that. Some kind.'

'So you know, if I see you once I'm out, I won't be quite so friendly.'

'There's no danger of that.'

'Just as long as we're clear.'

'I mean, we know all about that famous temper of yours, don't we?' A smile. 'The only reason I came back at all was to say thank you.'

'For what?'

'For giving me what I needed. For putting me on the right track.'

Now he doesn't much care whether he looks nervous or not. All these years saying nothing; not even *then*, after it had happened.

He hadn't let something slip, had he?

No, he can't have been that stupid.

He sits up straight and lays his hands flat on the table. He says, 'You hear stories inside about people like you.'

'Really? What kind of people is that?'

'People who get off on all this. Who just like being close to it.' Now, he leans forward, confident that he's hit a nerve. That he's back in charge. 'All this shit you've been giving me, all those questions, and I reckon you just want to know what it's like.'

'What it's like?'

'To kill someone.'

The visitor's face breaks into a grin. 'Oh, I wouldn't worry too much about that. I'll know for myself soon enough.'

PART ONE

THE BROKEN CIRCLE

THERE AND THEN

Tony De Silva stands and watches Robin and Heather drinking coffee decanted from the large vacuum flask he lays on every week. They're chatting easily and, as usual, Robin is helping himself to the lion's share of the biscuits. Tony decides that he will need to speak to him about that. Diana is a few feet away, looking out into the garden and cradling a mug of herbal tea, while Chris is already sitting down, his thumbs working at the screen of his smartphone. Tony strolls across and glances over Chris's shoulder to check that he is not playing any sort of combat game, which, for him, would not be permissible.

The use of phones will not be allowed once they get started.

Tony checks his watch. Six o'clock and it has been dark for an hour already, but outside the conservatory window the garden lights show up a scattering of frost on the lawn and across the bare, black beds.

'Looks like she's bottled it,' Chris says, well aware that Tony is behind him, keeping an eye on what he is doing.

'We'll give it another minute or two,' Tony says.

'You're the boss.'

Tony takes a swig from a small bottle of mineral water. He says, 'Wrong word.'

It's useful, he thinks, this ten or fifteen minutes before they begin. There are never any breaks during the session itself, so it's good to get the small talk and light refreshments out of the way. It's usually when toilet visits are made – to the downstairs cloakroom only, of course – and it gets conversation started, which he believes always make the session itself go better.

Diana turns from the window and smiles at him. She still likes to keep herself to herself in these informal moments, though she seems a little less anxious in the circle these days, which Tony is pleased about. On the other side of the conservatory, Heather says something which makes Robin laugh, and he spits crumbs which Heather stoops to gather up with her hands.

'We should probably sit down,' Tony says.

He tries to place the melody that's drifting down from upstairs, watching as Robin, Heather and Diana put their mugs back on the trolley and move across to take their seats in the circle. The chairs are identical, but each of them sits in the same position every week, their territory chosen early on and now carefully protected. Tony takes his usual seat, hangs his jacket over the back of it and looks across at the single unoccupied position in the circle.

'Shall I close it up?' Heather asks.

It's what they normally do, if there's a no-show. Better a smaller circle than an empty chair. Tony nods and Heather is pushing the chair towards the wall when the doorbell rings. She says, 'Sod's law,' and starts to drag it back into the circle again.

'Bang on the hour,' Chris says. 'This one's clearly got a *major* thing about punctuality.'

Tony stands up, walks quickly out through the kitchen and opens the front door to a woman who looks much as he expected, having spoken to her on the phone a few days before. She tells him who she is anyway, and they shake hands before he leads her inside and through into the conservatory.

Everyone except Chris watches her come in.

Tony takes the new arrival's coat and points out her seat. As she lowers herself into it, Diana and Robin, who are seated on either side of her, subtly shift their chairs away; just an inch or two.

'Welcome,' Tony says.

There are nods and smiles, murmured acknowledgements from most of those in the circle. The newcomer nods and smiles back, if a little nervously.

'Let's get the formalities out of the way,' Tony says. He looks towards the eldest member of the group, a man wearing a suit with an open-necked striped shirt. 'Introductions?'

'I'm Robin,' the man says. He smiles at the newcomer then looks to his left.

'Heather ...'

'You already know my name,' Tony says. 'But, once again, welcome.' He looks to the next chair, but Chris is staring into space, as though completely uninterested in proceedings. Tony waits a few seconds. 'Chris?'

'Oh for heaven's sake.' The woman to Chris's left shakes her head and turns to her new neighbour. 'I'm Diana,' she says. 'And if you want some early advice, you're best ignoring him. Some of us are rather more needy than others.'

'Somebody talking about me?' Chris says. He produces a radiant smile and turns it towards the newest member. 'My name's Chris.' He sits back, laces his fingers behind his head. 'Tennis pro, male model and part-time racing driver.'

'You're leaving "rent boy" off the CV these days, then?' Heather says.

Robin laughs, low and hoarse.

Chris beams and casually gives Heather the finger.

Tony waits.

When the woman opposite him realises that it's her turn, she sits forward. 'Caroline,' she says. A nervous laugh. 'I hope I can remember everyone's name.'

9

The names will come quickly enough, Tony knows, but getting to trust and understand these men and women with whom she has one crucial thing in common will be a longer and far more difficult process.

A respected doctor in his early sixties, with a history of addiction to a variety of easily available medications. A thirty-two-year-old woman once addicted to drugs and gambling. A young gay man, living in a series of hostels and shelters, his drug dependency now replaced by an addiction to computer games and online pornography. A well-heeled housewife who had drifted into alcoholism as her domestic life had disintegrated and now shops compulsively instead of reaching for a bottle of wine at breakfast.

There are many different roads to recovery.

'Right.' Tony reaches beneath his chair for a laminated sheet of paper and passes it to his left. 'Will you do the honours in a minute, Chris?'

Chris snatches the sheet.

Tony looks at Caroline. 'This is what's called a "slow open" group, OK? Meaning that I can bring new clients into the circle as and when, and therefore some members will have been part of the group a lot longer than others. Some have been in recovery much longer than others.' He looks to Heather first.

'I've been clean for nearly two and a half years,' she says. She looks to her right.

'Four years,' Robin nods, 'seven months and twenty-two days.'

Diana says, 'I haven't had a drink in nine weeks.'

They all wait for Chris. He grins, wolfish, and says, 'Well, it depends which time you're talking about.'

Tony shakes his head, having heard the same line from Chris the last time a newcomer was welcomed. He looks at Caroline again. 'We're here to work on a range of recovery skills and to offer relapse prevention support, and whether you've been coming three months or five minutes, everyone in the group has equal status and equal rights and is equally protected.' He nods at Chris.

Chris has clearly given the same spiel before or heard others do it. He does not need to look at what is printed on the sheet and speaks in a monotone, like a call-centre operative trotting out a compulsory legal declaration. 'This circle is a safe place. It cannot be broken or violated and that which is discussed within it should never be taken outside.' He puffs out his cheeks to demonstrate his boredom. 'Confidentiality is the fundamental principle that underpins these sessions and the only exceptions to this are where the revelation of a serious crime is made or where it is felt that a member intends to harm themselves or others. Then, the therapist is ethically bound to reveal only such information as is necessary. Blah blah blah.' Without looking, he holds out the sheet for Tony to take.

'Thanks, Chris.' Tony looks at Caroline. 'All good?'

She nods, looks around the circle. 'Everyone seems really ... different, which is good.'

'It's *really* good,' Heather says.

'So what's everyone's ... ? Am I allowed to ask?'

'Ask anything you like,' Tony says.

Caroline nods again, then, distracted, looks upwards. 'Who's playing the piano?'

Tony stares at her, takes a few seconds. 'I'm wondering why you would want to know that?'

'Is it your wife? Girlfriend?' She waits, but gets no answer. 'You don't want to tell me, that's fine.'

'Well ... by not answering the question, I just think I'm more likely to find something out about you.'

She shrugs, like she isn't bothered, then grins. 'Is it your gay lover?'

Tony sits back. 'See what I mean?'

'Boom!' Chris shakes his hand in the air, flicking the fingers against one another, like the black teenager he isn't. 'One nil.'

Caroline looks at him, unable to mask her irritation. 'Sorry?'

'It's not a game,' Tony says. 'And nobody's keeping score.'

'You can't mess with Tony,' Chris says. 'He's too good.'

'I took everything I could get my hands on,' Robin says, suddenly. 'To answer your initial question. And I'm a doctor, so I could get my hands on almost anything I fancied. Diazepam, morphine, pethidine. Fentanyl was a particular favourite.'

'Vodka and white wine for me,' Diana says. 'Though it was more or less whatever was going to get me pissed by the end. Actually, by the end, I wasn't getting pissed at all and that was the problem.'

'What about you?' Heather asks. She looks at Caroline.

'Oh, please!' Chris leans forward. 'It's not like you need to be Sherlock Holmes, is it? Look at her.'

'You are such a twat,' Heather says.

'I'm used to it,' Caroline says. 'Doesn't bother me.'

'That's good,' Tony says.

'Yes . . . I had a problem with compulsive overeating. I've always had . . . issues with food, with weight. Then, when the knees started to give out, I got hooked on painkillers. So . . .'

'Right,' Chris says. 'But it's really all about why your knees gave out, isn't it? Your basic addiction is to cake at the end of the day. Eating all the pies.'

'That's correct,' Caroline says. 'Wow, are you a therapist as well?'

Robin looks to Heather, then to Tony. 'I'm not sure he actually understands what the word "support" means.'

Tony has already turned to address Chris. 'I'm wondering why you're feeling the need to attack Caroline like this.'

If Chris is listening, he shows no sign of giving a toss. 'Truth is it's a bit of a pussy-arsed addiction, isn't it? Food. Not even sure it *is* an addiction, not a proper one.'

'You know the rules,' Tony says. 'If someone says they're an addict, they're an addict. Simple as that.'

Chris ignores him. 'It's all a bit amateur-hour though, don't you reckon?' His voice gets higher, camper as he talks faster and grows more animated. 'I mean, you have to eat food, don't you? You don't have to shoot up smack or guzzle gin, and let's be honest, a few extra helpings isn't going to kill anyone, is it?'

12

'Have you any idea what damage obesity can do?' Robin asks. 'Are you a complete idiot or just pretending?'

Still, Chris isn't listening. 'Sorry, I just think it's a bit of a joke, that's all. Weightwatchers, love, that's where you should be.' He looks around the room, ready with his killer punchline. 'I'd go as far as to say our newbie's a bit of a lightweight, except she'd think I was taking the piss.'

Caroline stares at her shoes, and save for the hiss of Chris sucking his teeth, unhappy with the reaction to his wit and repartee, the group falls silent. Tony waits, in accordance with the rule he'd learned years before, when he was sitting in a circle himself. The therapist will never to be the one to break a group silence.

After a minute or so, it's Diana who says, 'Perhaps we should start again.'

'Good idea,' Tony says. 'We got a bit sidetracked, I think. So ... everyone had a good week?'

Nods and grunted yesses. Five of the six in the circle know what the question really means. Caroline will catch on quickly enough.

'Good,' Tony says. 'Now, I wanted to raise an issue I've already spoken to Caroline about on the phone.'

'This shame business,' Caroline says.

'Right.'

'Shame?' Heather says. 'What about it?'

'I think we should start discussing it, opening up a little about what it is we're all ashamed of.'

'Who says we're ashamed about anything?' Chris asks.

'Of course we are,' Robin says. 'I think it sounds like a good idea. We talked about this a lot at Highfields.'

Highfields House is a residential rehab in which Robin has spent some time; a place from which many of Tony's clients have come in recent years. Others in the group have come to recovery via a very different route and Chris is one of them. He groans. 'Don't start with all that twelve-step rubbish again.'

'It's helpful,' Robin says.

'To you, maybe.'

'I'm game,' Diana says.

'Good.' Tony undoes a button on his shirt. The underfloor heating is cranked up a little high and it's starting to get warm in the conservatory. 'I think it will be helpful,' he says. 'I really believe that shame is at the root of a great many addictions.' He looks around, mindful as always of making eye contact, where possible, with each member of the group whenever he can. 'Shame about something we did. Shame about something that was done to us. I think that facing up to that shame and taking away the power it holds over us is a key recovery tool.'

'I'm ashamed that I was a junkie and an alcoholic,' Heather says. 'Simple as that. Same as most of us, probably.' Next to her, Robin nods enthusiastically. 'I reckon anyone who's half decent would be ashamed of that, right? I'm ashamed that I stole and lied all the time. I'm ashamed that I shat on people who cared about me.'

'That's all really positive,' Tony says. 'But I'm talking about the shame that drove you towards substance abuse to begin with.'

Heather opens her mouth and closes it again.

'Look, I'm not suggesting we dive straight into this, but I'd like us all to be thinking about it over the coming week and then maybe we can talk about it a bit more at the next session.'

'Who's going to go first?' Caroline seems anxious.

'Don't worry, it probably shouldn't be you,' Diana says. 'Not unless you want to. You've only just joined, so . . .'

'Well, don't look at me,' Chris says.

'Nobody was,' Heather says. 'Sorry, *darling*.'

'I'll go first.' Robin blushes slightly as all eyes turn to him. 'Well, somebody has to kick things off, don't they?'

'Thanks, Robin.' Tony scribbles something in the notebook he keeps on his lap. 'Like I say, think about it and we'll see how it goes. It's not a regime, it's just a suggestion.'

'Can I say something about the "here and now"?' Diana asks.

Tony nods, suppressing a smile. Whenever possible he tries to guide his clients from the 'there and then' to the 'here and now': to talk about the way things are in the present; their current lives as former addicts. Diana is, in many ways, a model client and is always keen to prove it. She has a noticeable habit of parroting Tony's favourite phrases and buzzwords back at him.

'Well, allowing for the fact that by "here and now" I mean yesterday, there was an incident in the supermarket I'd like to talk about, if everyone's OK with that.'

Heather, Caroline and Robin say that they are. Chris slaps his hand to his chest and says, 'Oh my God, had Waitrose run out of mangoes again?'

'My friend called me when I was in there,' Diana says, ignoring him. 'She was the one who first told me what my husband was up to. She'd seen him in a restaurant with his little bit on the side, you know?' Her mouth tightens briefly. 'Anyway . . . it must just have been that association or whatever it was. Like a sense memory or something, because without choosing to, I suddenly found myself standing in the aisle with all the booze . . . '

... THEN

Caroline, Heather and Diana walk up to Muswell Hill Broadway. Caroline had suggested the Starbucks nearby, but to her great surprise the other two told her they always went to the pub after a session, and clearly, sticking to a routine is important to them. 'There are some groups where you'd never be allowed to go somewhere "wet",' Heather said. 'The pub, I mean. Tony's a bit more relaxed about that kind of thing, as long as there's more than one of us.'

'I could never go into a pub on my own,' Diana had said.

Even though she's the only one with no history of alcohol abuse, and despite the others declaring that they have no problem if she wants a glass of wine or whatever, Caroline insists on buying a round of soft drinks.

'I know how I feel sometimes, if I'm watching someone putting a massive plate of fish and chips away,' she says.

They sit around a small table in the corner. Heather points out a bigger one, tells Caroline that's where they usually sit, if it's free and the whole group have come along. 'Robin and Chris come most of the time,' she says. 'Robin a bit more than Chris, probably.' Fifteen minutes earlier, leaving Tony's house, Robin had apologised and told them that he had an appointment, while Chris had jammed earbuds in and walked quickly away, clearly not in the mood for socialising.

'Yeah, what's his problem anyway?' Caroline asks. 'Chris.'

Heather rolls her eyes and looks at Diana. 'Bloody hell, where do we start?'

'You were right about him being needy,' Caroline says.

'He just wants attention all the time,' Heather says. 'Likes to show off.'

'Still no excuse for being rude though.' Diana tucks a strand of hair behind her ear. An expensive cut and dye job matches the high-end make-up which had been reapplied on the walk from Tony's. Her dove grey tracksuit, aside from being a fraction of the size, looks a damn sight more expensive than the one Caroline had bought at Sports Direct. 'Mind you, he would never admit to being an arsehole, he'd just say he was being "waspish".'

'He's gay, right?' Caroline asks.

'Oh yeah, very.'

'You just wait,' Heather says. 'A few sessions in and you'll be sick to death of hearing about Chris's bloody sex life. He likes to throw in as much graphic detail as possible, you know?'

'He thinks he's being shocking,' Diana says. She mimes an exaggerated yawn. 'All part of the attention thing. Actually, much as he gets on my tits, I think it's just a defence mechanism. You know, a wall he puts up.'

'He was just having a pop at you because you're new,' Heather says. 'Wanted to see if you could take it.'

Caroline sips her mineral water. 'I can look after myself. I've had plenty of it over the years.'

'Yeah, I bet,' Heather says.

The pub is getting busier, noisier, and Caroline has to lean in to make herself heard without raising her voice. 'Robin seems nice, though.'

'He is,' Diana says. 'He's very . . . keen.'

'So are you,' Heather says.

Diana reddens. 'You know what I mean. Like volunteering to go first with this whole shame thing.'

'Yeah, well.' Heather gives Diana a knowing look.

'Is that a South African accent he's got?' Caroline asks.

Heather nods. 'He came over when he was a teenager, I think. Went to university over here.'

'He *is* a doctor or he *was* a doctor?'

'He still is,' Diana says. 'But he stopped for a while.'

'What he was saying about how easy it was to get drugs?' Heather slowly stirs the ice in her drink with a straw as she speaks. 'When it got really bad he used to do this whole drug diversion thing, yeah? So, he'd give his patient a bit, find some excuse to leave the room, shoot a bit in his own arm then go back and give his patient the rest.' She sees the shock on Caroline's face. 'I know, sharing needles and all that, but it happens all the time according to Robin. With anaesthetists especially. Anyway, turns out he gave a few of his patients hepatitis C, which, you know, you can die from, and that was when he realised he needed to clean his act up.'

'He wasn't caught?'

'No, but he knew it was only a matter of time, so he took a "sabbatical" for a year and sorted his life out. Amazing, really.'

Diana nods her agreement. 'Robin's very passionate about being in recovery, very motivated. Still goes to a lot of meetings. NA and so on.'

'What about you?'

Diana shakes her head.

'Me neither,' Heather says. 'Just Tony's sessions. I meditate as well . . .'

Caroline thinks for a few seconds. 'What you were saying, about the moment Robin knew he needed to get clean or whatever? It was one particular photo for me. I couldn't bear to look at it. That and chucking down tramadol like they were Smarties.'

'Different for everyone, I suppose,' Diana says. 'There was one really bad week, I couldn't get the lid on the recycling bin. All the empties, you know?'

Heather lays a hand on top of Diana's, just for a second or two. 'I knew a junkie in rehab who decided to get clean when his mum died and the family wouldn't let him see the body.'

Caroline looks confused. 'Sorry, I don't . . . ?'

'They thought he might steal the jewellery they were laying her to rest with. Yeah . . . that's probably the worst one I've ever heard.'

'Jesus . . .'

Heather finishes what's left of her drink, then goes to the bar to get another round. She's short, thinner even than Diana, but there's little in the way of make-up and she has made no attempt to hide the smattering of grey in hair that is closely cropped. She wears skinny jeans and trainers, a sweatshirt under a bright orange puffa jacket.

'You got any kids?' Caroline asks.

'One,' Diana says. 'Grown up now, more or less.' She digs into her handbag for her phone. She stabs and scrolls, then leans forward to show Caroline a few pictures. 'She's in her second year at Exeter.'

'Empty nest,' Caroline says.

'Very.' For a few seconds Diana scratches at a stain on the table with a scarlet fingernail. 'What about you?'

'No, but I want to.'

'Well, you've got plenty of time.'

'Yeah.'

'What are you . . . thirty-something?'

'I'm twenty-seven.'

'Oh . . . sorry.'

'Doesn't matter, and you're right, I've got loads of time.'

Heather comes back with the drinks, muttering about the barman taking his time to serve her because she wasn't buying alcohol. She pushes Caroline's Diet Coke across, says, 'What were you two gassing about then?'

'Kids,' Caroline says. 'You got any?'

Heather blinks and hands Diana a glass. 'Always meant to, but it's hard isn't it, when the only meaningful relationship you've ever really had is with a chemical?' She sits down. 'It would be great, but you know, time's running out and buggered if I'm using a turkey baster.' She produces two packets of crisps from her pockets and tosses them on to the table. 'Hope you don't mind these. I'm starving.'

'Don't be daft,' Caroline says. 'You were fine about me having a drink if I wanted one.'

'Sure?'

'I think I can cope with people putting away a couple of bags of cheese and onion.'

Heather smiles, showing teeth that are far too straight and white to be natural. She tears open both bags of crisps lengthways and nudges one towards Diana.

Caroline watches them each digging in. 'I was thinking . . . bearing in mind that whole "what's said in the circle" thing, are we OK to talk about some of this stuff? You know, what you were saying about Chris and Robin.'

Diana grunts and quickly finishes chewing. 'Long as it's still within the group, it's fine, I think.' She looks to Heather. 'It's talking to outsiders about the group that's not allowed.'

'It's nothing Robin wouldn't happily tell you himself anyway,' Heather says.

Caroline nods. 'It's kind of like when they bend the rules in *Big Brother*, isn't it? You can't talk about the nominations to anyone else, you know, why you've nominated someone, but you can sort of talk . . . generally about them.'

'I've never seen it,' Diana says. 'It's a bit like experimenting on rats in a cage from what I've heard.'

Caroline laughs. 'Trust me, that session tonight made the *Big Brother* house look like happy families or something.'

'I thought it was all pretty relaxed tonight,' Heather says. 'Chris aside, obviously.'

'So, come on then, tell me about Big Brother.' Caroline grins and reaches across to take a handful of crisps.

'Tony?' Diana leans back, thinks about it. 'He's an interesting bloke, but he doesn't give a lot away. Well, you can't really, can you, doing what he does? They have to draw a line, I suppose, not allow their clients to get too close.' She turns to Heather again. 'You've been going the longest, what do you think?'

'His family's from Sri Lanka,' Heather says. 'But he was brought up in Scotland, I mean you can hear that, right? I know he used to be a bit of a songwriter, might still be for all I know. That's what the piano's about.'

'We still don't know who's playing it though, do we?' Caroline says.

'Well, we do know he's married, or has a girlfriend. We saw her once, when she came into the kitchen, didn't we?' Diana nods. 'I don't think Tony was best pleased, remember?'

'He went a bit quiet,' Diana says.

'There's a bit of stuff on Google if you want to have a look, but not much. The various therapy associations he's a member of, all that.' Heather nods. 'I did find one of his songs on YouTube once.'

'Was it any good?' Caroline asks.

'All right, I suppose.'

'Oh, I quite liked it,' Diana says.

Heather pulls a face. 'It was too hippyish for me. A bit James Bluntish.'

'Is that rhyming slang?' Caroline says.

Diana spits mineral water on to the table, which makes Heather laugh even more than she has been. When she has stopped laughing, Heather says, 'You are going to fit right in . . .'

An hour later, watching Diana walk back to where she'd left her car, Caroline says, 'She did well, didn't she? That wobble she had in the supermarket, staying strong, or whatever you want to call it.'

Heather shrugs. 'We all have wobbles.'

'I suppose.'

Having established that they are heading in the same general direction, they turn and begin walking towards the bus stop.

'You know, people or places that set you off,' Heather says. 'Stress is one of the worst things, money problems or whatever. Or it can just be something bad happening.' Hearing the familiar rumble of a diesel engine, she turns to see a bus coming. 'Shit.' With the stop still fifty yards away she looks at Caroline, but it's clear that, for one of them at least, running to make the bus is never going to be an option.

'You go,' Caroline says.

'No, it's fine.'

They carry on walking, say nothing as the bus sails past them.

'Thanks,' Caroline says.

'It's fine, I don't mind waiting.'

'No, I mean for being nice. Saying I'd fit in and everything.'

'Well, you will.'

'Hope so.' Caroline smiles. 'I'm really looking forward to getting to know you.'

Heather hums, non-committal suddenly.

'What?'

'Probably not a very good idea.' Heather shakes her head, walks on with her head down. 'If you knew me, you really wouldn't like me.'

... THEN

The escort had not been the one whose picture he'd chosen, but it had happened before and this one was pretty enough, so he hadn't been overly bothered. He *had* been a little annoyed that, in the usual broken English, she'd demanded more money for a few of the things he'd wanted, especially as she'd specifically promoted those services on the agency's website. It always amused him that these things were advertised in code. Did people seriously think that CIM might stand for 'covered in mud' or that 'watersports' had anything at all to do with boats?

Once she has gone, Robin takes a shower; his second one in an hour, since the girl had insisted on him showering before they'd got down to business. Again, all pretty standard. He changes the sheets, as there seems little point in being clean and climbing into soiled linen later on. He microwaves a lasagne, and once he's eaten, he stretches out on the sofa in his dressing gown, listening to Duke Ellington and trying not to think about how much he would enjoy a large glass of red right about now.

A nice shot of fentanyl or methadone.

Tonight's session with Tony had gone well, he thinks. The new girl seems sweet enough and, lying there, he wonders how she might react if he were to have a quiet word in private with her, talk her through some medically approved weight-loss treatments he would be able to recommend. On reflection, it's probably not a good idea. She's almost certainly on one diet or another anyway, and if she took offence it could make future sessions a little tricky. He likes to get on well with everyone, however difficult that is sometimes.

He is feeling slightly anxious about having put himself forward for the shame session the following week. He was only trying to help Tony out, because he could see that nobody else was in any rush to volunteer. He tells himself to keep calm about it, that he's got a week to think about how best to tell the story, that it will all go OK. The other reason he'd spoken up was because he'd known it would irritate Chris, which was always rather fun. Poisonous little so-and-so doesn't like him, has a problem with the way Robin talks about his recovery. Chris is not a fan of the twelve-step approach, of the passion and the proselytising. Robin asks himself why he even gives someone like that a second thought. After all, you did whatever worked and stuff anyone else if they didn't like it. How could Robin be any other way, considering where he'd been and where he was now? How close he'd come to losing everything.

Not that there hadn't been a heavy price to pay.

He'd just about escaped with his career, but more or less everything else had gone. Almost thirty years married, his wife had known what was happening very early on of course and had made it clear that it was her or the drugs. Gave him a simple choice, unaware that it was a contest she couldn't win. It had been ugly and rancorous, but how could he have expected anything else?

They had already been through so much together.

He had been furious at the time, as the scale of his losses had started to become clear, but somewhere between the lines of those legal letters and in the pauses during those frosty phone conversations there was always the suspicion that his wife could send a letter to the

General Medical Council any time she felt like it, have him struck off in a heartbeat. So, in the end, he'd been left with little choice other than caving in to everything her hatchet-faced solicitor had demanded. Thankfully, he'd clung on to his job by the skin of his teeth and had salted just enough away for a one-bedroom flat in an area that wasn't completely hideous.

He'd made the best of it, started again.

He looks around. The place is clean and well laid out, it has everything he needs, but Christ, it's so pathetically small. He has nobody but himself to blame, of course, but he can't help remembering. He would be inhuman if he didn't miss his study, his garden, his dog.

It's a struggle sometimes, not to be bitter, even if that goes against everything he's learned and come to believe about recovery. He has always tried to abide by the programme, though in at least one respect he knows that he's cheated. Making amends to those you've hurt is a step that's important and it sounds so straightforward; seems so easy when it's just a heading on a blackboard or a flip chart. But he has still not been brave enough to check on those patients he'd infected. He's far too scared about what he might discover.

It had been a death that had tipped him over the edge; that still lured him back towards it every day of his life. Any more deaths would be impossible to live with.

Robin closes his eyes, and when he opens them again an hour later, the music has finished and he's breathing heavily, sweaty beneath his dressing gown. Climbing into bed, he can still taste the girl, can smell her perfume on the headboard, and he lies there wondering why he bothered changing the sheets.

... THEN

Group Session: February 16th

New client (Caroline) started this evening. Seems confident, though may of course be front to mask predictable anxiety. Held her ground against Chris, who was oddly aggressive. Will explore this more next week.

Others in the group supportive, as expected. Especially Robin and Heather.

Suspect that Chris is still struggling with secondary addiction(s). Same goes for Diana and shopping compulsion. Will need to monitor this carefully.

Robin has volunteered to begin exploration of shame/underlying cause of addiction at next session. Believe this will be very helpful. Others more reticent, but may be more willing once Robin has kicked things off. Firmly convinced this approach will yield good results. Hidden shame = guilt/ anxiety/maladaptive behaviour (sexual violence, compulsion, addiction). Important to establish empathy in supportive atmosphere of group.

READING FOR NEXT SESSION
Shame: The Dark Core of Addiction (Hughes, Larner)
Hidden Shame and Rehab (Psych Review 2011)

Tony closes the file on his computer and turns round in his chair to look at the large calendar on the wall above the bookshelves. The week ahead is a busy one. He's got two other group sessions with different clients, a number of one-to-ones and half a day at a residential centre in Sussex. It's not untypical, but he's already thinking ahead, to warmer weather and an altogether different few weeks.

In three months he'll be travelling across Europe; a ten-city tour, as 'lifestyle consultant' to a well-known musician he has worked with for several years. Everyone in the star's inner circle knows exactly why Tony is there, of course, but to everyone else he's just another member of the entourage, working alongside the dietitian, the nutritionist and the personal trainer. It means great food and five star pampering in a series of nice hotels and Tony would be being dishonest if he did not admit that it was something to look forward to after a series of sessions in grim hospitals and underfunded residential centres.

That's not to say working closely with such a client, making sure he stays clean and sober for as long as he's on the road, is without its problems. Being on call twenty-four hours a day – ready to step in if there's a problem, or if the client just wants someone to talk to – can be exhausting. It has also brought him some unwelcome attention over the years. His name has been linked with a number of celebrities online and this has led to frequent calls from journalists as well as more upfront questions from several of his own clients.

Come on, Tony, is it really you know who? What's he really like? I bet you get up to all sorts on those tours ...

Tony says nothing; neither confirms nor denies. He could dine out for months on some of the stories he's able to tell, but breathing so much as a word would mean the end of a very lucrative gig.

The money's important to him. The self-esteem that's so very much tied up with it.

He gets up, closes the door behind him and walks up one flight to Emma's room at the top of the house. The music is loud enough to drown out the noise of his footsteps on the stairs, but he doesn't need to go in. The stench is incredible.

Walking back down to the ground floor, he remembers a night in Toronto a couple of years before. Sitting on the floor of a penthouse suite in the early hours, playing a borrowed guitar while a bored, insomniac, platinum-selling pop star sang one of *his* songs. Mangling his lyrics, but still . . .

A sliver of moon that bleeds through the blind,
Cannot light up the darkness in his mind,
A past unnatural and people unkind,
It's time to leave the world behind.

Just for a second, he thinks about going to the piano in the first floor sitting room and playing the song himself, seeing how well he can remember it. He decides that it's probably a bit late.

This is pretty good, mate. No, really. You should have stuck at it . . .

The memory quickly dissolves as he walks into the kitchen and sees Nina sitting at the breakfast bar. She has a large glass of white wine in her hand and her stockinged feet are up on an adjacent barstool. She's slowly turning the pages of a newspaper, keeping one eye on the TV screen that's built into the door of the stupidly expensive fridge she insisted on buying.

'You eaten?' he asks. When she doesn't reply, he picks up the TV remote and turns the volume down. He notices the spasm of irritation on her face just before he asks again.

'I got something on the way home,' she says.

It's after nine, but Tony is used to his wife getting back late. She often has to entertain clients or go for dinner with other execs at the ad agency. There are night shoots and awards ceremonies, movie premieres sometimes. Now and again she asks Tony if he wants to go with her, but he always says no. He thinks that knowing he won't want to is the only reason she asks in the first place.

He opens the fridge, peers in.

'How was your session?'

'Yeah, fine,' he says. There are some bits of salad, lots of jars; pickles and preserves. He pulls out a pizza that is probably meant for their daughter, but which she will never eat. 'Went well.'

'Good. So, how was your girlfriend?'

Tony turns, lets the fridge door close behind him. 'What?'

'You know exactly who I'm talking about,' Nina says. She cranes her head and stares past him, towards the TV screen. 'The tiny one who looks like a boy.'

'You're being ridiculous.'

'You didn't see the way she looked at me that time, when I came into the kitchen.'

'I'm not even going to talk about this.'

'OK.' Nina shrugs. 'But it's not like you haven't got form in this area, is it?'

Tony sighs, begins to tear at the packaging on the pizza box.

'Very unprofessional, if you ask me.'

'If it's the woman I think you're talking about, that was a long time ago.' He moves to stuff the plastic and cardboard into the recycling bin. 'She developed an attachment to me, that's all.'

'Which you did nothing about.'

'I was trying to help her,' Tony says.

'I think shagging her would probably have helped her enormously.' Nina sips her wine; precise, measured. 'You get too involved with your clients, that's the point.'

'How can I not?'

'What about the new woman? The one who came tonight.' She turns to him and smiles. 'She your type?'

'Trust me, no she really isn't.' Tony walks across and turns the oven on. 'And even if she was—' Nina's laughter stops him short. She either finds his protestations genuinely funny or else she is simply winding him up. Tony can no longer tell the difference. He opens one cupboard after another in search of olive oil and something different to talk about. 'Have you been upstairs yet?'

'I've only just got in.'

'The smell up there . . . Jesus.'

'Yes, well.' Another delicate sip. 'That's your area of expertise, Tony, not mine.'

'She not your daughter, then?'

'I don't know why you're being so dramatic. They all do it.'

'It's getting out of hand.'

'It's just an appropriate rebellion, that's all. Even I can work that much out. What do they say about a cobbler's children going barefoot?'

Tony closes the cupboard. He stands and studies his wife.

'I'm sure you'll sort it out with her.' Nina reaches for the remote and raises the volume of the TV. 'When you've got time. I think that's the attachment you should be concentrating on, don't you?'

HERE AND NOW

Nicola Tanner read through the email twice, then clicked on the attachment. She thought about the tens of thousands of other Londoners starting work in bland, open-plan offices much like this one, right about now. Many would be exchanging meaningless platitudes with workmates; chatting about what had been on TV the night before or complaining about the day ahead, just as several of her own colleagues were doing at desks nearby. Loosening ties and needlessly rearranging paperwork. Finishing overpriced coffees bought from chains on the way in, because they could not face the slop that squirted in fits and starts from the machine in the corner.

She clicked on the first picture, sucked in a fast breath.

Many of them would be working at computers, as she was, and might spend the first ten minutes weeding out spam or checking Twitter. Some might even ease themselves into the drudgery of the working day by checking out a few of the hilarious videos someone else thought they might enjoy.

She doubted that too many would be staring at pictures of dried blood and marbled flesh.

The next photograph was a close-up of the victim's face, its features ravaged. The lips gone, a yellowish trail of leakage from the nose ...

'All right, Nic?' DCI Martin Ditchburn dropped a meaty hand on Tanner's shoulder on the way to his office. Tiny, but, most important, with a door that could shut out the open-plan hubbub and provide a few precious moments of peace and normality. It was the perk of the chief inspector's rank that everyone coveted the most. Ditchburn called back as he walked away. 'You up to speed with that Victoria job?'

'Just looking through it now, sir,' Tanner said.

Catching a glimpse of the smile as Ditchburn carried on towards his office, Tanner knew exactly what her boss found so amusing. Among a certain sort of detective at least, such everyday deference to seniority was seen as a little 'old school'. Tanner knew that some found the simple use of the word 'sir' when addressing a senior officer unnecessary at best and ridiculous at worst, but she didn't much care. It felt ... correct. Perhaps foolishly, she expected the same from those of lesser rank than herself, but it rarely happened and only if she was in a particularly bad mood would she pull an officer up on it. Those few occasions had, she knew, been the cause of some resentment, bouts of mockery poorly disguised as banter, but Tanner had been in the Job too long to give a toss.

Straight out of university and twenty years in.

A little under ten more left and she was already starting to plan, because that was what she did. Thinking about what to do afterwards. There was a village in Wiltshire she and her other half had been visiting on and off for a while and she liked to imagine the two of them getting out of London and settling down in a place like that. Something part time maybe, to bring a few quid in and stop her brain turning to mush. Long walks and a decent garden to work on and no snaps of corpses waiting for her first thing in the morning.

She dragged her eyes back to the screen, thinking that she would happily have traded places with anyone responding to an email from a suspiciously generous Nigerian prince or an advert for penis enlargement. She might even have stooped to sitting through a montage of whimsical cat videos.

She managed half a smile. No, that would probably be going too far.

Tanner read through the email one more time, then dialled the number of the officer who had sent it. Marion Fuller had been one of the on-call inspectors for the Homicide Assessment team the previous night, and had been dispatched to an address in Victoria as soon as the body had been discovered. She had quickly ruled it a suspicious death and now the case was being passed across to a team at Homicide Command in Belgravia, specifically the one whose DI had the lightest caseload.

'Have fun with this one,' Fuller said, once she'd answered the call.

It was a routine handover, a process she'd been through many dozens of times, but Nicola Tanner was already starting to think that this was not her lucky day.

'Who found the body?' she asked.

'Local uniform put the door in just after midnight,' Fuller said. 'A neighbour rang in to complain about the smell. Had done so several days running, apparently.'

'Oh dear.'

'Yeah, so someone's on the naughty step.'

'How long are we talking?'

'A couple of weeks at least. One for the bug squad, definitely.'

The first piece of bad news. However brilliant a forensic entomologist was, they would be unlikely to establish a time of death any more precise than a two- or three-day window. This meant that identifying a suspect based on their lack of an alibi was almost impossible.

Tanner put her glasses on again and went back to the text. 'In the email you say "signs of a struggle".'

'Yeah . . . broken glass on the kitchen floor, plant pots and whatever knocked over. It was a right mess. You only had to see the blood, though, to know it was wrong.' The sound muffled suddenly; Fuller placing a hand over the mouthpiece to talk to someone else for a few seconds. 'Sorry . . . yeah, the skull looked intact, so stabbing's my best guess. Hard to be sure, what little there is left.'

'And no signs of forced entry.'

'Only what the uniforms did,' Fuller said.

So, a victim who was trusting enough to let a stranger in, or a killer who was known to them.

'Have we got a name yet?'

'We found a couple of credit cards, got a name from the landlord. You might be able to get a formal ID later on today.' Fuller gave Tanner the name and Tanner wrote it down.

'Next of kin?'

'The mother's dead and the father lives up north. He's on the way down, but like I say, he's not got a lot left to identify.'

Tanner knew it would come down to personal effects most probably, dental records to be absolutely sure. The correct way, and the kindest. No father should have to watch a sheet being pulled back, only to find himself staring down at bones and slop.

'A couple of weeks?' Tanner was scrolling through the pictures again. It never ceased to surprise her just how quickly a human being could be . . . reduced. Beneath a heavily stained white shirt, a chest collapsed in on itself; exposed flesh creamy at the edges and a glimpse of the cavity, blackened and hollowed out.

'Yeah.'

'And definitely not a missing person?'

'Nope. First thing I checked. Doesn't appear to have been missed by anyone.' Fuller sounded busy suddenly, keen to end the call and crack on with something of her own. 'Not yet, anyway.'

This was what disturbed Nicola Tanner the most, over and above the routine problems that went with the death of someone who lived in isolation. Most people were killed by someone close to them, but where did that leave those conducting the murder investigation when the victim did not appear to be close to anyone?

She thanked Fuller for the information and ended the call. She began to print out the pictures.

It was hard to imagine anything more wretched. This was not the natural order of things. A death, especially a violent one, should leave a hole in the lives of the bereaved.

Tanner trudged across to the printer feeling listless, heavy; nodded back at a colleague whose mouth was moving and whose eyes were turned in her direction.

A hole in *somebody's* life.

. . . NOW

It was at least ten hours since the forensic team had first arrived at the property in Victoria, and the crucial recording, collection and removal of potential evidence had already taken place. Given the choice, Tanner preferred access to an untouched crime scene, at least prior to the removal of the body, but a handover usually meant sloppy seconds. It was not without its benefits, though. There was something to be said for having the freedom to move around on her own, and she didn't miss the unseemly chit-chat or the stream of tasteless jokes. She was certainly happy enough not to be creeping about, all too aware of her own clumsiness, done up like an over-sized infant in a plastic Babygro.

'Going to need a fair few bottles of Mr Muscle to clean that lot up.'

Sometimes, there was simply no avoiding the chit-chat. It was not Tanner's strongest suit.

'Right,' she said.

'Not exactly fragrant in there, either.' The uniformed officer on duty outside the property seemed keen to continue the conversation, but Tanner kept her head down and went inside.

It was like a smack in the face, meaty and sickly sweet. Before pulling on nitrile gloves, Tanner dabbed Vicks beneath her nose and began to breathe through her mouth; slow and shallow.

She put her head round the bedroom door. The bed had been stripped, the wardrobes emptied. It was much the same story in the bathroom, and the whole place might have looked as if it had simply been abandoned in a hurry were it not for the state of the kitchen.

Broken glass crunched beneath her feet and she nudged a few of the larger shards to one side with the toe of her black brogue. The cupboards and worktops were dusted with fingerprint powder and there was dried soil in the sink from the toppled-over plant pot Fuller had mentioned. The pot itself had been removed, along with almost everything else by the look of it. Tanner could find no cutlery, no drawer containing tea towels or utensils. There were no storage jars, no toaster or knife block, and only a plastic kettle and a manky-looking washing up brush had been left behind. Such wholesale removals were becoming increasingly common. Some forensic teams preferred to take as much away as possible, to run the necessary tests in their own fully equipped laboratory, rather than using portable equipment in what was often limited space.

Or perhaps it was simply that there hadn't been a great deal here to begin with.

After staring at its rotting contents for half a minute, as though trying to figure out how she might knock up a spot of lunch, Tanner closed the fridge and turned to stare down at the human stain on the kitchen floor.

Ragged and shocking against the dirty white of flaking boards.

The classic 'outline' of a body was only ever seen these days on old film posters or the covers of trashy thrillers. Now there were digital recordings made from every conceivable angle, but who needed chalk anyway, when the human body did a very good job of leaving its mark behind in dried fluids and dead flesh?

Tanner looked at the brown-black shadow where one arm had been stretched out and the expanse of dried blood that had spread from where the torso had finished up. Fuller was almost certainly right about it being a stabbing. Though the pathologist would be left with little that might indicate defence wounds, Tanner could not help imagining those moments after the victim had first laid eyes on the knife in the killer's hand.

A friend or a furious lover. An acquaintance or a stranger welcomed in.

A scream and a struggle and that terrible realisation. Pots and glasses knocked over or sent crashing to the floor as the victim fought to stay alive. Scrambling, desperate, until there were only bubbles of blood and no breath left to beg with.

Tanner leaned back against the worktop and it was only then that she noticed a line of small drawings on the wall. Three of them, mounted one above the other in clip-frames next to the kitchen door. She walked across, taking care to avoid the outline of the body.

They were drawn in felt-tip pen; cartoonish, the borders shaded neatly in bright colours. A scattering of stars and smiley faces decorated a series of uplifting slogans.

WE SUFFER TO GET WELL

YOU ARE NOT ALONE

WE ARE ONLY AS SICK AS OUR SECRETS

Tanner straightened one of the frames which was hanging skew-whiff. She stood back and looked at them for a while, then left.

Outside, the uniformed officer said, 'Any joy?'

Tanner did not even look at him.

Back at the office, she looked through an inventory of everything removed from the crime scene, which had been sent across by the evidence officer. The details of what had gone where. Nothing seemed unusual or of particular interest and, in the end, all Tanner really had was a list of items needing to be tested or analysed and there was not a fat lot she could do until the relevant results were in front of her.

Her partner always said the same thing on the many occasions Tanner found herself in this situation and was complaining about it.

A nice big plate of wait and see pudding ...

She knew that even with a following wind, there would be no fingerprint results until the next day, so she put a call in to see if the forensic entomologist assigned to the case could provide even an approximate time of death. Dr Liam Southworth was in no mood to be rushed and said as much. Tanner pressed him. She knew that the entomologist's final report was unlikely to narrow the time of the murder down to a specific day or even a specific few days, so surely a best guess at this stage would not be asking too much. It was, Southworth told her. He was a scientist and he did not believe in guessing.

Searching around for someone else to bother, Tanner thought about two of the most important items that had been taken from the scene and rang the phone and computer forensic laboratory.

A technician named Appleton was rather more willing to share a few preliminary findings than the bug man had been.

'Not much on the computer,' Appleton said. 'Well not by the usual standards anyway. Email activity was not heavy, by any means. One of those who didn't bother to erase spam, so there's plenty of crap in the inbox, but sent email was sporadic and nothing of any real interest, I don't think. There's a Facebook page, but not a lot of activity on there, and there's not many friends.'

'Nobody on Facebook has any friends, do they?'

'Right, but none of these seem to be *actual* friends, if you see what I mean. There's a few private groups visited regularly and most of them seem to be concerned with recovery from addiction. People swapping stories ... drugs and booze, you know? Might be of interest.'

Tanner reached for a notebook and scribbled it down in capitals, the information appearing to confirm something she had already begun to suspect. 'That's great.'

'Aside from that, nothing I've come across so far is putting up any sort of red flag. Obviously we're examining the hard drive, but it really doesn't look like anything's been hidden.' There was a pause, a prolonged hum. He was looking through notes. 'The phone's a bit more interesting . . . '

Tanner said, 'Go on.'

'Well, the call history's thrown up a couple of things. Oh . . . I'm guessing you want to know the time of the last call made?'

Tanner said that she wanted to know very much and Appleton told her that the last outgoing call had been placed just after ten thirty pm, sixteen days previously.

'Nothing after that, and judging by the pattern of use that's probably the same night the murder took place, right?'

'Probably. Tell me about the call history. Things thrown up, you said.'

'We're still checking all the contacts, but in the final week, several calls were made to the same mobile number in the early hours of the morning. None lasted more than a few seconds, so looks like they all went straight to someone's voicemail. You want me to send all the info across?'

'Sooner the better,' Tanner said. 'But you might as well give me that number now.'

She wrote it down, underlined it.

'There was a diary on the phone as well,' Appleton said. 'Unused, except for the same appointment in there every week. No idea what it is, just the same time every Monday night and a name.'

Tanner took down the name, thanked Appleton for his time and said she'd be expecting his email.

Sixteen days. She turned back a few pages of her calendar to check when that was and scribbled down the date. She felt like calling that pompous entomologist back, telling him where he could stick his maggots.

. . . NOW

Fifteen minutes after the examination had been completed, Tanner sat down with the pathologist in an office adjacent to the coroner's at Westminster Mortuary. The room was cramped and chaotic. Files were piled high on several of the cluttered desks, illegible notes scrawled on a dusty whiteboard. A number of charts and health and safety posters had corners that were no longer fixed to the wall: torn or hanging loose.

Tanner tried not to let it bother her.

'The full report's going to take a while. Three or four days, probably.'

'For now, I only need the basics.'

'There's nothing I can tell you that you didn't hear while I was conducting the examination.'

'I wasn't taking notes,' Tanner said.

'OK, I can give you the headlines.'

'Thanks, Philip. I appreciate it.' She saw the pathologist lean back, failing to stifle a smile. 'What?'

'How many times have we worked together, Nicola?'

Tanner thought about it. 'Six or seven?'

'You're always so . . . formal. Only my mum calls me Philip.'

'You think it's wrong to be formal?'

'I'm just saying. It's unusual, that's all.'

'This is a serious business,' Tanner said. She sat and watched the man in the chair opposite flicking through his notes. She took out her own notebook and a pen while she waited, turned to a clean page.

'Nice notebook. Is that real leather?'

Philip Hendricks was not Tanner's favourite pathologist. There was no question about his competence or diligence, but he could be a little . . . flashy. Quite literally sometimes, if one of his facial piercings caught the light in the post-mortem suite. Who knew how many piercings, tattoos everywhere, the shaved head. It felt showy to Tanner, unnecessary. It seemed wholly unsuitable considering the nature of his job.

'So, we're looking at a body that's well past bloat and somewhere between decay and post-decay stages,' Hendricks said. 'Time of death isn't down to me on this one.'

'I've already spoken to Dr Southworth,' Tanner said.

Another half-smile. 'Yeah, he told me you'd called yesterday, pestering him.'

'I was hardly pestering him.'

'If you say so.' Hendricks pulled a face, like he was unconvinced.

Tanner hid her irritation. It was normal for the entomologist and the pathologist to confer, but something about the pair of them talking about her . . . *bitching* about her, disturbed Tanner. 'As it happens we have a reasonably accurate time of death now, so Dr Southworth can take as long as he likes.' She waited for Hendricks to look at her. 'The victim's phone.'

'O2 are putting us out of a job.' Hendricks smiled and went back to his notes.

'Multiple stab wounds,' he said. 'Three at least. One in the back, though it's hard to say if it was the first one or not, with the fatal wound puncturing the right ventricle. Death from a combination of external blood loss and haemothorax, which is a build-up of blood between the chest wall and the lung. Am I going too fast?'

'I'm fine,' Tanner said.

'Death would have been a matter of minutes.'

Tanner did not look up from her notebook. 'Right-handed, left-handed?'

'Wounds to the upper right chest would usually tend to indicate a right-hander. Impossible to say.'

'How forceful would you say the stabbing was?'

'Forceful enough.'

'Frenzied?'

Hendricks thought about it. 'No slashings ... well, none deep enough to mark bones, anyway. In and out.' He formed a fist and demonstrated. 'It's hard to say exactly how much force was used or to be very specific about the type of knife, because the decomposition has eliminated the puncture wounds. But no, I wouldn't say frenzied.'

'So could be a man or a woman?'

'Definitely one of those,' Hendricks said. He smiled; at his own wry wit perhaps, or the fact that Tanner's face had stayed so completely expressionless. He dropped his notes back on to the desk. 'So, toxicology back in a couple of days and the full report a day or so later. Is that it?'

'Any chance I could get the toxicology findings as soon as they come in?'

'I don't see why not. Looking for anything in particular?'

'Possibly ... '

Tanner had come across words similar to the ones in those frames at the crime scene several times before. She had seen them at rehab centres and halfway houses and, standing in the victim's kitchen, she had immediately begun to think that this murder might be drug related. People tended not to do drug deals in their own kitchens, but perhaps the killer was a disgruntled buyer or a user, already high and looking to steal. She had seen nothing to indicate that drugs had been found on the premises, but Tanner nevertheless considered it an angle worth pursuing. They were all worth pursuing, unless and until the evidence proved her wrong.

Tanner noticed a dirty mug on the desk Hendricks was sitting at. A caption on the side: I SEE DEAD PEOPLE.

Hendricks saw her looking. 'Not mine, but pretty funny.'

Tanner's contempt for the flippancy did not last long. She was still thinking about the slogans on the wall of that kitchen in Victoria.

Thinking about suffering and secrets and someone who had rotted into their own floorboards, as alone as it was possible to be.

On her way out, Tanner said, 'Doesn't anyone mind about all that?' She waved a finger towards Hendricks' face.

'Only you, Nicola.'

Tanner was concerned about hygiene as much as anything else. Earlier, in the post-mortem suite, she had imagined Hendricks bending over the slab and some stud or hook popping loose and dropping into a cadaver's guts. 'Don't the relatives ever say anything?'

Hendricks stood up and shook his head. The smile was still there, but thinner. He folded his arms.

'Really? Nobody ever complains?'

'Only my boyfriend.' Hendricks put his tongue behind his bottom lip, pushed out the pointed stud and leaned towards Tanner. 'If this gets caught on his ballsack.'

'Oh for God's sake,' Tanner said.

Walking back to the station, Tanner picked up a message from one of her DCs. Dipak Chall could do with a little more focus sometimes, but he was bright enough and was not a clockwatcher. She called him straight back.

'This is all sitting on your desk, ma'am,' he said, 'but I thought you'd want to know straight away. We got three matches on prints from the crime scene.'

'Three?'

'First one's our victim. Done for shoplifting seven months ago. A five hundred quid fine and community service.'

It had begun to rain. Tanner stopped beneath the awning of a café and dug her umbrella from her shoulder bag.

'The other two are a bit more juicy. We've got assault, solicitation and possession of class A drugs. That's all one person, by the way.'

'Good.' Tanner was pleased that her notion that the murder might be drug related was starting to look well founded.

'Left the best until last.'

Tanner said, 'Right?' and stepped out into the rain.

'Drugs again, this time possession with intent to sell. We're going back fifteen years, but considering what we know already, it's still the most interesting.'

'Because . . . ?'

Tanner kept moving as Chall gave her the name, the phone pressed hard to her ear, rain drumming against her umbrella. She waited for the pedestrian lights to change at Vauxhall Bridge Road, then picked up her pace.

Interesting was right.

... NOW

The tube journey home to Hammersmith was every bit as uncomfortable as it had been coming the other way, as it always was when Tanner was working days. Lucky if she got a seat, only to spend the journey tense and shifting position almost constantly so as not to let her feet or knees make contact with anyone. Worse still standing, crushed against the bodies of people every bit as miserable as she was; bags and hair and stink.

On the ten-minute walk from the station, she tried to shake off the stress of the journey and the day that had preceded it.

She wanted to take none of it with her into the house.

Her better half, while acknowledging how important Tanner's job was, had made it clear early on that there were things which had no place being discussed at home. 'Office stuff, gossip and whatever, that kind of thing's all fine, course it is, love, but I can't deal with anything ... squalid. It's not like I don't know what goes on in the world. How can you not? Just turn on the television, you can't get away from it. But that doesn't mean I have to deal with it while we're eating dinner or I'm lying next to you in bed at the end of the day.'

Tanner understood and, more than anything, she wanted to make the person she loved content, so she kept certain things – lots of things – to herself. It was tricky sometimes, especially on a day like the one she had just had. She had changed into a clean shirt and the spare skirt and jacket she kept at the office before leaving work, dropped the clothes she'd worn to the post-mortem off at the dry cleaner's near the tube station. There was simply no disguising that smell and everything it meant.

She pulled her purse out as she walked, opened it to make sure she had not lost the dry-cleaning ticket.

It was odd, admittedly, having conversations that sometimes made her feel as though she might just as well be working at an accountancy firm or a call centre. But things were good at home and it wasn't as though she herself had any desire to dwell on the more unpleasant aspects of the job. She wasn't one of those coppers, the ones who wallowed.

It worked, that was the main thing. You couldn't argue with almost fifteen happy years together.

'We must be doing something right,' Susan would say.

Coming through the front door, Tanner could hear the sound of the television in the front room. She dropped her bag and hung up her coat, then put her head around the door.

It was one of those programmes on the Lifestyle channel. Houses and holidays.

Susan had dozed off, the cat on her lap and an empty wine glass at her feet. Just as Tanner was backing out of the room, Susan opened her eyes and blinked at her.

'Sorry, love . . . just conked out.' She sat up. 'Good day?'

'It was all right, actually.'

'That's good.' She gently pushed the cat from her lap. 'Want me to make you something?'

'I'll do myself a bit of cheese on toast.'

'Sure?'

'Yeah, I fancy some,' Tanner said. 'You stay where you are.' She watched Susan relax back into the sofa, then lean forward suddenly to pick up the empty wine glass.

'Can you do me a top-up while you're out there?'

Tanner stepped across to take her girlfriend's glass, then walked out and across to the kitchen. She took the wine bottle from the fridge, examined it and saw that it was new. She poured out half a glass. She stepped softly back out into the hall to check that Susan was still in the sitting room, then went back into the kitchen and swiftly removed the smallest knife from the block.

She carefully scored a tiny mark on the bottle; an all but invisible scratch at the level of the remaining wine.

Susan shouted through from the living room. 'There's some new cheese, but finish the old one first . . .'

Tanner placed the bottle back in the fridge, then walked over and put the grill on.

... THEN

Diana sits and puts her make-up on, taking special care around her eyes and at the corners of her mouth, where the lines are. She applies the *Touche Éclat*, dabs at it with the tip of her little finger, then sits back and stares at herself. She applies a little more, goes through the process several times before she is happy. Or at least as happy as she will ever be.

Silk purse, she thinks. Sow's ear.

She stands and looks at herself in the full length mirror and wonders, as she does at this time every Monday, why the hell she goes to so much trouble to look her best. Who is she doing it for?

It didn't help her hold on to her husband, after all.

She opens her jewellery box, and while she's trying to decide which earrings to wear, she gives herself a good talking to. 'Stupid,' she says out loud. She's dressing to please herself and, right or wrong, that's what she's always done.

Even as the thought is taking hold and well before she can draw any strength from it, it begins to disintegrate and she can see nothing but her daughter's face. The accusation in it, and the blame.

She picks out the earrings, and as she's putting them in, she reminds herself to check her phone, even though she knows there's little point. There will be no missed calls and no messages. She remembers one of her friends telling her once that teenagers were only a hair's breadth away from being psychopaths. They were hard-wired to be selfish little bastards, the woman had said, and utterly without feeling for anyone but themselves. Her son, who was doing very nicely at Oxford thank you very much, had not called her in days, she told Diana. *Days.* Diana had smiled sympathetically and shaken her head, but something had tightened in her belly as she tried to remember her last conversation with Phoebe, how long ago that had been.

An argument, that went without saying. Some hideous variation on the bloodletting they had been engaged in ever since the split. Her daughter had always been a daddy's girl, but Diana had not been prepared for that kind of reaction.

Maybe if you'd made a bit more effort.

It's because you're so useless.

You drove him away.

Trying to stay calm as she watched the most precious thing she had left, the only thing, drifting from her grasp. Trying to explain that she hadn't done anything, that for heaven's sake, darling, he had been the one to have the affair.

You didn't leave him any choice . . .

Eighteen months now since her daughter had left home and she doesn't even bother calling to ask Diana for money. She always goes straight to her father for that. Diana lies awake at night imagining Phoebe and her ex-husband talking about her. Phoebe and her ex-husband's new girlfriend out shopping together. She lies awake and imagines all sorts of things.

She turns the bedroom light off and smooths the duvet before closing the door behind her. She's excited as always about the meeting, if a little scared, and it's around now that, in another life, she might have poured herself a glass, just to steady her nerves. She smiles at that, as she passes the large mirror at the top of the stairs.

50

She looks all right, she thinks. Bloody good for her age actually, and though Tony is far too professional to say anything, of course, she knows he thinks so too.

She makes an effort because this is the thing she cares most about now. The group is not her life, she's not melodramatic about it, but there isn't much else that's as important any more. She doesn't want to waste time having lunch with friends who will ask how she's doing without actually caring a great deal. The trips to the salons for hair and nails and feet are purely practical and the shopping gets her blood pumping a bit, that's all, though she knows very well that she needs to cut back.

At some point she needs to talk to Tony about that, one to one.

When she gets near the front door, her two dogs come skittering out of the kitchen, yapping and hopeful. They haven't had a walk in several days and Diana feels guilty. She can see that they're putting on weight. It's not her fault, she tells herself, because she always flags a little towards the end of the week, finds it harder and harder to drag herself out of the house.

'Tomorrow,' she says. 'I promise.'

The session always gives her a fresh burst of energy and hope. A shot of confidence way better than she ever got from red wine or vodka. 'Silk purse,' she says to herself as she sets the alarm. 'Silk purse, silk purse, silk purse . . .'

She'll give the dogs a good long walk in the morning.

Heather and Chris are smoking on the pavement outside Tony's house. It's drizzling, so they both have their hoods up; shoulders hunched, keeping faces and cigarettes out of the wind. A few cars slow down as they pass, the drivers taking a good hard look at them.

'Checking to see we're not undesirables,' Chris says.

Heather flicks her fag-end into the gutter. 'We *are* undesirables.'

'Speak for yourself.' He waits for the next car to slow them down then steps forward to give the driver the finger and laughs as he accelerates away. 'Yeah, on your way, mate.'

Heather shakes her head. 'That's not very respectful.'

'Fuck 'em,' Chris says. 'How respectful are they being anyway? Looking at us like we're dogshit.'

'Respectful to Tony, I mean. These are his neighbours.'

'Maybe he needs to move.'

'You should tell him,' Heather says. 'I'm sure he'd appreciate the housing advice, from someone who sleeps in hostels or on other people's settees.'

Chris narrows his eyes. 'Yeah, well, shows how much you know, because I'm getting a flat, aren't I?'

'Yeah, you keep saying that.'

'I swear. Hackney or Haringey or somewhere. I've got the letter if you don't believe me.'

'When?'

'The woman from social services says it might be next week.'

'Nice one.' Heather punches him gently on the shoulder. 'That's really great news.'

'Yeah, well.' Chris tosses his own fag-end away. 'All dependent on me being a good boy and all that, not doing anything stupid.'

'Which is why you're here, right?' She nods towards the front door of Tony's house. It's grey, with a large chrome knocker and there is a sign saying NO COLD CALLERS fixed to the wall on one side. The porch has leaded lights and box trees stand on either side in square wooden pots. To the right of the small patch of lawn is a metal gate, outside which a series of recycling bins – blue, green and brown – have been left for collection.

'Well it's not for the company, is it?' Chris says.

'Cheers.'

'The sparkling conversation, whatever.'

'Why were you so horrible to Caroline last week, by the way?'

Chris looks at her and shakes his head like it's a very stupid question. He takes the tin of pre-rolled cigarettes from his pocket, turns away from the wind and lights up again. He does not bother offering one to Heather.

52

He pulls hard on the skinny roll-up, then hisses out a thin line of smoke which is instantly whipped away across his shoulder. Now, he's ready to answer. He says, 'I was only being honest.'

'Pull the other one,' Heather says.

'We're supposed to be honest in there, aren't we?'

'Not like that.'

'Right, so you've got to be honest, but only up to a point.'

'You're pretending to be stupid now,' Heather says. She watches a Mercedes slow just a fraction as it passes and stares at the woman behind the wheel: blonde hair that kisses a collar as she turns her head; the soft blue glow from the instrument panel and the shining satnav. She looks back to Chris, tries to stay nice and calm. 'There's a difference between honesty and insulting someone because you're a knob.'

Chris smiles. 'I just think the rest of you are too scared to say what you're thinking. I haven't got time for all that fucking ... politeness.'

'We're supposed to be making connections and supporting each other.'

Chris shrugs.

'Say what you think if you want, but don't make it personal.'

'How can it not be personal?'

'Fine,' Heather says. 'Any idea how personal we could get with you, if we felt like it?'

'Bring it on,' Chris says. 'Like you don't do it anyway, when I'm not there.' He looks past Heather. 'Oh Christ, here it comes ... '

Heather turns and they both stand and watch Caroline coming down the hill towards them. Waddling. That's the word that occurs to each of them. She is wearing a duffel coat and has a transparent umbrella with patterns on it and she lifts a hand to wave as she gets closer.

'Seriously, though.' Chris drops what's left of his roll-up. 'The state of her. At least smack keeps you nice and thin, right?' He steps back, looks Heather up and down. 'You should count yourself lucky. Some women pile it on when they come off the gear.'

Heather nods, like she's grateful for the observation. 'Really? Actually, I was just thinking that you were chunking up a little bit.'

'Piss off, this is all muscle.' He rubs a hand across his belly. 'I've been working out.'

'Your wrist, maybe.'

'Blimey, it's horrible isn't it?' Caroline says when she reaches them. 'Hasn't stopped all day.'

'I haven't been out,' Heather says.

Caroline looks at her watch. 'Should we go in?'

'Probably should,' Chris says. 'You don't want Robin beating you to the biscuits.'

Caroline looks at him, expressionless. She says, 'Why are you such a hateful cunt?'

If Chris is taken aback, he doesn't show it. He cocks his head. 'I think it's just a gift.'

Heather pushes open the gate and starts walking towards the front door. She turns and shouts to Caroline over her shoulder. 'Honest, apparently. He's an honest cunt.'

. . . THEN

'So, everyone had a good week?'

Tony looks around the group. He makes eye contact with Caroline, who nods enthusiastically. By now, someone else will have filled her in, let her know that the seemingly innocent enquiry with which he always kicks things off is a well-understood code within the group for a rather more important question.

Have you stayed clean? Are you still drug and alcohol free?

Tony is less concerned at these sessions with those behaviours that have, in some cases, replaced the more dangerous ones. It was often the way it worked when you were dealing with addictive personalities. He remains concerned about Diana's compulsive shopping and he suspects that Robin is still regularly using prostitutes, but they are not the primary issue. Besides, not all these secondary activities have been shared with other members of the group.

Different therapists have different time frames. The one day at a time brigade usually demand that anyone attending a session must have been clean for the previous twenty-four hours, while others insist on a longer period of abstinence. Seven days works well enough for Tony. It's what he'd become used to when he was in therapy.

'Good,' Tony says. 'So let's crack on.'

A day, a week, a month. Whatever the time frame, it doesn't preclude simple dishonesty, of course. And addicts are very good at lying.

One member of the group will not make eye contact and Tony can't help wondering just how 'good' Chris's week has been. If he has done something rather more damaging than spending whole days playing video games or watching online pornography. Chris is the member of the circle Tony is most concerned about. He's the most unpredictable, the most chaotic. He decides to try and talk to Chris privately when their time is up and suggest a few one-to-one sessions.

'I'm wondering if maybe we should address one of the issues from last week.' Tony glances down at the notepad on his lap. 'There was a certain amount of friction between Caroline and Chris ...'

'No friction from me,' Caroline says. 'I was on the receiving end.'

'He was at it again when we were outside,' Heather says.

Chris mutters, 'Grass,' just loud enough for Tony to hear.

'What were you doing outside?' Tony asks.

'Just talking,' Heather says. 'Having a fag, you know? Then Caroline arrives and he kicks off with the fat stuff.'

'We don't want that kind of thing in here,' Tony says. He sits back, appearing genuinely saddened. 'Conflict is nearly always counter-productive and we do not reject people because of who or what they are, especially because at some point that's exactly what's happened to *us*. Right? Chris, come on, you know how we work. You're not a beginner.'

Chris looks at the floor, shrinks a little, like a chided schoolboy.

'Look, it's fine,' Caroline says.

'No, it isn't,' Robin says.

'He should apologise.' Diana looks for support. 'He should just say sorry and we can all move on.'

Tony acknowledges the nods and murmurs of agreement and looks to his left. 'Chris?'

It takes half a minute or so, then Chris raises his head and looks across at Caroline. He says, 'I'm sorry if you were upset.'

Heather snorts her derision. 'That's not an apology.'

'That's passive, Chris,' Tony says. 'You're not taking responsibility.'

'I wasn't upset,' Caroline says. 'Takes more than that, trust me—'

'Listen, I'm sorry, OK?' Chris sits up straight, rolls his shoulders. 'I'm really sorry I said what I said. It was out of order.' And he looks as though he means it.

'Not a problem,' Caroline says.

'Good for you,' Diana says.

Tony thinks of something and quickly scribbles a note to himself, while bodies shift in chairs and throats are cleared. When he's finished, he looks up at Heather. 'So, what were you talking about outside?'

'Sorry?'

'Before we started.'

'Just chit-chat,' Chris says, quickly bumptious again. 'Particle physics, the problems in the Middle East. Usual stuff.'

'Actually, we were talking about how much money you make,' Heather says. 'Trying to work it out. I mean, this is a massive house, so you're obviously doing pretty well out of it.'

'Exploiting poor helpless junkies.' Chris winks at Heather.

'I don't think it's any of our business,' Robin says.

'We were just talking.' Heather seems to be enjoying the whole conversation and Robin's objection, the stuffiness of it, makes it funnier still. 'You know ... thinking about what you probably get for an hour and a half like this, multiplying by five, then having a guess at how many of these sessions you do a week, plus all the other stuff.'

'Don't forget the songwriting royalties,' Diana says.

Tony does his best to smile. 'I don't think they'd pay for a new kettle.'

'That's all, really,' Heather says. 'That's what we were talking about. Just messing around.'

'I reckon you're on about two hundred and fifty quid just for one session.' Chris sighs and plasters on an expression of mock longing.

'I was thinking how long that kind of money would have got me high for a year or so ago.'

'Well, I know you like to exaggerate,' Diana says, 'but from some of the stories you've told us, I don't think it would have gone very far.'

Tony raises a finger. Just a small gesture, but he always likes to guide the discussions as subtly as possible. He fights shy of interrupting if he can possibly help it. 'Well, it's nice to know my financial situation is so interesting, but you're basing your calculations on a false premise, I'm afraid. The fact is, not all my clients pay the same.'

'What, us, you mean?' Heather asks.

'I'm not going to go into specifics,' Tony says. 'But look, some people pay me privately, others have the fees paid through medical insurance ... a few are supported by charities or funded by social services, so ...' He pauses for a few seconds, trying to decide whether or not to reveal the other crucial factor in how he makes his living. 'And whether the money's actually coming from the individual or the individual is supported in some way, the fact is I charge some clients a bit less than others.' He shrugs like it's no big deal. Because it isn't.

Nobody speaks for a few seconds, until Chris says, 'For real?'

'That's good of you,' Robin says. 'I think it's perfectly fair that there's a sliding scale. I don't mind paying because luckily I can afford it, but it's right and proper that those who can't should pay a bit less, or be helped in some way.'

'No, that's bollocks,' Chris says. 'A junkie's a junkie, right? Doesn't matter how much you earn, that fact should make everything the same. Obviously, because you're minted you could afford to take better drugs and you didn't have to rob anyone or do other shitty stuff like some of us did to pay for it. The world out there ain't fair, we all know that, but *this* is our world now.' He looks at Tony. 'We should all be equal in here.'

'We are,' Tony says.

'Doesn't sound like it.'

'I should stop gobbing off if I was you,' Heather says. 'You're probably one of the ones who gets charged a bit less.'

Chris looks at Tony.

'Like I said, I'm not going into specifics . . . '

Chris looks at Heather and, after a few seconds, begins to laugh. The pair of them trade stories for a while, the assorted scams and wheezes they've been involved in or heard about. The things junkies do to make the money they need. Tony tells the group about a former client – unnamed, naturally – who hit upon what he thought was a foolproof scheme after buying an extension lead from B&Q.

'He'd paid with a stolen credit card, but then he discovered that the branch had this policy of exchanging faulty goods for cash without needing to see a receipt.'

'Nice,' Chris says.

'Sometimes he wouldn't even bother leaving the shop. He'd just take off the label, break it there and then and march straight over to the returns counter. It worked like a charm for a while, until he found the police waiting for him at the desk one day. Apparently the manager got suspicious because fourteen extension leads had been returned to the same branch in three days.'

Everyone laughs. Tony has used the same anecdote with other groups. It's the kind of story that would probably raise no more than a smile with most people, but addicts always find it hilarious.

'That's junkies for you,' Heather says. 'Always get too greedy, and you're not exactly thinking clearly when you're off your face.'

Chris says, 'I don't suppose you happen to know which branch of B&Q that was?'

Everyone laughs again and, seeing the group in such high spirits, Tony decides that now might be a good time to take things in a different direction.

He raises a finger, nods towards Robin.

'Now . . . last week, Robin generously volunteered to kick things off in looking at how, for some of us, shame of one sort or another may be one of the deep-seated causes of addiction.'

'Still not sure I buy it,' Chris says.

'Well, maybe what you think isn't awfully important,' Diana says.

59

'It's fine, we're just feeling our way into this, OK?' Tony waits for things to settle, then turns to Robin. 'Whenever you're ready . . .'

Robin has been relatively quiet up until now; less happy than usual to chip in. Tony has noted it, well aware that the eldest member of the group is a little less garrulous than Chris or Heather at the best of times, and that throwing a comment in now and again is very different from being centre stage.

'Right then.' Robin straightens the crease on both trouser legs and sits up a little straighter. 'I've been thinking all week about how to tell this and I suppose the best way is just to pitch right in. It's a bit like an operation, I suppose. When you're doing one, I mean. No point standing there dithering with a scalpel in your hand, you've just got to stick the blade in.'

'All depends if the surgeon's on drugs,' Chris says.

'Please.' Tony turns to Chris. 'I think it would be better for all of us if members of the group can do this without interruption. OK?'

Chris sighs, nods.

'You all know I grew up in South Africa, right?' Robin looks from face to face. 'Well, it was a very different country then. Very different. When I was a child, my family had . . . servants. Black servants, goes without saying . . . that was simply the way it was. Now, of course, that sounds horrific, but right or wrong my father genuinely believed that he was doing a good thing, that he was giving people jobs. They weren't paid very much, but it was regular work and accommodation was provided and everyone seemed very happy.' Robin takes a breath and flattens his palms against his knees. 'We had one family working for us. Mimi worked as a maid and her husband did odd jobs, looked after my dad's car and so on and they all lived on the property. It was . . . well, now you'd probably call it a shed.' He stops, searching for words. 'They lived in a shed . . .

'They had a little boy who was the same age as me, maybe a little bit older, eight or nine. Jimmy. That wasn't his name . . . he had a Zulu name like everyone else, but we called him Jimmy. His mum called him that too, if my parents or I were around, you know?

60

'Jimmy and I were friends. We used to muck around together, get into the usual sorts of scrapes. There were a couple of boys from school I saw now and again, white boys, but Jimmy was always there and the truth of it is, I thought I could boss him around, decide what games we were going to play, that sort of thing. We were close, though. That's what I'm trying to say ... we talked about things, our parents, whatever.

'God, this is hard ...'

'Take your time,' Tony says.

'I stole some money.' Robin says it quickly, blurts it out, then seems to relax a little. 'Took it from my mother's bag. It wasn't much, fifty rand or something and I used it to buy sweets. I was showing off, trying to show Jimmy how rich I was, I suppose.' He shakes his head. 'Unfortunately, my mother noticed the money had gone and there was an almighty row and everyone got dragged into it.' He looks up and the smile he gets from Heather seems to relax him. 'I said Jimmy had taken the money, told everyone I'd seen him do it. I still don't know why, but he didn't even try to deny it and next thing his mother's dragging him off and later on I can hear him crying after she's given him a good hiding.

'My father let the whole family go a week after that. He told me how important trust was and that there was no point once it had been broken. Said what a shame it was it had ended up that way. I'd known he was going to do it because my mother told me and still I never said anything, never owned up.' He glances at Tony. 'I tried to find out what had happened to them. Later on, that is. Before my parents died I asked if they knew anything, but there was no way to find out and they barely remembered it, to be honest. By then, even people of their generation were happy to forget they'd ever had black servants, you know?

'I think about it a lot. A *lot*. What I did to Jimmy and to his family. What a liar I was and what a terrible coward. There are dreams and so on, but you don't want to hear about them. So ...'

Tony waits a few seconds until he's sure that Robin has finished, then thanks him.

Chris says, 'Is that it?'

'Sorry?'

'Big boo-hoo because you nicked some money and got a kid whacked when you were eight? Seriously? What about your son?'

'Oh, for pity's sake,' Diana says.

Robin leans forward. 'I've been very clear about this. Losing my son was a trigger, OK? A *trigger*.' His accent is stronger suddenly, the 'r' rolled. 'I'm not denying that's when I started using, but this is something else entirely.'

'What happened to your son?' Caroline asks.

Heather and Diana look at her and shake their heads.

'Robin let everyone know early on that he's not ready to talk about that,' Tony says. 'That's absolutely his prerogative. Everyone's free to move at their own pace.'

Robin is still glaring at Chris. 'What the hell has losing my son got to do with any of this?'

'You tell me,' Chris says. 'We don't know how he was *lost*, do we?'

Tony raises a finger. 'As Robin says, there's a difference between whatever triggers addictive behaviour and what might be underlying causes that are much deeper. That's what we're exploring at the moment.'

'So, it's all about something in your childhood, is it?'

'Not always, but for the shame to have its roots in childhood is certainly not uncommon.'

Chris shakes his head, begins speaking in a hoarse whine. 'I'm a junkie because I used to piss the bed. I'm a junkie because a big boy called me names. It's all a bit convenient, if you ask me.'

'Nobody is asking you,' Heather says.

Caroline leans towards Robin. 'I'm sorry for asking about your son,' she says. 'I didn't know it was something you weren't comfortable talking about.'

Robin smiles at her. 'It's fine. I should talk about it, I know. I think, because it's the reason I started taking drugs, I'm just scared that if I let myself go back there . . . you see?' The smile withers when he turns his eyes back to Chris. 'Anyway, it's not you I could happily strangle right now.'

'I really wasn't having a pop at you,' Chris says. 'It's not your story I've got a problem with, it's this whole shame thing.'

'So, have a pop at *me*,' Tony says. 'I'm the one who suggested we investigate it. And I'm not actually allowed to strangle my clients.'

'Bet you've wanted to,' Caroline says.

Diana laughs and leans towards her. 'If we're anything to go by, I bet there're times he's wanted to murder some of them.'

'Have you?' Heather asks.

Hundreds of times, Tony thinks.

'Only very rarely,' he says.

... THEN

'I just don't think he could face it,' Diana says. 'After telling that story, you know? Poor bloke looked knackered at the end.'

Heather and Caroline nod their agreement. 'He told me he had an appointment, same as last week,' Heather says. 'But I think you're probably right, he just needs to be on his own for a while.'

The three women are sitting in the same part of the pub as the previous Monday, and for the second week in a row Robin has apologised for being unable to join them.

'Servants,' Caroline says. 'How messed up is that?'

'Different time,' Diana says.

'I think I could handle having a servant.' Heather grins as she pours herself another glass from a large bottle of mineral water.

'Really?'

'Oh, definitely. I'm guessing social services are going to have to stump up for him, mind you.'

'You might win the lottery,' Caroline says.

'Unlikely.' She looks at Caroline, waits for the penny to drop.

It takes Caroline a few seconds to remember that Heather had mentioned a gambling addiction the week before. She says, 'Idiot,' and shakes her head, then mimes putting a gun to it and pulling the trigger.

Heather waves it away and says, 'Not a problem. Couple of years now since I was nutjob queen of the scratch cards . . .'

'So, tell us about this servant,' Diana says. 'I presume he's stripped to the waist, nicely oiled up.'

'Oh yeah,' Heather says. 'And doing a *lot* of bending down to pick things up.' She remains deadpan as Caroline and Diana laugh. 'I wouldn't take the piss, obviously. Just get him to pop to the shops for me now and again, run me a bath, iron my pants.'

'You should try having kids,' Diana says. 'Throw in cooking and being an on-demand taxi service and that's pretty much your whole life.'

'Maybe I won't bother then,' Caroline says.

'There are *some* good bits.' Diana swallows and moves fingers through her hair for a few seconds. She finally smiles. 'I can't think of any right this minute.'

'Liars and thieves, the lot of them.' Heather leans into the table. 'Remember Robin's story. Mind you, some of us don't grow out of it.' She lifts up her glass and turns to look at Chris, who has been pumping coins into a high-tech fruit machine since they arrived. She might be talking to herself when she says, 'Used to piss away plenty on them an' all.'

'Where's he get the money from?' Caroline asks, looking towards Chris. 'I don't get the impression he has any kind of regular job or anything.'

'I doubt very much that he's ever had one,' Diana says.

Heather turns back. 'Oh, I think he has, just not the kind you'd approve of.'

'Cash in hand, you mean?'

'All sorts of things in his hand.'

Caroline sniggers. It takes Diana a few moments to get it.

'Have you known him longer than everyone else then?' Caroline asks. 'I mean, it sounds like you have.'

'A bit longer,' Heather says. 'Not a lot. I think I understand him a bit better though.' She turns to look again and Chris notices that they are all watching him. He pulls a face, sticks up two fingers at them. It's camp and comical.

'I understand him perfectly well,' Diana says. 'He's self-destructive and immature.'

'Well, he is that bit younger.'

'He just doesn't know when to shut up.'

'Look, I'm not arguing.'

'If he didn't say such nasty things he wouldn't have to say sorry quite as much as he does.'

Heather holds up a hand. 'You should tell him all this, not me.'

'I will,' Diana says. 'I do . . .'

She watches as Chris ambles back to the table. Heather shuffles along to make room for him and he sits down next to her.

'I wish pubs still had those quiz machines,' he says. 'I used to make a fortune out of them. Go from pub to pub, emptying the bastards.'

'What was the scam?' Heather asks.

'No scam. The truth is, I am just shockingly intelligent.'

'Well I'm certainly shocked,' Diana says.

Heather laughs and Chris pulls a face and then the others join in. Chris seems relaxed and happy, the tense exchanges of an hour or so before at the session seemingly forgotten. It's not the first time Caroline has been struck by how quickly his temperament can change. She had said as much to Heather the previous week.

'He's quite . . . mercurial, isn't he?'

Heather had looked at her. 'Is that a clever word for moody?'

'I suppose.'

'Well, yeah then, he is.'

Chris is telling a story about some friend of a friend who tried to fake a urine sample by strapping a water bottle to the inside of his leg, but forgot that he'd filled it with orange juice. He's a great storyteller, doing the voices, acting out each part perfectly and clearly relishing the reaction he gets.

66

When he's finished, and before he has a chance to start another routine, Caroline says, 'So, what's the story with Robin's son?'

Heather and Diana turn to look at her. Chris rolls his eyes and says, 'Oh please, let's not go there.'

'I'm just curious, that's all.' She pulls her tomato juice towards her. Her mouth hovers at the tip of the straw. 'He's dead, yeah?'

Diana nods. 'That's about all we know, though.'

'I think he killed himself,' Heather says.

'Really?'

'Well, it must be something bad. I mean, worse than just some illness or something.'

'Robin will tell us when he's ready,' Diana says.

Caroline says, 'Yeah,' and sucks at her drink.

'I'm sure there's plenty of things the rest of us haven't opened up about yet.'

Caroline grunts her agreement, sucking until the juice has all gone. She straightens up as a barman stops at the table to collect the empties. She half smiles at him, but he doesn't respond.

'Maybe he topped himself because of Robin,' Chris says, when the barman has gone.

'You're an arse,' Heather says.

Chris yawns extravagantly, stretching his arms out so that one snakes across the back of Heather's neck and laughing as she cringes from it. 'Maybe Robin just bored him to death.'

'Oh,' Caroline says.

'What?'

She nods towards the door through which Robin has just entered and they all turn to look. He waves and hurries over, breathing heavily. His silver hair, usually carefully styled and lacquered, is all over the place. It looks as though he's been running.

'I thought you couldn't come,' Diana says.

'I put my appointment back.' Still panting, he takes off his coat and folds it across his arm. 'Couldn't miss this, could I?'

Diana gives a small cheer.

67

'We're a group, aren't we?'

'Right,' Heather says, looking around. 'We just need to find another chair . . .'

Robin shakes his head, bends down and squeezes in next to Chris. 'Listen . . . I want you to know that whatever gets said at Tony's has nothing to do with . . . this.' He gestures towards the others. 'With *us*, I mean. Naturally people are going to get upset in there and emotions are going to run high, but that's part of it. All part of the process.' His face is just inches from Chris's. 'It's all useful in the end, OK? No hard feelings on my part.' He puts a hand on Chris's arm and rubs. 'That's all I wanted to say. Family, yes?'

Chris stares straight ahead, unblinking, one finger drumming rapidly against the edge of the table, but when it becomes clear that Robin will not move until he's had an acceptable response, he says, 'Yeah.'

Robin closes his eyes for a few seconds, then turns to the others and claps his hands together. 'Right, then, who wants a wholly satisfying non-alcoholic beverage?'

A few seconds after Robin has taken orders and gone to the bar, Chris stands up and walks back to the fruit machine in the far corner. He jams in a few coins and begins stabbing at the buttons.

The three women watch him.

'What's the matter with him now?' Caroline asks.

Chris leans against the machine, that finger still drumming.

Heather says, 'He doesn't like being forgiven.'

. . . THEN

Group Session: February 23rd

Resolved issue with Chris and Caroline. Usual tricks from Chris throughout and my suspicions about his abstinence, or lack of it, are getting stronger week on week. He continues to play a 'role' – archetypal fear of authenticity – preferring to be disliked for who he pretends to be than who he really is. Suggested some more one-to-one sessions, but he didn't seem keen.

Exchange about cost of sessions initiated by Heather. Talked about fee differentials/support of outside services. Interesting exchange between Robin and Chris about 'equality' among addicts. Worth pursuing at a later session, I think.

Robin's S. Africa story was extremely revealing. Catharsis powerful and obvious. Chris still has doubts about relevance of shame in recovery process and was aggressive with Robin afterwards. Raised issue of Robin's son which heightened tension further. Good to see Robin on the offensive for a change. Empowered by his own revelations? More convinced than ever that this is a worthwhile exercise.

Did not ask for volunteers for next time. Would be good to draw Caroline out a little in future sessions, so may put her on spot. Thinking that spontaneity might be way forward. Given a week to prepare their stories, is it easier to self-censor?

Tony puts the radio on to drown out the music from the floor above him; the repetitive thumping only marginally worse than the smell. The associations that go with the smell.

He tunes to a phone-in, sits back and closes his eyes. The same station has a show on a different night which he listens to on catch-up if he can't be at home when it goes out. A therapy phone-in. Some cut-price Frasier Crane dispensing faux pearls of idiocy that might just as well have come from a Christmas cracker. It annoys him, but he listens nonetheless, enjoying the anger as it builds and comes to the boil.

How can you love others if you don't love yourself?

You need to get closure and move on.

Try smiling more often.

Jesus . . .

It's envy of course, pure and simple. He wouldn't be much of a therapist if he couldn't recognise that, though he doubts very much that the moron on the radio show could. He knows it's the kind of show he should be doing himself, knows how good at it he would be. He has some media experience, after all, and he was always very good in front of an audience. Well, perhaps not at the end, but by then he had a hard time remembering which city he was playing in.

Good evening, Birmingham.

Coventry, you twat . . .

A nice radio job would be handy in terms of money as well, no question about that. He thinks back to the session, his discomfort during the discussion about money. It was more than just the awkwardness he always feels when clients try to elicit personal information. They had touched a nerve, the five of them sitting in that conservatory paid for by his wife. The *house* largely paid for by his wife. He enjoys his work, values it, but he does not like being supported.

He particularly dislikes being reminded of the fact.

Some nice, ulcerating shame of his own.

'Get in touch with them then,' Nina says, whenever he mentions the radio show. 'Send a CV instead of moaning to me about it. You need to push yourself a bit more.'

70

She's always telling him that he isn't pushy enough, that he should 'sell' himself more and that it all comes from spending too much time listening to other people. He knows she's got a point. Trouble is, somewhere in whatever she's telling him, however encouraging she might sound, he can always detect a seed of doubt. Some sharp and tiny seed he imagines she's taking great care to plant, and nurture. If the subject of his past life ever comes up – if he happens to mention an old song of his, or a gig he once played – Nina always seems to find a way to pour cold water on it.

A few months ago, a singer he had worked with years before – who had supported him at a handful of shows – was playing at the Hammersmith Apollo. Tony had suggested to Nina that they go along, told her he was sure he could organise tickets and backstage passes. She had sounded keen, but only for a day or two.

'Wouldn't it be a bit . . . embarrassing though?' she had asked eventually. Her hand on his arm. 'Afterwards, I mean. Eventually, he's bound to ask you what you're doing now.'

He'd gone on his own in the end and enjoyed it. Paid for his ticket like everyone else and come straight home afterwards.

The radio host gives out the number for the phone-in again and Tony reminds himself that he needs to talk to Heather about the messages. He had been about to put it into his notes, but had stopped himself when it occurred to him that Nina might look at what was on his computer from time to time.

You know exactly who I'm talking about . . .

He's probably being stupid. Because he's becoming convinced, more so by the day, that his wife doesn't really care a great deal.

The one who looks like a boy.

Thinking back on their conversation in the kitchen a week before, it seems obvious to him that Nina was amusing herself. The pained accusations and the fake jealousy.

When a caller starts ranting about how the Polish have taken over Earls Court, Tony leans across and turns the radio off. Without being aware of it, his fingers begin tapping at the edge of his desk in time

71

with the beat from Emma's room above him. He looks up and sees the central light fitting moving gently over his head. A month ago it was reggae, which he could just about cope with, but this is mechanistic, ceaseless. It's like a furiously racing heartbeat and the smell tells him that his daughter's heart is almost certainly keeping time with it.

Thumping against her skinny chest, up to twice as fast as normal.

Tony gets up and opens his door, breathes it in. The same burned sweetness that was once the way his own world smelled. Him and his friends and every place they went. On his clothes, in his hair.

Now, it just smells like waste.

. . . NOW

Once Tanner had introduced herself and Chall, the man who had answered her knock drew the grey front door a fraction closer to himself. Narrowed the gap. It was the way many people would behave with Jehovah's Witnesses or salesmen, but in Tanner's experience it was not the normal reaction to a pair of amiable-looking police officers. In certain areas of London after dark perhaps, but not usually in the middle of the day and rarely on the doorstep of a house like this.

'Mr De Silva?'

'Yeah . . .'

Tanner held up a photograph. 'Could you confirm for us that this woman is a client of yours?' It was the picture held on record by the DVLA. They had not found a more recent photo at the victim's home and her father had been unable to provide any.

Now, De Silva opened the door a little further and straightened up. 'Ah . . . I hope you understand, but you clearly know what I do for a living and professional ethics mean that I'm unable to confirm or deny that. I'm sorry.'

Tanner nodded, expecting it. 'We're from the Homicide Command, sir.' She looked for a reaction, but none was apparent. 'I need to tell you that, unfortunately, the woman in this photograph has been murdered.'

A well-fed tabby cat appeared in the doorway and darted into the front garden. Chall smiled and turned to watch it go. De Silva ignored it, breath hissing from him like a punctured ball as his shoulders dropped.

He said, 'Right,' then stepped back, opening the door good and wide.

He led them into the kitchen, pausing to offer fresh coffee which Tanner unilaterally declined, then carrying on into a bright and spacious conservatory.

'Nice,' Chall said.

'Thank you.'

They sat in wide rattan chairs with deep cushions. An earthenware bowl filled with polished pebbles sat in the middle of a matching table.

'I have an office upstairs for one-to-one work, but this is a good space for group sessions.' De Silva looked around. 'We push these against the wall and bring in the chairs from the garage.' He sat back. 'They're not quite as comfortable, though.'

'These are great,' Chall said. 'I'm worried I might nod off.'

'My wife chose them.'

The therapist was tall and looked to Tanner as though he took trouble to keep himself in shape. He wore jeans and a red hoodie, and with greying hair cut close to the scalp he could easily have passed for a good few years younger than the forty-six Tanner knew him to be. He lowered his head for a few seconds, and when he looked up again the lines on his face were suddenly more evident.

He said, 'This is horrible.' There were tears gathering now at the corners of his eyes. He wiped them quickly away with a fingertip. 'I mean, you always have to maintain a professional distance, but there's still a bond, you know?'

'When did you last see her?' Tanner asked.

'About . . . three weeks ago. Yeah . . . the Monday night group.'

'Monday, March the twenty-second?'

'Sounds about right,' De Silva said. 'I can check my diary.'

'We're almost certain that was the same night she was killed.' Tanner glanced down at her open notebook. 'That evening or the early hours of the following morning.'

'We checked her phone records,' Chall said.

Tanner looked up, listened. 'Who's playing the piano?'

Chall said, 'Whoever it is, they're very good.'

'What's funny?' Tanner asked.

'Nothing.' De Silva crossed his legs and leaned back.

'You smiled when I asked, that's all.'

'Nothing, just ... it doesn't seem awfully relevant, that's all.' De Silva looked at his watch. 'I do have a session in half an hour, so—'

'Did you miss her?'

De Silva looked at her.

'If she was part of your Monday night group, she would have missed three sessions now.'

'Yeah, obviously I noticed she wasn't there. It's not unknown, but I did wonder what had happened.'

'Did you not try to contact her?'

'I called, but it went straight to her voicemail.'

'You weren't worried though.'

'Yes, of course, but like I said, it's not unknown. I've had clients who suddenly stopped coming to sessions and then turned up again eighteen months later like nothing happened. Some of them can be a bit ... unpredictable.' He waited for Tanner to say something. 'You do know I work with people in recovery from addiction?'

'Yes, we do know that,' Tanner said.

'And some of them are a bit more famous than others, right?' Chall ignored the look from his boss. 'One or two, anyway.'

'Sorry?'

'I googled you.'

'Oh.' De Silva shook his head in disbelief. 'That's what the police do now, is it? They just google people.'

'Not just, no,' Chall said.

Tanner glanced out into the garden. A pair of squirrels chased each other around the base of what was probably meant to be a relaxing water feature. She looked back to De Silva. 'So, did the rest of the group talk about why she'd stopped coming?'

'We talked about it, yeah.'

'Were they worried?'

'Of course they were. The group's like a family. But at the same time, everyone has issues and problems of their own and they understand the way it works. They know that people can drift in and out, can go off the rails. It might be them missing the next session, you know?'

Tanner nodded, like she did know. She wrote *others* in her notebook and underlined it. 'Was Christopher Clemence worried?'

De Silva looked down at his hands, laced his fingers together.

'Is Mr Clemence not also a member of that same group?'

'Like I said at the door. Professional ethics. I can neither confirm nor . . .' He stopped when he saw Tanner nodding.

'His fingerprints were found at the victim's home,' she said. 'At the crime scene.'

'Right.' De Silva sighed. 'Yes, Chris is one of the group.'

'We also found your fingerprints at the crime scene, sir.' Chall leaned forward. 'That's how we found you, matter of fact. Possession of a controlled drug with intent to supply.'

'Oh, for God's sake.'

'I know, a long time ago.'

'I think I nicked some sweets when I was eleven,' De Silva said. 'You might want to look into that.'

Chall didn't blink. 'Well, if you can give me the name of the shop, I'll see if they want to prosecute.'

'More to the point,' Tanner said, 'what were your fingerprints doing there?'

De Silva took a few seconds. 'Oh . . . she had a birthday party. Well, not a party, really. Just the group.'

'So, you're in the habit of going along when your clients have a party? What about that professional distance you mentioned?'

'I didn't go,' De Silva said. 'Meaning, I didn't stay. I just popped in with a cake. She'd made amazing progress. She was celebrating another year clean. I was just being supportive.'

'Nothing wrong with that,' Chall said.

'No, there isn't.'

Tanner looked down to her notebook again. 'Those phone records we mentioned.' She turned a page, studied it, turned back. 'According to those, she made a number of calls to you in the week before she was killed and several before that. Calls in the early hours. Most of these were no more than a few seconds in duration, so I presume you were in bed.'

De Silva nodded.

'Did she leave messages?'

'Just to call her back.'

'Do you still have them?'

'No.'

'And did you call her back?'

'Of course I did.'

'So your clients also have your personal number, do they?'

De Silva considered it, his expression pained suddenly. 'Well, actually it's something I've been wrestling with for a while,' he said. 'Several colleagues of mine already have two different numbers for exactly this reason and it's something I've been thinking about a lot. Getting these kinds of calls was starting to become a problem.'

'What did she want? When she called.'

The therapist shrugged. 'Just to talk. She was up and down, you know. She had problems with depression, which date back to before the drug abuse even began. She was taking prescribed medication.'

'Yes, we found it,' Tanner said. 'In her flat.' During the pause before she spoke again, she became aware that the music had stopped. 'And in her liver.'

'I didn't think you could do that,' Chall said. 'Take Prozac or whatever, if you're supposed to be keeping off drugs.'

'Ironically, that's one of the things that was making her anxious,' De Silva said. 'Narcotics Anonymous, one or two of the other groups, don't really approve. It's a major bone of contention, because a lot of people on those sorts of medication have problems with relapse.'

'You were actually the last person she called,' Tanner said.

'*What?*'

'The night she was killed. The last call was made to you, just after ten thirty.'

'Ten thirty-six,' Chall said.

'Do you normally go to bed that early?'

'Not as a rule.' De Silva looked shaken.

'You were at home, though?'

'Yeah, of course. I would have been writing up my notes on the session.'

'Was anyone else here?'

'Well, my daughter was almost certainly out. She usually is.'

'What about your wife? Was she at home?'

'Probably, I can't remember. I'll ask her to check her diary.' The therapist thought for a few seconds, then threw up his hands. 'I don't know . . . I must have just missed the call.'

Tanner closed her notebook. Said, 'Shame.' She sat back, the frantic blur of the squirrels busy at the edge of her vision.

'Right.' De Silva stood up. 'I really need to get ready for my session.'

Tanner and Chall stood up too. Tanner said, 'It would be a big help if you could give me the names of the other people in that group.'

De Silva was already walking back towards the kitchen. 'No, I don't think I can do that. I was willing to confirm that Chris was a client because you've already got his prints and you clearly believe that his criminal history might be of interest. If you want to ask him about others in the group, I can't stop you, but I've gone about as far as my code of conduct allows, I think.'

'We guessed you'd probably say that,' Chall said.

'Obviously if there's evidence that something or somebody in the group is directly connected to a serious crime, then that changes things. Otherwise, client confidentiality is paramount. I'm sure you appreciate that.' At the front door, De Silva said, 'Are you allowed to tell me how she died?'

'I'd rather hold on to that information for the time being,' Tanner said.

'Is that *your* code of ethics?' De Silva asked. 'Or just because you don't feel like it?'

'She didn't relapse,' Tanner said. 'If that helps at all. Aside from the medication she was taking for the depression, she was drug free when she was killed.'

De Silva nodded. As he pushed the door shut, he said, 'At least I'm doing something right.'

. . . THEN

She pulls the first sheet of paper across and takes out her felt-tips, an old magazine underneath so she won't mark the table. She lines them up, the colours in the same order as always. Black, brown, blue, green, red.

She still can't quite get her head around how expensive cards are. Two and a half quid a pop, some of them. Such a rip-off for a cheesy rhyme and a stupid picture with an even stupider joke. There are only five people to invite, but still, there's no way she's going to waste a tenner or more on that. That's money she won't be able to spend on food or drink and she quite fancies tarting the place up a bit if she has enough left. A few balloons or something.

Five people to invite, though she's only expecting four to come. Four at the most.

Not exactly a party like the ones she used to have, though they're all a bit of a blur these days. They just tended to happen anyway. A few people told a few more and they all pitched up knowing there would be plenty of gear around, enough cheap cider to float a battleship. Parties were never *for* anything.

You asked a hundred junkies when their birthday was, she wouldn't have expected a great many to know. Even fewer to care.

So, she might have been making the cards because of the money, but she thinks that hand-drawn invitations mean that bit more anyway. She likes drawing, always has. Only thing she ever really liked at school, and even when she was using she would try and find time for it. For a while, she thought about trying to be a graffiti artist, like Banksy or something, but the paints and the guns were pricey and it was just one more thing to risk getting nicked for, so in the end she didn't bother. That's what she told herself at the time, anyway. Truth is, just like every other junkie she's ever known, she'd made all sorts of plans and every one of them went straight out of the window the second she got high. The second she *needed* to get high.

She takes a black felt-tip to start on the borders. Neater that way, she reckons.

Not that she's got that many plans now she's clean, mind you.

She wants to get a cat.

She wants to get off benefits. She lost the last decent job she'd had after a stupid bit of nicking, then a couple of casual ones after that. She's sure it's because someone found out about her past, but she could never prove it.

She wants to meet a decent bloke, maybe have a kid.

Four friends. If you can even call them friends. Closest thing she's got though, beggars and choosers and all that. It seems like she had loads before she got clean, but back then the truth was she only really hung out with other people who were using.

They'd all had to go; that was how it worked. You said goodbye to the drug, which was far and away the major relationship in your life, and goodbye to anyone associated with it. She's pretty sure that a few of those ex-friends have gone for good by now, gone as in dead, and she knows bloody well that's probably how she would have ended up. She's thankful every day for that moment when she finally knew she had to make a choice.

The borders done, she picks out a red pen to start the decoration.

As she draws a star in the top left hand corner she thinks about her conversation with the new girl, Caroline. In the pub a week before, telling her the story of the junkie and the dead mum's jewellery.

She hadn't told Caroline that junkie was her.

She draws more stars and plenty of smiley faces, because they're her favourite. The invitations will all be basically the same, but they're hand-drawn, with each person's name on their own card, so she hopes they all recognise the work she's put in, when she hands them out at the next session.

She thinks about what else to draw.

She's about to do a nice shiny box, decorated with a bow, but she stops, thinking that they might take it as a hint to buy her a present. That would be nice, but she doesn't want it to look like she's angling for it. In the end she settles for a big bottle of champagne with a popping cork, but on the label it says, NOËT & SHAMDON. STRICTLY NON-ALCOHOLIC.

When she's finished decorating them, she puts a name at the top in capitals and then writes the message. In big, swirly letters, like she sees on the side of tube trains sometimes, a different colour for each invitation.

ANOTHER YEAR OLDER,

AND DEFINITELY A DAMN SIGHT WISER!

COME AND HELP ME CELEBRATE!

DRESS TO IMPRESS ...

HEATHER xxxxx

PART TWO

KING OF
THE WORLD,
PIECE OF SHIT

THE VISITOR

THE FIRST VISIT

He's been sitting there waiting for several minutes when his visitor arrives. He watches as one of the guards points him out among the crowd of other prisoners already deep in hushed conversations at tables with wives, mothers, children. He sits up straight, adjusts the green tabard he is wearing over the prison-issue sweatshirt.

The visitor sits, takes out a notebook and pen. Says, 'Thanks for this.'

'So, let's hear about this "project", then?' The prisoner holds up the letter his visitor had sent two weeks earlier. 'Sounds like crap to me.'

The visitor smiles. 'I'm writing a thesis on dubious convictions.'

'What's dubious about it?'

'Well, in this case I suppose I'm more concerned with the crime itself. The circumstances.'

He studies the person opposite him. 'Bit old for university, aren't you?'

'Mature student. Final year of my law degree.'

He grunts and takes out a scarred tobacco tin. He opens it and begins preparing a roll-up.

'So ... I've read the court transcript and the evidence seems fairly straightforward. Plenty of witnesses, murder weapon recovered at the scene and you seemed perfectly happy to plead guilty.'

'Happy?'

'You never disputed that you'd done it.'

'No point, was there? Like you said, plenty of witnesses.'

His visitor writes something. 'You had an argument with the victim in the pub.'

He nods, licks at the cigarette paper.

'What was that about? It doesn't say anywhere.'

'I couldn't remember. Still can't.'

Now, his visitor studies him. 'You were being accused of murdering someone after an argument and you couldn't remember what caused it?'

'It was a red mist type of thing, that's all.' He looks away, sees a prisoner from the landing next to his reaching to take a young woman's hand across an adjacent table. 'I've got a temper, all right?'

His visitor nods. 'Well, that's what really got me interested to begin with, I suppose. Your defence barrister kept talking about how out of character it was, the violence, losing your temper the way you did. That was virtually your whole defence. He repeatedly claimed that you'd never been involved in anything like this before. He made out like you wouldn't say boo to a goose.' A pause. 'That's what your friends and family say too.'

'Who you been speaking to?'

'Just some background research, that's all. A couple of phone calls.'

He looks down at the letter again, reads, mouthing the words. 'You a journalist or something?'

'I'm not a journalist.' A nod towards the letter. 'It's a personal project, I swear.'

He puts the completed roll-up back in the tin and closes the lid. 'We had an argument and I hit him. That's it.'

'Had you ever met him before?'

'No.' Quick and simple, because he's telling the truth.

'Had you heard his name mentioned before?'

He blinks, tucks the tobacco tin away beneath his tabard.

'I know the police asked you this, so sorry for going over it again, but if you'd just gone to the pub for a quiet drink and you didn't know the man you got into the argument with, why were you carrying an iron bar in your coat pocket?'

He shakes his head and looks up at the clock.

'You'll be out in what . . . a couple of months? I mean, you would have been up for parole a lot sooner if you'd ever shown the slightest bit of remorse, but that's up to you. All I'm saying is, what harm can it do to talk about it now?'

He smiles, for the first time. 'Maybe I'm not sorry.' He leans across the table, hisses it. 'Maybe that bastard deserved everything he got, all right?'

His visitor tenses and tightens the grip on the pen; smiles back.

. . . NOW

They came in numbers from behind burned-out cars and around corners, yelling and brandishing weapons. They were dressed in black, some with their faces hidden and others heavily bearded; as close to being Central Casting Islamic terrorists as their creators could get without being overtly racist. Chris Clemence made short work of them, putting the last one down in a noisy hail of rapid machine gun fire, with a satisfying eruption of blood and brain matter.

Mission completed.

Clemence casually entered his initials in the list of high scorers then climbed out of the seat and bumped fists with several of the boys who had been gathered around the machine to watch and shout encouragement. There were four or five of them; white, black and Asian kids. The logos varied, but the basic uniform of jeans, trainers and hoodies was the same as Clemence was wearing, though he was probably ten years older.

He turned and looked at the couple watching from near the entrance to the arcade. He waved, waggling fingers. There was a short, whispered exchange with some of the kids, a little more fist bumping, then he ambled over.

'Very impressive,' Chall said.

'Not really,' Clemence said.

Tanner raised her warrant card, but Clemence did not need to see it.

'Yeah, Tony called.' He looked around, as though eager to see who might be watching him having this conversation. 'He said you'd probably want a word.'

Tanner waited until she had his full attention. 'I want it somewhere a bit quieter, if at all possible.'

'There's a Starbucks over the road.' Clemence pointed. 'Only if you're buying, though.'

'I think we can stretch to that,' Tanner said.

They walked across Wardour Street into the coffee shop; a buffer between the blacked-out windows of an adult entertainment store and a high-end seafood restaurant.

'Can I get a cake as well?' Clemence asked.

Chall said, 'Now you're taking the piss.'

They carried their drinks to a table in the corner that gave them a view back across the street towards the arcade. A few of the boys Clemence had been talking to were still loitering on the pavement outside.

'This a normal Saturday morning for you, is it, Chris?' Tanner asked.

'I come a fair bit, yeah.'

'Nice to have a fan club.'

'Oh yeah, I'm like the Pied Piper, me.'

'Bit young, aren't they?' Chall said.

'Bit young for what?'

Chall nodded across the street. 'Younger than you, I mean.'

'So? They're gamers, same as a lot of kids that age. Would you be happier if they were out nicking cars or mugging people?'

'Still at school, I reckon, most of them.'

'I'm not sure what you're implying.'

'Sergeant Chall wasn't implying anything,' Tanner said. 'Were you?'

'Making conversation,' Chall said.

Clemence scooped the froth from his coffee with a plastic spoon and licked it off. 'I just like playing games.'

Tanner watched him tear into three sachets of white sugar then slowly pour one after the other into his cup. She said, 'More than *like*, by the sound of it. The woman we spoke to at the night shelter knew exactly where you'd be.'

'Creature of habit.' Clemence grinned. 'And as you very well know, I've had habits a lot worse than this one.'

'Still expensive,' Tanner said. 'What was that game, a couple of quid a time?'

'Yeah, but I'm good. Well, you saw. So I get twenty minutes or half an hour for that.'

'Eating into your benefits a bit though, I would have thought,' Chall said.

'Not really.'

'Wouldn't it be a lot cheaper to play at home?' Tanner could see that one of the boys from the arcade had crossed the road and was pulling faces at Clemence through the window. She looked at Chall, who stood up and waved the boy away.

'Would be if I had one,' Clemence said. 'Anyway, sometimes you need to get out and see people, don't you? It's all about making connections, right?'

'What is?'

'Having a life, moving on. Something Tony's always banging on about.' He turned his head to watch the boy go back to his mates. 'Trust me, there *are* things I prefer doing on my own.' He looked back to Tanner with a grin that was short-lived. 'But people like me aren't always particularly fond of our own company.'

'People like Heather, too?'

He shrugged, then nodded. 'So, what happened to her?'

'You know what happened, if you've spoken to Mr De Silva.'

'I know someone killed her.'

'Which is all you need to know for now.'

'Stabbed, was she? Strangled?' He waited, saw that Tanner wasn't going to bite. 'Don't suppose it matters, does it? Dead's dead.'

'Tell us about her.'

Clemence swirled coffee around in his mouth, swallowed it noisily. 'She was ... nice. A bit nutty sometimes, neurotic about things. Always doing things exactly the same way, you know?'

'Like OCD, you mean?' Chall asked.

'Kind of. Everything always had to be in order.'

Tanner looked down at her notebook.

'Don't know what else to say, really. I got on better with her than some of the others in the group. We took the piss out of each other, helped each other out.'

'Helped how?' Tanner asked.

'You know, if she was having a bad day or whatever, she might call and I'd try and snap her out of it. We'd go and have a cup of tea or something, talk bollocks. She did the same for me a few times. Just normal stuff.'

'Talk bollocks about what?'

'Anything. Telly or sport, something in the news. Things you never get to talk about in the group.'

Tanner looked up from her notebook. 'Anything you think we should know? Anything you think might be important, bearing in mind what happened to her?'

'Not that I remember.'

'Nobody she was involved with? Who she might have been worried about or frightened of?'

'Not now.' Clemence saw Tanner's reaction, shook his head. 'By which I mean, yeah, there would have been, but we've all had dealings with some nasty bastards over the years.' He smiled. 'One or two of them even had warrant cards.'

Tanner did not rise to it. 'Did Heather ever mention any names?'

'If she did I can't remember any, but she would have come across a few people you wouldn't want to mess with. Ex-junkies don't have too many saints in their address books.'

Tanner shifted her chair to allow a young woman to sit down at the next table. The woman immediately pulled a laptop from her bag and logged on. She caught Tanner's eye and smiled. Tanner looked back to Clemence. He had remarkably good skin, considering his history, she thought. Pale, but more or less flawless around the carefully groomed stubble. He had styled his hair every bit as carefully; blond streaked into the black, teased into spikes on top and squaddie short at the sides. His teeth were better than she might have expected too and he showed them off a good deal, well aware of his winning smile. Tanner could easily understand why other men might find him attractive. Women too, unaware that they were barking up the wrong tree, or simply wanting to mother him.

'Tell us what goes on in one of your sessions,' she said.

'In the group, you mean?'

'It would be helpful,' Chall said.

Clemence sat back and folded his arms. He appeared to think about it for a few seconds, but then shook his head slowly. 'I don't think I can. That's the one rule, you know.'

'Yeah, but murder trumps it,' Chall said. 'Don't you reckon?'

'I don't see how it's relevant.'

Tanner nodded. 'As far as we can make out, Heather didn't have too much else going on in her life outside the group you were both in with Tony De Silva. We're obviously looking at all sorts of things, but until we've got anything else concrete, those sessions might well prove to be extremely relevant.'

'Sorry,' Clemence said. 'We talk . . . well, you can probably work that much out, but I really can't tell you who said what. There are people in the group who'd want my balls on a plate. Tony for a kick-off.'

Tanner leaned forward. 'She wasn't found for a while, you know that?'

'What?'

'They didn't find Heather's body for nearly three weeks. Nobody reported her missing, because there wasn't anybody to miss her.'

'In the end, most of her just seeped through the floorboards,' Chall said.

'Jesus.'

'If you were her friend like you say, I would have thought you'd want to do anything you can to help us.'

Clemence grunted, tore around the cardboard rim of his empty coffee cup. 'What was her name?'

'Sorry?'

'That's how much of a friend I was, OK? I don't even know what Heather's second name was.' He carried on tearing, the cup getting stubbier, an inch at a time. 'First names only in the group, you see?'

'Finlay,' Tanner said. 'Heather Finlay.'

Clemence nodded. 'Sounds Scottish or something.'

'She was from Sheffield originally. Came down here for college then stayed on.'

'I knew it was up north somewhere,' Clemence said. 'Used to take the piss out of her accent. Eeh-bah-gum, all that. She used to do the same with me, told me I was like a camp cockney or something.' He smiled. There was almost nothing of the coffee cup left and he gently eased the debris to one side of the table. 'A pearly queen, she called me once.'

'While we're talking about names, it would be helpful if you could tell us who else was in that Monday night group with you and Heather.' Tanner turned a page in her notebook.

Clemence narrowed his eyes. 'What did Tony say about that?'

'He wouldn't tell us, but said it was fine if you did. Call him if you want.'

Clemence shrugged. 'Fair enough, but like I told you it was only first names.' He thought for a few seconds. 'Robin's probably your best bet, because at least I know what he does.'

'What does Robin do?' Chall asked.

'He's a doctor . . . an anaesthetist. A consultant, I think, or something high up anyway, because he always wants everyone to know how great he is. He mentioned the hospital once. The Royal something?'

'Thanks, that's extremely helpful.'

'I do my best.'

Tanner wrote the information down then looked up at him. 'What's that below your eye, Chris?'

'What's what?'

Tanner gestured vaguely towards what was clearly a bump beneath Clemence's right eye, bruising not quite faded around it. 'Been walking into things?'

'I'm clumsy,' Clemence said.

Tanner nodded. 'Are you clean at the moment?'

'Come again?'

She waited.

'Yeah, I fucking am. Like that's got anything to do with anything.'

'How long?'

He pushed himself back into the corner, the muscles working in his jaw. 'I have ups and downs, fair enough?' He took a few deep breaths then stood up quickly, stared out the woman with the laptop who had turned to watch. 'Can I go now?'

Chall got to his feet too. 'Scared someone's going to beat your high score?'

Tanner stayed seated. 'Before you head off, can you just tell us what you did on the evening of March the twenty-second?' She looked at him. 'If it helps you remember, that was the last session Heather attended.'

Clemence refused to look at her. A few more deep breaths as hands were thrust into pockets then taken out again. 'After the session, I went to the pub with everyone else, same as every other week . . . then I left.'

'To go where?'

'To wherever I was staying at the time.'

'The shelter at St Martin's?'

'Might have been, I move around. I'm supposed to be getting a flat, aren't I, but it's taking a while. Paperwork and all that.'

'Tell me about it,' Chall said.

Tanner closed her notebook. 'It's all important,' she said. 'The red tape, the paperwork. People doing things properly is what might get you a flat in the end.' She reached for what was left of her coffee. 'Doing things properly is how I'm going to find Heather Finlay's killer.'

. . . NOW

Tony's wife rang when he was in the queue for the checkout.

'We need fresh spinach,' she said. 'And pancetta.'

'I'm just about to pay.'

'Might as well get some more mozzarella while you're at it.'

Tony sighed and stepped out of the queue, asked his wife if there was anything else as he walked back into one of the crowded aisles. More often than not, the weekend shop on a Saturday morning fell to him, and though there were always crowds to negotiate and parking spaces to fight for he'd come to look forward to it. Once the shopping was done, he would deposit the bags in the boot of his car then enjoy half an hour or so in the Crocodile Gallery café with the newspaper. A double espresso and an almond croissant, then a crafty cigarette afterwards.

He relished the routine.

'Why were there police here yesterday?'

'What?' Tony waited for a shopper to move, then reached for the spinach.

Nina asked the question again.

'How did you know about that?'

'Emma heard them talking when she came down to use the bathroom. Weren't you going to mention it?'

'When, exactly?' Tony said. 'I was in bed whatever time you got back last night and you were asleep when I left this morning.' He realised he was heading in the wrong direction, executed a tricky turn and began pushing the trolley towards the deli counter.

'So, go on then.'

'A client died.' It was hard to manoeuvre with one hand, so he tucked the phone between his chin and his neck. 'Was murdered, actually.' He could not bear the unsteadiness, the feeling that the phone would slip and fall at any moment, so he stopped and pushed the trolley hard against the edge of the aisle. 'One of the women in my Monday night group.'

'Which one?'

Tony took the phone from his ear and looked at it. HOME. A picture of Nina and Emma. The duration of the call ticking by in seconds.

Which one? Not *Oh God that's terrible.* Not *Fuck* or *Bloody hell.* *Which one.* He became aware of a woman staring and mumbled a sorry as he nudged his trolley forward so that she could get at the tinned fish.

'Can we talk about this when I get home?'

'Whatever you like,' Nina said. 'Can you see if they've got any edamame beans? If not, they do them in Waitrose . . .'

Forty minutes later, Tony was unpacking the shopping in his kitchen: squashing down packaging into the recycling bin; balling up the empty carrier bags then pushing them inside a bigger plastic bag that was hanging in one of the cupboards.

'Which one was Heather?' Seated at the central island, Nina was looking at something on her iPad and brushing toast crumbs from her dressing gown.

'The one who gave you a filthy look, remember?' Tony held up a pot of edamame beans. Nina blew a kiss in his direction. 'The one you said looked like a boy.'

'Do they think it was drug related?'

97

'I don't know what they think.'

'Every chance though, don't you reckon?'

'Well, I'm sure it's something they're considering,' Tony said. 'But they know she definitely wasn't using when she was killed.'

Nina scrolled and swiped. 'Feather in your cap, anyway.'

'Yeah.' Tony carried the multipacks of bottled water through to the utility room. He felt a flush spreading across his chest, a shard of guilt pressing at his breastbone. He had said something similar, shutting the door on that policeman the day before.

'So what are you going to do?' Nina asked when he came back into the kitchen. 'About the group.'

'I've put it on hold for a while.'

'Probably a good idea. I mean, you're not a grief counsellor, are you?'

It still surprised Tony how little she understood the work he did, and he might have said something if he had the slightest interest in his wife's latest cutting edge campaign for bras or biscuits. The truth was that for many recovering from serious drug addiction, grief was exactly what they felt. Mourning the drug they had loved and been loved by; mourning the part of themselves that had died when they'd left it behind.

'No,' he said. 'I'm not.'

When he had spoken to each of the surviving members of the group the day before and broken the news about Heather, he had simply told them that they should take a short break while they processed their loss. Robin had been sanguine about it, but Tony guessed that was because he had NA meetings and other support groups in place. Caroline had said she understood, which was not surprising since she was still a relative newcomer and not as bedded in or dependent as some of the others. Diana and Chris had seemed the most disturbed at the thought of a hiatus, and, though he couldn't promise, Tony had agreed to try to fit in individual sessions for them both until such time as the group was reconvened.

Until he was ready to reconvene it, because the truth was that Tony himself did not feel able to carry on immediately.

'I can smell the cigarettes, by the way,' Nina said.

Tony turned away from her. He walked across to the sink and began washing his hands. 'I was stressed, all right? Upset. I've lost a client.'

'Well, what's that, thirty-five pounds a week? I'm sure you'll fill the gap quickly enough.'

'Are you joking?'

'Of course I am. And I meant, I can smell the cigarettes every Saturday.'

'Come on. Once a week.'

'Is that really a good idea?'

'It's a treat, that's all.'

'Oh, that's OK, then,' Nina said. 'You should probably have a few drinks while you're at it, maybe a line of coke, wake up in a skip.'

'You're being daft.'

Tony dried his hands on the tea towel; rubbed and rubbed long after they were dry and until he heard Nina say something about going for a shower. He turned round to see her hugging their daughter as the two of them passed in the doorway.

Emma mumbled a 'Morning'.

He walked across to hug her himself; squeezed and tried to remember the last time he'd felt her skinny arms curl around his back. Then he sat down and tried to stay calm while she made herself breakfast.

There had been a bout of bulimia several years before, and though that particular issue with food seemed to have passed, though his daughter was eating, watching her do so was like observing a series of delicate and defined rituals being carried out by a chimp.

It was precise, and utterly chaotic.

The ingredients of each meal would change every few months or so, but would remain constant for weeks on end, breakfast, lunch and dinner, until Emma finally grew sick of them or developed an obsession with something else. Today, it was – still – miniature frankfurters, cherry tomatoes, raw baby sweetcorn, finely sliced pickles. There were plenty of all these in the fridge as Tony had taken care to stock up at the supermarket an hour before. Though the components of the meal were all small enough to begin with – making his daughter's hands look like those of a giant as she worked at them – she took great pains to make each piece smaller still. The tiny sausages were cut carefully into tinier slices, the tomatoes into quarters that could be hidden beneath a thimble, and it was not until this work had been satisfactorily completed and each element of her meal comprehensively reduced that she would eat any of it.

Then the chaos would begin.

She ate with her fingers, or sometimes from the blade of a knife. She swigged water from a bottle and ate directly from whichever surface she was in front of, dispensing completely with crockery of any sort until, when she had finished, there was usually as much food smeared across whatever she was wearing as there was on the worktop or scattered on the floor around her.

'It's getting ridiculous,' Tony had told Nina. 'She's like a baby.'

'Your area, not mine,' Nina had said.

It was the cobbler's kid with no shoes again and Tony was growing tired of it. He wanted to talk about why, but fought shy of talking about the kind of female body image people in advertising traded in or bringing up the umpteen stupid diets Nina had been on since Emma had been born. No, his job was to sort out the mess, same as always, and it only served to highlight yet again, how little Nina understood what he did, or could be bothered to try.

Now, watching Emma pick up a slice of sausage no bigger than a penny and bite it very carefully in half, Tony remembered a session he'd done in a prison not long after he'd begun working as a therapist. Fresh-faced – well fresh-ish – and full of newly acquired buzzwords and homilies to go along with the piss and vinegar.

'I'm not interested in slapping on a sticking plaster,' he'd told them. 'I don't want to cover up the wound. I want to know why that wound's there in the first place so we can avoid another one.'

A prisoner who, up until that point had looked friendly enough had leaned towards him and quietly said, 'I'll wound you in a minute, you soppy twat.'

Tony had spent the rest of the session shaking so much that he could barely hold his notes.

'Mum says you could hear what those coppers were saying down here yesterday.'

He was a lot more resilient these days.

Emma glanced up. 'Yeah, but only a bit. I could see them outside though, when they left. They looked like coppers.'

Tony watched her eat for half a minute. A slice of pickle, a quarter of a tomato, a measured swig of water between each. 'Can you hear when I do my sessions?'

'What?'

'When we're in the conservatory. Sometimes we can hear when you come down to play the piano.'

'Is that a problem?'

'Nobody's told me it bothers them yet,' Tony said. 'I just wondered, if we can hear you, can you hear what's going in the group? You know, when you've finished playing.'

Emma shrugged. 'I usually go straight back upstairs.'

'What about the sessions I have in my office?'

She sighed. 'What about them?'

'Can you hear what's being said? I know you usually have your music on.'

'Why would I be interested in what you and your junkies are on about?'

'I just asked if you could hear, that's all. You do understand that these conversations are supposed to be confidential, right?'

Emma looked up at him, seemingly furious that he was continuing to interrupt precious eating time with inane questions. 'A. Why would I give a shit? And B. Who would I tell?'

'Fine,' Tony said. 'Good.' There was little point trying to read anything into his daughter's reaction. She would probably have been equally obstreperous had he enquired about her plans for the rest of the weekend or made some innocuous comment about the weather.

She was seventeen.

Emma finished eating and left without any further conversation. When she had gone, Tony spent five minutes cleaning up after her, then went upstairs to his office. The shower was still running in the en suite and he could hear the murmurings of his daughter on the phone in her room. He listened, but could make out no more than the odd word or exclamation.

He looked at the birthday invitation that Heather had given him weeks before, still pinned up on the cork board above his desk.

His name in swirly red and blue letters. Stars and smiley faces.

A few minutes after the shower stopped running, he heard Nina calling from the bedroom.

'Fancy going to the pictures tonight? Why don't you have a look, see what's on?'

Tony shouted back and told her that he would. Then he reached for the invitation, took it down and put it away in a drawer.

. . . NOW

'We could probably walk it in twenty, twenty-five minutes,' Chall said.

Had she been alone, Tanner would have made the journey from Soho back to the office on foot, without question. She had done so many times, in fact, coming back from the West End: along Piccadilly then down through the park and straight past Buckingham Palace. Tanner liked to walk, but any pleasure it might have given her would now be tempered by the need to make concessions. It was certainly not personal, because Chall was an officer in whose company she was generally more than comfortable, but twenty-five minutes was just too long a time to spend at the mercy of somebody else's walking pace. Their desire to chat.

'Nice enough weather for it,' Chall said.

Within a few minutes they were on a train heading west towards Green Park. Saturday lunchtime, and though the carriages were not quite as busy as they were during weekday rush hours, they were still crowded with excited tourists en route to Hyde Park or Harrods, as well as those heading further afield and already looking beaten down by the seemingly interminable Piccadilly line journey to Heathrow.

'So, you think he was high?' Chall asked.

They were strap-hanging by the small doors at the end of the carriage. The sergeant waited until the movement of the train eased him gently back towards his boss.

'Clemence.'

'No, I don't,' Tanner said.

'That kid certainly was. The one outside, pulling faces. Might explain why he hangs around with them.'

'The fan club?' It was the reason Tanner had asked Chris Clemence the question. Those who were genuinely trying to stay off drugs did not tend to associate with those who were still using them.

'When he says ups and downs, maybe he's talking about ketamine or MDMA. Easy route back in if that's what you're looking for and you haven't got much to spend.'

Tanner knew that Chall was right, because she had seen it before. Teenagers using drugs recreationally were much more likely to dole out a tab or two to a virtual stranger than any junkie would be to share gear with his closest friend. She nodded. 'Right, and even if Clemence isn't high now, who's to say he wasn't off his tits three weeks ago?'

At Green Park they changed lines, following the crowds heading southbound via Victoria. In a busy carriage they managed to bag adjoining seats opposite a young couple all but obscured by the large rucksacks on their laps. Tanner guessed they were heading for the coach station, which she knew well because it was virtually next door to the police station. Whatever time Tanner arrived at work, there would usually be a rat-arsed backpacker wandering around somewhere near the entrance to the nick.

It wasn't quite so easy to spot those whose purpose on the streets around Buckingham Palace Road was altogether darker, but Tanner knew they were there. Men and women waiting to offer a helping hand to the young boy with no money fresh off a coach from Leeds, or cut-price accommodation to the teenage girl just arrived from Glasgow and desperate for work. A 'welcome to London' smile from those looking to acquire human stock cheaply, for whom Victoria coach station was the closest thing the likes of them had to a cash and carry.

Tanner wondered if Victoria coach station had been Heather Finlay's first view of London when she'd arrived from Sheffield all those years before.

'What is it they're all so busy writing anyway?' Chall asked. 'On those bloody laptops.'

'Sorry?'

'People in coffee shops.'

'What about them?'

'What are they doing? Like that woman, just now. You can't get a seat most of the time because they're just sitting there for hours on end, tapping away like it's really important.'

'Sending email?' Tanner had never given the subject a moment's thought and found that she was unable to care about it now that she had. 'Watching porn?'

'Writing novels,' Chall said, nodding. 'Or *wanting* everyone to think they're writing novels. I mean, Jesus, if they can afford three and a half quid for a latte you'd think they could afford Wi-Fi at home.'

'Maybe some people need to get away from home.'

Chall thought about it, but not for very long. 'Write what you know. That's what they say writers should do, isn't it?'

'Is it?'

'Well, if that's true, how come there aren't a lot more novels about losers who spend their lives sitting in sodding coffee shops?'

Tanner had stopped listening, but smiled, because Chall was a decent bloke and the look on his face made it obvious that's what he was expecting.

A few minutes later, coming out on to the street at Victoria, she was thinking that, whether or not that advice was useful to writers, using your experience was what any sensible copper did. Tanner's experience still led her to believe that drugs had played some part in Heather Finlay's murder, and the fact that Heather had almost certainly

105

known her killer meant that Tanner was keen to track down everyone else in that Monday night recovery group. Perhaps Christopher Clemence was not the only one to have had ups and downs.

'I want a name and address for this anaesthetist by the end of the day,' she said.

'Shouldn't be too hard,' Chall said.

Tanner's experience told her that such confidence could often be the kiss of death, but on this occasion she chose to ignore it. Passing the coach station, she caught the eye of a young girl carrying a backpack almost as big as she was, smoking with friends near the entrance. Tanner didn't know if the girl had just got off a coach or was about to board one. She found herself hoping that it was the latter.

. . . THEN

'You've got an amazing house,' Caroline says.

'Thank you.' Diana looks a little embarrassed and quickly offers to take Caroline's coat as she shoos her dogs away. She holds out an arm to let her visitor know which way to go.

'I thought Tony's place was pretty fancy, but . . . bloody hell.' The exclamation comes as Caroline walks through into the kitchen and gets her first look at the garden. The dogs are still leaping up at her shins and yapping. 'It's like a football pitch or something.'

Diana opens the back door and marshals the dogs outside. 'Actually, Tony's house is probably worth a lot more than this one because of where it is,' she says. 'Muswell Hill's a bit more desirable than Barnet.'

Caroline walks towards the French windows. 'I didn't know you could even get gardens this big in London.'

'Yes, we're very lucky.' Diana reddens a little when Caroline turns to look at her and moves quickly to the other side of the kitchen to make drinks. As she waits for the kettle to boil and takes cups and saucers from a cupboard, she asks Caroline about her journey, if the directions she'd given her over the phone were OK. Despite the fact that Caroline has come on the tube and the bus, Diana talks, babbles, about how terrible the traffic can be, even on a Saturday, and there is a minute or two spent on the weather – 'How British am I?' – which has been pleasantly mild and allowed her to get out into the garden which she says she enjoys. She points out the carpet of snowdrops which has come into bloom at the base of a large hydrangea near the Wendy house.

She carries the drinks across to a scrubbed pine table that runs the length of one wall and pulls out a chair for Caroline. 'God, listen to me go on,' she says.

Caroline sits, though she needs to move the chair a little further from the table. 'It's fine.'

'Truth is, I'm not really used to having company any more. There always used to be people in and out, especially at the weekend, but not so much these days.' Diana lifts her cup and touches it to Caroline's. 'Anyway, I'm very glad you're here.'

'Thanks for asking me,' Caroline says.

'I wasn't sure you'd want to come.'

'Well, to be honest I wasn't sure if it was allowed. I didn't know if there were rules in the group about socialising. I know we go to the pub after the sessions, but apart from that.'

'Actually, Tony encourages it,' Diana says. 'I think the only thing that's really frowned upon is any kind of sexual relationship in the group, but that's quite common in rehab and recovery. Robin says it's an absolute no-no with the twelve-step lot.'

'Why?'

'I think it's all about focusing on yourself and not being able to handle the stress of a new relationship. Plus, if you get into a thing with someone else who's in recovery, there's always the danger if one of you relapses that the other will too. It's all a bit of a minefield.'

'Well, I don't think we need to worry about that,' Caroline says. 'It's just lunch, right?' She waits a few seconds, then grins and laughs when Diana begins to.

'Oh, I'd be *such* a rubbish lesbian,' Diana says. 'Though there have been times I've thought life might be a bit simpler if I was that way inclined.'

'I do wonder about Heather,' Caroline says.

'Really?'

'Well, just the way she dresses, I suppose. I know that doesn't mean anything, but . . . '

Diana sips her tea, shakes her head. 'Definitely not. Not considering how keen she is on Tony. Well, she could bat for both teams, but I don't think so.'

'She likes Tony?'

'Oh, she definitely fancies him. Well, he's an attractive man, isn't he?'

Caroline smiles. 'Actually, I thought *you* had a bit of a thing for him.'

Diana reddens again. 'Not really. It's just that stupid thing when you have a bit of a crush on a teacher, isn't it? Didn't you ever have one of those?'

Caroline nods. 'Mr Wilson. Taught us geography.'

'And obviously Tony's way too professional to be remotely interested anyway. So . . . '

The dogs are whining outside, jumping up to scratch at the back door. Diana gets up and takes treats from a ceramic bowl. She opens the door and tosses them out to the dogs, tells them to be quiet.

'I'm glad you're . . . gossipy,' Caroline says. 'I didn't really know what to expect and I didn't want to feel like I was out of my depth.'

Diana walks back to the table. 'What do you mean?'

'Well, I know what it's like when we're all in the pub, but when it's just two of you . . . I don't know, I thought you might want to talk about books or art or something.'

'Really?'

'You know, like one of those ladies who lunch.'

Diana smiles. 'Oh, I was definitely a lady who lunched once upon a time,' she says. 'Then I became a lady who drank lunch, and now . . . well God knows what I am now.'

'Better off,' Caroline says. 'You're better off.'

Diana nods and raises her tea cup. 'Talking of lunch, are you hungry?'

'Starving,' Caroline says.

'I made a salad. Is that . . . all right?'

'Yes, I mean—'

'I just thought—'

'Of course—'

'If you'd rather—'

'No, salad's fine,' Caroline says. 'Sounds lovely.'

They look at each other for a few seconds, then Diana says, 'Right then,' and hurries across to the fridge. She brings back a large bowl covered in cling film and a bottle of sparkling water, then goes back to fetch plates, cutlery and a plastic jug filled with dressing.

'Actually, I normally try and relax a bit about the diet at week-ends. I don't go mad or anything, but you need to have treats, don't you?'

'Oh, absolutely.' Diana pours the dressing on to what looks like a rather unappetizing green salad, then uses wooden spoons to toss it. 'How's it been going, anyway? Being off the painkillers.'

'Well, there's less pain as I lose more weight, which is great.'

Diana glances up. Says, 'You look like you've lost some since the last session.'

'A few pounds,' Caroline says. 'Long way to go yet.'

'As long as you're moving in the right direction.'

'The pain's getting easier to cope with every day, and Tony's made a few suggestions.'

'That's good.'

'He gave me the name of this acupuncturist.'

'How's that going?'

'I haven't been,' Caroline says. 'I'm terrified of needles.'

Diana spoons out a portion of salad on to each plate. 'That's a bit ironic, isn't it? Considering some of the people in our group.'

Caroline laughs. 'Actually, sometimes the pain's sort of ... good. It's a reminder of how bad I let things get and I know that while it's still there I've still got work to do. It spurs me on a bit.'

'No pain, no gain,' Diana says.

'Well, sort of.' Caroline nudges the salad round her plate. 'Is there any salad cream?'

Diana looks at the fridge. 'Sorry, I don't think there is. I've got some mayonnaise.'

'Yes please ...'

While Diana is fetching it, Caroline looks across to the collection of framed photographs on a wooden chest near the window. 'Nice pictures of your daughter,' she says.

Diana brings the mayonnaise and watches Caroline ladle a large spoonful on to her plate. 'Yes, somehow Phoebe always manages to look nice, even if she dresses like a tramp.'

'How often does she come home?'

'Not as often as I'd like.' Diana pops a cherry tomato into her mouth. 'But that's being a student, isn't it? There's always a party to go to, nights out in the pub with her friends. Now and again she might even have an essay to do.'

'Does she see much of her dad?'

Diana reaches for the water. 'I'm not really sure.'

'It was funny, before,' Caroline says. 'When I was saying how amazing your garden was and you said "we". "We're lucky" or something.'

Diana nods. 'I know. Stupid.'

'It's understandable,' Caroline says. 'Like when someone dies and for a while you still say "is" instead of "was".'

'Actually, that's exactly what it's like. A death, I mean. Sometimes I forget, even now, and find myself setting the table for him, or thinking that there's something on the TV he'd really like.'

'I hope you took him for everything you could,' Caroline says.

Diana looks up at her, as though a little shocked by the younger woman's directness. She shrugs. 'Oh, I did, but the strange thing is that now I almost resent the money.'

'Really?' Caroline's eyes widen. 'Well, I can take some off your hands, you know, if it'll help.'

Diana smiles. 'I know, it sounds stupid, doesn't it? Don't get me wrong, I take it, but it doesn't make me feel great. It magically appears in my account every month and all I can think of is him sitting there on his computer pushing the buttons, making the transfer and moaning to his girlfriend about what a scrounging bitch I am. Bleeding him dry. I think about him doing it in bed, tapping away on his laptop while she's lying next to him, slagging me off and playing with his tiny dick. She's the one I think about most, if I'm honest. She's the one I loathe. I know that's not very healthy and Tony's forever trying to bring me from the "there and then" when there was so much hatred and bad feeling, but the truth is there's plenty of hatred in the "here and now". How can they ruin people's lives, women like that?' She looks at Caroline as though waiting for a response, but does not leave time for one. 'And it's not because she loves him . . . certainly not because she fancies him. Pot-bellied shortarse, that's my ex. It's about money, isn't it? I mean, that's all it can be. Cars and handbags and nice holidays and do any of those things justify what she did to me or my daughter? Do they justify destroying a family?' She looks at Caroline again, waits this time.

'Course they don't.'

'Women like that are . . . sub-human,' Diana says. The tension leaves her face and she pushes a strand of hair behind her ear. 'Help yourself to some more.'

'Sure?'

'Come on, it's only salad, and it needs to be eaten. You can have your weekend treat tomorrow.'

'Oh, I will,' Caroline says.

. . . THEN

It's probably the warmest day of the year so far, though it's hardly balmy. The sun being out at all seems enough for most people though, happy to be leaving gloves and hats at home, the crowds overtaken by a kind of euphoria at only needing two layers instead of three.

Chris is wearing a denim jacket borrowed from a former boyfriend and never returned. Heather has a short suede jacket bought from a second-hand shop in Camden market ten years earlier. They are sitting on a bench in Hyde Park, watching dog-walkers and Frisbee-throwers, couples out with high-end strollers and kids kicking balls. People are lying on the grass reading books or listening to music. A large group sits around a chequerboard of blankets enjoying a picnic, and beyond the Serpentine, which is crowded with boats, the flags on Hyde Park barracks are unmoving.

Chris opens the Styrofoam container and takes a bite of his chicken burger. He says, 'I used here, once.' He nods towards a clump of trees near the group of picnickers. 'Over there. Got off my face and watched the ducks.'

'Anywhere in London you haven't used?' Heather reaches into her own takeaway bag and pulls out a handful of chips.

'Not really,' Chris says. 'Best one was in the toilets at Thames Magistrates' Court.'

'What?'

He looks at Heather. 'Afterwards, obviously, I'm not stupid.'

'Yeah, bit of a giveaway, I would have thought,' Heather says. 'If you shoot up before.'

Chris grins, chewing. 'Right. My brief laying it on thick. Giving it "My client is taking major steps to overcome his addiction to class A drugs" and me standing there in the dock, drooling like a nodding dog.'

There is a seagull nosing about near the bench. Heather throws down a couple of chips which are pounced on immediately. 'You still dream about it?'

'Oh, God, yeah. Don't you?'

Heather nods. 'Once a week, probably. It's usually a frustration dream, you know? Like I can't get any gear, or I do manage to get some but I can't find a needle. The other night I dreamt I'd got everything sorted, but the syringe was massively long and curly, like a weird rollercoaster or something, stretching right round the room. The needle was in my arm, but I couldn't reach to push the plunger.'

'It's shit, isn't it?' There is a second gull now, lurking near Chris's end of the bench. He stretches out his legs and it flutters away. 'There's those few seconds after you wake up, and it's great, like you can still feel it. Then you remember that you're clean. It's like dreaming about an ex or something. You're just having such great sex and then you wake up with a huge stiffy and remember he dumped you.'

'You can always have a wank.'

'Oh, I always do.' Chris shoves what remains of his burger into his mouth. 'Doesn't matter what I've been dreaming about.'

'It's like these people who've been in cults or something,' Heather says.

'What?'

'You know, you read about people who've been kept in a cellar for years or whatever. Then one day they get released and it's like "Oh, *this* is what the world is like".' She watches a woman walk past, a toddler clutching her hand. The child looks at Heather. She smiles, but the child just stares and aims a kick at one of the seagulls. 'When you're using, you don't care about anything. There's only one thing to worry about, which is where your next bit of gear is coming from. Then you get clean and suddenly there's all this other stuff to deal with ... and it starts to really matter, you know what I mean? Having somewhere decent to live, having a job that isn't completely rubbish, having a partner.' She looks at Chris. 'It hurts when you don't have those things.'

'Anaesthetic's worn off, hasn't it?'

'All the way through rehab they keep on telling you how much better everything's going to be, but they never tell you that a lot of the time it won't feel like it.'

'You feel conned, right?'

Heather stares at him. 'I'm not saying I'd want to go back. I'd never want to use again.'

'Course,' Chris says. 'Me neither.'

'Wouldn't mind a decent job, that's all.' She scrunches up her takeaway bag and stands up. 'So I could afford something other than KFC for lunch.'

Chris says, 'What, like Nando's, you mean? You've got ideas above your station.' He watches her walk to a litter bin twenty yards away. When she gets back and sits down again, he says, 'You should get yourself a rich boyfriend.'

'I'd settle for something with a pulse,' Heather says.

'Nice older man with a few bob tucked away. It's great for a month or two, like a holiday. Just close your eyes when it's time to do the business and imagine it's Hugh Jackman.'

'I don't think so.'

'George Clooney?'

'I want to be in love with someone,' Heather says.

Chris shrugs. 'Yeah, well we all live in hope.'

They say nothing for a while, watch the comings and goings, slurping at their fizzy drinks. Chris removes his jacket and lets his head drop back, enjoying the sunshine.

'You all set for Monday?' Heather asks.

'All set for what?'

'The shame thing.'

'Who says it's my turn?'

'Just in case it is.'

Chris sits up quickly and shakes his head. 'No way. Tony can't make me do anything I don't want to.'

'When has Tony ever made you do anything?'

'Still not convinced there's much point.'

'Robin thought there was. Said he found it really helpful.'

'Yeah, well,' Chris says. 'He's into all that sharing crap. Sharing some things, anyway.'

'Why bother coming to group sessions at all? If you don't want to share anything.'

'Not sure I'll stick it, to be honest,' Chris says. 'Not sure it's helping.'

'You told Tony?'

'Not as yet.'

'You shouldn't be afraid of it,' Heather says. 'Whatever it is you're ashamed of. I bet you, whatever it is, I can beat it.'

He looks at her. 'You reckon?'

'It's not like it's a competition, but yeah.'

'I'm looking forward to that,' Chris says. 'How come you aren't scared of telling everyone?'

'I'm shitting myself,' Heather says. 'But I know I'll feel better afterwards. I know I need to do it. I know you need to do it.'

'Not yet,' Chris says. 'Not ready.'

'That's fine,' Heather says. 'Don't leave the group though. Don't use that as an excuse for leaving.'

'Nothing to do with that,' Chris says. He turns to her and grins. 'It's the people I can't stand.'

'Cheeky bastard.'

'Imagine how boring it would be if I wasn't there. Just Dr Dull, the Desperate Housewife and Moby Dick.'

Heather smiles, in spite of herself. 'Haven't I got a nickname?'

'I'm still working on it.'

Heather stands up and buttons her jacket. Top button first, then the bottom, then the middle, same as always. There's no good reason, it just makes her feel better. She says, 'Come on. You fancy a coffee?'

Chris is watching the picnickers. 'Weird, isn't it? Remembering places you got high. What you took, who you were with. Like a great memory and a terrible one at the same time.' He stops, hearing Heather swear and turns to see her holding her arm out, staring at a glistening gobbet of bird shit on her sleeve. He starts to laugh.

'Piss off. This is my favourite jacket.'

Chris pulls a used serviette from his takeaway box and passes it to her. 'It's supposed to be lucky.'

Heather starts walking away. 'I need some water.'

'Lucky Heather!' Chris stands up and hurries to catch her up. 'There you go. That's brilliant.'

'You think I'm lucky?'

Back together, they walk quickly towards Park Lane. 'You're still alive,' Chris says.

. . . THEN

Diana had offered to drive her back to the tube station at High Barnet, but Caroline had insisted that there was really no need, that the walk to the bus stop would do her good.

'It all helps, right?' she had said. A smile, a blush and a palm tracing the sphere of her belly.

Now, she trudges back towards the High Street, breathing hard, feeling the sweat gathering on her neck and in the small of her back, in the creases behind her knees. Nylon sticking to her. There isn't a chance she'll walk off so much as a pound, not after all the mayo she'd slathered across that tasteless salad, but she might walk off a little of the envy.

She can feel it cool and begin to disperse in her chest, step by agonising step.

Embracing Diana on the doorstep, Caroline had sucked in what felt like a mouthful of something sickly that probably cost as much per designer bottle as she earned in a day. A week, maybe. Those stupid pedigree dogs still yapping outside as they said their goodbyes. That house, which Diana had copped for simply because her old man had found a younger model. All that bitterness, the tedious ranting about the woman who had stolen her beloved away and it wasn't like *she'd* married him for his good looks in the first place, was it?

Caroline slows a little, then stops. Her knees are killing her, so she reaches into her reasonably priced bag and feels for the small plastic bottle.

She wonders just how many lies she and Diana had told one another in the last couple of hours. Diana was good at it, no question. She had almost made Caroline feel sorry for her, all that horrible dirty money flooding in. What a nightmare that must be. The woman had a nice line in empty compliments, as well. A smile of what might have been admiration on her face, of pride even, when the truth was that Caroline hadn't lost an ounce since the last session, had put a bit of weight on, if anything.

Pity was all Caroline had seen, all she ever saw.

Maybe you just got better at lying as you got older, though Caroline knew that she was pretty damn good at it herself. All that rubbish about the pain, for a kick-off; how good it was. Yes, there were times she did her best to grin and bear it, but not for very long, because only an idiot would suffer when they didn't have to. Sometimes, she thinks, it's fun to lie just for the hell of it; when it means nothing. It hadn't been Mr Wilson she'd fancied at school, it had been Mr Roach, the music teacher, and she'd done a lot more than fancy him. She smiles, remembering, and continues to rummage.

A couple of kids whizz by on bikes, shouting something. The usual stuff, comments about the size of her arse, but she doesn't even look up.

Her fingers close around the bottle of painkillers.

The warmth of the plastic and the rattle of the pills inside feel almost as good as a chicken leg tastes, or a custard slice.

She starts walking again, just for a minute or so until she reaches the High Street. It's busy with Saturday afternoon shoppers, cars cruising slowly, seeking parking spots. Looking for somewhere she can buy a bottle of water to take her pills with, she sees a newsagent on the opposite side of the road, sandwiched between a bakery and a burger bar.

Fucking typical. Fucking wonderful.

The kids on the bikes have turned round and cycle past again to have another go. Sarcastic whistles this time, a barely literate comment about Jabba the Hutt. Caroline thinks about what she would like to do to them if she could catch them. She thinks about that dirty old bastard of a music teacher and the way he used to look at her.

How he would look at her now.

She can't be bothered to walk as far as the pedestrian crossing, so she waits for a good-sized gap in the traffic and crosses the road.

Tony has just said goodbye to his final client of the day, and when he takes his phone out he sees four missed calls from a number he recognises. He walks slowly back upstairs. He had heard the buzzing from his jacket pocket while he was trying to talk about methadone withdrawal to a nineteen-year-old girl. The girl had heard it too. 'It's OK if you need to get that,' she had said. She had nodded towards the jacket on the back of his chair, then looked away; wringing her hands, drumming the heels of her trainers on the stripped wooden floor.

Now, he dials the number as he walks back into his office.

'Oh, thank Christ . . . '

Heather answers almost immediately and begins jabbering. She tells him she's been desperate to get hold of him, that she doesn't know what to do. She tells him she'd been thinking of jumping on a bus and coming round. When he can get a word in, Tony tells her that he's been busy with clients, that he does have other clients, even on a Saturday. Keeping his voice nice and steady, he asks her what the matter is and when she tells him, he says, 'You're being ridiculous.'

'I'm not.'

'Heather, it's a jacket,' he says.

'I don't know what to do.'

'It's bird shit on a jacket.'

'You don't understand.'

Tony puts his head round the door, looks out, then closes it. He walks back to his desk and drops into the chair. 'Trust me, I'm trying to.'

'I bloody love this jacket,' Heather says. 'It's the nicest thing I've got. The only nice thing.'

'Yes, but it is just a thing.' Tony begins tidying his desk; straightening papers, popping pens into the old coffee tin next to his printer. 'That's the point. The best things in life aren't things.'

Heather does not appear to have been listening. 'Why shouldn't I have nice things? Don't I deserve nice things as much as anyone else?'

'Course you do.'

'So, why do they always get ruined?'

'Who says it's ruined?'

'It won't be the same.'

'It'll be fine.'

'Even if it looks the same, I'll know.'

'I think you're being overdramatic.'

Heather says nothing for a while. She sniffs, coughs. Tony can hear voices from her TV in the background. She sighs and says, 'I'm just so stressed, you know?'

'We've talked through your coping strategies, haven't we?'

'Yeah.'

'You remember?'

'Yeah.'

'But you won't need them, all right? Not today.' It's ridiculous, but Tony knows he needs to ask. 'You're not considering using, are you?'

'Course I'm not.'

'Good.'

'But it's the same ... feeling, you know? Like nothing's worth it, like what's the point?'

'Tell me what you mean.'

'Like what's the point of caring about anything? Like it was easier when I didn't give a toss. When I didn't care what I looked like, or how my hair was, or if I stank.'

'It's just a jacket, Heather.' Tony looks up at the calendar. Another ten weeks and he'll be in Venice or Berlin or Barcelona, eating sushi in a smart hotel. Sometimes he thinks that his screwed-up, egomaniac

121

rock star is far easier to deal with than most of the 'civilians' he treats. The rock star's word, not his. He lowers his voice a little. 'I know you liked it and I understand what you're saying, but what we're doing is trying to make you care about yourself, OK? When we've done that, you'll see that while it's great to have the nice things you're talking about, they're not the be-all and end-all. It's not how we measure self-worth.'

On Heather's television, someone is shouting. An audience whoops and cheers. 'Why do these things always happen to me, though?'

'I don't think it was personal,' Tony says.

'What?'

'The bird shit.'

Heather laughs, but she sounds tired. She says, 'Fucking seagull . . .'

'I need to go,' Tony says. 'I'll see you on Monday, OK?'

'You always make me feel better,' Heather says. 'Always.'

He glances at the door. 'That's nice to hear, but you need to know that this isn't why I gave you my number. Any of my clients.'

'What's that mean?'

'It's supposed to be for emergencies, OK? For when you're really in trouble. When relapse is a serious possibility.' He leaves a few seconds, wanting it to sink in. 'You can't be calling me about things like this.' He waits again. 'Heather?'

She takes another few moments. There's more sniffing and coughing, like she's hawking something up. She says, 'Tough love now, is it?'

'Heather, it isn't—'

'Tell me who else I'm supposed to call.'

. . . NOW

Dr Robin Joffe had said that he would prefer not to use his office, so came down to meet Tanner and Chall outside the entrance to A&E at the Royal Free Hospital in Hampstead.

'I hope you don't mind,' he said as they shook hands. It was drizzly and he began buttoning up his overcoat. 'No offence, but police officers tend to look like police officers in my experience.'

'And you'd rather not be seen talking to us,' Tanner said.

'Wouldn't most people?'

Joffe led the two officers out on to the road and began walking down Pond Street towards Hampstead Heath station.

'My mum was treated in there,' Chall said, nodding back towards the hospital. 'Knee replacement. You might have put her under.'

'When was she treated?'

'Oh . . . it was about ten years ago, I think.'

'I was working somewhere else then,' Joffe said. 'She was lucky.'

'Yeah, it's a good hospital, isn't it?'

'Lucky not to have me, I mean.' Joffe was walking quickly. He was stocky, a touch overweight, but still surprisingly fit. Though some people's hair went white a lot earlier than others', Tanner had him down as being somewhere in his early sixties. 'I wasn't exactly at my best back then.'

They stopped for traffic at the bottom of Pond Street, then crossed into South End Green, the confluence of several busy roads and the gateway to the heath. At its centre was a fenced-off area, with a pair of old-fashioned red phone boxes and half a dozen benches surrounding a large, Gothic-looking fountain.

'It's Victorian,' Joffe said. 'Listed, I think.' He began leading Tanner and Chall slowly round the fountain. 'Once in a while someone raises the money to get it working, but a few months later the council decides to turn it off again.'

Chall was doing his best to look interested, but Tanner was grateful that the circuit was no more than twenty or twenty-five steps. They were not here to go sightseeing. Looking down, she saw that every few feet, a quotation from a famous writer had been carved into the paving slabs beneath her feet. Orwell, Keats, Robert Louis Stevenson. She stopped to read the somewhat incongruous contribution from Agatha Christie.

If one sticks too rigidly to one's principles, one would hardly see anybody.

After wiping moisture away with a handkerchief, Joffe sat down on an empty bench and stretched his legs out. Tanner and Chall joined him, one on either side. It was warm, despite the drizzle, and most of the other benches were occupied. What looked like a pair of students ate salad from plastic containers, a teenage girl communed with her phone, and an elderly woman sat murmuring to a small dog.

Tanner took her notebook from her bag.

'This was all done up last year.' Joffe waved a hand towards the railings and the low hedge on the other side, beneath which several rows of tired-looking daffodils and tulips had been neatly laid out and had dutifully bloomed.

'Nice.' Chall nodded down at the uplighters built into the paving stones and the literary words of wisdom etched into the concrete around them. 'I read *Animal Farm* at school.'

'All about reclaiming the spot for the local community, apparently, but really more to do with getting shot of the boozers and junkies who were hanging around.' Joffe shook his head. 'Hence getting the special new benches.'

'They're comfortable,' Chall said.

Joffe stabbed a finger towards the raised metal ridges that divided the bench they were sitting on into three separate seats. 'Yes, they're OK to sit on, but they're designed to be impossible to stretch out and sleep on.'

'Ah,' Chall said.

'The locals can be a bit . . . intolerant,' Joffe said. He looked across at Tanner, as though she might find what he had to say next of special interest. 'They didn't want a new Sainsbury's either.'

Tanner managed a nod, which meant nothing. She said, 'We'll try not to keep you, Dr Joffe.'

'It's Robin.'

Tanner waited.

'Whatever I can do to help,' Joffe said. 'Whatever's going to help catch the person responsible.' He shook his head. 'I still can't quite believe it. Well, none of us can.'

Tanner asked the most important question first, hoping that Joffe's answer might speed things up a little.

'I went to the pub with everyone else straight after the session,' Joffe said. 'Same as we usually did. I left after about an hour, I think.'

Tanner asked for the name of the pub and wrote it down. 'What did you do after that?'

'I went home and was visited by an escort.' He stared at Tanner, waiting for a reaction. Next to him, Chall shifted in his seat. 'She was called Amber, though I'm sure that's not her real name because she's Eastern European. They all are. I'm very happy to give you the name of the escort agency so you can check all this out.'

'Thank you,' Tanner said.

'You're very . . . honest,' Chall said.

'I don't lie. Not any more.'

'Never?'

'Not about anything important.'

'What time did Amber leave?' Tanner asked.

'She was there about an hour,' Joffe said. 'And that included dinner.'

Tanner stared at him.

'Joke,' Joffe said. 'Seriously . . . I paid for an hour, but it didn't take that long. She probably left just before ten o'clock.' He watched Tanner writing in her notebook. 'It's become something of a habit, to tell you the truth. At the sessions with Tony I get certain things off my chest and afterwards I feel I need a different kind of . . . relief.' He looked at Chall. 'Routine is important when you're in recovery.'

'I hope the agency gives you some kind of discount,' Chall said.

Joffe smiled and looked back to Tanner.

'Do you remember what happened at that final session?' she asked. 'What people got off their chests?'

'I'm afraid not,' Joffe said.

'Anything that might be significant? You know, looking back on it.'

'I'm sorry, but I'm not really comfortable talking about what went on in any specific session. That's the only rule we have. It would be a betrayal.'

Tanner was not surprised. 'What happened to wanting to do whatever you could to help?'

Joffe took a few seconds. He straightened the creases in his dark trousers. 'I'm sure you'll get the same response from the others.' He glanced at Tanner. 'May I ask who else you've spoken to?'

'We've already interviewed Christopher Clemence.' She saw the doctor's reaction. 'What?'

'Well, let's just say that Chris and I don't exactly see eye to eye a lot of the time. It would be fair to say that, when it comes to the process of recovery, how we approach it, we're very much at either end of the "spectrum".'

'Chalk and cheese,' Chall said.

'One way of putting it.'

126

'And where was Heather, would you say?' Tanner asked. 'On this "spectrum".'

Joffe thought about it. 'She was the peacemaker, quite often. I mean she didn't take any crap and if she thought someone was in the wrong about something she would speak up, but most of the time I think Heather just wanted everyone to get on. Impossible, obviously.'

Tanner was still writing when the old woman with the dog got up from the adjacent bench and moved towards them. Her dog, a scruffy-looking terrier, stopped and began sniffing at Tanner's feet. When it began jumping and pawing at her shins, Tanner quickly raised her hands out of reach of the dog's face, held them up next to her own.

The old woman said, 'Come on,' and pulled the terrier away.

'Are you afraid of dogs?' Joffe asked.

'Sorry?'

'It's quite common.'

'No, I'm not.'

'I know a hypnotherapist who might be able to help.' He took his phone from his inside pocket and began scrolling as he spoke. 'This chap's excellent, really. He works with smokers, people with phobias, over-eaters. Actually, I recommended him to someone in the group.'

Tanner raised a hand. 'Thank you, but there's really no need.' She waited, then watched Joffe slip his phone back into his pocket. 'Now, if you aren't willing to talk in specifics about the group—'

'I can't.'

'Can you give us some idea of the kind of thing that went on? What a typical session might be like. It would be a big help.'

Joffe nodded. 'Well, the simple answer is that there's no such thing as a typical session. I've been in plenty of groups—'

'I'm only interested in the group that you and Heather were in. The Monday evening group with Mr De Silva.'

Joffe shrugged. 'Same thing applies,' he said. 'Sometimes it was an hour and a half's shouting match and sometimes we spent all our time laughing. It would depend on the make-up of the group that particular night, what mood everyone was in. It would only take one person to disrupt it, you know? To create a bad ... vibe or whatever.'

Tanner thanked him and made another note. 'We're keen to talk to everyone in the group and Mr De Silva has told us that if individual group members are OK with it they're free to give us the names. As I said, so far we've only spoken to Mr Clemence.'

'Right. Well, the only person whose full name I actually know is Diana Knight. We've had meals together a couple of times.' He smiled and glanced at Chall. 'Nothing like that, I should add. She lives in Barnet, so hopefully you'll be able to track her down.'

Tanner put her notebook away and lifted her bag up on to her lap. 'What did you mean before? When you said about not being at your best ten years ago.'

Joffe swept his hair back, straightened those trouser creases again. 'Well, you know I'm a recovering addict, so I would have thought you could work that much out for yourselves.'

'Alcohol?' Tanner waited. 'Drugs?'

'Drugs, primarily.'

For the first time since Tanner had clapped eyes on Robin Joffe, he was looking uncomfortable. She knew that the doctor did not have a criminal record, but now she thought she understood why he might be so reluctant to talk to police officers in his place of work.

She said, 'OK.'

'Is it relevant?'

'In the early stages of an investigation, it's hard to say what is and isn't relevant.' Tanner stood up. Joffe and Chall quickly followed suit. 'Clearly your support group was very important to Heather, so ...'

'Important to all of us,' Joffe said.

Handshakes were briskly exchanged for the second time. Tanner thought that Joffe's palm was perhaps a little clammy, but the drizzle had been getting heavier and the bench might well have been damper than it looked.

'I know you won't be able to go into any details.' Joffe shifted his weight from one foot to the other. 'About what happened to Heather, I mean. But can you at least tell me if was quick? Did she suffer?'

Tanner dragged the strap of her bag on to her shoulder and said, 'Yes, I think she probably did.'

The doctor muttered, 'Thank you,' but looked rather as though he wished he had never asked.

They watched Robin Joffe walking away towards the hospital, his dark coat flapping behind him as he trudged back up the hill.

'Want me to check out his alibi?' Chall asked.

'He hasn't got an alibi,' Tanner said. 'His friend Amber had gone by ten and we know from the phone records that Heather Finlay was still alive at half past.'

'What do you make of all that not lying stuff?'

'Everyone lies,' Tanner said. Simple, a matter of fact. 'And even if everything he says is the truth, it doesn't mean there aren't things he's choosing not to tell us.' She turned round and stared at the fountain. 'Call the escort agency anyway and see if you can talk to Amber, or whatever her name is.'

'Right.'

'And try not to get overexcited. If she says you're special and that she really likes you, she's definitely lying.'

'I'll bear that in mind,' Chall said. He pointed at the floor. 'You read any of her books?'

Tanner looked down at Agatha Christie's words carved into the shiny slab. She shook her head. The truth was that she'd barely read anything as a child, having been far more interested in rough and tumble with her two elder brothers. She didn't read much now, and certainly not crime. There was a time when she and Susan might have watched an occasional crime drama on TV, but Susan's tastes were distinctly cosy and Tanner had finally called a halt to the nonsense after seeing a victim on *Midsomer Murders* dispatched by a giant cheese.

'The little grey cells,' Chall said.

'What?' Tanner bent to pick up a crisp packet, caught in a sodden clump of fallen blossom.

Chall tapped a finger against the side of his head and said it again, this time laying on the cod Belgian accent good and thick.

Tanner straightened up and walked towards a litter bin. 'I don't think I've got enough of them,' she said.

. . . NOW

At the door of the church hall in Belsize Park, Robin was greeted by a reticent young man with bad skin who mumbled a welcome, but could not make eye contact. It was perfectly normal and Robin guessed that the woman looking at the floor when she was not dispensing hot drinks from a sagging trestle table was feeling equally awkward. Those still in their first ninety days clean or uneasy with sharing would often be allocated service posts. It left them little option but to meet people, to make contact with those who had once been where they were now.

Robin took care to say hello, to tell each of them they were doing a great job. The young man nodded and the woman's nervous smile showed what few teeth she had left.

As soon he had taken his tea and grabbed a handful of digestives, he went and sat down towards the back of the room. It was cold and overly lit. There were perhaps forty people scattered unevenly across seven or eight rows. There was a good deal of chair-scraping which echoed around the hall and a few fragments of whispered conversation, until a woman Robin recognised stood up from her chair at the front. As secretary of the meeting, she ran through the guidelines

131

with which he was well familiar. Shares, she said, were to be confined to those matters relating to and affecting an individual's recovery, and the twelve-step programme of Narcotics Anonymous. Everyone was to refrain from obscenity, abusive language and personal attacks and, in line with NA traditions, there was to be no expression of opinion on outside topics. Smiling, she confirmed that this was an open group, so Robin knew that not everyone present would be an addict. There might be the concerned parents of teenagers in attendance, or the odd Channel 4 documentary maker; friends there to lend moral support or simply those who were curious to see what went on. They were warmly welcomed, though all were required to identify themselves and none would be allowed to speak.

The secretary then introduced the chosen chair for the evening and an older man stood up and said how happy he was to be there, to have the chance to share his strength and his hope. In a thin, reedy voice, he talked for twenty minutes about his own journey, choosing to focus on the first step, the most important, he said more than once, and the one which he had certainly found the toughest: the admission that he had been powerless, that his life had become unmanageable.

Robin sat back and let the words sink in and soothe him, as such words always did.

Now he had the power back.

Now he could manage everything . . .

He had looked up the meeting in the where-to-find booklet that was always in his pocket. It was one he had attended once or twice before, but not on this particular day of the week. Normally he went to meetings a little closer to home, but this had been an emergency and so he had sought out the venue nearest to the hospital. The place he could get to fastest as soon as his shift had ended.

It was a long time since he had needed a meeting this badly.

He could not remember feeling so discombobulated, so jumpy. A few hours before, walking back to the hospital after the meeting on South End Green, he had felt his chest pulsing beneath his coat and jacket, his heart rate elevated as much by the conversation as it was by the gradient.

He still wondered how he had come across.

It was hard to be yourself at the best of times, talking to police officers, all but impossible when that self was still ... fractured; still in the process of putting itself back together. They knew how to throw people, of course; that was all part and parcel, wasn't it? Tanner had been especially good at that, he thought and he supposed that female officers were generally better than their male counterparts when it came to the psychological stuff. He well remembered the tricks his ex-wife had played when the wheels had come off his marriage. The passive-aggressive stuff and the threats so subtle that he had half thought he was imagining them.

You've worked so hard to get where you are. It would be a shame to throw all that away ...

He had tried to appear calm, back there on that bench, to gather his thoughts when he needed to and say only what was necessary. All fine and dandy until the end, when the woman had brought up his past. His own fault for mentioning it in the first place, but being happy with who he was now meant a blanket refusal to deny who he had once been.

I don't lie ...

Once the chair had finished, the secretary opened the meeting to the floor and the addicts began to speak up. They raised a hand and introduced themselves, were welcomed in that manner so parodied by sceptics and lazy comedy writers, then said whatever they had come to say.

I'm twenty-three days clean.

I want to get sober, but I'm scared of what I'll be like.

I don't really know why I'm here. I don't actually have a problem.

Robin had heard variations on that one more times than he could remember.

After hands had been joined and the serenity prayer spoken aloud, the meeting broke up and people began to drift towards the street,

133

most lighting cigarettes the second they were out in the fresh air. There was a good deal of hugging and chatter. Some walked away together in twos and threes, while others loitered awkwardly near the door, as though hoping to be spoken to or invited elsewhere.

The secretary laid a hand gently on Robin's arm. 'Not seen you here for a while,' she said.

'No.'

'Everything OK?'

Robin quickly assured her that everything was fine and said how much he had enjoyed the meeting. As soon as someone else joined the conversation he seized the chance to walk away.

I don't lie . . .

His hands were shaking. He thrust them into the pockets of his overcoat as he hurried towards his car. As soon as he had closed the door of the Audi, he reached for his phone and began searching through his list of contacts. The very least he could do was call Diana and warn her that the police would soon be knocking on her door.

It was only polite.

Neither had felt like cooking, so they ate at a small Chinese place on Hammersmith Grove. It was walkable, as well as being a damn sight cheaper than somewhere in the West End, and – though Tanner had tired of pointing out that there was probably a very good reason – they could always get a table.

Susan scattered slivers of spring onion into a pancake and reached for the last few pieces of the crispy duck they had been sharing. 'Paul Murphy was back on form again today.'

'Oh good. It's been ages.'

'Well, he was absent for a lot of the time.'

'Oh. That's a worry, isn't it?'

'Are you kidding? Never seen the staff room so happy.'

Susan taught at a primary school in Chiswick and the boy in question had been the subject of many of her favourite stories over the past couple of years. Most of them were hilarious, or had at least become so in the telling, though Tanner was convinced that the boy's often bizarre behaviour hinted at a home life that was anything but happy.

'He exploded in the bogs,' Susan said.

'*What?*'

'Well, as good as.' She took a bite of her pancake, and chewed fast, keen to tell the story. 'So, nobody can find Paul after lunch. Everyone's looking and they finally find him in the toilets and it's like he's ... exploded. I'm not kidding; there's shit everywhere.'

Tanner grimaced. 'Come on, Sue, not while we're eating.'

Susan grinned. 'I swear, it was like a dirty protest. So we called his mum ... have I told you about Paul's mum?'

'The one who looks like a boxer.'

'A very bad boxer. Anyway, so she comes steaming in half an hour later and he's still there sitting on the floor because nobody wants to try and clean him up ... she marches into the toilets, takes one look at him and says, "Fuck's sake, Paul, I told you fourteen peaches was too many."'

Tanner thought how good it felt to laugh. She had enjoyed the occasional bit of banter with Dipak Chall and one or two others over the past few days, but there had not been much cause for hilarity, not like this. Susan could always do that. It was one of the reasons Tanner loved her partner so much.

'Fourteen peaches!' Susan said and they laughed some more.

The waiter arrived to clear the starter away. When he had gathered up the plates and bowls he asked if they needed any more beers. Tanner said she was fine as she was, while Susan quickly downed the last of her Tsingtao and ordered another.

'I was at South End Green today.'

'At where?'

Tanner explained where it was, told Susan about the fountain she had never noticed before and the quotations on the ground around it. 'My murder case,' she said. 'The woman in Victoria.'

135

'Did you read any of those books when you were a kid?' Susan smiled as the waiter returned and put down her beer. 'Murders in vicarages and what have you.'

For the second time in one day, Tanner said that she didn't.

'I used to like the Secret Seven,' Susan said. 'The Famous Five and all that. I was always convinced that George was one of ours.'

'I was talking to a doctor,' Tanner said. 'That's why I was there. He was in a kind of support group with my victim.'

'What kind of group?'

'Just a general . . . therapy kind of thing.' Despite the fact that the only other occupied table was on the other side of the restaurant, Tanner leaned forward and lowered her voice. 'He told me he'd been taking drugs while he was still performing operations.'

Susan nodded, took a few pieces of cucumber. 'High functioning,' she said. 'That's what they call it.' She took a swig of beer. 'I don't get it.'

'What?'

'Drugs. Never have. Couple of puffs of dope when I was in the sixth form and that was me done.'

Tanner nodded. This wasn't anything she didn't know, hadn't heard before, but it was fine. Two people who had been together as long as they had were bound to start repeating themselves. Sometimes it was probably because they had simply run out of things to say, but often it was about reintroducing themselves. Replanting a flag. Each reminding the other that they had an opinion on something other than whether the kettle needed descaling and whose turn it was to take the rubbish out; views about one issue or another that still counted for something.

'Never seen the point,' Susan said.

'I know.' Tanner wondered how many times she had told Susan just what she thought about arming the police or capital punishment or the dangers of the internet. Then she thought about the things she had never told her.

'People make a choice, don't they?'

Tanner nodded again.

'I do that line of coke or I don't. I take that tablet or I don't, whatever. I know people talk about it being genetic or being about family and environment, but at the end of the day, they choose to do it.'

'Like which skirt should I wear today? Like whether I want salt and pepper squid or sizzling beef?'

'You know what I mean.'

'Maybe it's the only choice some people have.'

'What, like your druggy doctor? Operating on people while he's off his tits?'

'Some people,' Tanner said.

Like a young woman who finally made a choice to get clean; to reclaim her life. Only for someone to take it from her.

'I know you think I'm unsympathetic,' Susan said.

Forty minutes later they handed over credit cards, splitting things straight down the middle, same as always. They left enough change for a tip and each took a fortune cookie, to take the taste of the MSG away as much as anything. The stickiness on the teeth, the slick coating on the roof of the mouth.

Tanner's fingers pushed through the brittle, yellowish crescent as Susan read out her motto. Something about a long-awaited opportunity, a lucky number. Even as Tanner was unfolding her own thin slip of paper, she was thinking about a motto she had seen elsewhere, hand-drawn in felt-tip pen behind dirty glass. Bold and brightly coloured; fringed by stars and smiley faces.

We are only as sick as our secrets.

. . . THEN

To Tony's experienced eye, the body language and the enthusiasm of the responses around the circle when he asks the usual question suggest that everyone has genuinely had a pretty good week. Or that, at least, nobody has had a bad one. He looks once more at Chris to be sure; gets a roll of the eyes and a confirmatory nod.

'Excellent,' he says. He straightens the notepad on his lap, rolls the biro between his fingers.

'Me and Diana had lunch,' Caroline says.

· 'I have lunch every day.' Chris looks for someone willing to play along. 'Breakfast as well, sometimes. I'm a nutcase, me.'

'We had lunch together. At Diana's house.' Caroline looks at Tony. 'That's all right, isn't it?'

'I told you it was.' Diana sounds a little irritated that she was not believed, that the younger woman is insisting on checking. Or perhaps she just thinks that Caroline is sucking up to Tony.

'Of course,' Tony says.

'As long as we don't sleep together, right?'

'Is that likely?' Chris leans forward. 'Only I know people who'd pay good money to come along and film that. You know, for people with specialised tastes.'

'Don't start,' Heather says.

Caroline smiles. 'Water off a duck's back.'

'That's a lot of water,' Chris says.

Tony raises a finger, waits for silence, then looks at Caroline again. 'This group is all about learning that we're not alone, that others have been through what we have. Are still going through it. Interaction is a really important part of that process and if it carries on outside this circle, so much the better.'

Caroline says, 'Great,' and smiles at Diana.

'As long as it doesn't lead to the development of smaller groups within the larger one.' Tony lets that sink in. 'That's important, too. Cliques are never a good idea.'

'Me and Chris met up as well,' Heather says. 'Well, you know we sometimes do.'

Tony nods. 'Right, and that's absolutely fine, but the same thing applies.'

'I bet our lunch wasn't quite as swanky as yours though.' Chris looks to his left and waits for Diana to look back at him. 'Suckling pig, was it? Roast swan?'

'We had salad,' Caroline says.

Diana turns sharply to look at her. 'I was trying to ... cater.'

'I know. I didn't mean it to sound ...' Caroline reddens. 'It was lovely.'

When Chris has finished giggling, he nods across at Robin. 'What about you? Nobody want to have lunch with you, then?'

'I rarely have time to socialise,' Robin says. 'I work.'

'I work too,' Caroline says. 'Anyway, we had lunch on Saturday.'

'Tell us about your job,' Tony says. 'If you want.'

'Nothing to tell.' Caroline shrugs. 'Supermarket.'

'Nothing wrong with that,' Heather says.

'Never said there was.'

'I was sacked from a supermarket.'

'What for?'

'Nicking stuff.' Heather shakes her head. 'They make it so easy.'

'Can't have been that easy or you wouldn't have got caught.' Caroline laughs and Heather laughs along with her.

'Old habits,' Tony says. He sits forward. 'We've talked about this before, haven't we? Many of us have stolen or worse to feed our addiction, and even when we're in recovery the urge to do those things can still linger.'

'Sometimes I wish I'd got caught,' Robin says. Tony turns to him. 'Because I had access to whatever I needed, I never had to steal, or anything else. It was too easy to feed the addiction, basically. Anaesthetists don't even have to write prescriptions, they can just order up a bit more of this drug, a bit more of that one, no questions asked.' He smiles, but there's no joy in it. 'Possibly another reason why they have the highest suicide rate in the medical profession. Anyway, I'm just saying that perhaps if I'd been forced to break the law and been caught ... if I'd gone to prison even ... I might have got clean a lot sooner than I did.'

'That's interesting,' Tony says.

Robin nods. 'A wake-up call sort of thing.'

Chris barks out a dry laugh. 'If you think there's no drugs in prison, you're an idiot.'

'Chris.' Tony looks at him; a warning.

'Sorry. Just saying ... it's rife inside, mate. *Rife*. People go into prison clean as a whistle and come out as major league junkies.'

'Yes, I'm sure you're right,' Robin says. 'It wasn't a good example.' He stares at Chris. 'Have you been in prison?'

Chris looks at his feet, the toes of his training shoes tapping out a rhythm. 'I know, all right?'

The group falls silent for a while. They shift in their chairs and watch the day continue to dim outside the conservatory windows. Tony takes the opportunity to scribble a few notes. Heather stands up

140

and takes off her jacket. As she is hanging it carefully across the back of her chair, Tony looks across. He sees no sign of a mark on either sleeve. When Heather sits down she catches him looking and smiles. It looks like embarrassment, but Tony can see that she's pleased at the acknowledgement of their private conversation; this moment between them.

'I want to go back to talking about shame,' Tony says. 'The resolution of the shame in our pasts as part of the recovery process. As part of redefining ourselves.' He looks around the circle. 'Everyone still OK with that?'

'Absolutely,' Diana says.

Robin nods. 'I found it hugely helpful.'

Tony looks at Chris. Chris stretches his legs out and says, 'Yeah, whatever. I said my piece about this last week.'

'Say it again if you like,' Tony says.

'Not much point if everyone else is up for it.'

'We never do anything if it makes any member of the group uncomfortable.'

Chris waves away Tony's concerns. 'Whatever. Don't look at me though. All I'm saying.'

Opposite him, Heather begins to make chicken noises, quiet at first, then growing in volume. Chris puffs out his cheeks as though supremely bored and gives her the finger.

Tony stifles a smile. 'Nobody has volunteered to ... lead things off tonight, but I don't think that's any bad thing, as it happens. Preparing something often leads to a certain amount of ... self-censorship, which is never very helpful. With this particular part of the process, I'm wondering if being thrown in the deep end might actually pay dividends.' He looks around the circle again then extends a hand towards Caroline.

'Oh, God,' she says.

Tony holds up both hands. 'No problem if you'd rather not, but if that's the case, I think it might be useful to talk about why you don't want to.'

141

'It's not that I don't want to, but I really haven't got anything to say.' She looks at Robin, then Diana. 'Just so I'm clear, you're not talking about being ashamed of who we are now, right? What we've done . . .'

Tony shakes his head. 'Something more deep-seated than that. Something that we did, or perhaps something was done to us, that may well have been what led to the addictive behaviour in the first place.'

'And it's not always immediate,' Robin says. 'It can take years for that behaviour to surface.'

'You running this now?' Chris asks.

'No, he isn't,' Tony says. 'But what Robin says is bang on. Just think about his own story, what happened to him when he was a child.'

Caroline nods, understanding. She takes a deep breath, then shakes her head. 'There's nothing. Sorry.'

'Really?' Chris narrows his eyes and studies her. 'You seriously telling us that you never strangled the neighbour's cat or murdered your parents? Seriously?'

Caroline ignores him, keeps looking at Tony. 'I swear. I've been thinking about this since last week and I just can't think of anything. There's nothing I'm ashamed of, honestly. Is that . . . weird? I mean, is that not normal?'

'It's fine,' Tony says.

'Fine,' Diana says.

Heather leans towards her. 'And you've got nothing to be sorry about, either.'

Caroline looks relieved. 'You can ask someone else if you want to, but there is something I'd quite like to talk about, if that's OK.' She looks to Tony. He nods. 'I mean I know Chris was taking the mickey, saying that painkillers aren't really a proper addiction, you know . . . not hardcore, or whatever. Thing is, he's basically right. I took them and the pain went away, sometimes, but they didn't get me high or anything. So I wanted to ask the others what that was like. Well, maybe not Diana . . . obviously I know what being pissed is like.'

'I didn't get pissed,' Diana says, quickly. 'That was the problem. I told you that on your first night.'

'OK, sorry. Everyone else, then. When you take heroin. What does it do, exactly? How does it make you feel? I'm sitting here with you all every week and you're talking about these things and I've genuinely got no idea. I mean, is that . . . all right?'

Tony sits back. Robin appears to be thinking about it. Heather and Chris exchange a look.

'It's fucking fantastic,' Chris says, eventually. 'I'm not going to lie. It's the best feeling in the world. Why else would you do it?'

'Ignore him,' Heather says. 'He's talking crap and he knows he is.' She has been looking hard at Chris, but now she turns to Caroline. 'Yeah, it's good to begin with, but in the end you're not using to feel great. You're using to stop feeling shit.'

'Very different things,' Robin says.

'I don't think I ever used because I wanted to feel great.'

'You mean like you see in films?' Caroline asks. 'When they're throwing themselves around and screaming?'

'That's always such bollocks,' Heather says. 'Cold turkey isn't nice, but they always overdo it on TV and stuff. I'm talking about how you feel every day, when you need to score.'

'What's that like then?'

'You're a bit . . . spacey, you know? You wake up and it's like you've got the runs or something, but you haven't, because heroin makes you constipated. Then it's like you're *very* awake and you just feel like you've got flu.' She rubs her arm, remembering. 'You've got goose-pimples and you feel too hot, or too cold, and whatever you do you can't get comfortable. It's like your skin doesn't fit.'

'Greasy,' Robin says. 'Your skin feels greasy.'

Heather is still rubbing her arm. Chris is watching her.

'So, what's it feel like when you finally get it? When you shoot up?' Caroline puts the last two words in inverted commas, like she feels silly saying the phrase out loud.

'Weird thing is,' Heather says, 'all those symptoms go when you're about to fix. Just like that. Just knowing it's coming, you know? And the whole business is like this . . . ritual that you need. Spoons and

143

candles and all of it.' She laughs, shakes her head. 'When I was on methadone they used to give me pills, but I'd crush them up just so I could use a needle. A dirty needle was better than popping a pill. Like I was addicted to the works as much as anything else.

'Then you do it, and it's ... instant.' She snaps her fingers. 'The taste in the back of your throat, and the glow. This warm glow.'

Robin nods. 'Like those kids on the Ready Brek commercial. Remember?'

'What taste?' Caroline asks.

Heather thinks for a few seconds, then shakes her head. 'Can't describe it. It's ... heroin.' She cocks her head slowly right, then left, as though she's working out a stiffness in her neck. She says, 'What you said before, about the painkillers?'

'What?'

'It's no different, not really. Exactly the same thing applies to smack, or whatever else you're using.' Her eyes slide away from Caroline's. 'You take it and the pain goes away.'

'And you're the king of the world,' Chris says.

'Until you're not.'

Robin nods, knowingly. 'King of the world, piece of shit.' He looks at Caroline. 'It's something we say a lot. It's what junkies are, what they feel like most of the time. Always the two extremes.'

'What are you now?' Caroline asks.

'I'm a piece of the world,' Robin says.

Chris throws his arms wide. 'And I'm the King of Shit.'

As had happened the previous week, as often happens whenever part of the session has drifted into heavy territory, they spend the rest of the time swapping stories. Tony is happy with the shape of such sessions. The dissipation of any tensions that might have built up, the reassertion of the group as a unit before they go their separate ways for another week.

He listens as Robin tells them about a junior doctor who snorted coke off the belly of a coma patient and Heather talks about an old friend of hers, a woman smaller than she was who had once stolen a dumper truck and driven it into a chemist's in the middle of the night.

Tony keeps a careful eye on his watch and, with five minutes to go, he raises a finger. 'Now, before we call it a night, Heather has something she wants to give everyone.'

'Is it an STD?' Chris asks.

Even Robin and Diana can't help but laugh, but Heather ignores them. She takes a large envelope from her bag, then stands up and moves around the circle, passing out the personalised invitations.

Diana says, 'A party. That's fantastic.'

Heather hands Tony his invitation last. 'Not really a party. I mean it'll probably just be us. I wanted to celebrate with the group, you know.'

Chris pretends to fight back tears. 'That's beautiful.'

'Well, count me in,' Robin says.

Caroline tells Heather how nice the invitations are. She says she would love to come and asks if there's anything she can do to help.

'Not sure I can make it,' Chris says. 'I might be washing my hair. *X Factor* might be on.'

'And I might cut your balls off,' Heather says.

Diana says, 'Are you coming, Tony?'

'I'm afraid I can't.' Tony looks at Heather for a moment or two, then addresses the group. 'Not really ethical, you know? But I think it's a great idea.'

'Course he can't,' Robin says. 'Professional distance.'

'Right,' Chris says.

'Yeah, but it's her birthday,' Caroline says. 'What if one of your patients invited you to a party? You could go, couldn't you?'

'Yes, probably, but it's not the same. There isn't a relationship, as such. I don't anaesthetise the same patient every week.'

'I bet you weren't always so sure.' Chris is reaching for the small rucksack beneath his chair, the time almost up.

'Meaning?'

'Meaning you were so off your tits a few years ago, you could have knocked the same patient out every day for a month and you wouldn't have had a clue.' He's grinning, but there's an edge. 'Wouldn't have known one end of a body from the other.'

'If you're going to be an argumentative arsehole, I'd rather you didn't come.' Heather reaches for her jacket.

'Will there be nibbles?'

'I'm serious.'

'Jelly and ice cream?'

'See you all next week,' Tony says. 'I'll expect a full report.'

Chris stands up. 'Probably won't happen anyway.' He walks towards the door, swinging his rucksack. 'Some seagull will have looked at her the wrong way and she'll have chucked herself under a train.'

... THEN

They walk up towards the Broadway. Chris is out in front, twenty feet or so ahead of anyone else, though it is probably down to more than his naturally longer stride or any eagerness to get to the pub and order an orange juice. Caroline, Robin and Diana are behind and Caroline is well aware that the other two are deliberately walking more slowly than they might otherwise.

She nods towards Chris.

'You reckon he was overweight when he was a kid?'

Robin and Diana watch Chris striding purposefully ahead, increasing the distance between them. Robin shrugs.

'You know, the problem he's clearly got with fat people.'

'I think he's got a problem with almost everyone,' Diana says. 'You're too big, I'm too posh ...'

'There's a pattern developing,' Robin says. 'And I'm getting bloody sick of it. He says something to piss me off, to get a rise out of me, I make the first move to try and smooth things over and then the next week he's at it again. Well, I won't be doing it any more.'

'I suppose I should be relieved it's not just me,' Caroline says.

Diana has taken a compact from her bag and checks her make-up

147

as they walk. 'It's pretty obvious that he doesn't want to let anyone in. To get close, I mean.'

'Why do you think that is?' Caroline asks.

'I don't really care,' Robin says. 'Let Tony deal with it.'

Caroline glances back over her shoulder. 'What happened to Heather? I thought she was behind us.'

The other two look. Robin says, 'Maybe she forgot something.' When he turns back, he's surprised to see Caroline forging ahead alone. He can hear her panting as she almost breaks into a run. She shouts to Chris, tells him to wait for her. Chris looks round and scowls, then slows dramatically to let her catch up.

She puts an arm through his and he tenses.

'What you doing?'

Caroline all but drags him forward and they carry on walking. 'Why are you so afraid that someone might actually like you?'

'Nothing to do with being afraid,' Chris says.

'No, course not.'

'I just don't care.'

'Yeah, you do.'

'You don't know what you're talking about.'

It's cold, and Caroline gives a small shiver as she leans against him. 'I just save myself a lot of trouble and presume people won't like me. Easier that way.'

They walk on in silence towards the top of the hill, past the luxury cars and double-fronted Edwardian houses, some even grander than Tony's. A couple of million and change, every dozen steps.

Caroline says, 'I used to be exactly the same, you know.'

'Same as what?' Chris says.

'Not wanting people to get too close.' She is dictating their pace, but still breathing heavily. 'No self-esteem, probably; all that. I was always suspicious, always thinking people had some kind of agenda. If it was a woman, I always thought they just wanted to make themselves look better by having a fat mate, and if it was a bloke I'd think they were doing it for a bet or had some pervy thing about wanting to shag a fat lass.' She looks at him. 'You ever shagged a fat bloke?'

'Only for money,' Chris says.

'Some people like it.'

'Some people like all sorts of weird shit.' He looks at her. 'No offence.'

She nods, like she's impressed. 'Well, that's progress, I suppose.' They cross over and head left on the main road, walking a little faster now they're on the flat. 'You're right though. *I* think it's weird. I mean, don't get me wrong, I'll take it where I can get it, but I'd much rather be with someone . . . fit. You know, who can do it for more than five minutes without needing oxygen.'

Chris laughs. He says, 'I did have a bloke pass out on me once. But I think it was just that he'd never seen a cock that big before.'

Caroline laughs. She leans in even closer and says, 'Well, you know where I am . . . if you ever fancy batting for the other team.'

The Broadway is busy, music and chatter spilling out from a large pub that has opened in what was once a church, but they keep walking, on the opposite side of the road, arm in arm towards their regular. They can hear Robin and Diana, laughing about something, thirty seconds' walk behind them.

'Good thing about being clean,' Chris says. 'One of the good things. You get your sex drive back.'

'Really?'

He nods. 'When you're using . . . it's just something you do to pass the time. Like eating something with no taste. Like putting a rubbish jigsaw together.' He grins at her. 'Nice to actually enjoy it again.'

'One more reason I'm glad I never went down that road,' Caroline says.

'There's lots of good reasons,' Chris says.

In sight of the pub, Caroline slowly removes her arm from Chris's and runs pudgy fingers through her hair. 'Stupid, isn't it?'

'What?'

'Keeping people at a distance because you feel bad about yourself.'

'I don't feel bad about myself.'

She nods, indulging him. 'I'm talking about me. Took me ages to realise what an idiot I was being. It's why I joined the group, basically.'

Chris throws his arms out. 'To meet fabulous people, you mean?'

'To meet anyone,' she says.

'If you were looking for a social club, you could have done a hell of a lot better.'

'OK, not just for that.'

'Now, I could take you to some *seriously* great clubs . . .'

'I just wanted to get to know people who might have some of the same things going on. The same problems.' She straightens her dress, where the material has gathered in creases across her chest. 'To let them get to know me.'

'Don't worry,' Chris says. 'We'll get to know everything before we're done with you.' He pushes the door to the pub, holds it open for her. Caroline thanks him, then hesitates, just for a second, before entering.

'There's this one place.' Chris follows her inside. 'Trust me, you haven't lived till you've seen dwarves in tight leather shorts.'

Tony has heard the voices, and when he comes down the stairs he can see that Nina is at the front door, talking to someone. When she becomes aware of him, she opens the door a little wider to reveal Heather standing on the doorstep. Heather smiles and raises a hand. Nina throws Tony a look; no more than a glance, but one that makes it clear there will be words between them later on.

'For you,' she says.

'Right,' Tony says. 'Thank you.' He stands to one side as his wife turns to walk past him and up the stairs. He waits a few seconds before stepping forward.

'Sorry,' Heather says. 'I just—'

'Did you leave something?' Tony's voice is measured and very low.

She shakes her head. 'I just wanted to ask if it was about that phone call on Saturday.'

'I'm not with you.'

'The reason you won't come to my birthday party.'

Tony's head drops and he lets out a sigh. He's not at work now, he has a glass of wine on his desk upstairs, so there's less need to maintain a professional position, to rein in his feelings. When he looks up again, Heather is staring at him, hands thrust into the pockets of that bloody suede jacket.

'I explained why I can't come.'

'Sounded like an excuse to me.'

'Well it wasn't.'

'I said I was sorry on the phone.' She sounds sulky and she gently kicks her training shoe against the doorstep. 'I know I shouldn't have called, but I told you, you're the only person who can sort me out when I get like that.'

'I know,' Tony says. 'We sorted it out. It's fine.'

'So, why don't you want to come to my party?'

'It's not about whether I want to. It's what Robin said. There needs to be a professional distance.' He moves his hand back and forth in the air between them, emphasising the space. 'I'm the therapist and you're the client.'

'When we're in the group, yeah.'

'All the time, Heather.' She nods, as though she gets it. What he's saying, or what she thinks he *has* to say, considering the circumstances. 'Do you understand?'

'That we're not friends, you mean? That you don't like me?'

'I never said that.' Tony sighs again. He's thinking about his glass of wine getting warmer, that hotel in Venice or Barcelona.

'It's not about whether you want to.' Heather nods again, kicks the doorstep. 'That's what you said, right?'

'Correct.'

'So, *do* you want to? I mean, I get that you can't, but would you want to come otherwise?'

151

'It's a pointless question.'

'Still. Would you?'

'Why wouldn't I? I like parties as much as anyone else.'

This seems to satisfy Heather. She visibly relaxes a little. Tony half turns back inside, but Heather does not move. She says, 'Your wife seems nice.'

'What?'

'She clearly doesn't like me, but she seems nice, otherwise.' A car being driven too fast passes the house, bumping hard across one of the many sleeping policemen. Heather blinks. 'Is she?'

Tony's fingers tighten a little around the edge of the door. He shrugs. 'Of course she is, she's my wife.' He is watching closely for a reaction when Heather's eyes move suddenly to fix on something behind him and, when he turns, Tony sees his daughter standing in the hallway. He says her name. Then he says, 'Everything all right?'

Emma mutters what might be a 'Yeah'.

'Hello.' Heather cranes her head to get a better look inside.

Tony looks back sharply at Heather. He watches her smile and wave, but when he turns back to see how his daughter will react, she is already walking away towards the kitchen. He turns back to the door.

'Heather, look—'

'I should probably get along to the pub,' Heather says. She looks faintly pleased with herself.

'Yeah.' Tony nods and tries not to sound too relieved. 'The others will be missing you.'

'I doubt it.'

'See you next week then.'

'Yeah, course.' She hitches her bag on to her shoulder, narrows her eyes at him, mock-furious. 'I can tell you what you missed.'

'Right.' Tony takes half a step back from the door and watches Heather give the step a final nudge with the toe of her trainer. 'And listen, thanks for the invitation, OK? It was very thoughtful.'

152

'Don't sound so surprised.'

Tony says nothing; has no idea what to say. There had not been the faintest hint of anything like surprise in his voice. He closes the door, nice and gently, and lets out a breath. Halfway back up the stairs he stops and turns and, through the stained glass panels in the door, he can see that Heather is still standing there.

. . . THEN

Predictably, the TV in the corner is tuned to the Monday night football on Sky. The game is not due to kick off for another fifteen minutes, but the preening pundits are in full flow. It is make or break time, apparently. The big one; a must-win game. As usual, the only one showing any real interest is Diana, who glances up at the screen every minute or so from the group's regular table in the opposite corner.

'Do they have to take lessons or something?' Robin says. 'To learn how to speak in those awful clichés all the time? Somebody's going to be sick as a parrot in a minute.'

'Or over the moon,' Caroline says.

Chris sips his drink. 'I bet you there's at least a couple of junkies on that pitch.' He nods. 'Mate of mine says he was in rehab with a Man United player.'

'No way,' Caroline says. 'Who?'

They all look at Chris. He grins at their curiosity, then names the player and insists that plenty of top level footballers take drugs regularly. 'Worse than doctors,' he says. He smiles when Robin looks at him, lets him know that he is joking, that he has no agenda.

Robin nods and smiles back. Since his conversation with Caroline on the way to the pub, Chris appears to be in as good a mood as Robin can remember, and from the comments exchanged at the bar Robin is not the only one to have noticed. Chris seems genuinely interested in the conversation and, for once, his jokes – good and bad – have no discernible edge to them. Robin has not yet had a chance to ask Caroline what she and Chris had talked about, but he is waiting keenly for the opportunity. 'Well, footballers can certainly afford it,' Robin says. 'A hundred thousand pounds a week.'

'And the rest,' Diana says.

Caroline turns to her. 'So, how come you like football so much?'

'My ex-husband.' Diana taps a manicured nail against her glass. 'He likes it, so of course I pretended because I was a dutiful wife, and then eventually I did.' Her face changes suddenly, as though she has bitten into something sour. 'I wonder if she likes it. The new one. Or maybe he's pretending to like the things she likes. Facebook or what-ever.' She clears her throat, then looks up and around at the others. She shrugs, like it's no big deal, like she's being silly, but the bitterness in her voice charges the silence that hangs over the table for a few seconds. The others adjust their chairs. They stare into Cokes and mineral waters.

Chris says, 'Oh, you've decided to join us,' and they all look up, relieved, to see that Heather has arrived.

'Sorry,' she says.

'Did you forget something? Wasn't your precious jacket, was it?'

Heather grins, sarcastically. 'Tony wanted to talk to me,' she says. She asks if she can get anyone a drink, then heads to the bar to get one for herself. While she is gone, Caroline asks Chris if he knows about any other footballers with drug problems, while Diana talks to Robin about a persistent pain in her knee. Nobody speculates as to what Tony might have wanted to talk to Heather about.

'The way England play, I reckon they're all on Valium,' Chris says.

In the other corner, those gathered near the TV groan loudly as Arsenal miss a clear-cut chance to take an early lead.

'Sounds like you might have arthritis,' Robin says to Diana.

By the time Heather returns to the table, the group's conversation has fractured yet again. Chris is now talking happily to Robin, while at the other end of the table Caroline and Diana are leaning together.

Caroline says, 'I didn't mean anything, you know, at the session. When I said about the salad.'

'I know you didn't.'

'You seemed a bit pissed off, that's all.'

'Yes, sorry if I was a bit snappy,' Diana says. 'It's been rather an awful day.'

Caroline waits.

'Well, they're all awful at the moment, if I'm honest. I'm doing a lot of shopping.'

'Why not, if it makes you feel better?'

'It doesn't, though, not in the long run, but I can't help myself.' Diana shakes her head. 'Worse I feel, the more bloody shoes I buy. I can't imagine what Imelda Marcos must have been going through.'

'Who?'

Diana smiles and shakes her head. 'Anyway, it's no excuse for being a bitch, so sorry.'

'Is she a lot younger?' Caroline asks. 'The woman your ex-husband's with.'

Diana looks at her.

'What you said about Facebook.'

'Fifteen years,' Diana says. 'Younger, I mean . . . she's not actually fifteen. Though not far away.'

They both laugh, then Caroline says, 'Men are pathetic.'

'Yes, and they're predictable, and maybe that's why I don't really blame him. Who wouldn't want a newer car or a flashier house if they were offered it, but when a certain type of woman comes along and lays it all out on a plate—'

'A woman who hates other women.'

'Absolutely. With no thought whatsoever for the havoc they cause. The damage to so many others. It's completely unacceptable, don't you think?'

Caroline nods, largely because Diana is giving her little choice.

'It's . . . evil.' The older woman leans in even closer, and despite the designer clothes and the expensive hairstyle, it looks as though – were the target of her bile next to her at that moment – she would happily use the glass in her hand as a weapon. 'There are *rules*.'

A roar rises up from those watching the football and, startled by the noise and perhaps herself, Diana leans away quickly and turns around to look. The home side have gone a goal up. Caroline widens her eyes at Heather, but Heather is not close enough to have overheard the exchange and is busily eavesdropping on the conversation between Robin and Chris.

'You're in a good mood,' Robin says.

'It's the drink.' Chris raises his glass. 'Can't hold my orange juice.'

'Seriously, though. You had good news about your accommodation?' Robin suspects it isn't that, but it feels like a good place to start digging.

Chris is rocking very gently, as if in time to some music that nobody else can hear. 'I have good moods and bad moods, I suppose. Same as anyone else. Well, we're all a bit up and down, aren't we?'

'You more than most though, I'd say.'

Just for a moment there is a flash of the normal Chris; a narrowing of the eyes and something tight around his mouth. But then his face softens and he cocks his head. 'Yeah, can't really argue.'

'You can tell me to mind my own business—'

'Mind your own business.'

'Seriously . . . I was wondering if anyone had ever suggested that you might have bipolar disorder.'

Chris blinks. 'Bloody hell, do doctors ever take a day off?'

'It's only a thought. Might be helpful.'

'Tony mentioned it once,' Chris says. 'In a one-to-one.'

'Have you done anything about it?'

Chris shakes his head. 'It's meds, isn't it? Not sure I want to go there.'

'Medication isn't necessarily incompatible with recovery,' Robin says.

Chris does not look convinced. He says, 'Well, anyway, whether I'm bipolar or fucking *tri*polar, it's part of me, right? Makes me the lovable, glorious creature I am.'

Robin smiles and eventually touches his glass to the one that Chris raises towards him.

'Lovable, glorious arse a lot of the time, I'm well aware of that.' He doesn't bother with the pointless wait for Robin to contradict him. 'I shouldn't have said what I did at the session.'

'These things happen,' Robin says. 'Tony doesn't want us to self-censor.'

'Still. Must have been awful, trying to do a job like that. I mean having that responsibility while you were using. Most I ever had to worry about was finding somewhere to sleep.'

Robin nods, accepting the implicit apology, or simply remembering. 'It was my patients who suffered most of all. That's the worst part.'

'We've all done bad things,' Chris says.

'Relative, though, isn't it?'

Shouts for a penalty go up near the television, which quickly become pointless insults hurled at the referee when the decision is not given.

Once the noise has died down a little, Chris says, 'Would you have lost your job? If the hospital had found out?'

'Oh yes, immediately.'

'That would only have made things worse though, right? Better to be a junkie with a job.'

Robin shakes his head. 'I should have resigned.'

'Would you still lose it?' Chris has lowered his voice. 'If they found out now, I mean?'

'They wouldn't have any choice, would they?' A momentary tremor of pain distorts Robin's features. 'Then there's the inevitable lawsuits that would start flying around.'

'Oh right. Yeah ...' The shouting starts up again. Chris turns around and loudly asks the nearest fan to lower the volume. He gets a hard stare for his trouble, before turning back to Robin. 'Wonder how they'd feel if they knew their star midfielder was pissing all his wages away on coke?'

Caroline walks into the Ladies to discover Heather already in there. She is still at the sink when Caroline emerges from the cubicle and shifts across slightly so that Caroline can stand close to her, the pair of them looking at themselves in the small, cracked mirror like teenagers in a nightclub cloakroom.

'So come on then, what did Tony want?'

Heather's eyes shift to Caroline's reflection, clock the look on her face. 'Did Diana say something?'

Caroline is all innocence. 'No. Just asking, that's all.'

Heather shrugs and goes back to her own reflection, leaning in close and widening her eyes. She is not brushing her hair or applying any make-up. She stares as if simply to confirm that she's really there. 'Your guess is as good as mine,' she says. 'It's like he just wanted to talk to me, find out how I was doing.'

Caroline nods. She has taken out a small plastic make-up bag and is reapplying lipstick. 'I think I'm actually making progress with Chris.'

The eyes dart across again. 'How d'you mean?'

'Breaking down the barriers a bit, you know.'

'Yeah, well.' Heather does not sound altogether pleased. 'I did that ages ago. Not that hard, really.'

'Yeah. You two are obviously mates.'

Heather sniffs.

'I'm not trying to muscle in or anything.'

'It's a free country.'

'You know, if you think I'm trying too hard.'

'Chris can be mates with whoever he wants.'

Caroline says 'OK,' and after straightening her dress, she leaves to find Robin on his way out of the Gents. She puts a hand on his arm, as though pleased that she has a chance to talk to him alone.

'Listen, we could have lunch, if you want. Or coffee or something.'

Robin looks a little taken aback and it's a few seconds before he says, 'Why?'

'Why not?'

Robin says nothing.

'Just . . . in the session, you know.'

'I have got friends.'

'Course. I'd like it though. You know, if you want to.'

Robin fingers a shirt button. 'Yes, sorry. I just thought you were feeling sorry for me or something. Being a bit oversensitive.'

'Call it a date then,' Caroline says. She steps back as Heather comes out of the ladies and the two of them walk back towards the table together.

'He's nice, isn't he?' Caroline says.

'Got a thing for older men, have you?'

Caroline laughs, but she has reddened slightly. 'Not sure Diana would be very happy if I did. I mean he's not married, but it still might be against her "rules".'

Heather looks at her, confused.

'Just saying, I wouldn't want to get on the wrong side of her.'

. . . THEN

Group Session: March 1st

A useful session. The usual bickering, but no red flags. Caroline and Diana seem to have bonded, which is good. Chris less angry than in previous sessions despite the same goading of Caroline and a nasty attack on Robin towards the end. Heather seems calmer after midweek phone call.

Caroline unwilling to participate in the shame exercise. Adamant that it is not applicable to her, though not opposed in principle. Hard to gauge truth at this stage, after only three sessions with her. Shows no inclination so far towards one-to-one. Chris remains opposed and I fear that he may seek to disrupt further attempts with others in the group.

Interesting discussion at Caroline's behest about physical effects of H. Became revelatory exercise in sense-memory. Is she being voyeuristic?

Heather has invited group members to a birthday party, which could be tremendously useful in terms of forging stronger links. Discussion of my own ethical position vis à vis my inability to attend. Robin's comment about 'professional distance' sparked derisory remarks from Chris. Robin, as always, fighting the urge to retaliate.

Key Line: *'You take it and the pain goes away.'*

Tony had come sooner than he would have liked, surprised and excited by Nina's intensity, but she had urged him on, refusing to let him slow down or hold back, insisting that she had come twice already.

He has never really believed the suggestion that make-up sex is better than sex would otherwise be, but there is no denying that it was as passionate as he could remember. As it had ever been, in fact. As it was in those first few months clean, when he was nervous and horny as a teenager, and it felt like the two of them had just discovered what their bodies could do and must immediately make up for lost time.

Equally though, there is no denying that the argument preceding it had been every bit as passionate.

'You need to back away sometimes,' Nina had said; had screamed. 'You can't be their friend. Why the hell would you ever *want* to be their friend?'

Heather was not the first client of his to overstep the boundaries. Over the years, several had abused his accessibility. He had been accosted in the street more than once and there had been a number of unwelcome visits or phone calls far more inconvenient than Heather's. He had always believed that it was part and parcel of the job, even when he had discovered one of his clients hiding in the spare bedroom, several hours after a session had finished.

Something about Heather though had seriously rattled his wife's bars. The sight of her, standing on their doorstep, smiling as if she had every right to be there.

'As if I should have invited her in for dinner or something.'

Nina had a nose for these things; an instinct which, over the years, Tony had learned to respect, and be afraid of.

'She's way too needy.'

'They're all needy, and it's my job to help them. That's the point.'

'Right. A job. Not a mission from God.'

'She's no different from any of the others.'

'You didn't see the way she looked at me when I answered the door.'

'Oh, come on.'

'Don't tell me I'm being melodramatic – and don't you dare pull that shit about me not understanding because I've never been a junkie.'

'I wasn't going to.'

'Don't you fucking *dare* . . .'

Now, they lie a foot or so apart in the super-king-size bed that Nina had once slept on in a luxury hotel in Bath and insisted on buying. Still breathing heavily, still sweating. Tony could swear he feels the air in the bedroom moving against the skin on his arm, kissing his shoulder.

Nina says, 'Have a cigarette if you want one.'

He shakes his head. 'It's just a Saturday thing. If I start associating smoking with sex, I'm going to be on twenty a day again.'

Nina laughs and leans down to pull the sheet up, then slides a hand across until it finds his. She says, 'I do love you, you know. I know sometimes you don't think I do.'

'That's not true.'

'You're not exactly easy to live with though. I mean neither am I, but . . .' She sighs away the rest of it and pulls the sheet a little higher. There is laughter from a group of kids walking past outside and a siren screaming its way along the Broadway, then fading. 'Everyone's got baggage, I'm well aware of that, but just when I start to forget about yours I'm confronted with piles of it.'

'I'm Mr Samsonite,' Tony says. He puts on a deep, mock-sexy voice and turns towards her. 'Mr Excess Baggage.'

'Seriously, though. That business in the car.'

'Oh, please.' He rolls back again. 'Let's not talk about that again.'

'It was scary, Tony. It's always scary.'

The day before, driving back from the cinema, Tony had been cut up by some teenager in a VW Beetle. He had sounded his horn and flashed his lights and on seeing the raised finger had pulled in front of the car at the next set of lights and got out to confront the driver. There was a good deal of shouting. He had called the teenager an 'irresponsible little wanker', then slammed his fist on to the Beetle's bonnet hard enough to dent it, and when the teenager, who by then was looking understandably frightened, had threatened to call the police, Tony had told him to go right ahead.

'I was worried about you and Emma,' Tony says. 'Stupid idiot could have killed us.'

'He didn't though, did he? And if anyone looked like they were going to kill someone, it was you.'

'It's just road rage. It happens.'

'Rage is right,' Nina says. 'And I get why it's there, and I know you're going to tell me that a lot of ex-addicts have that kind of anger bubbling away inside them. Doesn't make it any easier to live with.'

'I know.'

They say nothing for a minute or so, then Nina leans to kiss his cheek and turns over. She reaches for the switch on her bedside light and prods her pillow into the required shape.

She says, 'Don't forget the recycling tomorrow.'

Tony thinks his wife is overreacting. Before the business with the Beetle driver, he cannot recall the last time he'd lost it like that. Perhaps a year before, when a neighbour had knocked on the door to complain about the noise from the top bedroom and had not accepted Tony's apology with sufficient grace. He keeps his temper as well as anyone else, he reckons; knows how to lay a damper on things when it looks like flaring up. There are exercises, mechanisms . . .

'I'm sorry, OK?'

Tony lies quite still, his light still on. He already knows that sleep isn't coming any time soon, that he will need to read for a while. Before too long he hears Nina's breathing change and he turns his head to look at her back and shoulders. She is slender and toned thanks to four sessions a week at the gym and is still brown from the week she has recently spent soaking up some winter sun in Dubai with two girlfriends.

164

He stares at his wife's body and knows how lucky he is. He loves his daughter and values his job and is deeply thankful for a life which, a few years ago, would never have seemed possible. So he cannot understand why he is wide awake at one thirty in the morning and thinking about a well-worn, brown suede jacket.

Heather, slowly taking it off.

. . . NOW

Tanner bought a sandwich from Pret A Manger, took it back to the office and spent the majority of her lunch hour catching up on paperwork. She disliked it less than a lot of her colleagues did, even if, admittedly, the two hours or more of it that was generated by every hour of what others called 'proper police work' was not necessarily the most sensible use of time or resources. Steps were being taken to address the imbalance by issuing some front line officers with tablets and equipping squad cars with laptop computers to speed up the admin process. It had done little beyond generating an outraged column or two in the *Daily Mail*, and Tanner was not sure she fancied lugging an iPad around in her handbag anyway.

Paperwork needed doing, so it had to be done; simple as that. She would not risk scuppering a prosecution by failing to properly liaise with the CPS. When an entire investigation could be jeopardised by failing to check and double check the dozens of individual reports pertaining to it, why wouldn't she do so?

In truth, she enjoyed filling in forms and always had. At home, the post would be opened and anything remotely official-looking would be handed silently to her across the kitchen table for completion. Bank correspondence, insurance documents, customer-service questionnaires.

Black ink and block capitals.

Slowly working her way through the sandwich and a bottle of orange juice, she typed out three different interview reports and made changes to some pre-trial documentation on a domestic she had been working since the turn of the year. She filed the application for her annual clothing allowance and filled in the first part of her holiday paperwork good and early.

With a few minutes of her lunch hour still remaining, she called home to see how Susan was feeling. Returning from her early-morning run, Tanner had found her partner still in bed, complaining that she was feeling nauseous and that her head was thumping. Saying she would need to call in sick.

'You still in bed?' Tanner asked now.

'Wrapped up on the settee,' Susan said.

'OK.'

'Jeremy Kyle isn't helping.'

'Drink plenty of water.' Tanner was thinking that Susan might not have been feeling quite as bad if she had done so the night before.

Susan said she would, then laughed softly. 'I'm lying here wondering how the supply teacher's coping with Paul Murphy.'

'Listen, call me if you need anything.'

'It's a migraine,' Susan said. 'Definitely.'

Tanner ended the call and turned to see Chall ambling towards her desk. He raised his chin and smiled at her.

'Well, we're bolloxed on the CCTV for Heather Finlay,' he said.

'Is that a technical term, Dipak?'

'It should be.' He sounded cheerful enough, despite whatever bad news he was about to deliver. 'Nearest cameras are on the main road, which doesn't really help us. We might have something down the line, once we know who we're looking for. That's if he's walked there of course; he might have driven, taken a cab, whatever.'

'Whoever did it knew her,' Tanner said.

'So?'

'So chances are they knew the area, knew exactly where the cameras were.'

'They'd only have taken the trouble to avoid them if they were planning to kill her, though. If it was a drug thing, isn't it a bit more likely that it was spur of the moment?'

'Possibly,' Tanner said.

'You want me to start looking at the phone records? De Silva's might be interesting.'

'Nothing to justify going down that road just yet,' Tanner said. Nothing worth the trouble and certainly not worth the cost. Some service providers were quicker than others when it came to providing their customers' phone records, but all of them made police forces up and down the country eat into their budgets for the privilege. 'Can't see the guvnor going for that as things stand.'

'It's all starting to look like one for the back burner,' Chall said.

'I don't think so.'

'Well you said yourself—'

Tanner was reaching for the phone that had begun to ring on her desk. She answered, said, 'Thanks,' then pushed her chair back. 'Diana Knight's waiting downstairs.'

Chall looked at his watch. 'Bloody hell, she's keen.'

'She's bang on time,' Tanner said. 'Which earns her brownie points straight away.'

'Or she's just trying to create a good impression.'

They began walking towards the stairs. 'The courtesy of kings.'

'What?'

'Punctuality.'

'Tell that to my wife,' Chall said. 'She couldn't be on time for anything if her life depended on it.'

Tanner said, 'I'd have divorced her years ago.'

'Sorry we couldn't find anywhere a bit nicer,' Chall said.

'It is ... what it is,' Diana Knight said. It sounded convincing

168

enough, but still she seemed a little wary as she looked around the room. Off-white walls with a window high up at one end and a camera mounted in the corner above it. A scarred, rectangular table. Two chairs on one side, a single chair on the other. 'How very different from the home life of our own dear Queen.'

It was an expression Tanner had heard before, though she was still not quite sure what it meant. She smiled anyway. As far as she was aware, the woman sitting across from her had never set foot in an interview room, so wariness to some degree or another was very much to be expected.

Chall said, 'We have got nicer rooms than this, but they're all being used, I'm afraid.'

The woman dabbed cautiously at the tabletop. 'It's exactly like it is on TV shows.'

'Except this isn't being recorded.' Tanner nodded towards the window. 'And there aren't any other officers looking in at us through there.'

'That's a relief.' Her hands moved instinctively to her elegantly styled hair, the only grey on show that of her skirt and matching jacket. Tanner clocked the delicate silver necklace and matching bracelet, the perfectly applied make-up. She decided that for a woman of fifty-three, Mrs Diana Knight was nothing if not well preserved.

She imagined what her mother would have said: *That woman's had no uphill* . . .

Tanner sat back and opened her notebook. Knowing why Knight was here, what her connection to the victim was, she guessed that, at some point, there had been plenty.

'Thanks again for coming in,' Chall said.

'Not a problem.' The voice was not overtly posh, but there was no discernible accent either. 'I got here early as it happens. Did a bit of shopping.'

Tanner nodded down at the two smart-looking shopping bags next to the woman's chair. 'Anything nice?'

'Oh, you know.' That slightly nervous smile again. 'Actually, I would have been happy to have come in first thing, but I was working, so this was the soonest I could do it, I'm afraid.'

Tanner did not remember anything about a job on the printout. 'What kind of work?'

'Just a local charity shop. A couple of mornings a week.'

'Good of you,' Chall said.

'Not really. There's precious little else to do. Plus, I get first crack at the bargains.'

Tanner said, 'A perk's a perk,' though she could not imagine that Knight did a great deal of shopping at Scope or the British Heart Foundation. She leaned forward a little. 'Now, you know we're investigating the sudden death of Heather Finlay.'

'Sudden death?'

'Murder,' Chall said. 'Police speak.'

'Oh. Right.' She tugged gently at her necklace. 'So, how's it going?'

'I'll be honest with you,' Tanner said. 'Right now, we need all the help we can get.'

'Oh.' It was said as though she had been expecting more; better. 'That's a shame.'

'Yes, it is.'

'I'll try, but the truth is I barely knew her. Only as one of the group, really.'

'What did you make of her?'

The woman thought for a few seconds. 'Well . . . she was a very . . . positive person, most of the time. Probably the most upbeat of any of us, when I think about it. There aren't too many glass-half-full types in these sorts of groups.'

'Most of the time, you said.'

'Yes, well, there were times she was down, too, but that's perfectly normal, isn't it? Recovery was very hard for her, I think.'

'She suffered from depression, is that right?'

'I'd rather not . . . it's tricky because . . . '

'It's fine,' Tanner said. 'I know there's an issue with discussing what was talked about during your meetings, but the medication was found during the post-mortem.'

'So you already know.'

Tanner nodded.

'Why did you ask me, then?'

Tanner was aware of Chall, smiling next to her. 'Without going into details, unless you'd like to, how did Heather get on with the other members of the group?'

There was more thinking. 'She got on very well with everyone most of the time. She was closest to Chris, probably. I think they'd had similar issues with their addictions and they were a bit closer in age. She bonded very early on with Caroline . . . she was friendly enough with Robin. And I don't remember her and me ever exchanging a cross word.'

'What about Tony?'

She looked at Tanner.

'How did she get on with him?'

'Well . . . look, she probably had a bit of a crush on him at some point. I mean so did I, when I first started going. So did Chris, for all I know. If they don't look like the back of a bus it's hard not to find yourself drawn to someone who's helping you so much.'

'I get it all the time,' Chall said. 'Nightmare.'

The woman smiled and looked down at the table, her fingers pulling at the necklace again.

Tanner wrote something down, then sat back. She said, 'Heather died just a few hours after the last session she attended with you all. You should know that, so you'll understand why I'm going to ask you about it.'

'Yes, but—'

Tanner held up a hand. 'Like I said, I'm not expecting details. Having spoken to Chris and Robin, I fully appreciate how important confidentiality is to you all. But it's my job to find out who killed Heather and there's a chance that whatever went on in that meeting had some bearing on what happened to her.'

Knight shook her head and laughed. 'No, that's ridiculous. Absolutely ridiculous.'

'People get murdered for the most ridiculous reasons,' Tanner said. She let it hang for a few moments. She looked down at her notebook, then back to Knight. 'As I said, I'm not expecting chapter and verse.'

The woman was fidgety while she considered her response. She fingered her necklace, straightened the shopping bags at her feet. 'There was some . . . shouting, I think, that evening. A few arguments.'

'About what?'

'There are always arguments and sometimes people lose their tempers. We talk about a lot of serious things.'

'Who was doing the shouting that night?'

She shook her head.

'Heather? You?'

'I can't . . . '

'Was anyone particularly angry with Heather about something?'

'You don't have to tell us what it was,' Chall said.

'I can't.' She looked at Tanner, then Chall, and the nervousness was suddenly replaced by determination. 'The group is hugely important to me, you need to understand that. To all of us. Hopefully we'll be starting up again soon and I simply can't risk being excluded from it. That's what would happen if I let outsiders into our confidences.'

'We're hardly outsiders,' Tanner said. 'It's not like you'd be blabbing to someone at a bus stop, is it?'

'I don't know how I'd get through the week if I didn't have the sessions to hold on to.'

'Right, and I'm guessing Heather Finlay felt very much the same.'

The woman looked pained suddenly and it took a few seconds before she began to shake her head again. 'It's too much to ask, I'm sorry.'

Tanner nodded as though resigned, but she was every bit as determined as Diana Knight. She began to fire questions across the table a little faster. 'You all went to the pub afterwards, right? Same as usual.'

'Yes.'

'And all of you were there for a while?'

'Yes.'

'Did you all leave together?'

'No. I think . . . Chris left first. Yes, that's right, then Heather. The rest of us stayed another half an hour or so.'

'And you went home?'

She nodded. 'The dogs would have been on their own for a good few hours by then. I needed to let them out.'

'Anyone at home with you?'

'I live alone,' she said.

'Thank you.' Tanner tried to look pleased, as though they were making excellent progress and what she was about to ask was of no great importance; trivial, almost. 'Can you tell us what you talked about when you were all in the pub?'

'It's the same thing.'

'I mean, did the arguments carry on?'

'I thought I'd explained—'

'It's the pub.' Chall's voice was raised. He looked at Tanner and puffed out his cheeks in exasperation. Tanner looked at her notebook, tapping her pen against a page that had no more than a few words scribbled on it.

'It doesn't matter.' Knight spoke slowly, a hint of condescension creeping in. 'Whether it's in Tony's conservatory or round a table in the Red Lion, what's said among the group can't go any further. It's the cardinal rule. People in the group need to feel safe.'

At least she had the decency to look momentarily embarrassed, so Tanner did not feel the need to point out the horrible irony in what she had just said. 'What if I told you that by not telling us, you're actively hindering the investigation into Heather Finlay's murder?'

'Is that what you're saying?'

Tanner waited.

'Well, I've said already that I think it's ridiculous to suggest there's any connection with Tony's group.'

'But if there was?'

'If you could show me a single piece of evidence to suggest that telling you these things would genuinely help catch Heather's killer, I'd tell you everything you wanted to know in a heartbeat. Of course I would. I'm absolutely certain that Tony would tell you himself.'

'But what I'm asking you to tell us could *be* the evidence. I'm really sorry if I haven't made that clear.' Tanner was not the least bit sorry and was feeling a powerful urge to lean across and grab hold of the woman by her fancy necklace.

'And I'm sorry, too,' Knight said. 'But, there it is.'

'Catch 22,' Chall said.

Tanner nodded, nowhere else to go, but she struggled to keep the irritation from her face. She had heard much the same things from Robin Joffe and Christopher Clemence. There was every chance she would hear them again. It was starting to wear very thin. 'Well, I'd like to say you've been a great help, but ... '

The woman reached down for her shopping bags.

'It's frustrating,' Chall said. 'That's all. The lot of you are spouting all this secrecy and solidarity stuff, refusing to tell us anything, and at the same time you're all claiming to be her friends.'

Diana Knight looked rather shocked. 'I told you when we started,' she said. 'I barely knew her.'

Walking back up the stairs towards the incident room, Tanner said, 'Right, one more to go then.' She looked down at the information provided by Diana Knight before she'd left. A first name and a north London branch of a low-cost supermarket. It was scant, but it would be enough. 'I'm not putting up with that confidentiality stuff any more, either. We'll need to go at things a different way next time.'

Chall took the scrap of paper. 'I'll find her.'

'Go and check out this pub as well. If they were all in there every Monday night, someone might remember them. Might at least remember if there was anything interesting going on the night Heather was killed.'

'It's as good an idea as any,' Chall said.

'I might go and talk to Heather's father, see if there's anything in her past that might help.'

They walked up another flight. 'So, what d'you reckon then?' Chall asked. 'Mrs Knight's tipple.'

'I've no idea.'

'Booze? Coke? Uppers? She didn't look much like an ex-smackhead.'

'What does an ex-smackhead look like, Dipak?'

'You know what I mean. Might have been sex, of course. She's a bit of a MILF . . .'

Tanner tried to look cross, but the attempt was unconvincing. 'I'm not sure that what any of them were into once upon a time is very important,' she said. 'I'm starting to think the addiction isn't the issue, but the group is.'

'Really?'

'Has to be.'

'Has to be, meaning you're sure it is? Or meaning if it isn't we've got bugger all else?'

'Both,' Tanner said.

. . . NOW

Diana had suggested the restaurant without thinking and regretted it
almost immediately. A family run Italian place, at the north end of
Upper Street in Islington, it was somewhere she had visited many
times with her ex-husband and she had not been there since he left.
She had driven past it several times, only to find herself wondering if
he ever ate there with the new woman, if she was now welcomed as
warmly as Diana had once been. She had consoled herself with vodka
or red wine and the thought that her replacement probably favoured
somewhere with a more relaxed atmosphere and a younger clientele.

Somewhere she could get a Happy Meal.

She walked in rather nervously, hoping that she would not be
greeted by anyone who might remember her. Who might cheerfully
ask where her other half was. To her relief, Robin immediately stood
up and waved from a booth in the far corner, allowing her to walk
quickly across to the table before encountering any staff she
recognised.

'Sorry I'm a bit late,' she said.

Robin drew her into a somewhat stiff embrace, then sat down
quickly. 'Only just got here myself.'

'Couldn't find a single yellow.'

'I was lucky,' Robin said. He nodded at her. 'You look nice.'

'Thank you.' Diana tried to sound ever so slightly surprised, like someone who had not spent two hours getting ready; swapping dresses and accessories, digging out bags from their velvet wrappings and shoes that had never been worn. Though this was most certainly not a romantic dinner, she had nevertheless relished the effort involved, the rituals of preparation. It had been far too long since she had needed to dress up for anything. Longer still since she'd been complimented for doing so. 'It's lovely to be out.'

'Long overdue,' Robin said.

'You've scrubbed up rather nicely yourself.' He was wearing a light grey suit and red spotted tie and, for a moment, she was pleased to think that he had made an effort too. Then she remembered that he had come straight from work. On closer inspection, the suit was one he had worn several times on a Monday night, sitting in the conservatory at Tony's.

Robin poured sparkling water and for a few minutes they exchanged chit-chat about the difficulties of parking in Islington, of parking almost anywhere, though both agreed that being no more than half an hour's drive from Barnet or the Royal Free, this was a handy enough location for both of them.

'Looks a nice place,' he said. 'Is this somewhere you've been before?'

'No.' Diana looked down at her menu. 'I heard good things about it, that's all.'

The restaurant was busy, with all but one table occupied: several other couples, a group of middle-aged men near the bar, one large family at a long table in the window. The volume of conversation from fellow diners was politely muted, though; no higher than that of the cod Italian music leaking from a speaker on the corner of the bar. A waiter, who seemed worryingly familiar but barely looked at them, took their order, and after he had deposited bread and olives Robin said, 'So, how are you doing?'

Diana let out a long sigh and shook her head.

'You don't have to ...'

She most definitely did have to. 'No, it's fine.' Painful as it was, she was delighted to have been asked, desperate to share her agonies and to revel just a little in them. The few one-sided phone conversations with friends had proved oddly unsatisfactory and, at home, she had found herself ranting at the dogs. 'Well, I say fine. Bad to worse, actually.'

'What now?'

'They're getting married.'

'Bloody hell.'

'Bloody hell is right. Unbelievable ...'

Robin picked up an olive, watched the oil drip from it. 'Is this because of the baby?'

'Oh yes. Whatever else my ex is, he's stupidly honourable like that. So, the little bitch has got exactly what she wanted, hasn't she? Got herself pregnant and now she'll get everything else.'

'What does Phoebe think?'

Diana laughed. A low, harsh bark. 'Your guess is as good as mine. One minute she's screaming at me about this baby, like it's my fault that she's going to be replaced in Daddy's affections, and the next thing I know she's shopping for a bridesmaid's dress. Obviously I didn't hear that from her.'

'When was the last time you spoke to her?'

The strange glee Diana had felt in venting her rage was gone in an instant as the punch of pain took the breath from her. She tore at the bread and squeezed it. 'Not since she rang to tell me about the baby. To tell me I'd ruined her life.' She shook her head and her smile was like a widening crack.

'You're all right, though?' Robin's question was coded, of course. The same simple code that Tony used at the beginning of every session. *You're not reaching for the Smirnoff?*

'Yes, I'm all right,' Diana said. She bit into the compacted chunk of bread. 'Sorry for ranting on.'

'Don't be silly.'

'I feel terrible, moaning on about the problems I'm having with my daughter. When . . . you know. Your son.'

Robin cleared his throat and looked to see if the waiter was anywhere close by.

'I can't imagine.' Diana waited, wondering if this might be the moment for Robin to finally reveal what had happened to his son. The incident that had triggered his own descent. She watched him raise a hand to gain the waiter's attention. 'It must be with you every day.'

When Robin turned back to her, he nodded slowly and loosened his tie. He said, 'I can't stop thinking about what Heather's poor father must be going through.'

'Tall skinny latte for Gunther.'

Chris had forgotten the name he'd given and it took him a few moments before he realised the coffee was for him and sauntered up to collect it. Lying when some spotty girl serving at Starbucks asked for your name was no big deal in anybody's book, but he couldn't resist it.

He'd lied about far more important things.

If he were being honest, he'd lied a lot before he'd ever taken drugs, and as part and parcel of the lifestyle that went with scoring and using on a daily basis he'd taken to it like a duck to water. Sometimes he thought it was what he was cut out to do, because even though everyone around him had been bullshitting about one thing or another all the time, he was far and away the best at it. The most creative, at any rate.

He carried his coffee back to the table in the window. From here, he could keep an eye on the entrance to the arcade, watch for the kid arriving.

He took out his phone, logged into the Wi-Fi and scrolled through his Twitter feed. He struggled to take anything in, one eye on the arcade and busy thinking about the last time he'd been sitting where he was now. The two coppers, opposite.

Are you clean at the moment?

At the moment. That was what was important, right? A few weeks before, right before the wheels came off, he'd been as messed up as he had been since he'd started recovery, but now he was back on the right track, so sod that dykey detective and her smartarse sidekick. Still struggling, still trying to get settled, but moving forward, at least.

He glanced out of the window. A few faces he recognised, but still no sign of the kid.

Nice enough lad. A computer freak, same as Chris, but nowhere near as good. Seventeen and clearly messed up about coming out, but more importantly, a kid who still lived at home and whose parents were away. He'd mentioned something about a bed being available for a few nights, dropped hints that were as subtle as a sledgehammer in the bollocks. All good with Chris, naturally. All better than good. A house was better than a hostel any day of the week, and a bed was better than a settee, was better than the floor, blah blah blah.

'There's PS4 set up on the home cinema too. You know, if you fancy it.'

'Sounds ace.'

'We can play all night, if you want.'

The kid wasn't Chris's type – too keen and a bit doughy and younger than he liked – but Chris would fuck him if it came to it. If that was what the kid was really after, which Chris presumed it was. He'd do that and make sure the kid had a nice time and he'd happily take the bed that was on offer, but that would be as far as it went. He wouldn't be nosing around, looking to lift a phone or a watch and sell them for a few quid. He wouldn't be pocketing any spare cash he found lying around the kid's house. He wasn't going back to that.

Are you clean . . . ?

What happened before Heather was killed had been a what d'you call it, a blip. No more than that. Nobody had ever said recovery was easy and unless you were a nutter about it, like Robin, there were always going to be a few bumps in the road, everyone knew that. A few enormous holes you didn't see coming.

Like the one Heather had fallen into.

He would lie to the kid, of course. About liking him, about seeing him again, being grateful for the bed, whatever. He couldn't imagine a day without lying, but that didn't make him any different from anyone else, did it?

The bankers and the politicians and everyone sitting in that circle round at Tony's place every Monday. The bloke on the next table and the spotty girl who'd given him his coffee and looked like she'd meant it when she'd told Chris to have a nice day.

Lying to the police, though. That had been stupid, even by his standards. He hadn't stopped thinking about it, had been worrying ever since because that woman, Tanner, hadn't looked like an easy touch by any stretch.

He had to try and put it right, but he knew he was going to need help. It was a big ask, but he didn't have a lot of choice. He couldn't think of any other way to avoid that big hole.

Chris took another look across at the arcade, then went back to his phone and scrolled quickly through his contacts until he found the one he was after.

He began writing a text to Caroline.

. . . NOW

When the plates had been cleared away, Robin said, 'So, how did it go with the police?' Nice and casual, as if he were asking if she wanted more water or had room for pudding. He thought he had waited long enough and done more than enough listening, considering this was the reason for asking her to meet for dinner in the first place.

'It was fine, I think.'

'Yes?'

'I wasn't there very long.'

Robin looked at Diana and found himself wondering if she could possibly think there was any other motive for his invitation. They had eaten lunch together before, but dinner was an altogether different matter. Was there perhaps a hint of romantic interest on her part? He had wondered about it before, that time she'd come to the hospital. There was no question she was an attractive woman and, though he was probably ten years older than she was, they were more or less on the same page.

He smiled at her and dismissed the idea immediately. Had they met at another time, in different circumstances, he might have considered making overtures. It had certainly been long enough since he'd done so. As things stood, though, there was no room in his life for anything that might complicate it. As far as female company went, he was perfectly content with Amber or Suzi or Caprice at £140 an hour.

He said, 'The woman, was it? Who interviewed you?'

Diana nodded. 'Her and an Asian bloke. A sergeant or a constable.'

'Seemed pleasant enough.'

'Yes, they were. Very interested in what goes on in our sessions, mind you.'

'I had the same thing,' Robin said.

'In the last session, especially.'

'Because it was the night Heather was killed.'

'They seem to think it has some bearing on things. On the murder.' Robin shook his head.

'I know,' Diana said. 'I told them it was ridiculous.'

'So, what did you tell them?' Robin looked down at the dessert menu. There was a time when he would have been watching his weight, prone as he was to piling on the pounds, but neither Amber nor Suzi nor Caprice seemed to care a great deal. 'About the final session.'

Diana looked a little shocked. 'Well, nothing, obviously. I mean, we're not supposed to, are we?'

'Absolutely not.'

'I certainly didn't go into specifics.'

Robin looked up. 'I'm not with you.'

'I told them there was some arguing and what have you, but I didn't go into any details.'

'Right.'

'You know, nothing they couldn't have worked out for themselves. You'd have to be an idiot to think we sit there every week playing Scrabble, wouldn't you?'

'Yes, but confidentiality still needs to be maintained.'

Diana's smile frosted over. 'That's what I told them.'

Robin nodded and hoped that his own smile might thaw hers out a little. 'You're absolutely right, of course. Completely ridiculous to think that the group has any connection with what happened to Heather.'

'Probably just some horrible random thing.'

'Right. Or she was killed by someone none of us knew anything about, and why would we?' Robin leaned forward a little. 'How much do any of us really know about others in the group? It's an hour and a half a week.'

'I think you know all there is to know about me.' Diana laughed. 'I go on about myself so much.'

'Nonsense,' Robin said. 'That's what we're there for. What I'm here for.'

'Well, thank you, but it feels like it sometimes.'

It had felt like it to Robin, too, for the last hour and a half. Diana was clearly still enraged at her husband for leaving and especially at the woman he had chosen to leave her for. She was understandably distraught at the damage inflicted on the relationship she had with her daughter, but still. Compared to what others in the group had gone through, were still going through, her life was a pretty bloody good one as far as he could make out. Though she had paid lip service to his own anguish, in a blatant effort to root out the cause, she had not got the faintest idea what he endured on a daily basis.

She needed support, yes, but more than that she needed to get a little perspective.

'So, are you going to get anything else?'

Diana pushed the menu away. 'I couldn't manage a thing.'

'Oh, did you say anything at all about the letters?' A last-minute thought, no more than that. Just something to talk about while they were waiting for the bill.

'No, I did not,' Diana said.

'Right.' Robin loosened his tie a little more. 'Thank you.'

'Why would I?'

'Absolutely.'

'What have they got to do with anything?'

'Well, I'm very grateful,' Robin said. 'But there is a . . . legal impli-cation, strictly speaking. Confidentiality is crucial, it goes without saying, but there might be an argument for saying that this sort of thing falls outside that. That the letters are not strictly a group matter.'

Diana waved a hand dismissively. 'I decided that mentioning them would do more harm than good.' She took a small compact mirror from her bag and checked her make-up. 'The police are trying to solve a murder, after all, and it seems as though they have their work cut out as it is. Why give them useless information that would only result in them wasting their time?'

Robin nodded enthusiastically. 'It *would* rather be leading them up the garden path.'

'Exactly.'

Robin signalled once again to attract the waiter's attention and mimed writing in the air. He reached into his jacket and produced his wallet. 'Let me get this,' he said.

'Are you sure?'

'My pleasure.'

Diana made no further effort to argue. As Robin laid his credit card down, she leaned across the table. She said, 'Anyway, we still can't be certain it wasn't Chris.'

Robin looked at her. '*What?*'

'The letters,' Diana said, quickly. She was flustered. 'I mean the letters.'

When Tanner got back to her hotel room, she took the till receipt from her purse and slid it into the brown envelope she kept for such things. Then she made a note in the back of her diary: date, location and *scampi and chips/sparkling mineral water: £8.75.* Tanner would no more dream of fiddling her overnight expenses than she would her tax return, though there were plenty who gave it a damn good try. She'd heard about an undercover officer who had claimed to need sports clothes to fit in with a local gang he was trying to infiltrate. This was readily accepted, until one of his receipts had been examined more carefully, and the full set of golf clubs stashed in the boot of his car had been deemed surplus to requirements.

As had he.

Scrupulous as she was, Tanner would have had difficulty using up even the most miserly allowance on this occasion. Always a budget hotel, of course, but she couldn't help wondering just whose budget places like this were tailored for. Tramps? Benedictine monks? She took off her shoes and lay down, fully clothed, on the bed. She turned on the TV and began to channel-surf, aimlessly. A famous comedian advertised these hotels on television, but looking around, Tanner doubted that he would find much to laugh about if he actually stayed in one.

It was perfectly clean and modern, but there was so little room that she had not bothered to unpack anything except a clean shirt for the morning. There wasn't even space in the bathroom for a basin, which was mounted instead in a corner of the bedroom, next to a small shelf laden with the proudly advertised 'tea and coffee making facilities' (kettle, sachets, miniature milk cartons).

She settled on Sky News and did her best to plump up her pillows. The TV screen was tiny and the bed was no more comfortable than she had expected.

Still, she was happy to be spending a night away.

She had called home from the station, just before getting on the train. Susan had sounded better, had told Tanner she had spent the day catching up on some marking. The migraine had eased, she said, and the day away from school had given her a chance to recharge her batteries.

Tanner had called again to let Susan know she had arrived in Sheffield. A short conversation had been enough to let Tanner know that the bottle she had marked in the fridge the night before had already been replaced.

'Don't go picking up any strange women,' Susan had said.

Tanner had said she would try not to.

There had been no women – strange or otherwise – in the small bar downstairs. A smattering of businessmen had given Tanner good reason to eat her dinner as quickly as possible, laughing too loudly at their own jokes, shiny-suited and red-faced as the beer began kicking in. Of course, they might not have been businessmen at all. They might just as easily have been architects or hitmen, and had Tanner attracted their attention for as much as a moment, she doubted very much that they would have been able to tell how she earned her living either.

What she would be doing to earn it the following morning.

It was the pictures she dreaded. There were always pictures. Photographs in frames, cardboard or chrome, and you said something because you were expected to and perhaps you picked one up to look at if it seemed appropriate. You did not talk about their grief. Not unless they wanted to, and even then you did not attempt to quantify it or talk about a process, because grief was not a series of steps. It was a mess, ragged and random, and it inflicted its pain on each person differently. A blade, a hammer, a stone pressed across a chest. Grief was as individual as a fingerprint.

So you waited. You ate and drank whatever was offered and you allowed the next of kin those few moments until the sobbing or the shouting had subsided. You listened, then you gave as much comfort as you were able, and you tried not to think about what you needed from the supermarket or when your parking ticket was going to run out.

In the end, most of her just seeped through the floorboards . . .

You tried not to let them know what you were thinking, at any rate.

Tanner watched the news until the same story rolled round again. She thumbed the greasy remote for another minute or two and then began to get undressed. Ten minutes later, the alarm on her phone had been set and she was lying in the dusty dark, her legs restless beneath the thin duvet, trying to settle.

Thoughts, scattershot . . .

Those businessmen would certainly have looked twice at Diana Knight.

An industrial sander would get the blood off.

A librarian. They would have thought she was a librarian.

. . . THEN

As always, walking through the front door, Chris breathes the house in and it feels as though he's twelve or thirteen again. Somewhere round there, anyway. The smell is enough to do it every time – furniture polish and boiled vegetables – and some part of him wants to bolt straight up the stairs, slam the bedroom door behind him and listen to Eminem or Chemical Brothers, good and loud.

Some Pink, maybe, if he was in a very different mood. Or Christina Aguilera. The stuff his mates had never known he liked.

Back then, his mother would have been shouting at him from the foot of the stairs, urging him to turn the racket down. Now, she just beams at him and reaches out to pull him to her skinny chest, and again it's the smell that transports him.

Pears soap and moisturising cream from the market; that hairspray that makes his nose tickle.

She's no more than a few years older than Robin, Chris thinks, but Jesus, it looks like an awful lot more. Clean living is one thing, but working as hard as she has for so long has caught up with her good and proper. Thirty years running around after Chris's father, cooking two hot meals a day, washing and cleaning for him and still managing to work part time doing much the same for other people, a few miles up the road in Greenwich or Blackheath. It's worn her down ... *he's* worn her down, and Chris doubts that she'd have the strength to shout up those stairs any more, even less chase after him. His hand moves softly across her shoulder blades, then he pulls away for fear of squeezing her too tight.

'Are you hungry, love?' She turns and walks towards the kitchen. 'I've got some leftovers in the fridge.'

Course she has.

'Soon warm them up for you, if you like.'

He says, 'That'd be great, Mum,' and goes through to the lounge to wait. He drops on to the settee, spreads his palms out and strokes the familiar brown velour. The room hasn't changed any more than anywhere else and he wonders if his *Gladiator* and *X-Men* posters are still on the walls of the box room at the back of the house.

Nobody was to know it wasn't actually the movies he liked, of course. He's not even sure he knew, not back then. He smiles, remembering a conversation with Heather about it. He'd told her that he wouldn't kick any of them out of bed and she'd made him laugh by talking about the mess Wolverine would make of the sheets.

From the kitchen, his mother asks if he wants tea with his dinner and he tells her that he does. Dinner at lunchtime, tea at dinner time. Something else he left behind.

'I've got some of those mini trifles in,' she shouts. 'From Sainsbury's.'

Somehow, his mother appears to have found room for even more of the hideous china figurines she loves. They are carefully arranged on the mantelpiece above the coal-effect gas fire and on top of the television. Dogs, horses, milkmaids. He knows she'll have dusted every one of them this morning, right before getting the vacuum out. A flurry of activity in between clearing the breakfast things away and settling down in front of *This Morning*, or that show with the bald bloke who chases after scam artists and cowboy builders. He knows she's got a soft spot for him.

190

She brings his food in on a thin wooden tray and sits in the armchair opposite to watch him eat. Gammon and mashed potatoes, runner beans and parsley sauce. Chris gets stuck in.

'You've missed your dad,' she says.

He grunts, mouth full.

'You should say when you're coming, love. Shame to come all this way and not see him.'

Chris nods and swallows. He doesn't make the journey back to Plumstead very often, not for six months or more, but when he does he is always careful to come at a time when his father won't be at home. He knows very well that at this time of day the old man will be happily ensconced in the pub, talking nonsense to his mates and blowing every penny of his pension, as well as any other bits he's managed to pick up cash in hand, doing odd jobs or getting lucky at the bookie's.

His mum is different, though; careful with what little she gets. His mum has always salted money away.

'It's difficult,' he says. 'I never know when I'm going to get time off, you know.'

'Work has to come first,' his mum says.

'Unfortunately.'

He carries on eating. He can't remember when he last ate anything like this, the last time a meal came on a plate.

'You been to see your brother?'

'No,' he says.

'Not at all?'

'No.'

'That's a shame.' She watches him, smiling, her eyes following the fork as it moves from the plate to his mouth. 'Me and your dad can't really get up there. The cost and what have you, and it's such a long way. I mean, we talk to him on the phone, obviously.' She leans forward to straighten papers and magazines on the coffee table. The *Daily Mirror*, the *TV Times*, *Puzzler*. 'I think a few of his mates visit from time to time, but it's not the same as family, is it?'

Chris doesn't look up. 'I don't really want to go.'

She nods, but it's apparent that she's not really listening. 'I suppose that's because of work as well, is it? You're so busy and everything.'

'Yeah.'

'I saw one of your things on TV the other night,' she says. 'That one about the scientist. The one that's handicapped, with the funny voice. That was one of yours, wasn't it? Your producing company.'

'Production company.'

'I thought it was,' she says. 'I told your dad.'

'We've just finished working on another film with that same actor,' Chris says.

'Him that played the scientist?'

'And we might be getting involved with the next Tom Cruise film. It's all in the early stages at the moment, you know. A bit up in the air. Endless bloody meetings.'

She sits back and shakes her head. 'I don't know ... all these film stars you must get to knock about with and you haven't once brought one of them round.'

'I'll have a word with Tom Cruise.'

She laughs. 'Can you imagine?'

Chris laughs. 'You never know.' He holds up his fork. 'He might be a big fan of gammon and mash.'

'Seriously, can you imagine though? The neighbours would go bananas.' As if the thought has prompted her to check on the houses opposite for some reason, she gets up and walks to the window. She stares out and watches a car pull up. 'Who's that, then?' Satisfied that it's nobody of any interest, she walks back to her chair. 'You still in the same flat?'

Chris nods, busily polishing off what little is left on his plate.

'I showed those pictures to one of the women I clean for. Over near the observatory, remember? She said it looked amazing.'

'I've actually done it up a bit since then,' Chris says. He had brought the pictures over last time he had visited. Stills from an article in a magazine he'd found in some waiting room or other.

'We'll have to come and visit one of these days.'

'I'm never there,' Chris says. 'That's the problem. All the travelling's getting on my nerves, tell you the truth.'

'I can't remember the last time we went up west,' she says. 'Probably when you got us tickets to that show, remember?'

Chris nods, struggling to remember the name of the dancer he'd been seeing at the time. Someone he hadn't thought about since. A few complimentary tickets to some shitty musical was just about all the tedious little wanker had been good for.

He leans forward and puts the tray on the table. 'That was great. Thanks, Mum.'

'You sure you've had enough?'

Chris lies back and pats his belly. He groans happily, then sits up as though he's just thought of something. 'Oh, listen, Mum.' He looks at her; she's still smiling. 'I don't suppose you could loan me a bit of cash, could you? Just fifty or something, and I'll send you a cheque or whatever.'

His mother's smile fades and she reaches down for the handbag next to her chair. She lifts it on to her lap. 'I don't understand,' she says. 'With films on the telly and all that. I probably said that last time, didn't I?'

'I thought I'd explained.' He leans towards her, shaking his head. 'It's all about cash flow. You know what cash flow is, right?' He doesn't wait for her to say that she doesn't. 'It's the way a company like mine works, how all the decent companies work. As soon as the money comes in from one project, we invest it in another. It's always tied up in the company, that's the problem. You see what I'm saying?'

She nods, but she has already taken out her purse and is staring into it. She says, 'I don't think I can, love.'

'It's only fifty. Or whatever you can spare, you know.'

'I know, but everything's spoken for, see?' She prods a finger inside the purse, as though hoping to find some notes she didn't know were in there. 'There's what I put away for the holiday every week, and the shopping, and we've just had the gas bill come in. It's a bad time, you know? I'm so sorry, love.' She shakes her head, and when she finally snaps the purse shut she looks devastated.

'Don't worry,' Chris says. He sits back again and tries to look as though he's already forgotten asking, but he can only think about his old man pissing fifty pounds up the wall in some pub in Torquay or Weston-super-Mare and how much those stupid figurines cost and the seven quid he's wasted on tube and bus fares to get here.

'Next week, maybe. If you still need it.'

'It's fine.' Probably a fiver apiece. Each of those ugly milkmaids and poxy poodles.

They sit in silence for half a minute, then his mother stands up and bends to pick up the tray. Holding it, she looks down at him. 'Now then,' she says. 'What about one of those trifles?'

... THEN

Learning to budget was something else you needed to do during recovery. A new and important skill to master. After all, being sensible about making your resources go where they should was rarely a pressing issue when you were using.

Twenty pounds to cover food and buy heroin: spend it all on heroin.

Ten pounds to buy food: spend it all on heroin.

Heather has become fiendishly efficient when it comes to budgeting. Not only does she make sure to allocate enough of her benefit money to cover essentials, she makes sure she allocates *exactly* enough. This amount covers food and bills, but also includes treats: chocolate, magazines, the occasional takeaway. Once all those things are covered, the last thing she wants or needs is money left over.

However committed you are to resisting it, temptation is always best avoided.

She had got everything sorted: rent, bills, the lot. She had worked out every last penny that would be needed to get the things for the party she had spent so many hours agonising over. It was all going to be perfect and now sodding Caroline has come along and spoiled everything by being nice.

Heather walks into the shop, still frantically doing her sums, trying to rejuggle things. Why does someone always have to stick their oar in and screw her plans up at the last minute? This is something she has been looking forward to for days – moving slowly through the shop, crossing things off her list as she goes – but now she's nervous and sweaty, because this isn't the way things had been supposed to go.

She has too much money to spend.

'I'm really happy to help,' Caroline had said. 'It's no big deal.'

'It's fine, honestly. I've made a list.'

'Yeah, but why pay for stuff when you can get it for free?' Caroline had explained that the supermarket where she worked gave away loads of food to their staff at the end of the week; gave it away or sold it to them for next to nothing. 'I can get all sorts of stuff,' she'd said. 'Sausage rolls, mini quiches, all the usual party food, you know? I mean some of it might be a day or two past its sell-by date, but it's fine, I promise.'

What could Heather say?

I don't want your shitty free food. *I've made a list!*

It's a big place, and open until very late; not quite as cheap as Lidl or Aldi would be, but a damn sight cheaper than the fancier supermarkets and only five minutes' walk from her flat. It's run by a Turkish family. There are two married couples, or maybe they're all brothers and sisters, Heather has never quite worked it out, but they're friendly and they always talk to her when she comes in. How's life, the weather, all that.

One of the men waves to her from behind the till. She smiles at him and grabs a basket, then walks quickly out of sight into the first aisle.

'I can come along early if you like,' Caroline had said. 'Help you get everything set up. We'll have a laugh.'

'Yeah, whatever.' Heather had stopped listening by then. She had already begun to panic, started recalculating.

She walks slowly up the first aisle. She has no intention of buying any cleaning products or kitchen towel, but she never misses an aisle out. Up one, then turn and down the next; it's the way she always does it. The basket is still empty, but it feels heavy already and she knows that in all likelihood she will require several. It's just drinks, basically. Soft drinks and a few balloons. There's nothing else she needs to get now, thanks to bloody Caroline.

One of the Turkish women, sister or wife, is kneeling at the top of the aisle, busy with a pricing gun. She nods as Heather walks past.

'You shop for your party?'

Heather grunts and turns the corner, in no mood to talk. Why had she been so stupid as to mention it last time she'd been in? She'd been excited, that was why, eager to let the woman know what she'd be doing next time she came into the shop. She should have known that something would happen to balls it all up. Something almost always does.

She slows at the drinks section and takes a good long look at the shelves. She might as well put some thought into what little she can get.

She loads Coke and Diet Coke into the basket, two large bottles of each. She picks out some fancy fruit juices in cartons – mango, guava, peach – and some weird-sounding cordial in a funny-shaped bottle. She carries the basket across to the till, picks up an empty one and goes back into the aisle again. She fills the basket with bottles of water, fizzy and still, and piles on a few random cans of drinks she's never heard of.

She goes back to the till again for a third basket. She might as well make it look as though she has a lot to buy.

The man at the till says, 'You live far?'

Heather looks at him. What the hell does he want to know that for?

'Is a lot to carry.'

'I'll be fine.' Heather moves away into the next aisle. 'I'm stronger than I look.'

There's not much, a lot less than there'd be in Tesco or whatever, but she knows exactly where everything is. She'd mapped out her route last time she was in the shop. Now she heads for the section she had planned to leave until last.

Balloons, hats, a banner. At least Caroline doesn't get any of this stuff for nothing. It's probably the only fun Heather's going to have.

Why shouldn't she have fun? It's her birthday, for God's sake, her party.

She picks out half a dozen hats and a big bag of assorted balloons. These are definitely going to be down to her. She looks at the different shapes in the bag, presses her thumb against them through the plastic and remembers what Chris calls Caroline. She allows herself a smile.

Moby Dick wouldn't have enough breath to blow up a condom.

Carrying her final basket back to the till, she decides that she'll make the banner. They haven't got one anyway, but she'll get out her felt-tips later and make something far better than anything she'd be able to buy. Something that will be the first thing people see when they come in. Something that's going to attract far more attention than old sausage rolls and mini quiches.

'Finished?' The man comes round from behind the till and heaves up the first basket. He begins ringing up the various bottles, talking as he passes each one across the scanner, but Heather isn't really taking any of it in.

She's looking at the display next to the till. She has too much money and she cannot take her eyes off the large plastic dispenser and the rows of brightly coloured cards.

Lucky Doubler. Super 7s. Cash Cow.

The owner of the shop comes round for her second basket.

Heather is suddenly thinking of all the things she could buy that would really make her party one to remember. A decent music system for a kick-off and fantastic presents for all her guests. She could forget all about mouldy supermarket food if she had enough cash to go on holiday somewhere decent, or get herself a car, maybe.

'Anything else?'

She hears him, but his voice is coming from a long way away, and the fact that her heart is dancing in her chest might be terror or might be excitement, but she tells herself that it doesn't really make a lot of difference and none of this is her fault anyway.

She tells herself that she can afford it.

She points at one of the scratch cards. It has pound signs and coloured balls and smiley faces.

'I'll have twenty-five of them . . . '

. . . NOW

There weren't any photographs, not that Tanner could see anyway. She felt relieved at not having to go through the usual routine, though the guilt at feeling that way was marginally worse. It was clear that Malcolm Finlay had seen her looking: the space where photos of his daughter should have been.

'I can't bear to have them out,' he said. 'Pictures of Heather.'

Tanner said, 'I understand,' though she didn't, of course.

'Not for now, anyway.'

'Right.'

'It's hard to be surrounded by pictures of how she was, you know? When all I can think about is how she ended up.'

Tanner leaned forward to lay her glass down on the table. Finlay had offered her tea and Tanner had asked for water. He'd said, 'Tap OK?' and Tanner had assured him that it was, while she'd struggled to remember the last time she'd drunk tap water.

Her mother's voice. *No uphill* . . .

The house was at the end of a terrace, ten minutes' taxi ride from the station, and as Malcolm Finlay had led her inside Tanner had been immediately impressed by how neat and tidy everything was.

Perhaps the man had always lived that way, Tanner thought, or perhaps he had been forced to do so after his wife had died. He might well have been a complete slob when his wife had been around to clear up after him. It was amazing how men who liked to appear domestically helpless could fend for themselves perfectly well when they had no other choice.

There was a sofa and an armchair and the thick lines around them showed that the dark red carpet had been recently vacuumed. A small flat-screen television stood on a cupboard in one corner and a modern pine bookcase in the other was well stocked with paperbacks. Choosing her moment, Tanner craned her neck to look at the names: Wilbur Smith, Ken Follett, Robert Ludlum.

'We weren't very close for a lot of years,' Finlay said. 'When it was bad. She didn't make much effort to keep in touch back then, and when she did it was always awful. I wasn't very sympathetic, you know?'

'Must have been hard,' Tanner said.

'Oh, yeah.' Finlay nodded. He was tall and well built; powerful. He still had a thick head of hair, though most of it was grey, as was the hair that sprouted at the vee of his open-necked shirt. 'It was horrible.' For a big man his voice was oddly light, thickened only by the hint of a rasp and the heavy Sheffield accent. Like someone Tanner had heard on the radio once, talking about gardens. 'She just cut herself off from everyone for a while. The family, all her old friends. I remember some poor girl she was at school with ringing me, all upset. Asking me where she was, what had happened.'

'What did you say to her?'

'I just said Heather was having a few problems, something vague like that. Said she was down in London, you know? I was too embarrassed to tell the girl she probably knew as much as I did.'

'It sounds like things got better though,' Tanner said.

'Oh yeah, once Heather had sorted herself out.' Finlay sat back in the armchair. 'Don't get me wrong, it wasn't overnight, nothing like that. She was a bit all over the place to begin with, and it took me a while to stop thinking she'd go back on it.'

'Understandable.'

'Most of them do, don't they?'

'Some do.'

'I couldn't let myself believe I was getting the old Heather back. I was trying not to get too excited about it, in case it was only going to last a week, or a month or whatever. Scared of getting my hopes up.'

'She didn't, though,' Tanner said.

'What?'

'She didn't go back. She stuck at it.'

'Oh, yeah.' He smiled, for the first time since Tanner had arrived. 'She did amazing.'

'Did she start taking drugs at college?' Tanner asked. 'When she moved to London.'

Finlay shook his head. 'Don't think so,' he said. 'I mean, she caned it a bit. They all do, don't they?' He looked at her. 'You got kids?'

'No.'

He nodded, said, 'Right. Well, it was just the usual stuff, I think: drinking cheap beer in the student union. Maybe a bit of weed. But no, I don't reckon that was when she started on the nasty stuff.'

'When did that change, then?'

He thought for a few seconds. 'It was about ten years ago. There was a problem with some bloke she was seeing. It all got a bit heavy.'

Tanner's notebook was on her lap. 'What was his name?'

Finlay didn't hear the question or ignored it. 'There was a young bloke she used to knock about with before all this at college and he was really nice. Spoke to him a few times on the phone. You know, when I rang and he was round at Heather's. I don't know how serious that was, but it all went out the window when this new bloke came on the scene. That's when everything went downhill, definitely.'

'Do you remember his name?'

'Never knew it,' Tanner said. 'Heather only mentioned him once, was a bit secretive about it. For some reason I think he was a bit older than she was. Maybe she said something, made me think that. I can't bloody remember.'

202

'No worries,' Tanner said.

'I do know that I wasn't happy about it. I mean, whatever went on it was making her miserable.'

'He ended it, did he? This older man?'

'No idea what happened, but next thing I know she's not returning phone calls, she only gets in touch to scrounge money and the first time she came home afterwards ...' He shook his head, blinked slowly. 'I hardly recognised her.'

Tanner said nothing.

'She'd always looked like her mum, Heather had, but now ... THEN, I mean ... she looked like her mum had done when she was ill. Just before she died. It was a shock, I can tell you that much. What she'd done to herself.'

Tanner watched Malcolm Finlay slowly raise his mug of tea, then pause and stare at it, as though he had momentarily forgotten what it was, what it was doing there. His mouth opened and closed, and then he drank.

'Is there someone else Heather might have talked to about this man she was seeing?'

'Maybe. A friend at college or something.'

'What about family?'

Finlay looked at her.

'Her sister, maybe?' Tanner knew there was a sister who lived in Scotland. A secretary at an engineering firm.

Finlay shook his head and leaned forward to put the mug down. 'They weren't close,' he said. 'Even before Heather went off the rails. Her sister's always been the sensible one. Always had a job and a family, even though, to be honest, it was Heather who was the bright one. I think she was a bit jealous because Heather was always the one who wanted attention, you know?'

'She's younger than Heather?'

Finlay nodded. 'You know what she said when I told her about Heather? What had happened?'

Tanner waited.

'She said, "Typical".' Finlay grunted. 'It was just, what do you call it, a gut reaction. I know she was upset, because I could hear it in her voice, but that was the first thing out of her mouth. Typical . . .' He found a thin smile from somewhere and leaned forward to brush at something on his trouser leg. He said, 'Is any of this helping? Is it of any use to you?'

'Everything's useful,' Tanner said. 'It's about building up a picture.'

'That stuff about the bloke Heather was seeing. You think it might have anything to do with what happened to her?'

'I've no idea.'

'It was a long time ago.'

'Ten years, you said.'

'There or thereabouts.'

'People can harbour grudges for a lot longer than that,' Tanner said.

Finlay sat back again, nodding as though he could see the sense in what Tanner was telling him. He suddenly looked like someone who was harbouring a grudge or two of his own. He said, 'They reckon that with these things, with murder and what have you, most of them are solved quickly.'

'Who reckons?'

'The first twenty-four hours or something.' He glanced towards the bookshelf. 'I must have read it somewhere.'

'It's not true,' Tanner said. 'I mean, sometimes, yes.'

'It gets harder though, presumably. The longer it drags on.'

'It takes as long as it takes.' Tanner swallowed and found herself studying the marks on the carpet near Finlay's feet. She wondered if perhaps she had sounded a little offhand. Flippant, even. 'It will get solved though,' she said. 'We will catch whoever was responsible for your daughter's death.' She slid her notebook into her handbag. 'Then maybe you can get those photos out again.'

Within five minutes of the train pulling away from Sheffield station, Tanner had visited the buffet car and was back at her table with a gin and tonic. Opposite her, a man in a smart suit worked furiously at a tablet. Swiping, tapping. It might have been spreadsheets or Twitter or Temple Run, there was no way to tell. Tanner decided that she would sneak a look when she visited the toilet.

It made her angry with herself, how badly she needed to know.

Malcolm Finlay had been right to question her about how helpful his information could possibly be. Was it really likely that something which had happened to Heather all that time ago was somehow connected to her murder a decade later? Could whatever – or *who*ever – made her turn to drugs for escape or comfort in the first place, have been responsible for her death?

It was possible, of course. Anything was possible.

She looked across at Tablet Man. He glanced up, then went back to his screen.

Tanner decided that she would try to talk to some of the people Heather had known ten years before. It would not be easy, as she had clearly lost touch with them, but Tanner would try to find someone who might put a name to the older man Heather's father believed she had been seeing.

She took out her notebook, intending to jot down a few ideas, but it lay unopened and the gin got drunk, and Tanner quickly found herself struggling to stay awake, staring out at the Yorkshire countryside and thinking about family.

Listening to Malcolm Finlay talk about the relationship between Heather and her younger sister, Tanner's face had betrayed nothing, but stories like that were something she always found hard to comprehend. Tanner had two elder brothers and they had always been thick as thieves. They talked on the phone every week. They spent Christmases together. She had been to dinner with one of her brothers only a week before and the other one and his wife had come away on holiday with her and Susan the previous year.

Stories like the one Finlay had told were sadly all too familiar though. Blood might be thicker than water, but so was bile. She knew very well that most people did not live like the Waltons, and her job brought her into contact with more dysfunctional families than she might otherwise encounter. All the same, Tanner couldn't help feeling that she and her brothers were the strange ones. The freaks, the oddballs ...

She was thinking about calling Susan again, steeling herself for it, when her phone rang.

'I talked to some of the staff in that pub,' Chall said. 'They all knew exactly who I was talking about and one of them said he remembers that night really well. Said there was usually a lot of laughing or whatever, but not that particular Monday.'

'An argument?' Diana Knight had said something to that effect.

'Several,' Chall said. 'This bloke in the pub told me he'd had to go across and ask them to keep the noise down. Chucked one of them out.'

'Chris?'

'Fits the description.'

'Good stuff,' Tanner said. 'Well done.'

'Oh, and I've managed to track down the final member of the group, too.'

'Right, we'll have a crack at her tomorrow.' Tanner felt the tiredness start to lift a little. The man from Heather Finlay's past was definitely worth checking out, but she still felt that Tony De Silva's recovery group was the most promising area of inquiry. She stole another glance at her fellow passenger, tried and failed to read his expression. 'Different approach this time,' she said.

It gets harder though, presumably. The longer it drags on.

'No more buggering about.'

... THEN

Caroline is as good as her word and arrives more than an hour before anyone else is due, beaming and laden down with plastic supermarket bags. She hugs Heather warmly and gives her a card.

'It's only a silly one,' she says. 'You've got to have a laugh, haven't you?'

Heather opens the envelope in the kitchen: a cartoon kangaroo in a party hat saying 'Hoppy Birthday, mate!' Heather says, 'Thanks,' and lays the card on the worktop. Caroline immediately picks it up and walks across to place it next to the only other card she can see, which is sitting on top of a bookcase. She points at the home-made *Happy Birthday* banner hung across the window and says, 'That's great,' then she walks back and begins taking food from the bags.

'Probably brought way too much.' She produces large packs of sausage rolls, quiches and pork pies. There is an assortment of dips and crackers, spring rolls, mini pizzas and a big box of chocolate biscuits. 'You can always freeze some of it, eat it whenever you fancy.'

'I suppose.'

'Probably last you the rest of the week.'

'You could always take some home.'

Caroline laughs. 'Last thing I need is all that stuff looking up at me every time I open the fridge,' she says.

'Oh, yeah. Sorry.'

Heather fetches plates from the cupboard and watches Caroline set out a selection of the food; arranging the sausage rolls, carefully laying out the crackers in circles, taking the lids off the dips. She hands Heather the items that need heating up. 'We can put these on when people get here,' she says. 'They can help themselves.'

'I might take them round on plates,' Heather says.

'Good idea,' Caroline says. 'Like a proper posh do.'

Heather puts what is not yet needed into the fridge and, when Caroline comments on the quantity of drinks in there, asks her if she wants something. Caroline asks for a Diet Coke, and once the drinks are poured into paper cups, the two of them lean back against the worktops and look at one another.

'So, get anything nice?' Caroline asks.

'Sorry?'

'Presents.'

'There's nothing I want,' Heather says. 'My dad sent some money.'

'Nice.' Caroline glances towards the card sitting next to her own on the bookshelf. She has already seen what is written inside.

Love Dad.

Heather's father is clearly a man of few words.

Not even a kiss . . .

'So, you excited then?'

'If anyone comes.'

'Don't be daft,' Caroline says. 'Everyone's well up for it.' She looks around. It's not a big flat, just a kitchen and a small living room divided by a row of cupboards, one bedroom and one bathroom off the hall. 'So, who else is coming then?'

'It's just us,' Heather says. 'The group.'

Caroline smiles, to show she's fine with that. 'I was hoping there might be some fit blokes.'

'Robin?'

Caroline grins. 'I was only messing about.' She wanders across to the door. 'Chris is good-looking, but I think I'd need to get him *really* drunk and there's not much chance of that.'

'Stranger things have happened,' Heather says.

Caroline throws her a look, expressionless, then turns away and points up at the frames hanging near the kitchen door. The slogans, drawn and decorated. 'Do these help, then? Just looking at them, I mean.'

Heather glances at her watch. 'There's another one I'm going to do. *A journey not a destination.*'

Caroline stares at her.

'Recovery.'

'Oh, right.' Caroline cocks her head and claps her hands together. She nods at the frames. 'Anyway, we can forget about all this for one night, can't we? We are having a *party* . . . '

Heather watches as Caroline drops her empty paper cup into the kitchen bin. She walks across to straighten one of the frames, moves it just a fraction and says, 'It's times like this I really need to remember it.'

They all arrive within fifteen minutes of each other, though predictably, Chris is the last one to turn up. There are more cards to put on the bookcase and Robin and Diana have brought presents, each one beautifully wrapped. Heather opens them while they watch: an expensive set of soaps and bathroom smellies from Diana; a red leather iPhone case from Robin.

'They're gorgeous,' Heather says, quietly, looking away as she tears up.

Robin smiles and lays a hand on her arm. Diana smiles too, but it seems like an effort, a bad mood hanging over her like a small, black cloud.

'Blimey, that's quite a spread.' Robin nods towards the plates of food on the worktop. 'Must have taken you ages.'

Heather looks quickly to Caroline, but the younger woman says nothing. Just winks.

'Thank God,' Chris says. 'I'm bloody starving.'

'Dig in,' Caroline says.

As Chris starts loading up his plate, and Robin and Diana move to sit down, Heather gathers up her presents together with all the shiny wrapping paper and walks quickly away into the bathroom, so they won't see her crying.

'She's having a baby,' Diana says. 'Can you believe it? That woman is having my ex-husband's baby.' She and Robin are sitting close together on the sofa, paper plates of food on their laps. Heather and Chris are talking in the kitchen, while Caroline is smoking in the far corner of the living room, blowing her smoke out of the open window. 'Phoebe called me, absolutely furious.'

'Understandable,' Robin says.

'Not with her,' Diana says. 'Not with the woman he left me for. With *me*. Yet again, this is somehow all my fault, because I wasn't a good enough wife to hold on to him.'

'You shouldn't let it upset you,' Robin says.

'Really?' She turns to look at him, horrified. 'That's all you've got to say? That's being supportive, is it?'

'You're being rather unfair.'

'Am I?'

'We're not actually in a session, Diana.' He gestures towards the *Happy Birthday* banner. He holds up his untouched plate of food to illustrate his point, but Diana is determined to make one of her own.

'We're supposed to be a group though, aren't we? A family. This is my "here and now", OK, and some support would be very much appreciated. This bloody nightmare is my "here and now".' She glances up and can see that Heather and Chris are looking at her. 'I don't know what the hell I'm going to do.'

'As long as you know what not to do,' Robin says.

'I really don't need a lecture.'

'Times like these are the most dangerous.'

Diana barks a short, bitter laugh and shakes her head. 'You don't have to worry. If I'm reaching for a bottle, it's only so I can go round there and smash that bitch over the head with it.'

She looks up to see Caroline walking across, sighs and sits back. As well as a voluminous polka-dot dress, the newest member of the group is now wearing a pointed party hat and, ominously, two more are dangling from her fingers by thin elastic. She grins at Robin and waves one of the hats, but the look on his face tells Caroline all she needs to know, so she turns and walks away towards the kitchen.

Heather has made a playlist and now her phone is docked with a pair of portable speakers set up on the kitchen worktop. She has put together a collection of music from the year she was born – Depeche Mode, The Police, Billy Joel – as well as all her favourite songs from her time at school and college.

In the middle of the living room, Chris is dancing to 'Tubthumping' by Chumbawamba. He is acting out the lyrics as he throws himself around, arms flailing, taking a whisky drink, a vodka drink, a lager drink, a cider drink, and pretending to get increasingly pissed as he does so.

Heather is watching from the kitchen and laughing hard, loving it. She shouts at him over the music. 'That's hardly very appropriate, is it?' He gives her the finger and that makes her laugh even more. She calls him a wanker and, without looking at her, he grins and spins away and 'drinks' another drink.

He is reeling about the room by the time the song fades out, pulling faces at Robin who is sitting alone in the corner. The track is replaced by 'Bitter Sweet Symphony' by The Verve and instantly Chris changes tack. He begins to sway and writhe, throwing elegantly dramatic shapes as though completely transported by the music. His movements become steadily more ornate and manic, but as the song reaches a climax, he throws a sly glance towards the kitchen and looks fiercely disappointed to see that Heather is no longer watching.

Instead, she is walking across to join Caroline and Diana, who are talking by the bookcase. They both tell her what a great party it is and the three of them stand and laugh at Chris for a minute or two.

'You've got a lot of books,' Caroline says.

'Yeah, I love reading.' Heather reaches out and touches one of the cracked spines. 'Get that from my dad.'

'That's nice.' Diana picks out a book and studies the back cover. 'I was actually in a book club for a while, but it was just a bunch of women in full make-up who talked about whatever novel it was for two minutes, then sat round drinking wine and yakking about house prices. Don't get me wrong, I was one of them, but I do like to curl up with a good book. Plenty of time to do it now, as well.'

'I haven't read a book since school,' Caroline says.

'Really?'

'I like magazines and stuff, but books seem like such hard work.'

Heather shakes her head. 'Not if you find the right book. You can really get lost in it, you know? Best entertainment there is, if you ask me, and it's free. Well, good as. Most of this lot were thirty pence each from the charity shop.'

'Oh.' Diana looks at her. 'I work part time in a charity shop and we have a huge books section. If you tell me the sort of thing you like, I can keep an eye out.'

'Yeah, cheers,' Heather says.

'It's really not a problem.'

Chris moves across to join them, then stands there, hands on hips, nodding his head in time to Ace of Base, until they are all looking at him. He says, 'Talking about me?'

'Talking about books,' Heather says.

'Bloody hell,' Chris says. 'Party's not got that bad, has it?'

Heather leans towards Caroline. 'He's not a big reader. Not unless you count cereal packets.'

'I prefer films,' Chris says. 'It's a more kinetic medium.'

'A more what?' Caroline says.

'Yes, I like films too.' Diana is actually tapping her feet to the music now and seems finally to be enjoying herself. She replaces the book she has been looking at. 'What's your favourite?'

Chris thinks about it. 'Well, there's one called *The Sperminator* I'm rather fond of. Oh, and *Raiders of the Lost Arse* is an absolute masterpiece.'

Diana says, 'You're disgusting,' and looks as though she means it, but Caroline and Heather are already giggling and, after a few seconds, Caroline has to spit some of her drink back into her cup.

Nobody is quite sure how long the doorbell has been ringing. When Heather finally hears it, she immediately panics and rushes to turn the music down. She stands frozen in the kitchen and tells everyone to be quiet. Convinced that someone has come to complain about the noise, she sends Robin to the door, deciding that if she is in trouble, he is the person best equipped to get her out of it.

'I can't lose this flat,' she says. Diana puts an arm around her. Heather is actually trembling.

'It's probably just a Jehovah's Witness,' Chris says.

'Seriously, I just can't.'

'If he's fit, can we invite him in?' Caroline asks.

They wait in silence for a few seconds, until Robin reappears. He has an odd look on his face, a half smile. He says, 'Guess who' and a cheer goes up from the others when Tony emerges from behind him.

'Brilliant,' Heather says.

They all move towards him and Diana says, 'I thought you couldn't come.'

Tony holds up a box. 'I just dropped in to deliver a cake.'

Heather rushes forward to take it from him then turns back to kiss him on the cheek. 'So glad you came,' she says.

He has reddened. 'I can't stop.'

'You've got to have some cake at least, seeing as you brought it.'

213

Heather lifts the cake from the box. It certainly doesn't look as though it has come from a chain bakery. She shakes her head in disbelief and opens a drawer to get a knife.

'I bought some candles too.' Tony takes a paper bag from his coat pocket and hands it across. 'They didn't have enough for the number of years.'

'It's not that many,' Heather says, laughing. 'Cheeky sod.'

'Just put one in the middle,' Caroline says. 'One candle for one family.'

Robin nods his approval. Tony says, 'Very nice idea.'

Once the candle is lit, Caroline launches into a rendition of 'Happy Birthday' and the others join in. Diana's voice, a high trill, rises above everyone else's and Chris tries and fails to sing a harmony line at the end. Everyone claps and after Heather has blown out the candle and wiped her eyes, she steps forward to cut the cake.

'Looks amazing,' she says. She glances at Caroline, takes care to only cut five slices.

Chris turns the music back on, and Heather quickly nudges the volume down a little. Robin and Diana carry their cake into the living room and sit down.

Tony looks around, at the balloons pinned up in the corners of the room and on the door, the banner that has started to sag a little. 'Looks like you're all having a great time.'

'Oh yeah,' Chris says. 'The joint is jumping.'

Heather is still grinning. 'We had dancing.' She moves closer to Tony and hands him the plate with the biggest piece of cake. 'I bet you're a good dancer. Being musical and everything.'

'You should have brought your guitar,' Caroline says.

Chris rolls his eyes and heads towards the bathroom.

Tony has just taken a bite. He shakes his head, grunts and swallows. 'I don't think so.'

'Maybe one Monday night. You could give us a private concert.'

'It's not really why we're there,' Heather says.

'Afterwards, obviously.'

'Still, not really fair to ask.'

'I should get going.' Tony lays his plate down, the cake unfinished. 'Got a client later on.'

Heather's smile falters for a moment, but then she puts her own plate down and wipes her fingers on her T-shirt. 'I'll show you to the door.'

She follows Tony out into the hall. He stops at the front door and turns to see that she is close to him.

'Thanks for coming,' she says. 'For breaking the rules or whatever.'

'Well, not rules exactly.'

'It means a lot.'

'I just thought you ought to have a cake.'

'Doesn't matter what the reason was. Just happy that you decided to come.'

'That was the reason, though,' Tony says. 'The cake.'

She looks at him.

'Happy birthday, anyway. And well done.' He turns and fumbles for the lock. Heather leans past him and opens the door.

Once she has watched him walk away and closed the door, Heather stands leaning back against it for a few seconds. An Atomic Kitten song is playing in the kitchen: 'Whole Again'.

She remembers slow-dancing to it, with the boy she was seeing back then.

She listens and licks the sugar from her lips.

She is startled as the bathroom door opens suddenly and Chris emerges. He sniffs a couple of times and looks at her. He raises his eyebrows.

'There you go,' he says. 'You got what you wanted for your birth-day after all.'

. . . NOW

The supermarket manager's office was bland and functional: white-board, metal filing cabinet and glossy black desk. It was not a great deal bigger, Tanner thought, than the one her chief inspector took such pride in, and was even less homely. Just about the only indication that a human being actually worked in it was a mug, still half filled with tea, standing next to the computer, and a sign on the back of the door: a cartoonishly buxom woman puckering up.

DON'T FORGET TO KISS THE BOSS!

Having already met the charmless Yvonne Segal, Tanner decided that, were she an employee here, it would certainly be the one thing she would do her very best to forget.

'No mirrors in her house then,' Chall said, when Segal had left the room.

Tanner smiled. 'Yeah, the make-up *was* a bit Coco the clown.' She was seated behind Segal's desk, with Chall on a chair at one end. A third chair was sitting empty on the other side of the desk. It was this chair that Tanner and Chall found themselves glancing at when the door opened and Segal ushered Caroline Armitage into the office.

Both were asking themselves if the chair would be big enough.

'Right then,' Segal said. 'I'll leave you to it. Give me a shout if you need anything.'

Armitage walked forward and Tanner invited her to take a seat.

'This shouldn't take long,' Chall said.

Tanner had wrestled with weight problems of her own for a few years. A succession of yo-yo diets as she'd tried and failed to shed those unwanted pounds, until she'd eventually settled on a regime of regular exercise and cut down on takeaways. Until she'd accepted that there were jeans she was simply never getting back into again.

'Don't do it for me,' Susan had said, back when Tanner was struggling. 'I like you as you are.'

'I'm doing it for me.'

'I think that's bollocks. It's always about how other people see you.'

There was little question as to how other people would see Caroline Armitage. She was seriously big; twenty stone or more, Tanner reckoned. She watched the woman settle herself in front of the chair, take the weight on her arms and lower herself slowly into it.

'This is about what happened to Heather, right?'

'Correct,' Chall said.

Tanner had deliberately not given Caroline Armitage any warning of their visit, but still she was thinking that the girl's intonation had been a little odd. As though she were checking that the police did not want to talk to her about something else entirely, that her manager had not caught her dipping into the till.

'It's just a few questions.'

'No problem.'

Tanner watched the girl shift in her seat, heard the soft *shush* of the nylon. 'We want to talk about an evening you and several others spent in the Red Lion pub in Muswell Hill. A Monday evening, just over four weeks ago.'

The girl nodded. 'Heather's last session.' she said. 'We went to the pub afterwards.'

The blonde hair was almost certainly dyed, Tanner thought, but there were no dark roots showing. She wasn't wearing quite as much make-up as Yvonne Segal, but it was a close thing. Presuming that she would not go as far as to actually kiss her, Tanner wondered if Armitage was trying to emulate her boss.

'Regular night out, wasn't it?' Chall asked.

'Yeah, but we didn't exactly do a lot of drinking. Trust me, I could really have done with one sometimes.'

Armitage smiled and Tanner suddenly saw how pretty she was. She guessed that it probably took most people that long to see it. She wondered if that made the weight problem easier or harder to bear. She said, 'Do you remember that night?'

'Oh yeah,' Armitage said.

'Any particular reason for that?'

'Yeah, because it was the last time I saw Heather ... the last time any of us saw her.' She turned up her palms, as though it were obvious. 'I've thought about it a lot.'

'There was quite an argument,' Chall said.

Armitage looked at him.

'We spoke to the staff in the pub. Several arguments by the sound of it.'

Tanner watched Armitage hesitate. 'Listen, we know all about the confidentiality, how important that is to you all, but we're not here to talk about your session with Mr De Silva.' Tanner was now as sure as she could be that whatever went on in the pub was a direct result of what had occurred during the session earlier the same evening. Finding out what had been said in the Red Lion would tell her as much as she needed to know about what had preceded it. 'We just want to know what happened in the pub.'

Chall moved his chair a little closer to Armitage's. 'You need to tell us what those rows were about.'

Armitage nodded understanding, then finally shrugged. She said, 'People were angry.'

'With Heather?' Tanner asked.

'Not all of them, and not just with Heather either.'

'Who else had fallen out?'

Another hesitation. 'It had all been kicking off between Robin and Chris for a while. Kind of building up. Things had got a bit nasty in the pub the week before.'

'Any particular reason?'

'There'd been some letter. I told Robin he was way off, you know? He had his own ideas as to who was responsible, so . . . '

Tanner nodded. She wanted to know what the letter was about, but there were other ways of finding out – most obviously by talking to Robin Joffe again – and she was wary of pressing Armitage too early. 'What did Chris make of all this?'

'He had other things to think about. They'd had it out already a few times and yeah, he thought Robin was a dick, but it wasn't really him he was pissed off with that night.'

'Heather?'

Armitage nodded.

'Why was that, Caroline?'

She looked away, her lips kissing one another softly as she searched for the right words. 'He was a bit all over the place and he was taking it out on Heather. He blamed her for . . . something she'd made him do. That's how he saw it, anyway. Shit, I'm going to be in all sorts of trouble for telling you any of this.'

Once again, Tanner was tempted to push for details, but she was sure she could get them from others. 'You said *people* were angry with Heather, like it wasn't just Chris.'

'Yeah, well, Diana had one on her as well, but that was just stupid if you ask me.'

'I'm sure it was.'

'It was all about something Heather had said during the session. I'd really rather not say what that was . . . '

'Fine,' Tanner said.

'It's just like it touched a nerve, that's all.' Armitage shook her head, remembering. 'Diana looks all posh and polite and all that, but she's got a hell of a temper on her.'

Chall watched Tanner scribbling in her notebook. He turned to Armitage. 'What about you?'

'Sorry?'

'Were you angry with Heather about anything? Sounds like most of the others were.'

'Yeah, I was, as it happens,' she said, 'but by then I was pissed off with almost everybody. I was upset, because we were all supposed to be supporting each other and suddenly the group was tearing itself to pieces.' She tapped her fingers against the arm of her chair. The pink polish could not disguise the fact that the nails had been bitten down to nothing. 'I wondered if it was me, you know?'

'What do you mean?' Chall asked.

'Because I was the new girl. Because maybe I'd changed the dynamic or whatever. I don't know that it was all sweetness and light before I joined the group, but it all turned to shit pretty fast after I did.' Her fingers were still tapping. 'I was thinking about leaving. I was going to talk to Tony about it.'

'So, are you going to?' Tanner leaned back in her chair. 'Mr De Silva says he'll be getting the group back together soon.'

Armitage shook her head. 'I've given up on stuff way too many times.'

Tanner and Chall exchanged a glance. They were almost done. 'What did you do after the pub?' Tanner asked.

'I went straight to see Chris,' Armitage said. 'He'd sort of stormed out before anyone else.'

'Stormed out or been thrown out?'

'Yeah ... a bit of both, I suppose. So I met up with him later to see if he was all right.'

Once again, Tanner looked at Chall. She said, 'Mr Clemence didn't tell us that he'd seen you after he left the pub.'

'Oh.' She looked confused. 'Well, that's his business, I suppose. I don't know . . .'

'Don't worry about it,' Tanner said. She had already decided that she would be talking to Chris Clemence again and now there was something else to ask him about. She said, 'Right then,' and stood up, and immediately began rummaging in her handbag. It felt polite to look away as Caroline Armitage got out of her chair, with considerably more effort than had been needed to get into it.

'Interesting,' Chall said, when Armitage had left.

'Certainly plenty to think about.'

'Bunch of nutters, the lot of them.'

'Not very PC, Dipak,' Tanner said. 'But I'm not going to disagree with you.' She had not given up on the idea of tracking down people Heather Finlay had known ten years before; trying to put names to the two men she had been seeing. For now, though, her priority was finding out exactly what had gone on between the members of Tony De Silva's group. Why some had chosen to withhold information and why others had simply lied. There were people she wanted to re-interview, perhaps more formally this time, and the therapist was one of them.

There was no sign of Yvonne Segal as they left her office.

'OK,' Chall said. 'If you had to. Armitage or her boss?'

Tanner popped a mint into her mouth. 'Neither.'

'Come on.'

'It's a stupid question,' Tanner said. 'If I *had* to, I'd shag *you*. But you'd need Rohypnol. And a gun to my head.'

Caroline pushed through the heavy PVC strip doors into the loading area. A lorry was backing up and a forklift was moving into position, ready to unload the pallets of baked beans or bog roll. She waved to the driver, then took out her cigarettes and her phone. She had one lit by the time her call was answered.

'I saw the police and I told them what you wanted me to,' she said. 'Happy now?'

'You're a superstar,' Chris said.

'I'm a mug, is what I am.'

'It'll be fine. I'll just tell them I panicked or something. Make up something.'

'Why don't you try telling me what you actually did? After you left the pub that night. I mean it might be a good idea, now you've got me to lie for you.'

'Look, it's not a big deal,' Chris said.

'Maybe not to you.'

'I wasn't exactly being a good boy, OK? I just didn't want those coppers doing me for something stupid. That's all.'

He was lying to her, Caroline knew, but clearly he was not going to elaborate. She took a deep drag. She said, 'Just so you know, if this turns nasty, I'll tell them you asked me to cover for you.'

'Why should it turn nasty?'

'Just telling you. Why should I get myself into any more trouble than I'm probably already in?'

'Because you're a nice person?'

'Yeah, right.'

'Because we're a group and all that? A *family*?'

'Now I'm just feeling sick,' Caroline said.

'Seriously, I'm really grateful, OK? I owe you one.'

'Big time, you do.'

Caroline put her phone away. With the cigarette in her mouth, she leaned down to rub at her knee, which had been hurting more than usual all day. Smoking, she watched the forklift weave between the stacks and wondered what that bossy cow Yvonne would have to say about the visit from the police.

. . . THEN

It isn't as though there is much clearing up to be done. The food left on the paper plates goes straight into a black bin bag, as do the plates themselves and the paper cups. It's hard for six people to make too much of a mess, especially when nobody is drinking. All the same, Caroline has volunteered to stay behind after everyone has left, to help Heather get the place straight again.

Within a few minutes, it's pretty much done and Heather is wiping the worktops in the kitchen. The music is still playing, more songs from her playlist, and she sings along quietly when she remembers the words.

Caroline stands in the middle of the living room, looking around. She picks up a paper cup that has been missed. She points. 'What about the banner?'

'What?'

Caroline walks across, but it's too high to reach. 'And the balloons?'

'I think I'll leave them there for a bit,' Heather says.

'Yeah?'

'Cheers the place up a bit.'

'Fair enough.' Caroline walks back into the kitchen and watches Heather finish up. 'Pleased with how it went?'

Heather folds the dishcloth across the edge of the sink; picks it up again and refolds it until the square is perfect. 'Yeah, I think so. It was all right, wasn't it?'

'It was great. Chris was on good form.'

'Well, that's always a bit worrying,' Heather says. 'When he's that hyper it usually means there's a major low coming.'

'Diana seemed to cheer up eventually. Had a face like a slapped arse when she arrived.'

Heather nods. She had spoken to Robin and knew exactly why Diana had been so upset. 'Can't be easy for her, what's going on.'

'Not unheard of, is it?' Caroline knows too, and she shrugs. 'Horny old blokes and girls with daddy complexes.'

Heather looks at her, a little shocked. 'A baby, though. Must be tough.'

'Well, shit happens, doesn't it? She's always the one who says *Chris* is a drama queen.'

'She's lonely,' Heather says.

'Aren't we all?'

They say nothing for a while, listening to the music. There's nothing else to do, but Caroline does not seem in any hurry to leave. She says, 'So, what about Tony, then?'

'What about him?'

'Turning up.'

'Oh yeah. Really nice of him.'

Caroline grins. 'Made *someone's* day.' She stares as though she's waiting for a reaction, but Heather just smiles and starts singing along to the chorus of a Gorillaz hit.

'This the stuff you were into at college?' Caroline asks.

Heather nods. 'This was always on at the clubs.'

'Never went, myself. College, I mean.'

'Seems like forever ago.'

'Not much of a dancer, either.' Caroline holds out her arms. 'For obvious reasons.'

'No reason you shouldn't dance,' Heather says. 'It's got nothing to do with . . . you know. It's good exercise.'

'Knees are buggered,' Caroline says. 'Even if I wanted to.' For a few seconds she watches Heather, who is nodding her head, transported. 'Bit of a clubber, were you, back then?'

'Not really,' Heather says. 'I mean, sometimes.'

Caroline smiles and nods. 'I bet you were into all sorts.'

'I wasn't.' Heather laughs.

'I heard that you sleep with more people in those couple of years, at college or uni or whatever, than you do in the whole of the rest of your life. Main reason I wish I'd gone.'

'Well nobody told me.' Gorillaz give way to S Club 7. 'Don't take the piss,' Heather says, laughing again. 'I used to love this.'

'Do you fancy going out?'

'When?'

'Now.' Caroline nods, excited. 'Why not? We could go to the pictures or something. I just got paid, so I'm happy to stump up for it.'

'Sounds great, but I'm knackered,' Heather says. 'I think I'll just get an early night.'

'Fair enough.' Caroline is still nodding. 'We should do it one of the nights though.'

'Definitely. Sorry . . .'

Caroline is already moving towards the hall, having taken the hint, and Heather follows her out.

'See you Monday, then.'

'Yeah.'

'You should bring some of the leftovers along. Not for me, obviously.'

As soon as Caroline has left, Heather helps herself to another piece of her birthday cake. She puts on the Atomic Kitten song and carries the cake across to a chair. She doesn't bother using a plate.

The rush from the first mouthful is instant and does not fade – the sugar, and the music and that look on Tony's face when he had held

225

out the box to her – as she takes out her phone and starts to send him a text.

She wants him to know just how much today has meant to her.

Robin had gone straight from work to the party, so he collects that day's post on his way back into the flat, drops it on the coffee table then puts an M&S risotto into the microwave. Aside from a mouthful of birthday cake, he hadn't eaten a lot at Heather's; unable to stomach too much of that cheap party crap. He lays out a plate and fork on the small table in the kitchen and checks his watch.

Half an hour until Suzi is due to arrive.

The party had been OK, and Robin has always prided himself on his ability to talk to anyone, but he couldn't honestly say that he'd enjoyed himself. Even though he never feels like the oldest at the sessions, the music and the dancing had set him a little apart from most of the others. All that silliness. It wasn't surprising that he'd spent most of the time talking to Diana. She usually made a beeline for him, even when they were just doing the tea and biscuits thing before a session started. Truth be told, she was starting to get on his nerves. All that whining, all that me, me, me.

In the end, he'd stayed no longer than he'd absolutely had to. He hadn't wanted to offend Heather.

He walks into the bedroom and checks that everything is ready. He smooths out the duvet and straightens the book that is sitting on his bedside table; lays his glasses on the top. Stupid really, that he takes so much trouble. Suzi and her colleagues probably spend most of their time working in places that make his little flat look like the Ritz.

They must feel right at home here, Robin thinks. It's more like a hotel room than anything.

He checks that everything he needs is in the drawer by the bed – the toys, what have you – looks to be sure he has enough cash in his wallet, then goes back into the living room and flicks through the post while he's waiting for his dinner to cook.

As much junk mail as ever, a credit card statement he does not bother to look at, and it's only the white, hand-addressed envelope that appears to be of any interest. He tears it open and removes the single sheet of paper that's inside. He unfolds it, then sits down, ignoring the *ping* of the microwave.

The letters aren't cut out of newspapers, but they might just as well be.

Scrawled capitals . . .

HOW BAD WOULD IT BE IF YOUR FRIENDS AT THE
HOSPITAL FOUND OUT WHAT YOU'D DONE?
HOW MUCH WOULD IT BE WORTH
TO STOP THAT HAPPENING?
FIVE HUNDRED QUID, DO YOU RECKON?

Robin is still staring at the note, sweating and furious, when his doorbell rings.

. . . THEN

They talk about the party and what a great time they all had, though it doesn't escape Tony's attention that Diana is tense and Robin seems unusually muted. Instead of biscuits they eat some of the leftover sausage rolls and mini pizzas that Heather has brought along, and when they finally take their places in the circle Tony says, 'That's a very nice way to start the session.' He opens his notepad and looks around. 'And hopefully Heather's party will have been the high point of a good week for everyone. Yes?'

'Fantastic week,' Heather says. 'Thanks to you. To all of you.'

There are the usual nods and murmurs of affirmation from the others, but before Tony has a chance to note down the response, Diana is speaking up.

'A good week in the sense of staying clean and sober, absolutely,' she says. 'But otherwise a particularly shitty one.'

'OK.' Tony waits.

'Well, the woman my husband chose to leave me for has got herself pregnant.'

'I don't think she got *herself* pregnant,' Chris says.

Diana ignores him. 'It's utterly horrendous and to make matters worse my daughter's antipathy towards me has only worsened. I didn't think the situation could be any more intolerable, but it looks like I was wrong.'

'You've done well to come through it,' Tony says.

'I'm not sure I have.'

'In terms of not drinking, I mean.'

'Well, if I began drinking again, she'd really have won, wouldn't she?'

'Didn't we go through all this at the party?' Robin says, suddenly. He undoes the top button of his shirt. He is sweating a little. 'It's all you talked about.'

Diana turns and stares at him. 'Yes, but as you said yourself, that wasn't a session, was it?'

'Felt like it.'

'I think Robin's got a point though,' Caroline says. 'Do we really want to listen to you moaning about your ex-husband and his girl-friend any more?' She smiles at Diana. 'I'm sorry if that sounds mean.'

'I agree,' Robin says.

'Broken bloody record,' Chris says.

Diana looks to Tony. 'My relationship with my daughter is the most important thing in the world to me and it feels like it's been stolen. This is my "here and now" and I thought that's what you wanted us to talk about.'

It's not the first time Diana has misinterpreted an important prin-ciple of Tony's work in the sessions. 'The "here and now" literally means that,' he says. '*Here* and *now*. What's happening in the group, what's going on between the members of the group, and not what's happening to any individual outside it. Their feelings about what you're talking about are precisely the "here and now" and I can't ignore them.' He looks to Chris, to Caroline, to Robin. 'There are some fairly strong feelings, by the sound of it.'

'I need to talk about this.'

229

'This is group therapy, Diana, not individual counselling with people watching. It's not a one-to-one session with an audience.'

Diana says, 'Fine.' She sits back and folds her arms like a scolded schoolgirl. 'Whatever's best for the group, obviously.'

'Thank you,' Tony says. 'I am looking forward to hearing from you later on, though.'

Caroline looks at Diana. 'Your turn tonight, is it?' She widens her eyes. 'Another tale of shame.'

'If Diana thinks it will be useful.'

Diana says nothing.

Tony waits to see if anyone has anything else to contribute, then says, 'I'm wondering if you're OK, Robin.'

Robin says, 'I'm fine.'

'You do seem a bit stressed,' Heather says. 'Everything all right?'

Everyone is looking at him. He is bolt upright in his chair, knuckles white against the armrests. He nods and says, 'Stressed is perhaps putting it a bit mildly. What I'm trying to do right now is keep a good deal of real anger in check and it's not easy, I promise you.'

Tony can see it. 'So, I'm wondering where that anger's coming from?'

Robin stares at the floor and shakes his head for a few moments. Then he looks up again and his eyes have narrowed. 'It's about feeling betrayed. It's about being threatened, because frankly there isn't any other word for it.' Now, his hands are fists, bouncing against his knees. 'And the ugly truth is that someone in this circle knows exactly what I'm talking about.'

The others begin looking around.

Caroline says, 'Who you on about?'

'What's happened?' Heather asks.

Tony is quick to raise a hand. 'OK ... I have to hold myself partially responsible for this, because I've been happy to encourage a degree of socialising outside the sessions ... but now clearly an issue of some sort has arisen.' He looks around. Robin is staring at Chris. 'When there is tension between people that has developed in their own time, it simply can't be allowed to come to a head within the circle.'

'Don't worry,' Robin says.

Tony hasn't finished. 'It's very serious. Something like this is simply not fair to those who aren't involved.'

Chris stares back at Robin and holds up his hands. 'What are you looking at me for?'

'At the risk of sounding like a pub landlord,' Tony says, 'you really have to take this outside. I don't mean now, either. Whatever's going on, it needs to be resolved, but not in group. I can't control what happens in your own time, but perhaps I need to seriously reconsider the policy of group members' meeting up during the week, certainly in terms of my best advice.' He shakes his head and begins writing in his notebook.

Caroline says, 'Was it always like this?'

'What do you mean?' Diana asks.

'I'm starting to wonder if this is something to do with me, that's all. Me joining the group.'

'Don't be daft,' Heather says.

'It's not your fault,' Tony says. 'Yes, any new member will naturally change the dynamic of a group to an extent, but it's always been ... feisty.'

'*Feisty?*' Caroline shakes her head. 'Bloody hell.'

Tony lets the silence hang for a few moments, then looks at Robin. 'I'd like to move on, if everyone's OK with that.'

'Understood,' Robin says. 'I didn't mean to disrupt things.'

Tony nods and looks to his left, but Chris just shakes his head, still apparently confused. It has begun to rain outside, noisy against the glass all around them.

Tony tries to instigate a general discussion about the positive effects of happy memories, but only Caroline and Heather seem enthused. Heather says that having the rest of the group there to celebrate her birthday will be a happy memory to look back on and Caroline talks for a while about a camping holiday with her mum and dad when she was a girl.

231

Tony winds the discussion up after fifteen minutes or so, and looks at Diana. He says, 'So what do you think, Diana? Is there a story you'd like to share?'

'Well, only if it's all right with everyone,' she says, through a thin smile. 'I don't want to get on anyone's nerves more than I already have.'

Heather leans towards her. 'Don't be like that.'

'It's always counter-productive to harbour a grudge,' Tony says.

'Nobody was trying to be nasty.' Caroline looks around the circle. 'Were they?'

Robin manages to summon a smile. 'Of course not.'

'It's just about mixing things up a bit. It would be like me talking about my bloody diet all the time. How boring would that be?'

Chris nods and yawns theatrically. 'Right. Or me banging on about my numerous sexual conquests.' He grins. 'OK, bad example.'

Diana says, 'Well, all right, then,' but her body language belies her apparent reluctance and Tony can tell that she is itching to talk. 'It goes back to when I was a lot younger.' She glances at Robin. 'Rather like yours. Back to when I was at school.'

'Private school?' Chris asks.

Heather looks at him. 'Who cares what kind of school it was?'

'Yes, private,' Diana says. 'But that's not strictly relevant, because what happened goes on at every school.'

Tony throws a warning glance at Chris, who is clearly desperate to make some remark about sex and bike sheds. He nods at Diana to continue, his pen poised.

'There was a girl at my school who was not exactly everybody's favourite, shall we say. Not hugely popular, not good at games or particularly bright or anything. She was big, you know?' She looks at Caroline. 'Not . . . *big* . . . I mean she was tall for her age, a bit clumsy.' She sits back and clears her throat. 'She wasn't exactly thrilled about any of this, so she took it out on other girls. Girls who were that bit younger, who she thought were prettier than she was. She was a bully, basically, and she was clever about it. Sly, you know?

232

'There was hair-pulling and pinching and that kind of thing, but it was never when there were others around to see it. Sometimes it was worse than that. A compass in the back of the leg, breaking other girls' things, taking money from them . . . and sometimes, when she really got angry, the violence would . . . escalate. Kicks and slaps and so on.' Diana's hand moves slowly to her face and presses. 'You could see the marks of her fingers afterwards, the outline of it . . .

'It was the emotional stuff that was the worst though. That's what she was really good at. Turning one girl against another, or two against one, then standing back to watch them tearing each other to pieces. She could make someone cry with very little effort. She had a talent for it. She would seek out the weaknesses in those girls who seemed to have everything going for them and just . . . reduce them. A couple of the girls she targeted had to leave in the end. She was actually proud of that, if you can believe it. Better than being popular or being in the hockey team or whatever.'

She lets out a long breath and swallows hard. 'She was truly vile. Back then, there wasn't such a fuss made about bullying, so the stupid thing is she got away with it. For years, she got away with it.'

After a moment or two she looks at Tony, to let him know that she's finished, but he is busy writing.

'That's horrible,' Caroline says. 'I hate bullies. They're basically just cowards.'

'Why didn't you ever tell anyone?' Heather asks.

Tony looks up. 'I think Diana is trying to tell us that she was the bully.' He looks across. 'Correct, Diana?'

She nods.

'I got that,' Chris says, pleased. 'I'd worked that out.'

The others are looking at Diana. Robin leans across. 'Well, cowardly or not back then, *that* was brave,' he says. 'Thanks for telling us.'

Tony closes his notebook. 'I'm wondering, Diana, bearing in mind what you wanted to talk about at the start of the session, if you think it's relevant that the girls you targeted back then were younger than you. Younger and prettier, you said. Is that something you'd agree is worth thinking about?'

Diana smiles. 'It's something I think about every day,' she says.

Chris folds his arms and lets out a whistle. 'Well, I'd be worried,' he says, 'if I was that young piece your ex-husband's got up the duff. Seriously, I'd be shitting myself.' He looks around. 'I'd be watching out for a compass in the back of my leg.'

... THEN

On a different night, they might have kicked things off by pulling Diana's story apart, demanding more detail from her, more disclosure. The session would have continued, albeit more informally and without its leader. The mood around the pub table is that little bit darker tonight though, the conversation subdued and unusually prosaic.

Heads are down.

Diana is all but wrung out, or giving a good impression of it. She chips in now and again, nods and smiles, but to all intents and purposes, she is elsewhere. Next to her, Robin contributes even less than she does. Though there is a drink in front of him, he has not touched it and he does not react when Heather or Caroline looks towards him or provides a verbal cue that he might normally pick up on, trying and failing to drag him into the conversation. He is animated only briefly, once every few minutes or so, when he turns to look at Chris, who is busy at the fruit machine on the other side of the pub.

This does not escape anyone's notice, but they try to ignore it. Heather and Caroline – who are doing enough talking for everyone – have taken Diana's story as the starting point for a series of largely comical reminiscences about their own schooldays. They swap tales of dodgy teachers and classmates, bad behaviour on school trips and assorted academic disasters.

'Did you have a nutter at your school?' Caroline asks. Seeing Heather think about it, she says, 'If you didn't, it was probably you. Come on, there's always a nutter. We had a kid called Mickey Fox, who'd do anything you told him to. Literally, anything. He chucked his entire desk out of the window once because someone told him to. Kicked a squirrel to death in the playground one morning.'

'I don't think we had anyone that bad,' Heather says.

'He got done for stabbing a taxi driver after he left school.' Caroline nods. 'Should have seen that coming, I suppose.'

'We had a bullshitter,' Heather says.

Caroline laughs. 'Yeah, so did we. There's always a nutter and there's always a bullshitter.'

'Colin Goodman.' Heather smiles, remembering. 'Came back after the holidays and told us he'd shagged his scoutmistress. Gave us all the juicy details. We were only eleven, or something. Told us his mum was in a James Bond film and his dad invented the PlayStation.' She shakes her head. 'He just lied about everything, all the time.'

'He's probably an MP or something now,' Caroline says.

They laugh and drink. They each cast a glance towards Robin and Diana, then further, to where Chris is slamming his hand against the fruit machine in frustration.

'Was it hard for you at school?' Heather asks.

Caroline looks at her. 'Not particularly.'

'You never got ... picked on?'

'No more than anyone else.'

'Because of being big, I mean.'

'No, because I wasn't actually overweight at school.'

'Oh ...'

'Not for most of the time anyway. Actually I was pretty sporty, in all the teams and that. I didn't start overeating until I was sixteen.'

'I should probably go,' Diana announces, suddenly.

Heather and Caroline both look across, then look at each other. 'Don't be silly,' Caroline says.

'It's really hard to just sit here, that's all, after you've told a bunch of people something so horrible.' Diana empties her glass and dabs at her hair. 'Wondering what they must think of you.'

'There's no judgement,' Heather says. 'Never. Nobody is forced to say anything and nobody can judge them for anything they do say, or punish them for it.' She waits until Diana finally meets her eye. 'You know that. You've heard Tony say it a dozen times.'

'Nobody can stop you judging yourself, though. Doesn't matter what the rules are.'

'I think that's all part of it,' Caroline says. 'What we're there for. Maybe not judging, but trying to understand ourselves at least.'

'Well, I'm certainly not there yet,' Diana says. 'I'm a long way—'

She stops when Robin pushes the table away and gets quickly to his feet; when he says, 'Right, that's it,' and turns to walk quickly towards the far corner of the pub. The three women watch him go and it is all too clear who he is heading for.

Heather starts to stand up. 'I should stop him.'

'Don't,' Caroline says. 'Whatever the hell this is about, I wouldn't get involved. I think Robin can take care of himself.'

'It's not Robin I'm worried about,' Heather says. 'Did you see his face?'

Chris is digging into his pocket for more coins when he catches Robin's approach from the corner of his eye. He turns to face him, grinning, ready to ask if Robin has any spare change. Then he sees the expression and takes a step back, until he is hard against the fruit machine.

'You're not going to get away with this, you know,' Robin says.

'Oh, I've been getting away with it for years, darling.' Chris looks for a reaction, but it's not a comforting one. Robin appears ready to kill. 'What's your problem?'

'You. You've always been my problem.' The South African accent is suddenly more pronounced, that dangerous-sounding rolling R.

'This is something else, though. This is a threat, pure and simple. Well, let me tell you that I've been threatened before and I didn't cave in then, and I will not cave in now.'

'You've lost it, mate,' Chris says. 'You back on the drugs?'

'You'd like that, wouldn't you?'

Chris looks at him.

'Might be able to up your price if I was using again.'

'What price?' Chris laughs, quick and nervous. 'I've got no idea what—'

'Trust me, I've never thought more clearly in my life. I know exactly who I am, even if you don't, and I will not be threatened by a worthless piece of scum like you.'

'When am I supposed to have threatened you?'

'I'm not scared, you know,' Robin says. 'You carry on with this and I'll go straight to the police.'

Chris throws up his arms. The nerves, the apparent confusion, have now been replaced by irritation. 'Do what the fuck you want. I haven't got a clue what you're banging on about, mate, so why should I give a toss what you do?'

'You've been warned,' Robin says.

'I'll bear it in mind.'

'Are we clear?'

'Oh, definitely.'

Robin nods, his point made. He jabs a finger towards Chris, then turns and marches away.

'I don't suppose you could lend us a few quid?' Chris shouts after him. He looks past Robin to the table from where Heather and the others have been staring. Seeing them, he raises his arms again. He laughs and shakes his head and the four of them watch as Robin stops, turns and pushes through the pub door, out into the street.

. . . THEN

Group Session: March 8th

Interesting group response to Diana's desire to talk about ex-husband, daughter etc. General unwillingness to collude in avoidance of group work which is very positive. Diana still struggling with here and now concept as are others. Will focus next session on H&N exercises.

Robin extremely angry about situation that has developed outside group. No surprise that Chris seems to be the focus, but I refused to allow this conflict to be brought into the circle. Sure it will surface next week during exercises, but will try to harness it.

Diana's story about bullying at school extremely illuminating. Shame is still triggering angry responses to her current situation. Disclosure will be positive for her at this stage. Caroline and Heather both supportive. Group seems to be learning that I am not the only agent of help within the circle.

Chris clearly thrown by Robin's anger but continues to maintain façade. Jokes, cutting remarks, non-verbal responses etc. Still unwilling to face rejection for who he really is. Perhaps his own story will help him come to terms with it. Will speak to him during the week to encourage this.

Despite degree of external conflict, I feel that enough trust and cohesion has been established to allow more provocative positions to be taken during sessions. Group feels not just ready for confrontation but actively seeking it.

When Tony steps out of his office, the stench of weed from his daughter's bedroom is almost overpowering. Nina is cooking dinner downstairs, but he knows she will probably be able to smell it, even above the onions and the garlic. She will want to talk about it when he goes down, to hector him. It's his job, after all. His area of expertise.

He's tired, and he can't face another argument, at least not one with Nina.

It seems like as good a time as any.

He climbs the short flight of stairs to the top floor, where his daughter's room sits next to a spare room filled with Nina's gym equipment and a second bathroom which Emma is supposed to use, but never does.

The music is almost as overpowering as the smell, so Tony knocks hard. He waits, knocks again, then opens the door.

Emma is lying on her bed. Her eyes are closed, but Tony doesn't know if that means she's unaware of his presence. He quickly clocks the remnants of the joint in the ashtray, the tobacco tin, the hash pipe on her bedside table.

He says his daughter's name, then shouts it. She opens her eyes and he shouts again. 'Turn it down, please.'

She fumbles for a remote and lazily points it at the music system that he and Nina bought her at Christmas; the system that cost way more than his own. Tony can't remember the last time he sat and listened to anything properly: Bowie or Dylan or one of the old Nick Drake albums he loves so much. He listens to music in the car sometimes, but it's not the same. Even thinking it, wishing there was more time to relax and enjoy something that means so much to him, he realises that he associates all the music he really loves with being high.

Is that how his daughter will be in years to come? When she looks back and thinks about whatever the hell it is she's listening to right now?

She turns her head and looks at him. Her pupils are dilated, the whites splintered red all around them. She says, 'What?' and the smile

240

makes it clear that she finds his very presence amusing, as though a mysterious figure of fun has walked into her room. Not for the first time, Tony asks himself how his daughter sees him, high or otherwise. How old does he seem to her? How stupid? How ludicrously out of touch with . . . everything?

'I'm wondering why you feel the need to smoke quite so much weed,' he says.

'What?'

'Look, generally we don't have a problem with it, in moderation. You know that. I'm well aware that all your mates do it.' He stops. His daughter is shaking her head and the smile has gone. 'What?'

'Why the hell are you always talking to me like I'm one of your patients?'

'I don't have patients. I have clients.'

'Whatever they are.'

'I'm not.'

She lowers her voice and it drips with mock sincerity. '"I'm wondering why you feel the need" . . . you should listen to yourself.'

Tony steps over a pile of discarded clothes. He picks up a tangle of headphones, an empty water bottle, a magazine, and puts them on Emma's desk. 'And you should see yourself.' He takes care to sound nice and calm, reasonable. 'Really, Em, I mean it. It's got out of hand now and if you're not careful you're going to screw everything up. School and uni, everything.'

'Here comes the lecture,' she says. 'It's so boring.'

'Do you not think I know what I'm talking about?'

'That's the whole point,' she says. 'Why should I listen to you when you've done so much worse than this . . . and please don't give me any of that gateway drug stuff, because you know it's not true.' She raises her head from the pillow, but she is speaking slowly, as though the words are an effort. 'I've read all the stuff on the internet, so I know that's rubbish and I also know that weed is way less harmful than booze, so maybe it's Mum you should be talking to and not me.'

'Look, I know it sounds stupid, coming from me, but the stuff you're smoking is so much stronger than it was in my day.'

Again she mimics him. 'In my day ...'

'Seriously, there's a lot of research out there linking it with latent psychosis, all right? The worst that could happen back then was the munchies.'

Emma laughs; a moment of connection. 'Oh yeah, I get them as well.'

'I'm not joking,' Tony says. 'And why the hell should we be paying for this, anyway? Giving you money just so you can get off your tits and treat us like shit?'

She looks at him, then blinks, as though she's only just remembered that he's there; that they are in the middle of an argument.

'You're so sad,' she says.

'Am I?'

'And you're only taking it out on me because you're scared of Mum.'

'Taking what out?'

'The fact that you can't have any of the fun you used to and your life is completely boring.'

'You don't know what you're talking about.' There's a beanbag a few feet away and Tony fights the urge to kick it across the room. 'And anyway, I stopped listening to people who were stoned a long time ago.'

'Exactly,' Emma says. 'You've got nothing in your whole life that's exciting. That gets you off. You sit there and listen to people who are struggling and fucked up and maybe it makes you feel a bit better about yourself, but all the time you're thinking about how great it was to get off your face back then.'

'You really don't know what you're talking about.'

'So the closest thing you can have to any excitement is to suck up a bit of theirs ... to listen to their stories and flirt with that skinny junkie, the one with the short hair.'

'*What?*'

242

'But you can't have her either, can you? Because you're stuck with us. Poor old Dad.'

'Where the hell do you get this from?'

'You know exactly who I mean.'

'Really, I don't.'

'The one Mum's got such a thing about.'

'*Heather?* You mean Heather? Oh, for Christ's sake . . . '

'Thank you *so* much for coming to my party.' The cod northern accent is laid on thick. 'It meant *so* much, and that birthday cake you bought was *gorgeous.*'

Tony stares. Has she been reading his texts? Or perhaps she overheard a phone conversation. Something that was said at the session.

Emma nods, knowingly. She moans and says it nice and slowly, like the name itself is enough to turn him on. 'Heather . . . '

Tony struggles to find the right words, to comprehend the level of hatred he feels for his own daughter at that moment. He watches her smile, sees her dark eyes narrow and focus on something behind him, before slowly closing. She lays her head back down, and when Tony turns round to leave, he sees Nina standing in the doorway.

. . . NOW

'It's a different world down here, isn't it?' Chall said.

It was hard to disagree as Tanner drove them slowly towards the centre of leafy Barnes, passing the hundred acre wetland centre in the loop of the Thames, then crossing the common. Though Tanner's place in Hammersmith was no more than ten minutes away, directly opposite them on the north side of the river, they might as well have been in a different city.

Chall stared out of the passenger window as they passed a deli, an organic butcher's, an estate agent that looked as though it could have been Grade Two listed.

'Fancy a game of "Spot the Asian"?'

'I don't think we've got enough time,' Tanner said.

Chall laughed and Tanner became acutely aware of the fact that, despite having worked with him for almost eight months, she had no idea where her sergeant lived. Or if he had kids. Not for the first time, she told herself that she should make the effort to get to know those she worked alongside better, to socialise more. The last thing she wanted was to let on that she didn't know, so she made a mental note to ask one of the team what Dipak Chall's domestic set-up was.

'So how did it go with the boss then?' Chall asked.

'Just the usual,' Tanner said. Within five minutes of arriving at work, she had been standing in DCI Martin Ditchburn's office, updating him on progress with the Heather Finlay case.

It had not taken long.

She told him that they had managed to track down a woman the victim had been at college with ten years before. Joanne Simmit had seen Heather's name in the papers, she said, and had been wondering if it was the same one. After telling Tanner how awful it was, how full of life Heather had been back then, she went on to tell more or less the same story as Heather's father had. Heather had been seeing a boy for six months or so, Simmit said, though she did not know if he was a student, or someone she had met outside. She thought he might have been called John, but it was a long time ago. Then a bit later there had been another man about whom she knew next to nothing. She had seen him and Heather in a restaurant once, which is the only reason she knew he was older, but she had never spoken to Heather about it.

In truth, they had not been particularly close friends.

'I'm not sure there's much down that road anyway,' Tanner had said. She'd told her boss that she did not believe someone from Heather Finlay's past had suddenly resurfaced and was responsible for her death. That she was sure her killer had been someone rather more familiar to her. 'I still think this group is our best bet.'

Ditchburn had faith in her, Tanner knew, but she also knew how many plates he was juggling.

'Don't bet on it too long,' he'd said.

They turned off Upper Richmond Road into a wide street lined with perfectly trimmed trees and imposing semi-detached houses. When they pulled up outside the address they were looking for, Chall said, 'What d'you reckon? Three million?'

'Probably.'

'Landed on his feet then, our friend.'

'Let's see,' Tanner said.

*

Christopher Clemence answered the door in tracksuit bottoms and a white vest. He was barefoot. He looked shocked, then angry, though above all he seemed mystified as to how anyone had managed to find him.

'We're police officers,' Tanner said, answering the unspoken question.

Clemence turned and walked back into the house, and Tanner and Chall followed him into a large sitting room. He flopped down on to a deep three-seater sofa, put his feet up and pointed to the matching chairs. 'Make yourselves at home,' he said. 'I'd love to offer you a drink, but I don't think I should abuse my host's hospitality.'

'I reckon we'll survive,' Chall said.

Tanner looked around and it was evident that Clemence had not fought shy of abusing the hospitality himself. There were empty glasses and dirty plates on the floor in front of the sofa. Socks and training shoes were dotted about. A pair of game controllers lay on the polished floorboards in front of the wall-mounted flat-screen and Tanner saw the boxes of several hardcore gay porn films scattered among those containing computer games.

She said, 'Just so you know, we got the name of your . . . host from his friends at the arcade and then we went to see him at school. That's how we got this address.'

'Very enterprising,' Clemence said.

'He's seventeen.' Now Chall was staring at some of the DVDs on the floor, the photos on the front of the boxes.

'Yes, which explains why he's at school.' Clemence sighed and stretched out. 'Now, last time I checked, which I do on a daily basis, the age of consent was sixteen.' He smiled at Chall. 'So you know what you can do with your moral outrage.'

'I'm not outraged in the slightest,' Tanner said. 'But I might take rather a dim view if I look into your arrangements a bit more and find out you're taking advantage of this boy financially.'

'Look all you want,' Clemence said. 'It's not my fault if he wants to spend all his pocket money on games, is it? If he wants to buy takeaways and enjoys the pleasure of my company.' He held up a hand, as if on oath. 'Nothing underhand going on, Inspector, on my life.'

'His parents know he's got a house guest, do they?'

'No idea, but I'll be gone by the time they get back in a couple of days and I can promise you they won't even know I've been here.' Clemence grinned. 'Well, they might want to change the sheets.'

Tanner smiled back. 'Why did you lie to us, Chris? About what you did after you left the pub on the night Heather was killed.'

'You've been talking to the Michelin woman, then.'

'We've talked to everyone. Caroline tells us you were with her.'

'Yeah, I was. She was worried about me, bless her.'

'You didn't mention that.'

'Not the same as lying, is it?'

'And living off a seventeen-year-old boy with wealthy parents isn't quite the same as stealing from him,' Chall said. 'But there's not much in it.'

Clemence smiled, but it looked forced. 'I've never exactly seen eye to eye with the police, put it that way. Nothing against you two, but a few of your mates in the Drugs Squad haven't exactly played fair with me in the past, when really I shouldn't have been done for anything. So, you learn that you can get in trouble if you're being naughty and you can get in trouble if you're squeaky clean. In the end, it doesn't matter who you're dealing with, whether it's a copper or a junkie. Someone like me, you learn to lie, and you keep a few things to yourself. It's kind of your default position.'

'You're saying you're never honest with the police.'

'Especially with the police,' Clemence said.

'This isn't about drugs,' Tanner said.

'Doesn't matter.'

'I think it does. Someone close to you was murdered, and you chose to withhold information rather than give yourself an alibi.'

'Why would I need an alibi?' Clemence swung his legs to the floor, flexed his bare feet. 'I haven't done anything.'

'So why not just tell the truth?'

'Is it just me?' Clemence asked. 'Or are we going round in circles?'

Tanner was feeling every bit as dizzy as Clemence clearly was. She opened her notebook and said, 'Is there anything else you'd like to tell us, Chris? I'd advise you that now's the time.'

'Such as?'

'Anything you think we should know about anyone else in the group?'

'Not especially.'

'What happened between you and Heather in the pub?' Chall asked.

Clemence shrugged. 'She pissed me off. We pissed each other off a lot.'

'Something she made you do, wasn't it?'

'Who told you that?'

'What might that have been?'

For the first time, Clemence looked really uncomfortable. He sat back and folded his arms. 'No.'

'No, it wasn't something she made you do?' Tanner looked at him. 'Or no, you're not going to tell us?'

Clemence said nothing.

'What about Robin Joffe?' Tanner asked. 'Some kind of altercation between you, wasn't there?'

'Robin's a tedious arsehole.' Clemence seemed in more relaxing territory suddenly. He pointed towards Tanner's notebook. 'You might want to write that down.'

Tanner closed her notebook and dropped it into her handbag. She stood up. 'Your face is looking better, by the way,' she said. 'That was a nasty bruise. How did you say you got it?'

Clemence made no attempt to get up. 'I didn't.'

'He told us he was clumsy,' Chall said.

Walking towards the door, Tanner stopped by the sofa and looked down at Clemence. 'Clumsy's right,' she said.

She looked for a moment as if she felt rather sorry for him.

*

'However this pans out, can we find something to do him for?' Chall keyed the remote and the car's indicators blinked. 'Cocky sod.'

'He's still lying.'

'Maybe he can't help himself.'

'Maybe,' Tanner said.

. . . THEN

It had been Caroline's idea to meet Robin near the hospital and her suggestion that they go for a stroll on Hampstead Heath, but even getting to the nearest entrance involves a five minute walk that is largely uphill, so by the time they have been on the heath for a few minutes, she is out of breath and keen to stop for a while.

'Sorry,' she says. 'Bloody ridiculous.'

Robin seems perfectly happy either way, so they sit down on the next bench they see, content to watch others do the walking for a while.

'None of us are as fit as we were,' he says.

It's one of those early March days that cannot quite make up its mind. It had been raining half an hour before, but is now clear, the sky almost cloudless. It's still far from warm, but that doesn't stop Caroline pulling off the thin jacket she is wearing in an attempt to cool down. She reaches behind her to lay it across the bench, revealing sweat patches the size of dinner plates beneath her arms.

'I need to do this,' she says. 'I know it's not great for my knees, but ultimately the only thing that's going to sort them out is shifting some weight.' When she looks at Robin she seems close to tears. 'This is less painful than not eating. Just.'

Two women jog past, one hard behind the other. Lycra, headphones, the works; a fierce focus etched across their thin faces. Caroline watches them until they disappear round a corner.

'Have you thought about hypnotherapy?' Robin asks.

'I've thought about everything.'

'I know a good man, that's all.'

'He's not going to make me start quacking like a duck, is he?'

Robin smiles. 'Not unless you want him to. Let me give you his number and you can think about it. I'll have a word, tell him you might call . . . I'm sure he can sort out mates' rates.'

Caroline thanks him and takes out her phone. Robin texts her the number. She stares at it and says, 'Well, I've tried almost everything else.'

'I want you to know that it's only your health I'm concerned about,' Robin says.

'I know.'

'I'm not making any other kind of judgement. It's certainly not about how you look.'

Caroline nods. She says, 'Judge away, mate. Trust me, I don't want to look like this. I try to have a laugh, don't get me wrong, that's one of the reasons I joined the group . . . for the social side. But the last thing I am is one of those jolly fat women. You know? I can't stand all that.' She stares at her feet, the ankles bulging above the cheap training shoes. 'Truth is, I'm as miserable as sin.'

'All of us get down from time to time,' Robin says. 'That's why I still find meetings so useful. We get depressed and we crawl into our respective holes or we get angry and lash out.'

Caroline looks at him.

'Well, yes, you saw.' He takes off his glasses and reaches into his jacket for a cloth to clean them with.

'You and Chris made friends yet?'

'That's never going to happen.'

'OK . . .'

They can hear enthusiastic shouting from a hundred yards or so away to their left and, rising suddenly above the brow of the hill, a stunt kite soars and swoops like a brightly coloured bird.

'He's trying to blackmail me,' Robin says.

'Chris?' Caroline almost laughs, but then sees that Robin is most definitely not joking. 'How?'

Robin tells her about the note, his confrontation with Chris in the Red Lion. 'My wife hinted at much the same thing back when we got divorced,' he says. 'Going to the medical authorities and telling them about my history. At the time, I was terrified. I would have done anything she wanted to prevent that happening. Now, strangely, it doesn't scare me in the same way. Now I'm just raging. I will not be threatened, least of all by someone like him.'

'You can afford it, though,' Caroline says.

'That's not the point.'

'So, what are you going to do?'

'If I don't hear any more, then I'll probably leave it and move on. The anger is something I'll simply have to deal with in my own time. I'm not sure whether he and I will be able to sit in the same room any more, but I won't be the one who leaves, I'm damn sure of that.'

'What if it doesn't stop?'

'I'll go to the police.' Robin shrugs. 'What else can I do? I know everything will come out about my past and it will probably mean the end of my career, or worse, but I don't really have any choice.' He looks at her. 'What's the point in any of us going through the recovery process if you can't live with yourself?' He sits back. 'We all have to complete a moral inventory.'

In the distance, the multicoloured kite has been joined by a second. For a few seconds they dance around one another, before colliding and disappearing quickly from view.

'How can you be so sure it was Chris?' Caroline asks. 'Why couldn't it be someone from one of the other meetings you go to? NA, or whatever.'

'It's only in Tony's group that I've talked about working when I was still using drugs. Infecting patients.' Robin shakes his head. 'Ironically, it's the only place I've felt safe enough.'

'OK, but why does it have to be Chris?'

'Who else could it be? I think I put the idea in his head myself when I told him about my ex-wife making similar threats. Rather more veiled, mind you, but basically the same. Aside from anything else, who else would need the money badly enough to do something like this?'

'Diana's certainly got plenty.'

'Yes, and you have a job.'

Caroline laughs. 'You got any idea how much I get paid? Trust me, I certainly need the money.'

Robin smiles and lays a hand on her arm. 'I think I'm a rather better judge of character than that. I know very well that neither you nor Diana nor Heather would ever stoop to something like this. To try and ruin someone's life.'

'I still think you're jumping to conclusions,' Caroline says. 'What happened to seeing the best in people? All that stuff about faith, that's part of the whole step thing, isn't it?'

'It's funny,' Robin says. 'When you're finally able to look at yourself, to really look, you get an awful lot better at seeing others for what they are.'

'I suppose. I still can't believe it was him, though.'

Robin smiles at her naivety. 'I think I've always known what Chris was. I mean, it's not like there haven't been enough clues.'

'Oh . . .'

He turns to Caroline, sees the look on her face. 'What?'

'It's nothing.' She reaches behind for her jacket. 'Come on, let's see if I can manage another ten minutes without collapsing.'

'What's the matter?'

She slumps back in her seat. 'Oh shit. It's . . . nothing, like I said.' She seems frightened, suddenly. 'Just something I saw at the party.'

... THEN

Chris leans in close, his breath fogging the glass, and peers at the yellowing skull. He moves back a few steps so as to take in the full length of the skeleton inside the case, then turns to Heather who is on the other side of the room looking at a display of knives, saws and what look frighteningly like pliers.

'You are seriously weird,' he says.

She waits for him to walk across, unwilling to raise her voice because several other people are also looking around the room.

'It's interesting,' she says.

'If you say so.'

They are visiting the Old Operating Theatre, a museum of surgical history housed above St Thomas's church in Southwark. For the past few minutes they have been walking around the herb garret, the province of the apothecary in what was once part of St Thomas's hospital and which now houses a permanent exhibition of instruments, physical specimens and gruesome-looking medical paraphernalia from almost two centuries ago.

Chris looks down at the display. 'Tell me why we're here again.'

'Because I like this stuff. Well, not *like* . . . but I've always been sort of fascinated by it. Always wanted to come.' She looks at him. 'Anyway, it's a nice change to go somewhere in London where you haven't shagged anyone or got high.'

She walks across to another cabinet, this one dedicated to samples of the ancient herbal remedies that were used in healing. The blue, green and yellow jars sit alongside an arrangement of artefacts associated with rather more drastic treatments: trepanning, bloodletting, and, of course, the laying on of leeches.

'See?' Heather says, pointing.

'Christ on a bike,' Chris says.

'They do these re-enactments,' Heather had told him excitedly, reading from a leaflet as they'd climbed the steep spiral staircase from the church lobby. 'Every Saturday, apparently. They use actors or whatever to show you what the operations were like, and . . . oh my God, they do live *leeching*.'

Chris's reaction now is much as it had been then. He stares at the cracked earthenware bowls labelled *Deer Horn*, *Wormwood* and *Snail Trail*. He wrinkles his nose at the smell which still lingers after two centuries, and says, 'How much did it cost us to get in?'

'Six-fifty each.'

'Bloody hell, we must be mad.'

'What do you mean *we*? I paid for you, remember.'

A middle-aged man comes and stands a little too close for conversation to feel comfortable. He nods, in acknowledgement of their shared fascination, and Heather nods back. She leaves it a minute or so, then moves sideways to another cabinet. Chris follows her.

'Yeah, since when were you so flush?'

Heather leans closer to the display. 'I had a bit of luck, that's all.'

'Lucky Heather,' Chris says. He leans down too, so that his face is only an inch or so from hers. 'Lucky enough to lend me twenty quid?'

'Nowhere near.' Heather goes back to her leaflet, but glances up after a few seconds and sees the profoundly miserable expression on

Chris's face. She points to one of the pages, stabbing at it, like he will be interested. 'When they first restored this place they found dried poppy heads in the rafters.' She looks at him expectantly. 'For making opium.'

The mention of the drug does the trick and quickly drags Chris from his sulk. 'Nice. You ever had it?' He doesn't wait for an answer. 'I had it a couple of times. Bloody lovely.'

Slowly they move on past a large oak dresser crammed with all manner of peculiar odds and ends – antlers, ostrich eggs, a pair of stuffed baby crocodiles – and arrive at a display case full of truly grisly-looking devices. The labels alone are disturbing enough: *Piercer, Scarificator, Decapitation Hook*.

Heather points down at what might almost be an antique egg-whisk, were it not for the fact that each thin piece of metal attached to the handle ends in a vicious-looking hook. 'If I was to use that on you, d'you think you might tell me what happened with you and Robin?' She smiles and claws her fingers, then inches them towards his groin. 'Come on . . .'

He backs away, his face a blank.

She has tried once already – on the walk from Borough tube station – and got nowhere. Chris had said only that there was nothing to tell and changed the subject when she'd pressed him. It was strange, considering how much Chris loves to tell a good story.

'I told you to leave it,' he says.

'All right, blimey.' Heather pulls a face. 'Just looked nasty, that's all.'

'I don't like being accused of things. Leave it at that, OK?'

'Accused of what?'

In spite of his obvious irritation, Chris can't quite suppress a smile. 'What part of "leave it" don't you understand?'

They walk up another flight of creaky stairs to the operating theatre itself. At its centre is the wooden operating table, surrounded by ranks of raised benches and railings, from which students would have watched and tried to learn, while others there merely to observe would simply have been trying to hang on to whatever they had last eaten.

They walk slowly round the table, Heather pointing out the box of sawdust that would have presumably been there to collect the blood, running her fingers across the worn-down patches in the wood. Chris goes across to study yet another skeleton, this one suspended from a hook. He reaches out to delicately touch a rib, while Heather studies a picture of a patient struggling on the table, six men fighting to pin him down before the surgery, such as it was, could begin. 'Bear in mind, this was all before anaesthetics,' she says. 'Can you imagine having your leg sawn off or whatever? Just a stiff brandy and something to bite on.'

'I've had a few sexual encounters like that,' Chris says.

'Amazing how far things have come though, when you think about it.' She walks towards him. 'Wonder what they'd have done with the likes of us back then?'

'Maybe leeches were good for withdrawal,' Chris says. 'Maybe badger spunk was like methadone. Maybe they could drill a hole in your head to let the demons out. How the hell should I know?'

'Easier ways to get inside people's heads now.'

'Not sure that's progress though.' Chris starts slowly climbing the benches. He shouts back to her. 'I don't think I want anyone inside my head.'

'That's your problem.' Heather follows him up and sits next to him on the topmost bench of the theatre. They stare down at the operating table.

'I'm not stupid, you know,' Chris says.

'Never said you were.'

'I know exactly why you wanted to go out today.'

'I told you, I always wanted to come here.'

'Yeah, but you didn't have to drag me along.' He lets his head drop back and stares up through the enormous skylight above them. He closes his eyes against the sunshine. 'You want to have another go at me about this shame shit.'

'It's not shit,' Heather says.

'You think it helped Diana last week? She didn't look very happy about it when she'd finished.'

'Nobody says you're going to be singing and dancing afterwards,' Heather says.

'Who says I'm going to do it?'

Heather turns to look at him. 'Shame is primitive,' she says. 'That's why it's so powerful. It's all tied up with why we feel unworthy all the time, why we feel bad about who we are.'

'You been borrowing some of Tony's books?'

'Look, the only way you're going to learn your own pain isn't shameful is by connecting with other people's. That's pretty bloody obvious, isn't it? I know you're scared about it, because so am I, but you have to expose yourself.' He turns, grinning, but she holds up a hand before he can exploit the unintentional double entendre. 'Being scared of showing who you really are is what leads to all the lying. Lying to yourself as much as anyone, which is the stupidest thing of all, when you think about it.' She reaches across and takes his hand. 'You've really got to do this.'

'I haven't got to do anything.'

'All right, you *need* to do this ... both of us do. And if you don't, how do you expect me to have the bottle?'

'Since when does what I do matter so much?'

'Please,' Heather says.

There's half a smile as Chris turns away and stares down into the scrubbed and airy well of the theatre. It isn't hard to imagine the place crowded with people, stinking of blood and piss and loosened bowels. The squeak of the drill or the grind of the saw against bone; the screams of the hapless patient and the grunts of effort from those trying to hold him down.

'I think I'd rather be strapped to that table,' he says.

. . . NOW

Robin Joffe opened the door to his flat and looked at them. He blinked and said, 'Oh.'

'Sorry to drop in unannounced,' Tanner said. 'We were in the area anyway and we just have a couple more quick questions, if that's all right.'

Joffe nodded and glanced back into his flat.

'Is now not a good time?' Chall asked.

'Not particularly, no.'

'Expecting company?'

'Not tonight.' Joffe looked right back at him. 'But I'm going to a meeting in twenty minutes, so I don't have a lot of time.'

'We don't need much,' Tanner said.

Joffe showed them in and led them quickly to the living room. He turned off the music that had been playing – something jazzy – and sat down. He said, 'There isn't even time to offer you a drink.'

'It's fine,' Tanner said.

'I don't know why people always do that,' Chall said. 'I know they're only being polite but we don't need endless tea and coffee. We're coppers not builders.'

'How can I help?' Joffe focused on Tanner.

'"I don't lie". That's what you said when we talked to you last time.' Tanner looked at him.

'I don't and I didn't,' Joffe said.

'Well, we don't have time to get into what defines lying, but let's just say we're concerned about what you didn't tell us.'

'I didn't tell you lots of things.'

'You know what I mean.'

'My favourite cricket team or the date of my mother's birthday.' Joffe looked irritated and confused. 'I answered all your questions as well as I could. I explained about the importance of confidentiality when it came to the sessions themselves, but otherwise I told you everything you wanted to know.'

'All right then, let's talk about what you chose not to tell us. You chose not to tell us about the situation between yourself and Christopher Clemence. We're keen to know why, that's all.'

'Situation?'

'The letters.'

It was immediately clear that Joffe was desperate to know who had told them, but he fought the urge to ask. Instead, he said, 'Why on earth should it matter? Why would something that was going on between myself and another individual have any bearing on what happened to Heather?'

'We believe that whatever was happening inside your group ... between the members ... had a lot to do with it.'

Chall glanced at Tanner. It was news to him that they believed any such thing. He'd been told it was no more than one line of inquiry, but he was certainly not about to question his boss.

Joffe shook his head. 'Yes, after you talked to Diana she told me she thought you were taking this approach. Well, I can only say to you what I said to her, which is that it's completely ridiculous.'

'I appreciate your honesty,' Tanner said.

'You're wasting your time while whoever murdered poor Heather is still out there.'

Tanner took a few seconds to look around. The flat was actually no bigger than Heather Finlay's and was laid out in a similar fashion, with the living area and the kitchen sharing the same open-plan space. The furnishings in Dr Joffe's flat were rather more expensive, of course, and the kitchen was decidedly more luxurious. The leather armchairs sat on bleached boards and designer rugs, while on the other side of a partition made of glass bricks, marble floor tiles reflected the gleam of glossy cabinets and high-end appliances.

'Tell me about the letters,' she said.

Joffe sighed and folded his arms. He looked at his watch. 'They were more like notes, actually. Blackmail notes.'

Tanner leaned forward.

'I was told to pay five hundred pounds if I didn't want the medical authorities to be informed about my past. A thousand, the second time.'

'About the drugs.'

'Yes, obviously, the drugs.'

'And you believed that Clemence was responsible for this, did you?'

'To start with, I certainly did.'

'Any particular reason?' Chall asked.

'Because of the kind of person he is.' Joffe's mouth twisted in distaste. 'Because he clearly needs the money. Because I didn't think it could possibly be anyone else.'

'So you confronted him in the pub, did you?' Chall could see that Tanner was busy scribbling in her notebook. 'That what the big row was about on Heather's last night?'

Joffe shook his head. 'No, the altercation with Chris was actually a couple of weeks before that night. A few days after Heather's party. I'd only received one letter by this point, but I told him straight away that I wasn't going to sit back and be threatened. I told him to drop it or I'd go to the police.'

'You'd have done that, would you?'

'In a heartbeat,' Joffe said.

'You said you thought it was Clemence to start with.' Tanner looked at Joffe, her pen still poised. 'Does that mean you came to believe it was someone else?'

'I considered the possibility, yes.'

'Who?'

'Heather.' Joffe watched Tanner write. 'It was something Caroline told me. She said that while she was at the party, she'd seen all these scratch cards in Heather's bin. Lots and lots of them, she said. I mean, I knew Heather had had a problem with gambling in the past, because she talked about it in the sessions . . . ' He stopped himself, took a few seconds. 'Now, it looked like she was doing it again.'

'That made you suspicious, did it?'

'If there's one thing I know about a gambler, especially one on benefits, it's that they're always on the lookout for money.'

'So, after what Caroline Armitage told you, you stopped thinking Chris was responsible for the note and decided it must have been Heather.'

'It wasn't quite as clear-cut as that,' Joffe said. 'I was . . . thinking about it for a while. Trying to weigh things up.'

'Did you talk to Heather about it?'

'I was certainly going to.' Suddenly, Joffe looked genuinely upset. 'I didn't get the chance though, did I?'

'But by that time . . . by the time Heather was killed . . . you had decided she was the one trying to blackmail you?'

Joffe smiled. 'I realise that this is probably a stupid thing to admit in the circumstances, but yes. I thought she probably was.'

Tanner waited.

The doctor shifted in his seat. He crossed his legs. 'Let's just say that by then I'd discovered what she was capable of.'

'Because . . . ?' Tanner left it a few seconds, then gave the answer that she knew Joffe would not. '. . . of something that happened in one of Mr De Silva's sessions.' She studied Joffe's face. 'In that final session?'

Joffe said nothing.

'Can we take that as a yes?' Chall asked.

'No, you can't.' After another cursory glance at his watch, Joffe stood up. 'I'm sorry but I'm going to have to throw you out.'

Walking to the door, Chall said, 'Do you go to a lot of these meetings? NA or AA or whatever?'

'At least once a week,' Joffe said. 'More, sometimes, if I feel I need them.'

'Why might that be?'

'Could be anything,' Joffe said. 'You go to extra meetings if you're stressed, or if there's some problem with work or something. You go to reassure yourself, when you're feeling vulnerable.'

'What about since Heather Finlay's murder?' Tanner asked. 'Been going to a few more meetings?'

Joffe already had one hand on the door. 'About average,' he said.

. . . THEN

It's a long time since Chris has done this, but it's not like he's forgotten how. It makes riding a bike look like rocket science; doesn't have to come back, because it's never really gone away. While it's not exactly comfortable, it all feels very familiar and he knows he hasn't lost the knack as he walks into the bar; as he looks around and is looked at. He knows it will be easy enough, because he's good at it, and even though, more than anything, he does *not want to do it*, there's still a part of him, deep down somewhere, that's excited.

There's a rush, and it's like kissing an old mate he hasn't seen for far too long.

He tells himself it isn't his fault he's back here again, back on display. His mum let him down badly when he needed her and Heather's as tight as a duck's arse, which is ridiculous because she should know more than anyone what difference a few quid can make to someone like him. Why is everyone else so much better with this stuff than he is? His mum putting it away for this and that and Heather accounting for every last penny, while his benefit cheque is always cashed and gone halfway through the week.

It's honestly not like he's pissing it away. He just can't hold on to it, that's all. Yes, you need to try and be careful and he knows that self-denial isn't something he's ever been good at, but why the hell should recovery mean living like a hermit?

Like a loser.

This isn't somewhere he's visited more than a couple of times before, but it works the same as anywhere else. Back in the day, he would probably have been somewhere predictable in Soho – Comptons, maybe, or Circa on Frith Street – but tonight he's chosen to come down to Vauxhall, where there isn't usually as much competition. Where the business is a little less obvious.

The bar isn't quite as 'scene' as a few other places and, most important, it's close to the flat that'll cost him fifty for a few hours' use.

He stands at one end of a crowded bar with an orange juice, then pushes his way to the other end and stands there for a while. A man he knows vaguely, a friend of a friend of someone he slept with once, comes across to say hello. It's a very one-sided conversation. Chris stays just the right side of surly, but makes it obvious that he's got more important things to do and the man quickly melts back into the crowd.

It's annoying, because although the chances had always been slim, he'd been hoping he wouldn't bump into anyone he knew. It's not like he's been giving friends the same story he spins his mum, but still, most of them would be shocked if they saw him out and about doing this again. Even if it is just a one-off. A quick blast from the past to tide him over.

In the bar, looks are traded and smiles exchanged and it doesn't take too long before Chris sees a reaction he recognises. One that counts. That says, yeah, I'm up for it, of course I am, but don't worry, I know that all the things I'm thinking right now that I'd like you to do to me are going to cost me something.

Job done. Well, the tricky bit, anyway.

It's a mild evening, so Chris wanders outside and within a minute, the man has joined him.

They talk, but Chris knows that later on he won't be able to remember very much about the conversation. While he smiles when he needs to, touches and leans in when he should, he's busy thinking about how he's going to spend the money this man has in his wallet. He's already shopping.

New jeans.

CDs.

That flash new sushi place in Covent Garden.

As punters go, this one's fairly typical. He doesn't give anything away, but an accountant or a frustrated City boy is Chris's best guess. A smart suit and spreadsheets all week, then desperate to get out and spread something else on a Friday night. He's somewhat nervous and he's certainly not a looker, which probably explains his willingness to shell out for something a little out of his league. Bulky and badly dressed, but not big or hairy enough for those who like that sort of thing.

They don't bother to finish their drinks.

Walking to the flat, the man says, 'I've never done this before.'

Chris nods. As lines he's heard more times than he can count go, it's right up there with *I can stop any time I want to*, or the old chestnut, *I don't even know what I'm doing here. I haven't got a problem with drugs.*

'Neither have I,' he says.

When it's finished, mercifully quicker than Chris could have hoped, the man steps back and turns away to zip himself up.

Chris gets to his feet and walks to the sink. He spits and wipes his mouth. He says, 'Was that OK?'

Behind him, the man grunts, like he's desperate to be gone.

'Glad to hear it.'

Chris washes his hands and tries not to think too hard about why he still needs the praise, why he seeks validation for such things, least of all in a situation like this.

It's all tied up with why we feel unworthy all the time . . .

Of course, he's pretty sure that Heather would have something to say about it. Plenty, in fact! He turns from the sink, thinking about her and the fit she had about the bird shit, and the weird thing she has for old hospitals, and he's smiling when the man he can still taste steps smartly forward and hits him in the face.

. . . THEN

Robin opens the door and leads Diana into the room. A couple of his colleagues are talking at a table in the corner, while a third sits alone with a newspaper. He introduces Diana as a close friend and all exchange greetings. He gestures towards the couple of slightly thread-bare sofas and armchairs, a hot drinks machine against the wall and a second that dispenses cold drinks and snacks. 'So this is the consultants' coffee room,' he says. 'Not quite the lap of luxury, but we like it.'

Diana nods. 'Very nice.'

'There's another one closer to the theatre that everyone uses, but this is where the consultants can come to take a breather. Let off steam, that kind of thing.'

'Have a good old moan,' the one with the paper says.

'That too.' Robin looks at Diana. 'Shall we . . . ?'

He says a perfunctory goodbye to his colleagues and escorts her out of the room. They walk back towards his office.

'Thanks for the tour,' Diana says.

Robin nods to a nurse as she passes. 'Pleasure. I'm only sorry there wasn't an empty theatre to show you. Next time . . . if you want to come back?'

'Yes please. It's nice of you to ask me.'

'I thought you might be interested.'

'Yes, I am . . . but for lunch, I mean.'

'Well, I wanted to say sorry for being a bit snitty at the last session.'

'Oh, it's all forgotten, honestly.'

'No.' Robin sounds insistent. He lays a hand on her arm as they begin climbing the stairs. 'It was wrong to criticise you for wanting to talk about your daughter. It was selfish and unsupportive.' He looks at her. 'Am I forgiven?'

Diana smiles. 'Well, let's see how good lunch is, shall we?'

At the top of the stairs they turn on to the corridor where the anaesthesia department is housed. Diana points towards Robin's neck. 'This is snazzy, by the way.'

His hand moves to the black and white spotted bow tie he is wearing. 'Ah, yes . . .'

'You don't see them around much any more.'

'To be honest, I hate them,' Robin says. 'I think they look bloody ridiculous, but I don't have a lot of choice.' Having reached his office, he opens the door, then steps back so that Diana can enter. 'I like to wear a tie, because I think they look smart and I believe that gives the patients confidence.' He closes the door and walks across to his desk. 'But thanks to health and safety regulations, the apparent "danger of infection spread" or some such bloody nonsense, you can't have anything . . . flappy.'

Diana is laughing as she sits down.

'Yes, it sounds funny, but every morning I put on a proper tie, then when I get here I have to take it off and put on one of these stupid things.' He points towards a drawer in his desk. 'I've got a selection of them in there.'

'Well, I think they look distinguished,' Diana says. While Robin is dealing with some last-minute paperwork, she looks around the office that he shares with two other consultants. There is not a lot of space, with three desks crammed in, but the smell of leather and polished wood imbues the room with a sense of achievement and, as far as Diana is concerned, conveys the high status that is richly deserved.

That merits the brass nameplate on the door.

'I can see why losing all this would be so painful,' she says.

Robin looks across. He had told Diana about the blackmail note within minutes of her arrival. He could see no reason to keep it a secret, he had said, having already discussed it with Caroline. Now he nods, sadly. 'Everything I trained for up in smoke,' he says.

'He won't get away with it.'

'I hope not.'

'I mean it.' Diana had put two and two together very quickly once Robin had mentioned the letter that had been waiting for him at home after the party. She had realised what he and Chris had been arguing about in the pub after the last session and told him that, for what it was worth, she thought his suspicions about Chris were well founded. 'We can't let him.'

Robin nods again. He has not yet told her what Caroline had said about Heather and the bin full of used scratch cards.

'It's your career we're talking about,' she says.

'I'd let it go though.' Robin slams a desk drawer shut. 'If it came to it, I'd take that risk. I won't be bullied.'

'Maybe he'll just drop it. Now you've told him you'll go to the police.'

'We'll see,' Robin says, getting to his feet. 'Every morning I go to the letter box and I'm shaking like a bloody leaf in case there's another one.'

'I can see why you're scared,' Diana says. 'But you're certainly doing the right thing by standing up to him.' She watches as Robin straightens his waistcoat, as he pulls his shirt sleeves down and buttons the white cuffs. 'A lot of people would just roll over and hand over the money, because that would be the easy thing to do, but I think that everything you've been through, the drugs and so on, has made you far stronger and more principled than you might have been otherwise. Does that make sense?' She sits back and breathes in the leather and the polished wood. 'It's . . . admirable, Robin, it really is. I mean that.'

'Thanks. That's . . . I appreciate it.' Robin walks across and reaches for the jacket that is hung on a stand in the corner of the room. 'I'd like to keep all this between ourselves for now, if that's all right. Obviously Caroline is aware of it, but I certainly don't want Tony knowing what's going on. I don't want any of this to disrupt our sessions.'

Diana nods, but it is not altogether clear that she has been listening. She says, 'There are too many weak men in the world.'

Robin hums tacit agreement, unsure how else to react. He tugs at his cuffs, then holds out his arms. 'Right then. Lunch?'

'Yes, please.' Diana stands up and steps towards the door.

'Oh, wait a minute.' Robin reaches for his bow tie. 'Just let me take this stupid thing off.'

'No, please keep it on,' Diana says. 'I like it.'

'Well . . . if you say so.'

'I do.' She waits until he reaches her and puts an arm through his. 'Have you ever thought about getting one that spins round?'

They are waiting to see what the weather is doing, trying to decide between a nearby pizza place or getting something they can eat outside, as they walk out of the hospital and turn towards South End Green.

That's when they both catch sight of the man hurrying across the road towards them. When they realise, within a few moments of one another, who it is.

When they freeze.

Diana says Robin's name and holds his arm a little tighter.

Robin says, 'It's all right.'

'It was terrifying enough as it was,' Diana will say to Caroline later on the phone. 'Bearing in mind what Robin and I had just been talking about. But until he got close to us, I actually thought he was wearing a . . . mask.'

By the time Chris is within a few feet of them, they can both see what the mask really is. The ragged map of bruising, shiny and crimson below a half-closed eye and lips heavily swollen on one side.

'What happened to your face?' Diana asks.

Chris is now blocking their way and staring at Robin. 'Ask your boyfriend.'

'What are you talking about?' Robin asks.

'Were you mugged or something?' Diana stays where she is, but there is genuine concern in her voice.

Chris hesitates. 'I was attacked.'

'Have you been to a doctor?' Robin lets go of Diana's arm and takes a step towards him. 'Something might be broken. Why don't you come inside and I can get someone to take a look at you?'

'I think you've done quite enough,' Chris says.

'Are you trying to suggest that Robin was in some way responsible for this?'

'He as good as threatened me in the pub the other night,' Chris says. 'You were there.'

'You've lost your mind,' Robin says.

'Warning me. Telling me I'd be sorry.'

'I didn't say any such thing.'

'Well, now *I'm* the one who's got a good mind to go to the police.'

'Do you seriously believe I got someone to beat you up?'

'I know that one minute you're accusing me, saying you won't put up with being threatened.' Chris touches a finger to his face. 'And the next . . . *this*.'

'Look, I'm sorry about the other night,' Robin says. 'Perhaps I did go a little over the top.'

Diana looks at him.

'I'm sorry I lost my temper.'

'People like you, people with money, you think you can do what you like.' Chris is shouting. There are tears welling up. 'You think you can get away with anything.'

272

'Oh, come on, Chris.' Diana holds out a hand, but Chris slaps it away.

'Leave him.' Robin takes Diana's arm and draws her back to him, then leads her purposefully around Chris who is refusing to step aside. 'This is completely insane.'

'Fuck you,' Chris shouts after them. 'Both of you.'

As they walk quickly away down the hill, Diana turns and looks back. Chris is pointing at them, kicking out at fresh air. She watches a young couple passing him and trying not to stare as he sinks slowly down on to the pavement and gently brings his hands up to cover his face.

. . . THEN

'Well, I think it's fairly obvious that at least one of us hasn't had the best of weeks.'

Tony's remark does not succeed in lightening the mood as he had been hoping. Before the start of the session, there had been a great deal of concern expressed at the injuries to Chris's face, and even though he had clearly not wanted to talk about it, certain members of the group had continued to press him. While Robin and Diana had stayed uncharacteristically silent, Heather and Caroline had insisted that – whatever the circumstances – he had been the victim of a vicious assault and at the very least, he should go to the police.

'I'll go with you, if you want some support,' Heather had said.

'Me too.' Caroline had nodded across the room to where Robin and Diana were standing together, drinking tea. 'Or maybe Robin would. You know, because he's a professional.'

Now, Tony looks at Chris. Like everyone else in the group, he has focused his attention on the extra chair that has been brought in. The circle has been opened out and, though each member of the group is still in the same position relative to everyone else, they are now seated in a wide semicircle with Tony and Chris in the middle, each with a view of the single chair that is, as yet, unoccupied.

'I want to concentrate on the "here and now" this week,' Tony says. 'I think there's been some misunderstanding as to how this principle operates within the group, so I want to try and move things on a little.' He looks around. Eyes are still fixed on the chair. 'We've been working on the basis that what happens in the group is more important than what has happened to any individual in their past or what is happening to them now. Everyone needs to focus on their immediate feelings inside the circle. Their feelings towards the other members of the group and towards me.' He leaves another pause. 'With a few exceptions, we've been doing this pretty well, but now it's time to move on to what people like me rather grandly call the "illumination of process". OK?' Another glance from face to face. 'We need to honestly and openly examine ourselves and how we interact with one another. That way, we perform a self-reflective loop, and it's only then that we can really understand what these feelings are telling us.'

'Bloody hell,' Caroline says. 'All sounds a bit complicated.'

'Well, I'm sorry if I've made it sound that way, because it really isn't.' Tony nods towards the chair. 'We're going to start with a simple hot-seating exercise.' He looks to his right. 'I think you've done this before, Robin.'

Robin nods.

'And you, Heather?'

Heather says, 'Once,' as though that was one time too many, but produces a smile when Tony catches her eye.

'How does it work?' Caroline asks.

'It's probably easier if we just plunge in and find out,' Tony says. 'Robin, would you mind kicking things off?'

Robin gets up, walks across to the empty seat and sits down.

'Usual rules apply,' Tony says. 'No dirty fighting and no interrogation. If someone says something that upsets you, we need to talk about why you're upset and not waste time scoring points or playing tit-for-tat. Everyone OK with this?'

Nobody says that they aren't.

Tony leaves a few seconds, turns to a fresh page in his notebook, then says, 'Robin, I wonder if you can remember the last time you lost your temper. At work, perhaps, or with a family member.'

Robin nods, thinks about it. 'Well ... I try not to lose my temper, but last week there was an altercation with one of my colleagues.'

'Which made you angry.'

'Yes.'

'OK. Now, if someone in the group were to make you feel like that, who is it most likely to be?'

Robin does not hesitate. 'Chris.'

Chris is staring at the floor. He nods, unsurprised.

'Why does Chris in particular make you angry?'

'Just the way he is. The things he does.'

'He pushes your buttons.'

'It's all fake,' Robin says. 'The tiresome jokes and the sex stuff. The confidence.'

'You think it's a lie?'

'Sometimes, yes. A lot of the time.'

'And you don't like liars.'

'No.' Robin swallows and crosses his legs. 'I don't.'

'We can all remember your story about what happened when you were a child.' Tony looks to the others; inviting their participation. 'I'm wondering if your feelings towards Chris, towards anyone you perceive to be untrustworthy in some way, are connected to the lie you told back then. To the fact that it's the lie that you are most ashamed of.'

Robin says nothing, so Tony turns to Chris.

'Chris, how do you feel about Robin saying he thinks you're a liar?'

'I don't feel anything,' Chris says. 'I don't really care.'

'If you did care, if you maybe start to care when you get home tonight, what might the things Robin said make you feel?'

'I'd probably just feel like laughing,' Chris says. 'At all the rubbish coming out of his mouth. Yeah, I lie, but so does everyone else. So does he.'

'People lie hundreds of times a day,' Caroline says. 'I read it somewhere. Literally, hundreds.'

Tony looks at Robin. 'You said that you try not to lose your temper. I'm wondering if it's the loss of control that you're frightened of.'

'Yes, of course.'

'Why's that?'

'Because it's . . . ugly.'

Tony waits.

'Because I spent such a long time completely out of control, when I was using, and I never want to go back there. Exercising a degree of self-control is something I take great pride in.'

'Hasn't everyone in this circle been out of control at some point?'

'Big time,' Caroline says.

'Maybe that's why it's so important,' Robin says. 'Why I don't trust people without it.'

'Trust is important to you,' Tony says.

'Very.'

'Which member of the group would you say you trusted the most?'

'Diana,' Robin says.

Diana says, 'Thank you,' but Tony raises a finger. At this moment, he senses that conflict will be of rather more use therapeutically than backslapping.

'And who do you trust the least?'

Robin looks down for a few seconds and shifts in the chair. Then he says, 'Heather.'

'I think I'm close to everyone,' Caroline says. 'In different ways.'

'If you had to choose one member of the group you felt closest to *now*,' Tony says, 'who would that be?'

'Probably, Robin.'

'OK . . .'

'You know, the whole father-figure thing.' Caroline laughs. 'Sorry, Robin.'

'Do you find yourself looking for a father figure in other situations?'

'No, I don't think so.'

'Is your father still alive?'

'No, he isn't.'

'You were close to him, though.'

'Course.'

'And you feel as though Robin's a father figure to the whole group?'

'Well, probably not to Chris.'

Diana stifles a snort. Chris is leaning back, his legs stretched out in front of him. He acknowledges the namecheck with a nod, as if he feels rather proud of the recognition.

'Do you think Robin is the person in the group who would influence you the most?'

Caroline cocks her head, thinking about it. She seems quite comfortable at being asked the questions; enjoying the process. The smile has not left her face. 'Not necessarily,' she says. 'I think I probably looked up to Heather at the beginning.'

'Not any more?'

'No, I don't mean that. She was really nice when I first started coming, that's all. She told me she thought I'd fit in.'

'Do you think you fit in?'

'Yeah, I do. I mean I'm no more screwed up than anyone else, am I?' She turns in her chair, tries to look at everyone else, as though seeking affirmation or laughter.

'So, if Robin's a father figure, do you see other members of the group as ... siblings?'

'Yeah, I suppose. Heather and Chris ... a bit, because we're a bit closer in age. And the whole love/hate thing.'

'Your feelings towards them swing between those two extremes?' Tony asks.

'Not literally. Just ... I'm not always sure if Heather actually likes me and sometimes I want to smash Chris's face in when he makes some comment about how I look. But then he makes me laugh or something . . . and it's not like I don't know why he's doing it.'

'Why do you think he's doing it?'

'Because he's insecure.'

'Is that something you recognise?'

'Yeah, course.' The smile falters and for the first time she begins to look slightly uncomfortable. 'Isn't everyone?'

'Is there anyone in the group who makes you feel more insecure?'

'I said. When Chris makes fat jokes.'

'Anyone else?'

'Not really,' Caroline says.

'Who would you say is the most secure person in the group?'

'Probably Robin again. That's how he seems, anyway. What do I know, though? He might go home and cry himself to sleep every night.'

'Is that what you do?'

'No.' The smile returns. 'Not every night.'

Tony smiles back. He says, 'If you *were* to go home and cry yourself to sleep, who is the person in the group who would probably be responsible?'

'I don't know.' She drums her fingers against her thighs. 'I mean, it could be anybody, couldn't it? Like I said, I feel close to everyone, so that means everyone's equally likely to upset me, doesn't it?'

Experience tells Tony that blanket statements like this are rarely, if ever true. He needs to come at the issue another way. He says, 'How about if I asked you if there was someone in the group who you're not quite as close to as you'd like?'

Caroline puffs out her cheeks then lets the breath out slowly. Her face creases, as though she's reaching for the one fact that will win her a million on some game show. Eventually, she says, 'Maybe Diana.' She turns immediately and says, 'Sorry, Diana, I had to say somebody.' She looks back to Tony. 'Bloody hell, this is really difficult. It's like the vote-off in *X Factor* . . .'

*

Tony scribbles in his notepad, then looks up.

'Is there someone in the group who you feel tends to dominate the sessions?'

'Well, probably Chris,' Diana says. She folds her arms. She appears relaxed, confident. 'In that we have to spend so much time dealing with all his nonsense.'

'You resent that?'

'Yes, a bit . . . no, a lot, actually. It's like we have to confront it all the time. The nasty comments or the filthy jokes. And if he's in a bad mood it's like we're walking on eggshells.'

'Because it's always about him.'

'Yes. Whole sessions sometimes.'

'You feel that sometimes the group gets waylaid?'

'Yes, and if I'm honest Caroline does it too, sometimes.' She turns her head, though not quite far enough to make eye contact with Caroline. 'And I'm sorry if it sounds like I'm just saying that because of what she said about me. She talks about Chris making fat jokes, but she brings the subject up herself all the time. Poor me, you know? Poor . . . obese me.'

Caroline laughs, but clearly she is not finding this funny. 'Am I missing something, here?' She looks around. 'This is exactly what *she* does. Come on, Robin, you said so yourself.'

Robin does not look back at her.

Tony allows himself a sly smile and looks at Diana. 'Do you think perhaps that Caroline's feelings are valid?'

'No, not really.'

'Only I'm just wondering if you dislike the tendency some people have to talk about themselves and their own problems all the time because perhaps you recognise it in yourself.'

'Takes one to know one,' Caroline says. 'That's basically what he's getting at.'

For half a minute or more, Diana stares at a spot just to the right of Tony's head. Then she says, 'Yes, all right. Perhaps.'

Tony nods, pleased. 'And why do you think your typical way of relating to the group is to talk about your problems outside? To consistently present the ongoing problem you're having with your ex-husband and your daughter?'

The shrug is momentary, the smile no more than a slit. 'Because I'm a silly, selfish bitch?'

'Is that what you really think?'

Diana shakes her head. 'No. But I can see why other members of the group might feel ... trapped, though. Or somewhat limited.'

'Do you think anyone in particular has felt like that?'

'All of them, at one time or another, I should think. Robin, certainly.' She turns in Robin's direction. 'I'm sorry if I made you feel like that, truly, I am.'

'It's fine,' Robin says.

'You're not here to apologise for anything,' Tony says. 'Not unless you feel you really need to.'

'What I need is reassurance, I suppose,' Diana says. 'Deep down that's probably what I'm after.'

'What kind of reassurance?'

'That I'm right to hate her. The woman who took my husband and as good as took my daughter at the same time. I want people to tell me that all this rage is justified and that I'm not just losing my marbles.'

'That's how you'd describe it? Rage?'

'There isn't another word for it.'

'Boring?' Chris says.

Tony does not take his eyes off Diana. 'Can I suggest that rage is only part of it?'

'It's needy,' Heather says. 'I really don't mean that in a negative way, I promise. Obviously you feel angry, but I think you basically want to be reassured that it wasn't your fault. That's what the drinking was really about.'

Diana's head drops slowly, as though she is falling asleep.

281

'How does that make you feel?' Tony asks. He waits a few seconds. 'What Heather just suggested.'

For a while there is only the sound of bodies shifting in chairs, and distant traffic. When Diana finally looks up, her perfectly applied mascara is bleeding on to her cheek.

'Yes, I want someone to tell me that my daughter's wrong,' she says. 'That he didn't leave because I wasn't a good enough wife. What's wrong with that? I want to be told that I'm worth a bit more than dog-walking and watching daytime TV and wasting time in that stupid charity shop. That I'm still attractive, and that I might be quite interesting, if anyone could be bothered to find out and that maybe, instead of people feeling sorry for me and telling me that time is a great healer and how everything happens for a good reason, someone somewhere might actually want to fuck me now and again.'

'Bloody hell,' Chris says.

Diana reaches into one pocket and then another, and Tony finally passes across the box of tissues that is always sitting under his chair. She dabs at her eyes and sits back, almost breathless.

'This is the first time I've ever cried at a session,' she says. 'All these months and this is the first time.' Her smile is wonky, but determined; her face flushed as she continues to wipe the tears away. 'That's supposed to be good, isn't it?'

'I don't think I've ever felt happier,' Heather says. 'Not since I've been clean, anyway.'

'Why were you so happy?'

'Because you were all there, celebrating with me. Everyone came and it was a great party and there was no fighting.' She smiles. 'Not that I was aware of, anyway.'

'Who were you most pleased to see?' Tony asks.

Chris makes a noise, somewhere between a cough and a splutter; wanting to be seen stifling his laughter. Tony ignores him.

Heather glances away, momentarily. 'It was nice that *you* came,' she says. 'Only because you told us you wouldn't, you know?'

Tony looks down at his notebook and scribbles something quickly. A doodle, to kill a few seconds. 'Do you think there's too much fighting between members of the group?' he asks.

'I don't know what's a normal amount.'

'You don't like it when people in the group argue with one another?'

'Well, I know that sometimes there's confrontation and that's normal. I know there has to be, but it doesn't mean it isn't upsetting.'

'Why does it make you so upset?'

'It's never nice watching people tear each other to pieces, is it?'

'Isn't it?' Chris asks.

'Well, maybe some people get off on that, but it just makes me freeze up a bit. Plus it's usually me that has to try and sort it out.'

'Like a peacemaker, sort of thing?'

'Yeah, and I don't think that's fair. I had to do it with my mum and dad and I hated that it was me who had to be the grown-up.'

'Are there moments in the sessions when you feel like that?'

'I suppose when Robin and Diana are going at each other. Yeah . . . just because they're the oldest.'

'I'm starting to feel positively ancient,' Diana says. She looks to Robin, but he is watching Heather intently.

Tony stays focused on Heather. He says, 'Who do you think is the most confrontational in the group?'

Chris says, 'Have a guess.'

'Well, I don't want it to sound like we're ganging up on him.'

'Fill your boots,' Chris says. 'I'd probably be upset if you said someone else.'

'He's the one who makes me angriest, but that's probably because he's also the one I'm closest to, I think.'

'Bless you,' Chris says.

Tony throws Chris a warning look. He does not want this to become a dialogue. 'Why do you feel particularly close to Chris?'

Heather shrugs. 'I'm not really sure. Because he knows what I'm really like, I suppose. People outside the group haven't got a clue, have they?'

'Are there people in the circle you don't think know you very well?'

'None of them do,' Heather says. 'Not really.'

'Because they aren't making the effort?'

'No, it's not that.'

'Maybe you aren't letting anyone get close,' Tony says. 'Maybe you don't think you're worth getting to know.'

'Probably because I'm not.'

'King of the world, piece of shit,' Robin says.

Heather looks at him. 'Maybe.'

'What did you feel like when Robin said you were the person he trusted least?'

Heather is still looking at Robin. Her face is expressionless. 'Made sense.'

'Why?' Robin asks.

Tony holds up a hand and leans towards Heather. 'Who would *you* say is the least trustworthy member of the group, Heather?'

She sits back and cocks her head as though weighing it up. 'I'd probably have to go with Robin on this one, and say me . . .'

'Heather's a doormat,' Chris says. 'Robin's a boring know-it-all with hairy ears, Caroline's a fat cow and Diana's a spoiled bitch with too much time on her hands. Can I go back to my seat now?'

'Yes, if you want to,' Tony says. 'But you're pretty much dying on your arse so far. I mean, nobody's laughing, are they?'

Chris brings his hand to his face and lays it gently against the side that is damaged. 'So?'

'Oh, was that not the reaction you were after?'

'It doesn't matter what kind of reaction he gets,' Diana says. 'As long as he gets one.'

'Nothing wrong with that,' Chris says. 'Somebody needs to mix things up a bit, don't they? Get this group's blood pumping. I'm only saying the things the rest of you are too scared to say.'

'I'm not scared to say anything,' Caroline says. 'I just don't say controversial things for the sake of it.'

284

'Neither do I,' Robin says.

Tony writes, then looks back to Chris. 'You think the group is too passive?'

'Some more than others, yeah.' He nods in Heather's direction. 'Nobody's asking her to be a peacemaker or whatever. She's only doing it to be liked, anyway.'

Heather shakes her head.

'Do you not want to be liked?'

Chris hesitates, then gathers himself. 'I want to be *loved*, Tony. Or better still, worshipped.'

'But it doesn't bother you if you're *dis*liked.'

'Not particularly.'

'Not when Diana says you dominate the sessions?'

'Maybe she likes to be dominated.'

'Not when Robin calls you a liar?'

'Like I said, we're all liars. I'm a particularly good one, I don't mind admitting that.'

'What's the biggest lie you've told in one of our sessions?'

Again, Chris seems thrown, but only momentarily. 'Well, I lied when I said I had a huge cock. Actually . . . '

'It's massive,' Tony says, nodding.

'Your punchlines are becoming rather predictable,' Robin says.

'At least I've got some.'

'You're the lie,' Heather says, quietly.

Tony looks at her and nods; encouraging her to continue.

'Everything about you is a lie. Everything you pretend to be.'

'Here we go,' Chris says. 'Blah, blah.'

'It's so obvious it isn't even funny.'

Chris looks at her. 'You want to talk about what's obvious?'

'This is something you've heard before?' Tony asks.

'Am I really supposed to think this is some amazing insight?' He looks back and stares at Tony. 'Seriously, is this some shit on one of your tablets of stone?' His voice is getting louder, edgier and though he is leaning forward, his shoulders are hunched and he has slowly

285

drawn his knees up. He looks defensive, suddenly; foetal. 'I'm not an idiot. It's not like I don't know this stuff. The number of times this crap got trotted out in rehab.'

'So, you know that people in recovery often adopt different personalities because deep down they're afraid of being disliked? Afraid of being ridiculed for who they actually are?'

'Yes.' Chris nods, like a good boy. 'I'm aware of that theory.'

'It's not a theory,' Tony says. 'It's something I've seen time and time again, for as long as I've been doing this. Clients who'd rather be disliked for being this ... character they've taken on than reveal who they actually are.' He waits. 'Is there a particular member of the group who you think would be more likely than others to ridicule you?'

'You're having a decent crack at it yourself.'

'Anyone more likely to humiliate you in some way?'

Chris says nothing. His head has begun to drop.

'The dread of self-disclosure, of *real* self-disclosure, needs to be overcome if there's going to be genuine recovery.' Tony's voice is lower suddenly, and he is talking as though there is only him and Chris in the room. 'We all pretend to be something we're not now and again. I try not to sound posh when there's a workman in the house, or sometimes I make out that I like a fancy restaurant when actually I'd much rather be having fish and chips. We do it to fit in, or to please other people, and it's perfectly normal. But hiding who you really are *all the time*, because you're scared or ashamed, is hugely counter-productive and can do serious psychological damage long term. You need to let your true self out into the light before it gets lost altogether. Before you disappear. Chris ... ?' Tony waits until Chris is looking at him. 'Now might be the perfect time for you to talk about what it is you're most ashamed of?'

'No.'

'We talked about this,' Heather says. 'You promised.'

He turns, snaps at her. 'No, I didn't.'

Tony raises a finger. 'Does anyone have a hand mirror? Diana?'

'Oh, right.' Diana reaches for her bag and quickly pulls out a compact. She stands up and hands it to Tony. He thanks her and immediately passes it across to Chris.

'Look at it,' Tony says.

'You want me to do my make-up again?'

'Please.'

After a few moments, Chris raises the compact and stares at himself. The egg-sized lump and the blotch of discoloration, the ring-ripped flesh below the eye.

Tony sits back. 'Something to think about,' he says. 'However bad you think your face looks … unless you start to be honest with yourself about these things, about who you really are … that's how your head's going to be on the inside.'

. . . THEN

Chris lets out a long sigh. He sits back hard and folds his arms. He says, 'I don't know what the hell you're all expecting.'

'We're not expecting anything,' Tony says.

'Seriously, though, all these confessions and shameful secrets. What's the point? So, we know that Dr Robin told a little white lie and got his little black friend into trouble. We know that Diana stuck a compass into girls who were fitter than she was.' Chris shrugs and sneers. 'How does that help any of us?'

'It's not about helping other members of the group,' Tony says. 'It's what talking about these things does for you. It's about owning your shame.'

Chris rolls his eyes. He leans forward slowly, takes a breath, leans back again. Tony has watched many people in this position going through the same deliberations more times than he can remember; the same agonies. It always reminds him of someone creeping to the edge of the high diving board and looking down in horror at the water so far below them. Wrapping goosepimply arms around their chest, then stepping back again.

He says, 'There's no hurry, Chris.'

He knows he can only wait and will him to jump; to find the courage. He looks away and becomes aware of Heather, rocking gently in the seat next to him; pulling at her fingers, mouthing, 'Go on . . .'

A minute crawls by before Chris snaps his head forward suddenly and begins to gabble.

'Look . . . it's not like it's going to make anyone throw their hands in the air and go, "Oh my *God*, I never imagined it could be anything like *that*, how unspeakably horrible!" Well, it might, I suppose, but what planet are you living on, because I mean it's everywhere now, isn't it? It's part and bloody parcel. You can't open a paper or watch the news and people sit around laying bets on who's going to get rumbled next. Which pop star or which TV presenter or which conveniently senile MP? Which childhood hero . . . ?'

He looks at them all, one by one. He feigns a theatrical incredulity at having to spell it out.

'I had what you might call a hands-on dad, fair enough?' He tries to smile, but it freezes midway there and becomes a grimace. 'Very hands-on.' A few moments later he starts to nod slowly, showing no sign he's aware that Tony is the only one still able to look at him. 'Don't get me wrong, we had all the good stuff as well, me and my brother. The football games with the old man and the fishing trips, and a tent in the garden we could sleep in if the weather was good. We had picnics in the park and sometimes we got to stay up late and he was never stingy when it came to bedtime stories. That was usually when things got a bit iffy . . .'

There's a long pause.

'They were great though,' he says. 'Those stories. The Famous Five and Harry Potter and then there was his particular favourite, which was all about how if he reached under the duvet and played with our tiny little cocks for a bit, it would help us sleep. Come on, isn't that a cracking story? There was the other one, of course, which he liked even more, all about how he would sleep much better if we did the same to him. Not just touching, you know . . . ?

'Thing was . . . it's like it became my favourite story too. It was a way of being close to him for once, I suppose, and we were all sharing this special secret. Yeah, I know, how mental is that? I looked forward to it and after a while I started to get . . . hard. Maybe that's when I found out I had a thing for blokes, I don't know.' His voice is lower than normal now and he is talking a lot more slowly, the London accent more pronounced. 'I remember lying there with my heart smashing against my chest, listening for him coming up the stairs, and I got jealous if he picked my brother instead of me. He didn't usually do us both at once.' He tries to smile again. 'He wasn't a monster . . .'

Tony leans forward. 'Chris, victims of abuse often come to believe it's their fault somehow. Like they invited it. It's perfectly normal.'

Chris doesn't seem to hear. 'We had these bunk beds. You know, with a wooden ladder? I'd nabbed the top one straight away, because it was exciting being high up. Then when the stories started . . . Dad's special ones, I mean . . . my brother would come up too and we'd lie squeezed in there together like sardines, trying not to breathe. Like he might not bother if there were two of us in the same bed. Then after a while . . . I don't know, a year or something . . . I moved down to the bottom bunk, so he'd get to me first.'

'You were trying to protect your brother,' Heather says. 'Even if that's not how you remember it.'

'What I remember is wanting it and hating it. Spending nights locked in the toilet and hours and hours just staring at myself in the mirror on the inside of the wardrobe door and wondering who this sad little ghost was. I remember lying in the bath until the water got cold and holding my head under and when I talked to myself it was like this echo inside my head.' He looks at Heather, a note of anger creeping in for the first time.

'I remember all sorts of things.'

Tony has lowered his eyes to write something, and when he looks back, Chris is weeping. There had been nothing audible to indicate its onset; no gasp, no explosive sob.

Tony wonders if crying silently is something Chris had learned to do a long time ago.

Chris mutters, 'Soft cunt . . .'

Robin clears his throat. 'Do you mind me asking how old you were?'

Tony watches Chris bring his hands up to press tears away. Without thinking he drags fingers down his damaged cheek and winces at the pain. 'Sorry,' Tony says. 'I'm not sure Chris should have to field questions at this point.'

'It's fine,' Chris says, sitting back. 'Bring it on. I've started, so I'll finish.' He looks at Robin. 'Eight or nine, thanks for asking. My brother was a year and a bit younger.'

'How did he deal with it?'

Chris blinks slowly. 'He's different from me. So he went off the rails in a very . . . different way. I haven't seen him in a long time.'

'Do you think your mum knew?' Caroline asks.

'No.' Quick and definite. 'There's no way, because she would not have let that happen. She would have taken a knife to him, opened the old fucker up like a bag of crisps.'

'Don't you feel like she should have known, though? Don't you blame her a bit?'

Chris looks away and down. His hand moves to his face again and now he pushes at it, as though he wants the pain; the distraction or the high. He says, 'She didn't know.'

After ten, fifteen seconds, when it's clear that Chris has nothing else he wants to say, Tony raises a finger. He looks at his watch and says, 'We've still got another ten minutes. So, is there anything anyone has wanted to say and not had the chance?' He looks around. Nobody seems keen to say another word. 'OK . . . I think this has been a hugely productive session, really. Everyone's made enormous progress tonight, and I know you all enjoy getting together in the pub afterwards, but on this occasion I would suggest that it might not be such a good idea.'

Caroline says, 'Oh.' She sounds disappointed.

'Sometimes a post-mortem's no bad thing,' Tony says, 'and it's always nice to wind down a bit. But the nature of the hot-seat process can lead to a fair bit of . . . accusation, afterwards. People demanding explanations for things that were said and getting upset. I'd rather that didn't happen without me being there.'

'So, come to the pub,' Caroline says.

Tony smiles and closes his notebook. 'I don't think so.'

As Robin and Diana reach for their jackets, Heather gets up, steps across and kneels in front of Chris, who is still looking at the floor. She says, 'You did brilliant, Chris. Really, that was amazing—'

Chris looks up fast; teeth bared suddenly, eyes narrowed.

He tells Heather to fuck off.

Chris leaves quickly, without saying another word to anyone, Tony's front door slamming behind him before any of the others have even got their coats on. As soon as they are all outside, Robin heads off in the opposite direction, en route to another of his 'appointments', leaving Caroline, Heather and Diana to walk slowly up the hill together, towards the main road.

It's a clear night, but cold suddenly.

They walk in silence, wary of venturing into the territory Tony has warned them about. Nothing is said, but smiles and sly glances are exchanged as they each begin to explore that dangerous terrain inside their heads.

Why doesn't he trust her?

That's the last time I get asked over for lunch.

I am not a doormat . . .

As soon as they reach the Broadway, Diana gestures towards her car. She mutters something about her dogs being alone and the hugs before she leaves are perfunctory.

Caroline nods in the direction of the Red Lion. 'Just you and me, then.'

'What about what Tony said?'

'I'm sure it's fine if it's just two of us.' Caroline shoves her hands into the pockets of her duffel coat. 'Come on ... I could murder a drink. A proper one, I mean. If that's OK.'

Heather says, 'Up to you.'

'I don't think I can remember needing a drink this much.'

'Just half an hour then,' Heather says. 'And we should probably avoid talking about the session.'

They start walking.

'Last thing I want to talk about,' Caroline says.

. . . THEN

Group Session: March 15th

Extremely positive results from hot-seat session designed to illuminate H&N process. Group successfully drawn into self-reflective loop with only limited resistance. A few outbursts of temper and accusation but ultimately revelatory. Real progress.

Robin confronted issues with control and trust (surprising that Heather is person he trusts least). Diana admitted need for reassurance and validation after prompting from Heather. Drinking allied to self-worth. Caroline revealed desire for stability – view of Robin as father figure. Diana as mother substitute? Heather unhappy at being made to adopt peacekeeping role. Adamant that nobody in group knows her well, but Chris probably closest. Predictable dread of self-disclosure from Chris, eventually persuaded to participate in shame exercise.

Chris's story confirmed long-held suspicions about sexual abuse, but survivor guilt/blame even more deep-seated than I had thought. Extremely unhappy at end of session. Anger aimed primarily at Heather.

As per standard protocol after hot-seat, group advised not to participate in usual post-session PM.

Key Line: *'It's never nice watching people tear each other to pieces.'*

294

Tony closes the file on his computer, pulls on his jacket and walks quietly out of his office. He stops on the first floor landing and listens to the house. Emma is out, so it is quiet above him, and the sound of the television from the floor below tells him that Nina is in the living room.

He walks slowly down the final flight of stairs, still listening as the sound gets louder. Some American drama everyone is talking about. He suspects that Nina is watching, not because she loves it, but because she doesn't want to get found out next time it comes up in conversation at a party or an awards ceremony.

He stops at the bottom of the stairs and stands in the hallway.

He is still buzzing.

His job is relatively unusual, he supposes, but it's the same as any other in many ways. When it's a slog, he can't wait to put a day – or evening – behind him; to wind down and lose himself in music or a book. There are other times though, when things go the way they did tonight, when it's hard to switch off. It was an incredible session. Electric. Sometimes it's like wading through treacle, when he's no better than a referee or merely there as a facilitator; laying down the rules, setting the agenda. Sessions like tonight's, though, help Tony remember what he loves about the job. The rush that comes when he really feels he is helping. He hopes that the members of the group are feeling the same buzz as he is. They've certainly earned it.

Moving silently towards the living room door, he thinks about the notes he's just typed up. Sometimes it's impossible to curb a simple human curiosity at the revelations. Often things are said out of spite or a desire for revenge and he's learned that they should be taken with more than a pinch of salt. Tonight though, it felt as though there was a good deal of honesty in what people were saying to each other, certainly more than he might normally expect from a group of recovering addicts. Truth itself had been a major theme of the session. Why Chris isn't telling it, why Robin is so obsessed by it. He can't help but wonder what Heather has done to make Robin so mistrustful of her, what exactly is happening between Caroline and Diana . . .

295

He leans close to the living room door. A lot of swearing, something being broken. Nina will have plenty to talk about.

He steps away and moves quickly through to the back of the house. He quietly opens the door out into the garden and, without turning any lights on, he walks around the side of the conservatory to where there is a designer fire pit and seating area; an enormous cream umbrella and a table and chair set that cost an arm and a leg.

He sits down and takes out his phone.

'It's Tony,' he says, when the phone is answered. He knows that she has his number programmed in, will know who is calling, but still it might have felt a little odd to say, 'It's me'.

Heather says, 'Hi.' Surprised but clearly pleased.

'Everything OK?'

'Yeah. Hang on, let me go somewhere a bit quieter.'

Tony can hear music and chatter. He can hear Heather clearing her throat as she walks.

'That's better.'

'Didn't listen to me about the pub, then?'

'Caroline wanted to come,' Heather says. 'I'm just keeping her company really. We're not talking about the session, I promise.'

'I didn't mean to get heavy about it.'

'It's fine. You know what's best for us.'

'Anyway . . .' Tony glances back into the house through the conservatory windows. If Nina were to come out she wouldn't see him from the kitchen. They haven't really said a lot to each other since the scene in Emma's bedroom. Just the necessary domestic dialogue. Shopping lists, school runs, bills. 'I just called to see if you knew how Chris was doing. If you'd spoken to him.'

'Oh. Did you not try calling him?'

'It went straight to his answerphone.' Tony is surprised and a little excited at how easily the lie comes. He smiles, imagining how outraged Robin would be. 'I thought you might have talked to him.'

'I was going to call him when I get home,' Heather says.

'OK, not to worry.'

'Shall I tell him you were trying to get hold of him?'

'Don't worry. I'll try him again tomorrow.'

'I could always call you later,' Heather says. 'If I get to talk to him.'

'No, it's fine.' Tony glances towards the kitchen again. He says, 'You were great tonight.'

There's a pause. Distant music and laughter. 'Was I?'

'What you said to Diana about neediness. That was very percep-tive. Very helpful.'

'It just seemed obvious.'

'Not to everyone. She really opened up after that.'

'Yeah, it was good, wasn't it?'

'It was better than good,' Tony says. 'You should be really proud of yourself.'

In the pause that follows, Tony imagines her leaning against the wall in some corner of the pub, one hand in the pocket of her suede jacket. He can picture that smile on her face.

'You know that a fair few ex-addicts go on to make good therapists, don't you?'

'Really?'

'Yeah. Well . . . me, for a start.'

Heather laughs. 'Yeah, obviously.'

'I've always thought the best therapists need to have gone through this stuff themselves. If they want to have real empathy.'

'It makes sense.'

'You might want to think about it.'

'You serious?'

'Why not? You'd just need to do the training and I'd be happy to help . . . if it was something you fancied having a crack at. Like I said, have a think about it.'

'I will, yeah. Definitely.'

'You've certainly got the right instincts and that's all you need to begin with.'

'I've got a great teacher,' Heather says.

Tony presses the phone harder against his ear. Now he can imagine that smile broadening, the tip of her tongue just visible. He casts one more look back into the house.

He says, 'Maybe we could meet up during the week and talk about it . . .'

When Heather gets back to the table, Caroline is already into her second bag of crisps. Heather sits down. She lays her phone on the table in front of her; nudges it once, twice, until it is perfectly straight.

Caroline wipes salt from her fingers and reaches for her glass. She says, 'Bloody hell, somebody looks pleased with herself.'

. . . NOW

'Not got your partner in crime with you today?' De Silva asked.

Tanner followed him into the kitchen, having gratefully accepted his offer of coffee. She put her handbag down on the central island and watched De Silva pop an espresso capsule into the gleaming machine. 'We don't always travel in pairs,' she said.

'No?'

'You're thinking of Mormons.'

'Isn't it a safety thing?'

'Sometimes.'

'Presumably you don't think I'm particularly dangerous.'

Tanner watched De Silva move the small cups across, empty the used pods into a small brown recycling bucket, take a plate down and lay out a few biscuits. His movements were precise yet oddly graceful. He was wearing jeans and a plain black T-shirt, loafers without socks.

'I've got mace in my bag,' she said.

They took their coffee through into the conservatory and sat down on chairs every bit as comfortable as Tanner remembered. She glanced out of the window, but today there were no squirrels scampering around the water feature. Just grey skies, and trees waving slowly through a curtain of drizzle.

'It was my daughter playing the piano,' De Silva said.

'Sorry?'

'Last time you were here. You asked.'

'Oh.' Tanner remembered the man's knowing smile, but was no wiser as to the reason for it. 'Not here today, then?'

'She's at school.'

Tanner looked towards the ceiling and summoned a knowing smile of her own. 'But the smell's still there. I mean . . . I presume she's the smoker.'

De Silva nodded.

'Smelled it the first time,' Tanner said. 'You can't miss it, to be honest.'

'You bothered?'

Tanner shrugged and shook her head. It was not something she would be concerned about anyway, least of all when she was investigating a murder, but it hadn't hurt to mention it. To put the therapist on the back foot. 'So, I've talked to everyone in the group,' she said. 'Managed to track them all down.'

No thanks to you.

'Right.'

'I had to talk to some of them more than once, in fact. Let's just say there were a few things they decided not to tell us, for one reason or another.'

De Silva said nothing.

Tanner took out her notebook and began to leaf through it. 'I'm not sure how much you're aware of what's been going on between them. Outside your sessions.'

'Only what they've chosen to tell me,' De Silva said.

'Did you know Robin was being blackmailed by someone in the group?'

De Silva looked genuinely shocked. 'No, I didn't.' He took a few seconds longer to process the information. 'It explains one or two

300

things that have happened in our sessions, though. Do you know ... who?'

'Robin still isn't sure,' Tanner said. 'He thought it was Chris at first, but then he thought it was Heather.'

'Really?'

'What do you think?'

'I'd be ... surprised,' De Silva said.

'You know she was gambling again. Before she was killed.'

De Silva looked more disappointed than anything, though Tanner could not tell if it was simply professional pride that was wounded. 'That's a shame.'

'And it's fair to say that Chris has been a little ... unstable.'

De Silva nodded. 'I'd been concerned for a while, but it became very obvious at that last session.' He saw the look on Tanner's face and smiled. 'I'm only confirming something you already know, so I'm not betraying client confidentiality.'

'Yes ... that last session.' Tanner looked at De Silva. '*Heather's* last session. Nobody has been willing to go into any details about that.'

'They wouldn't.'

'And you still won't.'

'Well, not unless I'm genuinely convinced that it has a bearing on what happened. If so, as I've said, I have an ethical obligation to reveal the details, but not until then.'

'I have reason to believe that it does,' Tanner said.

'Reason to believe is not enough, I'm afraid. Have you got evidence?' De Silva nodded, Tanner's silence enough to confirm his suspicions. 'I'm sorry, but I can't reveal confidential information about five clients based on a hunch.'

'One of them is dead,' Tanner said. 'The one that was murdered, remember? I'm not sure she'd care a great deal.'

'Even if it was just one client. I know you think I'm being difficult.'

'You're being professional,' Tanner said. 'I get that.'

'Good.'

301

'Do you keep notes of the sessions?'

'Of course.'

'Could I see them?'

'How is that any different?'

'I thought perhaps you might feel less ethically . . . compromised.' Tanner watched De Silva shake his head and stifle a smile that looked somewhat patronising as he reached for his coffee. She said, 'It's easy enough to apply for a court order and seize the notes. It wouldn't take long.'

De Silva shrugged and looked away. He took a fast slurp of coffee, as though he were sitting at some Milanese pavement café.

Tanner put down her notebook.

'What exactly is it you do, Mr De Silva? Sorry, is it mister or doctor?'

'I'm not a doctor.' He smiled. 'I'm not sure what you mean.'

'Well, I can't get specifics, in terms of what goes on in these group sessions . . . not yet, anyway. So, I'm just trying to get a better idea generally, that's all.'

'You want to know what a therapist does?'

'What *you* do.'

De Silva nodded and sat back. 'I lead the group,' he said. 'It's my job to establish an environment that's healthy and functional. I provide a structure. Limits and goals, you know? In some ways a group's like a laboratory, to investigate and explore interpersonal relationships.'

'You make it sound scientific.'

'In a lot of ways it is. I suppose I'm as much an engineer as anything.'

'So what makes a good therapist?'

'Someone who's empathetic,' De Silva said quickly. 'That's probably the most important thing.' He crossed his legs, stretched his arms out, nice and comfortable. 'It's what makes us different from other animals, you know that? Getting a sense of what someone else is thinking or feeling. Being able to get inside a fellow human being's head. Not that everyone can do it, not even those who literally get inside people's heads . . . some of Robin Joffe's mates at the hospital.'

'But you can do it.'

'I certainly do my best. Yeah . . . I think I'm pretty good. I listen to what's being said and what's not being said, and that means verbally *and* non-verbally. I look at the process of the group. Who chooses to sit where. Which people are sitting together and which of them sit as far apart as possible. Who's deliberately sitting close to me and who tries their best to sit as far away as they can. I explain, I clarify, I provide emotional stimulation . . . but most importantly, whatever is said, whatever is confessed or revealed, I don't judge.'

'There must be some interesting things . . . confessed,' Tanner said.

'Oh yeah.'

'Tricky though, I would have thought . . . working with addicts?'

De Silva cocked his head, gave a so-so shrug. 'Addicts are defensive by nature,' he said. 'That's the challenge.'

'Of course.'

'They deny. It's what they do, what they've always done. If it's run properly, group therapy can break through that defence system.'

'You think it's a disease?'

De Silva looked at her.

'I mean, some people might say it isn't, because the person's made a choice and it's clearly something that gives them pleasure.'

'Well, I'm not altogether sure how any of this is helping with your investigation, but by that definition syphilis wouldn't be a disease either.'

Tanner nodded. 'I've heard people say it, that's all.'

'People say all sorts of rubbish.'

'Some programme I saw about alcoholics.' She picked at a spot of lint on the collar of her jacket. 'Just wondered what you thought.'

'I think we need to ask ourselves questions. Like why people recovering after operations, being pumped full of morphine for a week or whatever, which is way stronger than street heroin . . . don't come out of hospital as hopeless addicts.'

'Never thought about it,' Tanner said.

'Because most of the time they're surrounded by caring staff, by friends and family who love them. It's lack of connection, that's the problem. That's why people become drug addicts, alcoholics. One reason, anyway.'

'That's interesting . . . '

De Silva said nothing for a while. Then he sat slowly forward. 'Are you married, Inspector?'

Tanner hesitated, but only for a second. 'No.'

'Boyfriend?'

'No.'

Tanner could feel the skin tighten around her mouth. If the therapist had asked about a girlfriend, she would have answered him honestly, but he did not. She could not help thinking that he already had the answer he was looking for.

He looked . . . satisfied.

'Alcoholism is a disease, pure and simple.' De Silva spoke slowly, his voice softer suddenly, his eyes fixed on hers. 'Once you have it, it can't be cured, it can't be controlled, and the only treatment is abstinence, whatever anyone says.' He raised a finger. 'Whatever anyone tells you.'

Tanner was aware of the colour in her face as she gathered her handbag and stood up, and, as she thanked De Silva for his time, she turned to look out at the curtain of rain, now a little heavier.

He told her he was happy to help.

Walking back into the kitchen, Tanner said, 'Oh, there's one more thing . . . '

De Silva smiled. 'Columbo.'

'Yes . . . it was just that you were going to talk to your wife or have a look at her diary, remember? To check if you were alone at home after the session on March the twenty-second. The night that Heather Finlay was killed.'

De Silva's smile evaporated. 'Yes, I checked,' he said. 'My wife was out that evening.'

'Do you happen to know what time she came home?'

'It was very late.'

Tanner nodded and thanked him again. She stopped at the door and mustered the considerable effort necessary to turn on some charm. 'Last chance to let me take a quick look at those notes. I wouldn't even need to take them away. Save me a whole lot of messing about.'

'Get your court order,' De Silva said.

PART THREE

PLAY THE INNOCENT

THE VISITOR

THE SECOND VISIT

His visitor does not need to be shown the way a second time and sits down as if they are old friends; begins to talk about the weather, the hassle coming through prison security, the long drive up from London.

'We've only got an hour,' he says. 'We can piss it away with chit-chat if you want. No skin off my nose.'

'Sorry.' The visitor takes the notebook and pen out, lays them on the table and flicks through the pages. 'You must be counting the days now.'

'Ever since I came in.'

'I bet. So why didn't you do something about it?'

'Such as?'

'Making it a bit easier for the parole board.'

'Yeah, well.'

The visitor looks at him. 'What you said last time, about not being sorry, what did you mean by that?'

A shrug as the tobacco tin comes out. 'That I wasn't.' He snaps off the lid. 'Sorry.'

'Don't suppose you fancy telling me why?' The wait for a response is not a long one. 'Thought not.'

'All this going to help you get a law degree then, is it?'

'Hopefully.'

'Funny old job, a lawyer,' he says. 'Defending people who you think might be guilty or else trying to put innocent people away.'

'Not much doubt where you were concerned though, was there?'

'Suppose not.'

'I'm actually far more interested in why people do things,' his visitor says. 'Motives.'

He says nothing.

'Money, sex, jealousy, hate ... love.' The visitor watches as the prisoner begins to assemble a cigarette. 'There's loads of reasons, but they're probably the big ones.'

He looks around, fingers working at the tobacco. 'All sorts in here.'

'Yeah, but I don't reckon losing your rag because someone spills your drink or looks at you the wrong way comes very high on the list, do you? I should think that puts you in a minority ... if that's what the reason was.'

'Told you last time, I can't remember.'

'Can you remember what actually happened? You taking that iron bar out, starting to hit him with it.'

'Not really.'

'Did you enjoy it?'

'*What?*'

'Well, you said last time he was asking for it.'

'I don't remember saying that.'

'Deserved everything he got, you said.'

'I was talking bollocks, making conversation, that's all.' He lifts the tin and smacks it back down on the table. 'Look, I just want to put it all behind me and get out of here, all right? Start again.'

The visitor nods, says, 'Course you do,' and sits back. 'Anyone waiting for you when you come out?'

'Yeah, course.'

'I don't mean your mum and dad or whatever. I mean anyone special.'

His face changes, as though he's trying to suppress a smile, and the visitor sees it.

'Maybe,' he says.

'Funny.'

'What?'

The visitor seems confused and starts looking back through pages in the notebook. 'Nobody in your family mentioned a girlfriend or whatever. You know . . . when I talked to them on the phone. Someone secret, is it?'

He picks up his tobacco tin and pushes back his chair. 'I think I've had enough of this.'

'Was it really one of those big motives, after all?'

'This has got sod all to do with any university, has it?'

The visitor starts to reel off that list of motives for murder again, a finger raised for each one. The prisoner gets to his feet, but hard as he tries, he cannot stop the blood rushing to his face when his visitor reaches the last one.

Love . . .

... NOW

'You did the right thing,' Weston said.

'Yeah?'

'Absolutely.'

The small tapas bar in Crouch End was a place Tony had eaten at often, usually with Nina and Emma, but it had been a long time since they had all been there together. Several years, now he came to think about it. It had been a favourite of Emma's when she was younger; the staff making a fuss of her, plying her with fizzy drinks and giving her pictures to colour in while they were busy preparing the plates of chorizo and *patatas bravas* she always insisted on eating. Tony had ordered both dishes for himself today and when the waiter had asked after Emma, Tony had promised that he would say hello to her for him.

'I don't know why you're wasting time worrying about it.'

'I'm not worrying.'

'We're professionals, Tony, and that's the way professionals behave.'

Tony nodded at his lunch companion and took a mouthful of the spicy potatoes. He imagined Emma at the table with them, as she was now, cutting each potato into a dozen tiny pieces, and he found himself wondering whether he and Nina had somehow made an unspoken agreement to avoid the place. The memories of their daughter, before things had become difficult.

'She definitely wasn't happy about it though,' Tony said. 'The copper. She probably thinks I was just stringing her along. Making her jump through hoops.'

'Who cares? Jumping through hoops is part of her job. You were protecting your clients and that's always our primary concern. Right?' The man opposite Tony – tall and smartly dressed – took a sip of water, then leaned across to touch his glass to Tony's.

'Cheers, Greg,' Tony said. 'Thanks.'

He and Greg Weston had met sharing a room in rehab. They had attended methadone clinics and group sessions together, then started out on the very path Tony had talked to Heather about the week before her death and taken the decision to train as therapists at the same time. Both had now been working for fifteen years, and both specialised in addiction recovery and relapse prevention, but they were very different practitioners.

Tony knew his colleague to be somewhat more beholden to ortho-dox psychotherapeutic theory than he was. That was the assertion, anyway. A few years before, he had visited the office that Weston rented in Marylebone and been shocked at the number of heavyweight textbooks lining the shelves. Freud, Jung and Adler, obviously. Yalom, Frankl, Laing and a good many more Tony had never even heard of. He still suspected that most of them were unread, there to impress clients just as they had impressed him, but he was always left with the feeling that Weston believed himself to be rather more serious in his approach to the job. They would meet up a few times a year, for lunch usually, like today, and Tony would always come away with the impression that his friend thought him a fraction too theatrical in his methods. A little less rigorous than he should be. It irked him; both the judgement and the fact that it bothered him so much.

'He's just jealous,' Nina had told him once. Back when she took the trouble to make him feel good about what he did. 'Because you have such a good rapport with your clients and he's too busy being up himself.'

Tony knew that she had a point, but today, as usual, it had begun to niggle before they had even sat down at the table. The truth was, Tony had only told Weston about his refusal to hand over notes to the police because he thought it might redress the professional balance between them a little.

'So, do you think it would help her? The notes.'

'No idea,' Tony said. 'I don't really know what she's hoping to find.'

'The dead girl's last session, you said.' Weston carefully cut off a small piece of Spanish omelette. 'Her shame story.'

'I suppose.'

'What was it?'

Tony looked at his colleague. It had long been understood that such discussions between them were strictly in the interests of improved practice and thus were in no sense a breach of client confidentiality.

So, Tony told him.

'Hell of a story,' Weston said.

'Yeah.'

'A confession, in every sense.'

'Certainly a notch or two above what the others had come up with. I mean the childhood abuse stuff we had the week before was nothing you and I haven't heard dozens of times, right?'

'What happened afterwards?'

'It was like a grenade going off,' Tony said. 'That silence when she'd finished, you know? You could still sense the ... carnage, though.' He described the reactions of others in the group that night and some of what he had been told had happened in the pub later on.

'Well, I can see why the copper thought it might be interesting.'

'Maybe.'

'The girl *was* murdered the same night.'

'Still, not sure it's going to be a great deal of help.'

'I suppose it depends how good a copper she is.'

314

'Oh, I think she's probably very good,' Tony said. 'Got a few issues of her own though, mind you.'

'Really?'

Tony waved the question away. He wasn't there to talk about Nicola Tanner. They ate in silence for a minute or so.

'Anyway.' Weston grinned. 'You can put all this behind you when you're off swanning about with your rock star pal.'

Tony looked up, shook his head like he hadn't quite understood.

'That's quite soon, isn't it?'

Another bone of contention. The implied assumption that Tony would only ever be a lightweight, because he wasted his expertise, such as it was, on showbiz types who could afford to pay him exorbitant fees.

'It's hardly swanning about,' Tony said.

'I'm only winding you up,' Weston said.

'I treat all my clients equally, you know that, whether they can play the guitar or not.'

'Don't be so touchy.' Weston popped an olive into his mouth, shook his head. 'You seem a bit rattled, mate. Seriously, are you OK?'

Tony ignored him. 'Anyway, I've got plenty on before that. I've got one-to-ones coming out of my ears and they want me to speak at a new residential centre in Brighton.' He swallowed, took a sip of water. 'And I think I'm going to reconvene the Monday night recovery session.'

'Really?'

Tony nodded.

'The dead girl's group?'

'Heather's group, yeah. What's left of it.'

'Are you sure that's a good idea?'

Up until that moment, Tony had been far from sure. He had been concerned that bringing them all back together after what had happened six weeks before might do some of them more harm than good. But the arrogance of Weston's question and the condescension in the smile as he asked it had made his mind up.

'It's time,' Tony said.

*

315

He watched Greg Weston get on to his bus, then turned to head in the opposite direction. It was a nice enough day and he decided to make the most of it by walking home. Nina was at work and he had no appointments until early evening, so there was nothing to rush back for.

He would call each member of the Monday night group on the way.

He headed south to begin with, then picked up the Parkland Walk on Crouch End Hill. Four miles or so, this was the route of an old railway line from Finsbury Park to Alexandra Palace, the development plans abandoned almost eighty years earlier at the outbreak of the Second World War. Now, the old trackbed was a popular haunt of ramblers and dog-walkers. A peaceful green corridor twisting through the hilly parts of Haringey and Islington, home to a huge variety of wildlife and dotted with crumbling bridges and half-demolished platforms and station buildings.

Tony began to walk north, the cutting opening out ahead of him, and wondered why he didn't walk a damn sight more than he did these days. It had always been something he'd enjoyed, that had invigorated him and kept his head clear in those first few years clean.

Are you sure that's a good idea?

Tony looked across at the grey peaks of Hornsey Ridge rising away to his right. Did working with a rock star once in a while make him any less good at what he did? He might not have read most of the books gathering dust on Greg Weston's shelves but he knew the ridge's layer of blue clay was the stratum beneath the city in which the underground was built. He knew these hills were called the Northern Heights and that Muswell Hill was largely formed by glacial debris, the terminal moraine of an ice-sheet that had once covered most of the country.

So, fuck you, Greg.

The dead girl's group?

He stopped on the narrow bridge above Northwood Road, a single line of traffic crawling beneath him, and called Diana.

'That's wonderful news,' she said. 'Will the others be coming?'

316

'You're the first person I've called,' Tony said. He could hear a dog yapping in the background. Diana shouted at it to be quiet.

'Thank you. For carrying on, I mean. I wasn't sure you would.'

'Oh, I was always going to continue with the sessions. It was just a question of when, that's all.'

'Well, you've made my day,' Diana said. 'Oh, and just so you know, things are still OK, touch wood. It's been a few weeks, but they've all been good weeks . . . '

The next call went straight to voicemail, but Robin rang back before Tony had reached the other side of the bridge. He sounded equally enthusiastic.

'I'm sorry for calling you at work,' Tony said.

'No problem,' Robin said. 'Best news I've had in ages.'

'That's nice to hear.'

'I'm going to plenty of other meetings, obviously, and I know we had some ups and downs, but that group was special.'

'I'll see you at the session, then.'

'Got plenty of biscuits in?'

'Of course.'

'Heather would have wanted us to carry on. Don't you think?'

The ground on either side of the path rose rapidly as Tony walked on, and a few minutes later the portals of what were once the Highgate tunnels came into view. In the decades since the closure of the line nature had stepped in to reclaim the land and now a tangle of dark roots twisted up through the collapsing brickwork. Cherry, rowan and hawthorn trees lined the trackbed and Tony had seen a family of muntjac deer at this very spot a few years before. He remembered holding his breath, reaching gingerly for his phone, desperate to get a picture for Emma, but the animals had gone before he'd had the chance.

'I'll be there,' Caroline said. 'But don't expect me to be in a good mood.'

'Everything OK?'

'Oh yeah, apart from being sacked everything's brilliant.'

317

'Sorry to hear that,' Tony said.

'Stupid cow said it was because of the police coming in, but she was just looking for an excuse, if you ask me. Not good for business, is it, having someone like me sitting at a till? Like a fatso at the checkout is going to stop people buying cakes.'

'Sounds to me like you might have a case for unfair dismissal.'

'Probably,' Caroline said. 'Can't be arsed.'

Striding on towards Queen's Wood, on a trail that would eventually bring him out on Muswell Hill Road, he arrived at another bridge, or what remained of it. He could smell mould and piss. Those bricks not lost beneath a wall of ivy were decorated with brightly coloured swirls of graffiti.

Leering faces and illegible messages; stars and smiley faces.

Doesn't matter what the reason was. Just happy that you decided to come . . .

Tony stood in the shadow of the overhang, sweating slightly and suddenly aware of how spooky the place could be. He remembered telling Emma the tale of the dreadful Goat-man, a figure from urban myth who was supposed to haunt these unlit pathways which local kids dared one another to walk at night. She had been frightened and upset, and it had taken him a good while to convince her that it was just a stupid story.

He wasn't expecting Chris to answer his phone, not when he saw who was calling, so he thought through his message for a minute or two before ringing and leaving it.

'Chris, it's Tony. I know things were a bit difficult for you at the last session and I hope you understand that you didn't really give me a great deal of choice. But I wanted to let you know that the Monday night group's starting up again, week after next probably, and I'd really like you to be there. Fresh start, OK? I hope you're doing well and don't worry, it's fine if you don't feel like you want to come along. If you do . . . great. Call me either way.'

Moving out of the semi-dark, Tony started slightly when he saw a figure crouched against the wall at the far side of the bridge. When he stepped closer it was clear that it was no ghostly Goat-man, and though there were no needles to be seen on the floor Tony did not need telling that the man was high: rocking slowly, his shaved head lolling, like he kept waking for a second or two before nodding off again.

Winos and drug addicts made good use of the place too. The so-called Friends of the Parkland did their best to move them on, to keep the place 'clean', but still, junkies were a lot more common than muntjacs.

Tony thought about Chris.

He really hoped he would make it to the meeting, but he wasn't holding his breath. It would be understandable if Chris wanted to forget all about the group and the people in it. To pretend that the events of that last Monday evening had never happened.

For very different reasons, Tony wanted to do exactly the same thing.

. . . NOW

Tanner closed the file on her computer, sat back for a minute or two then began to tidy her desk. She straightened papers and lined up pens, opened each of the drawers in turn and rearranged the contents. Then, for the third time since sitting down, she drew a stapled set of documents towards her and began to read.

It didn't take long. Still nothing . . .

'Somebody got out the wrong side of bed,' Susan had said. On her way to school, a few hours before, driving Tanner to the tube; negotiating the drizzle and the creep of rush-hour traffic in Hammersmith. 'Got *in* the wrong side last night, thinking about it.'

Tanner couldn't argue. Well, she could have said something about the fact that Susan could not possibly have known exactly what kind of mood she'd been in the night before. Not considering how much Pinot Grigio she'd put away in the course of the evening. Instead, she said, 'I know, sorry. This bloody case.'

'The girl in Victoria?' Susan leaned on the horn, swore at a cyclist.

'What?' Tanner was staring out of the passenger window. The shop fronts drifting past, pedestrians mooching along, looking no keener to get to work than she was.

'The drugs thing?'

They had not spoken about the Heather Finlay case since the discussion in the Chinese restaurant the week before. That night, Susan's less than sympathetic views on drug addiction had caused a good degree of friction and had almost led to a row. Tanner thought that sometimes Susan wanted a row, enjoyed blowing away the cobwebs, certainly when drink had been taken. Tanner preferred a quiet life and refused to rise to the bait on such occasions. There was more than enough shit to wade through at work.

'I thought I was on to something,' Tanner said. 'Well, I still do, but it's not that ... clear cut.'

It had taken longer than she would have liked to get De Silva's notes. Because they were designated as 'excluded material' under the Police and Criminal Evidence Act, Tanner had been unable to obtain a warrant in the usual manner. The district court judge had accepted her application for seizure and readily granted the necessary order, but this gave De Silva seven days to produce the material and granted him the right to object to its use in court. Though he had raised no such objection, he had seemed in no huge hurry to hand the notes over, and after three days Tanner had run out of patience and sent a uniformed officer round to collect them. Photocopies had finally been delivered to Tanner's house the night before.

Now those pages sat in the middle of her nice, tidy desk and they might just as well have been expenses forms or health and safety guidelines. Tanner had imagined marching into Ditchburn's office and dropping them on to his desk, hard evidence of her suspicions at the very least and, at best, grounds for arrest.

The meeting had not exactly panned out that way.

She looked up to see Chall by her desk.

'Not a lot in there, is there?'

'There's plenty, but not what we need,' Tanner said.

'Has Ditchburn seen them?'

'If you mean Detective Chief Inspector Ditchburn, yes, obviously.'

'So ... '

'He was ... disappointed,' Tanner said. 'He agreed it was a setback and suggested I concentrate on the other open cases I've got, each of which is every bit as important as this one.'

'Right.'

Dead end was the phrase Ditchburn had actually used, more than once, and, as far as those other cases went, it had been rather more of an instruction than a suggestion. Tanner rubbed her temples. She could feel a headache gathering strength.

'So, what are you going to do?'

'I'm going to work on my other cases, because that's what the DCI told me to do.'

Chall nodded, but showed no inclination to move. 'What about Heather Finlay?'

Tanner turned her head slowly to look at him. 'Do you know what multitasking is, Dipak?'

'Not really,' Chall said, grinning. 'I'm a bloke.' He watched Tanner turn away from him and jabbed a finger towards the notes on her desk. 'Bloody hell, though, I thought people like him were supposed to keep proper notes.'

'Depends on the therapist, I suppose.'

'So what, he's just a lazy bastard?'

'Lazy, pushed for time, who knows?'

'When he's talking about Heather's story, there's no names, no dates, nothing.' Chall was expressing all the frustration, all the disappointment Tanner was doing her best to keep to herself.

'Maybe she never mentioned them.'

'Or maybe she did and he just chose not to write them down. Maybe all that information is inside De Silva's head.'

Tanner thought about that.

'We can get his crappy notes, but how can we make him tell us?'

When Chall eventually wandered away, Tanner picked up the sheaf of notes again. It was the lack of detail that was the issue, no question about it. But even the broad strokes of the therapist's notes on that final session were enough to convince her that it was not quite a dead end, that as she'd said to Ditchburn, this was still their best bet. Best and only. There was certainly enough motive in Heather Finlay's story for any number of killers.

Adultery, false accusation, murder.

Reading De Silva's sketchy summaries one more time, she had little doubt that, whatever the details of Heather Finlay's confession, it had seriously upset other members of that group, even before whatever had taken place in the pub later on. Made one of them angry enough to lose control perhaps and decide to take revenge.

Flipping back through the pages, it was apparent to Nicola Tanner that many of them were unstable enough already.

... THEN

It is no more than a few seconds before Diana speaks, from the moment she opens the door and the woman standing in front of her introduces herself, but it feels like far longer. Time slowing and stretching, like woozy minutes sinking slowly beneath the surface of a dark pool; fighting the urge to scream and take in that fatal lungful.

A few seconds during which she decides she will probably need a nice long day at Heal's and John Lewis when this – whatever it turns out to be – is done with. She is already feeling that urge to spend, to acquire; to cram more things she will convince herself she wants into already overstuffed drawers and cupboards until she starts to feel better.

'I know who you are,' Diana says. Calm and cold, breaking the surface, sucking in air.

The woman ... the girl, shows no sign of surprise, although they have never actually met. Diana knows her name, of course, and has always known what she looks like. More than once, especially in the early days, she had driven to the house this girl and her ex-husband are still sharing; sat in the car and waited for a glimpse. A shape drifting past a window, lowering a blind. Once Diana had watched the girl emerge from the house and drive away in a shiny new Range Rover. She had followed at a distance, a few cars back the way they do on TV shows, with no idea what she would do when the journey ended. Eventually she had lost the Range Rover at some lights and pulled into a side street to cry, the bottle in the glove compartment within easy reach.

'I just thought we should talk.'

Diana says nothing.

'Obviously you know about the baby, so ...' The girl shifts her weight from one foot to another as though she's waiting for congratulations. She attempts a smile. 'It can't hurt to try and be civilised.'

Diana hopes that the scream is only inside her head. She says, 'Civilised,' and suddenly the word sounds very strange.

'Yes, don't you think?'

'Does he know you're here?'

'It was his idea, actually.'

'Well, that's all right then.' Diana's grip tightens on the edge of the door. 'Whatever's best for him.'

'So, can I come in?'

Diana stares past her, towards the enormous ash tree at the end of the drive. It seems like only a few weeks ago that its branches were bare, but now the familiar explosion of green is shading the front lawn. It might even need cutting back a little. From the corner of her eye she sees that the girl is about to speak again, so she stands aside to let her in.

God, the state of me. Why did I put on this hideous old skirt this morning? Why didn't I get my hair done yesterday?

She walks past the girl and leads her into the kitchen, hearing the pleasing hum of admiration behind her at the first view of the garden. Or perhaps it is the Poggenpohl units.

'It's lovely,' the girl says.

Diana half turns and acknowledges the compliment with a nod as she moves towards the table, but she knows very well what her visitor is really thinking.

I took him away from this.

'You can barely swing a cat in our kitchen.'

He left it all for me . . .

Diana pulls back a chair for herself and watches as the girl hesitates. Had she been expecting the offer of a drink? A plate of cucumber sandwiches, for Christ's sake? She stares, and sees the girl smile, every bit as embarrassed as she should be, before she walks to the table, her heels click-clacking on the terracotta tiles, and sits down.

'Look, I don't suppose we're ever going to be friends.'

'Oh, really? That's a shame.' The sarcasm is too heavy-handed and as she watches the girl's face fall Diana silently chides herself for the loss of control. She says, 'Sorry,' and hates herself even more for the show of weakness. The gutless . . . Britishness.

'It has been quite a while, after all.'

'I'm well aware how long it's been.'

'So, don't you think we should at least make an effort? The three of us, I mean.

'What?'

'For Phoebe's sake if nothing else.'

'Please don't talk about my daughter.'

'Well, she's not just your daughter, is she?' Now the girl is showing the steel that Diana has always known was in there. 'It's inevitable that I'll be seeing a lot of her, and us being enemies is going to be hard on her, that's all.'

Diana stares down at her hands.

Why didn't I do my nails this week? I look terrible.

'I'm only trying to help. Honestly.'

She must think I look like I've given up.

'He's always telling me what a fantastic mother you are.'

Diana looks up.

The girl nods. 'Honestly. He knows very well you're a better parent than he ever was. So, I thought, if we talked about things a bit, we might come to some kind of understanding at least, which would make things easier for Phoebe. Well ... for all of us. Make a truce or whatever. I know we haven't actually been fighting or anything, but you know what I mean ... '

Diana realises suddenly that she has been staring at the girl's chest, unblinking like a lecherous teenager, and that the girl is aware of it.

Comparing the girl's breasts to her own.

Imagining her ex-husband's hands on them, remembering what that felt like.

She pushes her chair back. 'Excuse me.'

She hasn't actually been sick, but it had felt as though she was about to be and she had not wanted to take the chance. To risk the girl seeing her struggle; her cheeks bulging, her hand across her mouth.

Him and the girl, tucked up in bed ...

'You're kidding!'

'Seriously. She was staring at my tits and then you won't believe what happened ... '

She breathes deeply as she watches herself in the mirror, as she runs a tap quietly and splashes water on to her face. She dries her cheeks with a flannel then throws it into the cupboard beneath the sink.

'You were right, darling. I think she's finally lost it.'

She stares at the bottle of bleach and imagines her knees on the girl's bony shoulders, forcing the neck of the bottle between those bee-stung lips, so much bigger and harder than her ex-husband's sorry little manhood. She wonders how long it would take. The agony would be immediate, she supposes, then presumably a long lingering death as the insides are burned out.

She closes the cupboard door and wipes water spots from the granite with her palm. She steps across to flush the toilet she has not used, then goes back to the mirror to quickly do what she can with her hair.

'We do PR for all sorts of people, actually. Arts organisations, charities, local authorities. All sorts.'

The girl is still sitting at the table, while Diana is busy making tea. Cups, not mugs. A tray, for pity's sake. That damned Britishness refusing to stay buried.

'I can't really blame you for thinking that I'm some sort of gold-digger, so I just wanted you to know that I actually work bloody hard. You know, give you some idea of what I do.'

'Do you take milk?' Diana asks.

The girl says that she does. Just a dash. 'We've got separate bank accounts too, in case you were wondering. It feels a bit weird telling you this stuff, but I want you to know that I pay my own way, that money's got nothing to do with it.'

'I've got some biscuits somewhere,' Diana says.

'I'm sure you were exactly the same, once upon a time. You used to work, didn't you?'

Diana nods, and now, with the kettle grumbling behind her, she is looking over at the knives. Japanese, expensive, razor sharp. In a tall earthenware jar beside the toaster, the meat tenderiser pokes its head above a tangle of utensils, and in the drawer beneath a set of hand-forged, stainless-steel kebab skewers sits in a wooden case. The handle of each is unique: a delicate twist of metal topped with a different semi-precious gem.

Garnet, amber, bloodstone.

'I like to think I'm a bit of a feminist,' the girl says. 'You know? So trust me, the last thing I want is to be kept by a man.'

It would be ironic, Diana thinks. Those lovely skewers. Fitting though, really.

They were a wedding present.

... THEN

'This is swanky,' Heather says.

'Not really.' Tony looks around. 'It's actually a bit tatty if you look closely. Mind you, that's why I like it.' The lounge area is all but empty. A couple of men in suits eating lunch at a table near the fireplace, another reading the newspaper in a large, leather armchair. 'None of those tossers with arty glasses and hipster beards, doing movie deals or whatever. Talking about recording contracts.'

'Must cost a bit, though.'

Tony shrugs. 'Not really.' In fact, it's one of the older and more exclusive clubs in the heart of Soho, whose 'tattiness' is artfully cultivated. Annual membership is more than a thousand pounds a year, but a well-known actor Tony worked with a few years before has blagged him a hefty discount. He often drops into the place to chill or drink coffee when he's in town. He meets prospective clients in there sometimes, a fellow therapist now and again. A month or so before, he'd had lunch with the rock star's manager in the dining room upstairs, to discuss his role on the forthcoming tour and to negotiate his fee.

'I love it,' Heather says. 'Thanks for bringing me, and thanks for ...' She nods towards the empty plates on the table in front of them. They'd both made short work of the club's signature Welsh rarebit, two cappuccinos each and carrot cake. 'I'm stuffed.'

'No worries,' Tony says. 'Now . . . listen. You've heard me bang on about boundaries often enough, and that's because they're important. Yes?'

When Tony leans forward, Heather does the same thing and now she nods, to show that she's taking what Tony is saying very seriously.

'That's why I wouldn't usually do this, OK? Be here with someone I'm actually treating. The only reason I've made an exception is because I meant what I said on the phone.'

'Really?'

'Why would I joke about something like that?'

'I don't know,' Heather says. 'I just thought maybe you were being nice. Like coming to the party.'

'That was different.' Tony leans closer to her. 'Look, you can learn the various techniques, the different approaches and so on, but basic empathy is there or it isn't and nobody can become a decent therapist without it. That's what I see in you every week and that's why I suggested it might be something you should think about.'

Heather laughs, nervous. She picks up the knife and fork that are already lying straight on her empty plate and lays them down again. Nudges them into line. 'You seriously think I could do it?'

'Yes, I do.' Tony shakes his head, like she's being silly. 'It's not just me, all right? I know at least half a dozen therapists who work in the same area I do who are former addicts themselves. I was in rehab with one of them and he's supposed to be pretty good. When you've been there and gone through recovery it gives you real insight about the best way to help others. I mean, that's common sense, isn't it?'

'I suppose so, but don't you need all sorts of qualifications?'

'Of course, and I'm not saying it's easy and that there isn't a shed-load of hard work and reading, because there is. But don't pretend you're too stupid to do it because that's a cop-out, and even if you do think you are, I can promise you that you're not. You can do it if you want to, I honestly believe that.'

330

Heather sits back. Her suede jacket is folded across the arm of her chair and she runs a palm along the length of one sleeve. She smiles. 'So, did you decide to do it when you were in rehab?'

'That's when I started thinking about it, yeah. Me and my friend Greg.'

'You didn't want to go back into music?'

Tony laughs, or sounds as though he's laughing. 'It was that world that got me into all the trouble to begin with,' he says. 'Why would I ever want to go back?'

'Shame,' Heather says. 'You were really great. I found some of your stuff on the internet.'

'Oh, God.'

'Don't you miss it? Even a bit?'

'I don't miss what it turned me into.'

Heather nods, then looks away and starts to hum a tune. She sings a few words quietly, just a phrase or two she can remember, then looks back at him. 'That one was my favourite,' she says.

'It's embarrassing . . .'

'I mean it. It's fantastic.'

Tony watches her fingers flutter at the sleeve of her jacket again, as though it's a comfort blanket. 'You've got a nice voice,' he says. 'Forget what I said about therapy – maybe you should be a singer.'

Heather stares at him for a few seconds, serious again, as though uncertain if he's mocking her. 'Did you mean what you said about helping me?'

'If you decide to train, you mean?'

'I don't think I'm stupid, but sometimes I don't have a lot of confidence, that's all.'

'Yeah, of course.'

'I know you don't have a lot of time or anything.'

'If you're prepared to commit to it, yeah, I'll do what I can. I promise.'

A waiter steps across to ask if they've finished, then begins to clear the empty plates and cups. As he's walking away, Tony steals a glance at his watch and Heather sees him. She says, 'Do you need to get off?'

Tony says that he doesn't, that actually there isn't anywhere else he needs to be for the rest of the day. 'What about you?' he asks. 'You got any plans?'

She laughs, puts on an affected accent. 'Well, I'll have to consult my diary, obviously.'

'Obviously.'

Heather laughs again.

'So, what do you reckon then?' Tony looks at her. 'You fancy going somewhere else?'

. . . THEN

In a noisy Thai restaurant on Chiswick High Road, Robin nods at the man opposite him, half listening; sitting at a large round table with six or seven others from the meeting, waiting for the mixed starter to arrive.

Each of the meetings Robin attends has its own post-session ritual. These people always come to the same restaurant and order the same starter to share, while those at a different weekly meeting in Camden go to a café that serves a full English breakfast twenty-four hours a day. On Monday nights, of course, after Tony's group recovery session, it's the Red Lion in Muswell Hill.

Just a few days now, until Robin will get his chance to confront Heather.

The man sitting opposite says something. Robin leans forward because he can't hear properly.

'It was good tonight,' the man says again.

Robin says, 'I needed it.'

The man reaches across to lay a hand on Robin's arm. 'You need to stay strong.'

At the meeting, Robin had stood up and talked about what was happening to him in another group. The threat from one of them to expose his history with addiction; the danger of losing his job if he refused to comply. Almost everyone who spoke after he had finished had expressed their disgust and sympathy and had urged him to stand up to his blackmailer.

A blackmailer who had now sent a second demand.

'You've come too far to lose everything,' one had said.

'Fuck the scumbag, whoever he is.'

'Addiction is nothing to be ashamed of.'

They were right, Robin knows that, and their support is like oxygen. Whether the blackmailer calls his bluff and goes to the police or Robin reports what is happening himself, he will, in all likelihood lose his job, but so what? Yes, it will be tough financially, but he has learned how to tighten his belt before. He survived the pasting he took during the divorce, so he tells himself that he can do it again. He has a little money put away and he is only a few years from retirement anyway, so what does it really matter?

And the truth is, he is ready to stop.

He is tired.

Physically, he has been feeling his age for a while and his exercise-free lifestyle is not exactly designed to slow that process down. His arthritis is getting worse by the day. He seems increasingly prone to infections and both eyesight and hearing are deteriorating alarmingly fast.

The creeping failure of precious mental faculties, though, are, for him, far harder to live with than dodgy knees.

He knows ex-addicts a lot younger than he is, whose brains are so scrambled that they can barely remember their own names any more, and up until recently, he had thought he had got away with it. Now, memories are starting to scatter; the synaptic connections sporadic, like an unreliable phone signal. The remembrance of certain events he had thought were safely filed away for ever have become like the disconnected fragments of a dream.

Much of his time at university, a holiday in France with his ex-wife, treasured moments shared with his son.

He had talked about Peter too, at the meeting.

The waste and the blame.

The stupid, senseless death that had never been paid for.

'Finally,' says the man opposite.

Robin looks up as the food arrives and is laid down, and the volume of conversation drops a little as people dig in.

Within a few minutes of starting to eat, Robin can feel the heat spreading through him, but he has eaten here often enough to know that it is not the spring rolls or the spicy Thai fishcakes that are causing the sweat to prickle on his back or the blood to rise to his neck.

The validation he is getting from those all around him is firing him up, he is sure of it, allowing free rein to a powerful anger he has been struggling to keep in check. That has not surfaced again since that evening in the Red Lion with Chris.

Back when he thought Chris deserved to be the target of it.

No, he will not let ... whoever is responsible for these threats get away with it. They must not be *allowed* to get away with it.

Losing his job or, worse, being struck off, is simply unacceptable. His professional reputation has been hard earned and he will not sacrifice it. As far as the money goes, who the hell does he think he is trying to kid? The nice cosy pension will go as well as the salary and it is simply idiotic to think he can easily recover from a financial hit like that. It's bad enough living the way he does now, like some student in that poky flat. He will not take a step down from there.

His mind is racing as he eats, as he nods along and pretends to pay attention to the chat around him.

Perhaps the answer is a counter-threat. All he needs to do is find something that his blackmailer would prefer to keep secret. If it is Heather, he doesn't doubt that there will be something there to find. There has to be a solution that doesn't involve ... the kind of thing Chris accused him of, that he believes him to be capable of.

People cannot threaten and harass with impunity. They cannot behave in such a way and not accept that there will be consequences.

'You all right, Robin?'

He looks up at the man who is now pointing and grinning at him from across the table.

'Looks like you've eaten a chilli, mate.'

Such things have to be paid for.

... THEN

Chris must have said something or made a noise; a low moan or a grunt of frustration, something. The boy, sitting shirtless on the floor, turns from the vast screen on which Nazi zombies are being ruthlessly dispatched and says, 'Calm down, for fuck's sake. He'll be here in a minute.'

'It's been hours.'

'It's been twenty minutes.'

'Look at you.' The boy turns back to his game. Woody, whose contact details Chris had wiped from his phone a long time ago because he was told to. Whose number it had taken him many hours to track down the night before, when the idea had first taken hold and quickly become something stronger.

When the niggle had become a need.

Walking and walking, waiting for Woody to call back, and all the while the memory of so many similar moments flooding his mind with all the things that would inevitably follow. The need to get high again. The urgency to find the money and all the things he will do to get it, so that he can get high again after that, and again, and on and on. The bed he will be refused at the hostel and the tiredness and the cold streets. The look of disgust he will get from others and from that thing with eyes dead as buttons and see-through skin when he stares into a mirror.

That was then, before the itch became something he knew he would have to tear into hard, and now he's sitting on this ratty sofa, his belly drum-tight, rubbing then scraping at his arms and his nails aren't long enough and the flesh feels like chickenskin.

'Have that, you fucker,' Woody shouts at the screen.

Chris thinks he's been in this room before, but he's not sure. He wonders if Woody's redecorated, then laughs because it's such a stupid idea.

'What?' Woody turns round again.

Chris shakes his head, gets up and begins to walk around the room, from wall to wall.

Woody laughs. 'Same as you always were.'

'What?'

'Gagging for it.'

And Chris isn't sure if it's Woody saying that or Heather and the noise of the explosions and gunfire from Woody's game is deafening, so he tells Woody to turn it down because they might not hear the doorbell. Woody swears and tells him that he hasn't missed this shit. He says that the other side of Chris's face is going to get messed up if he doesn't put a sock in it, but the instant he nudges the volume of his game down the bell goes; screams.

'Fucking told you,' Chris says, running for the door. 'Christ knows how long he's been out there ...'

The two of them are scrabbling for the cash as they open the door and, in the minute or so the whole business takes, the only word the dealer utters is 'Nice', when he sees what level Woody is at in his game.

As soon as the dealer is gone and the door is closed, the two of them retreat to opposite sides of the room.

Animals with meat to protect.

Now, it's just the ritual, and the sense-memory of pain – the cramp in his stomach, the stinging on his skin – miraculously vanishes as he takes out the spoon; the lighter and the cigarette filter and the vinegar to help the mix.

Didn't Heather say something about this, a few Mondays back?

Fucking Heather. He remembers saying her name as he'd walked and walked the night before. Shouting it out loud and making a woman who was passing jump back into the road.

Being scared of showing who you really are is what leads to all the lying. Is it, Heather? Fucking *is* it?

The syrupy smell as the brown liquid bubbles in the spoon makes him forget every single one of those stupid ... consequences. The hostel and the money and the looks of disgust. They do not matter any more and he is certain they never really did, because now there are other thoughts that need to be wiped away.

Bunk beds and bedtime stories. A locked bathroom door and his guts running out of him like water.

The blood blossoms in the syringe and when he pushes, and pulls and pushes, it's instant. A murmur, and then the roar of it coming and a surge of sweet who-gives-a-shit that is over him like a wave.

'Yeah,' Woody says, hoarse and slow, from a long way away.

And Chris is already in that wonderful place, where he doesn't have to think or pretend, to feel anything.

Somewhere he's perfectly alone and empty.

... THEN

There's not a great deal of light in the small alleyway, though business is still brisk on Gerrard Street; in the restaurants and supermarkets of Chinatown, from whose back doors and greasy windows the smell seeps like smoke. Roasting meat, fish and hoisin sauce.

The stink that will linger in their clothes for days.

Tony says, 'I want to get high with you.'

'No, you don't.'

'I won't ... but right now, I feel like I really want to.' Tony pushes his tongue back into Heather's mouth, his fingers a little further inside her knickers.

The metal fire exit clatters when Heather leans back against it. They freeze, just for a second, as something skitters behind one of the bins a few feet away. Tony's left hand is moving slowly inside Heather's bra, the fingers of his right still working as he tries to ease the material of her jeans away. Heather's palm moves up and down the length of his erection and she stops only when her fingers flutter to feel for the zip.

'This is pretty fucking close though,' Tony says.

They kiss again, hard and wet, then stop to suck in a fast breath, their faces pressed together. 'To what?' Heather asks.

'To being high. To not . . . Jesus . . . '

There are voices from the street just thirty feet away, shouting and laughter, but still the sounds the two of them make seem loud; lips pushed against ears inside the dimly lit doorway. Tony's low moan. Heather saying, 'There', and the high gasp that follows.

Tony adjusts his stance, spreading his legs so that Heather can take his cock out, and as soon as she has she lets go of it to push her jeans down across her skinny hips.

'We could go somewhere,' she says.

Tony takes her hand and puts it back, moves it for her.

'We could go to my place.'

'No . . . this is good,' Tony says.

For a few minutes they work at one another, quick and rough. They do not stop at the sound of a doorway opening further down the alleyway, and the footsteps have not yet faded away when Tony leans forward to brace himself against the metal door and Heather sinks slowly to her knees.

... NOW

Tanner was talking to Diana Knight in the station's reception area when Caroline Armitage walked in. The detective enjoyed the look of surprise and confusion, of something that might have been panic on each of their faces when they saw one another.

'Oh,' Knight said. 'I hadn't realised.'

'I thought it might be useful,' Tanner said. 'If there's two of you, you might help one another remember things. That's all.'

'Doing us both together?' Armitage asked when she reached them. She smiled as she wiped a forearm across her forehead and Tanner thought she could detect something salacious in the girl's tone; a suggestion that she'd got Tanner's number, in one way at least. Tanner had no intention of acknowledging it.

'So, you understand that you're going to be interviewed under caution, this morning?' As per procedure, each woman had been sent a letter requesting her attendance.

'Actually, I'm not sure I do understand,' Knight said. 'Not unless we're actually suspects.'

'I suspect there are still things you haven't told us,' Tanner said.

'Because we couldn't.'

'You know why,' Armitage said.

'Yes, but still, I'm entitled to interview you under caution if I believe that doing so might reveal further lines of inquiry.' Tanner reeled it off with a degree of relish; content and confident in her enforcement of interview guidelines. 'If it gives me the chance to gather information I can't get in any other way, which may prove relevant to any subsequent prosecution.'

'Well, if that's what you think,' Knight said.

'I think that one or both of you, unwittingly or not, may have been involved in a major offence. Either way, I've reason to think that offence was committed by someone in your group.' Tanner looked at the two women. Knight was dressed immaculately, muted tones and expensive fabrics; her appearance exuding confidence, even though, of the two, she seemed to be more nervous. Armitage wore a volumi-nous grey shirt over leggings and dirty trainers. She looked like she didn't give a toss. 'Interviewing the two of you formally might also bring home to you how seriously I'm taking this. The therapy group.'

'Yes, well, someone was murdered,' Knight said. 'I do understand that's quite serious.'

'Are you waiting for legal representation to arrive? I hope you understood that you're entitled to it.'

'I didn't think it would be necessary.'

'I didn't think about it at all,' Armitage said.

'Right. Well, I appreciate you coming in.' Tanner had one hand on her lanyard, ready to swipe her ID and go inside. She looked at Caroline Armitage. 'And I'm sorry if you've had to take time off work.'

'I got sacked.'

'Ah.'

'Oh, that's awful,' Knight said.

Armitage was still looking at Tanner. 'Down to you, according to my boss. Not good for business when the staff are questioned by the police on company premises.'

'She can't do that,' Tanner said.

'Oh, I'll pop in and tell her, shall I?'

Tanner watched Diana Knight reach across to rub the younger woman's arm as though she were comforting a distressed child.

'Right, let's get this done, shall we?'

In the interview room, which Knight said was marginally nicer than the first one she'd been in, Chall prepared the recording equipment while Tanner ran through the women's rights. She told them they were being interviewed in accordance with Code C of the Police and Criminal Evidence Act. She made the usual speech about not having to say anything, the possibility of silence harming their defence, anything they said being used in evidence. She made sure they knew that the interview was to be recorded on both tape and DVD and that they were free to leave at any time.

Free to leave, but she would want to know why.

Once the familiar tone had signalled that things were officially under way, Tanner formally introduced herself and Dipak Chall. She reminded her interviewees of their right to seek legal advice, then asked each woman to state her name, address and date of birth. She thought Knight winced a little at revealing her age and told herself not to smile.

'I'm not going to waste time asking again about what exactly was said and by whom during the session on March the twenty-second. Mainly because you're both still within your rights to refuse to tell me, but also because I now have a reasonable idea, having seen Mr De Silva's notes.'

Tanner was expecting a pause, and got one.

'He gave them to you?' Armitage asked.

'He had no choice.'

'You twisted his arm.'

'The court did.' Tanner leaned forward, keen to move on. 'So, instead let's talk a bit about what everyone's mood was like that evening. Before the session, I mean.' She looked from one face to another, picked. 'Diana?'

Knight stared at her.

'Do you mind if I call you Diana?'

She said no, but looked as though she minded a great deal. 'All right ... I think it would be fair to say I was ready for some support that night. Actually, I still am, which is why I'm so grateful that Tony's starting the group up again.'

'Really?' Tanner glanced at Chall, who, in accordance with her instructions, had sat there looking serious and said nothing. 'The Monday night group?' She was genuinely surprised, and interested. De Silva had given her no indication that he intended getting them all back together so soon.

All bar one, of course.

'Yeah, week after next, I think.' Armitage rolled her eyes. 'Should be ... interesting.'

Tanner was sure that it would be. She looked back to Diana Knight. 'So, March the twenty-second? You needed some support ...'

'Yes ... I'd been going through a difficult time,' Knight said. 'Things weren't exactly helped by my ex-husband's girlfriend popping in to see me.'

Now it was Armitage's turn to wince, rather more theatrically.

'Can't have been much fun,' Tanner said.

'That's putting it mildly. Why on earth would anyone do that?'

'I know.' Armitage nodded, enthusiastic. 'It's against the rules.'

Knight evidently caught something in the other woman's tone and turned to stare hard at her.

'Come on, that's definitely against your rules, isn't it?' Armitage looked at Tanner. Said, 'She's got rules.'

'Right,' Tanner said.

'About other women and how they're supposed to behave as far as other men go. Older men, that's a definite no-no, and married men, bang out of order. Married *and* older' – she pursed her lips and sucked in a breath – 'that's rule number one.' She leaned towards Tanner and mock-whispered, as if it was no more than a silly joke. 'That one gets her really riled up.'

'You're being unfair,' Knight said.

'Come on—'

'You try going through it.'

'I'm only messing around.'

'They're not rules.' Knight adjusted the thin scarf at her throat, used the few seconds to calm down a little. 'They're standards.'

Tanner had guessed there might not be too much love lost between these two very different women. At worst, she knew they would have almost nothing in common, save the reason they were there. She had not expected conflict to surface quite so soon, but now that it had, she was hoping it might shake a few things loose.

She looked to her left, watched the digital display count the seconds. She said, 'What about you, Caroline?'

Knight looked at Armitage, happy that it was the younger woman's turn.

'Well, look at me. Laugh-a-minute fat lass, happy as a pig in shit. Right?'

Tanner waited.

She shook her head. 'Wrong. Trust me, when I get a cob on, I really get it on.' She nodded towards Knight. 'And as it goes, she wasn't the only one who wasn't in the best of moods that night.'

'Because?'

Armitage smiled and closed her eyes just briefly, as though anticipating the reaction to what she was going to say; as if she couldn't quite believe how good it was. 'Well, whose fault is it we're here?'

'I'm not sure I—'

'You mean *Heather*?' Knight looked shocked.

Armitage looked at Tanner and reddened a little. 'I don't mean "fault", that wasn't what I was trying . . . but yeah. She was the reason I was so pissed off that night.'

Knight was still staring at her. 'What did Heather do?' Her voice fell a little when she mentioned the dead woman's name and it was hard to tell if the small show of respect was involuntary.

'More like *who* did she do.' Smiling again, Armitage reached for the bottom of her shirt, lifted it and flapped as though she was feeling the heat. 'I met up with her the day before and she was full of it. Walking around like a dog with two dicks, I swear.'

'Why were you so angry with Heather, Caroline?' Tanner asked.

'Because of what she'd done.' She glanced across at Knight. 'You are really going to love this. Talk about your rules.'

'What?' Knight asked, a little impatient.

Armitage took another second or two then turned her eyes on Tanner, and suddenly she was dead serious.

'She'd broken every bloody rule in the book.'

. . . THEN

Twice, Chris has walked from Holland Park tube station to Ladbroke Grove and back again. He thinks that certain buildings and shop-fronts are a bit like others he has seen recently, notices that a newspaper seller looks familiar, but is otherwise oblivious to the details of his journey or the fact that he is repeating it. Most of the time he is looking down at the ground moving beneath him. He doesn't step aside for people. He doesn't distinguish between the pavement and the road and he is unaware that when he stops to stare into shop windows – at naked mannequins with no arms or electrical goods or the reflection that looks like a ghost – he is sometimes standing there for ten or fifteen minutes at a time.

He can't even remember how he came to be in west London to begin with.

He remembers that at some point there was a phone conversation with Woody and he supposes that he was the one who had made the call. A promise to hook him up again that's probably worth nothing, but it's all he has.

He's coming down, but still high enough, and he's smart enough to know that now's the time to arrange his next fix. He's been caught out like that plenty of times before. Call me whatever you like, he thinks, but you can't accuse me of not planning ahead.

Whatever you like . . .

Gutless arsehole.

Waste of DNA.

Sad, stupid fucker.

These are among the many bad things he calls himself as he trudges the streets, but they're only words; just sounds that are immediately lost inside his head. Wheeling away into the darkness as other ideas, other certainties speed into focus, and stick.

She did this, not me. She wanted this to happen.

'Watch yourself, mate.'

He stops and looks at the man whose shoulder he has banged into. A man with a big, silly shoulder bag and a blue hat. Bag man . . . stupid hat man. Angry twat in a twatty hat.

He can't help laughing.

'You're not looking where you're going.'

'She tell you that, did she?'

'Sorry?'

'Yeah, well she's always got loads of opinions,' Chris says, unaware quite how loudly he is speaking. 'Plenty to say about other people, but maybe she needs to look at herself a bit more, don't you reckon? Stop making other people do things they don't want to, because the fact is she hasn't thought it through. Because she's selfish and maybe she wants other people to do these things, to face up to all the crap in their lives, when they were kids, whatever, because actually she's too scared to do them herself.' He nods, holds up a hand. 'Don't worry, you don't need to say anything to her, because I'm going to tell her all this myself tomorrow night. Right to her filthy stupid face in her precious circle . . .'

The man is out of sight well before Chris has finished, but in the few seconds before he had hurried away Chris had recognised the look. The man had been frightened, white-faced with it he was, below the peak of that twatty hat.

Chris laughs again and moves on.

A skinny little poof like me and now all of a sudden I'm dangerous . . .

Plenty of looks as he walks. Some of it's down to his face, he knows that, the bruises you can still see from half a mile away, but mostly it's the general . . . state of him. Shock, anger, revulsion, all the old favourites. Sympathy even, now and again, and he thinks that goes to show how sound a lot of people are, well in London, anyway. It's funny how quickly he's become used to those looks again and how, just like before, the only one he can't stomach is pity.

He's got more than enough of that for himself, thank you very much.

He crosses one road and then another, heading aimlessly back towards Ladbroke Grove and racking his brains for alternatives if Woody doesn't come up with the goods.

Dredging up names, characters.

Spike, Billy Whizz, that mental bloke in Dalston who always carried a briefcase with a knife in it . . .

Waiting for lights to change he walks on the spot, then freezes when he sees them talking outside a coffee shop. A pair of them and he's pretty sure already, but when one glances across at him he knows beyond a shadow of a doubt that they're Drugs Squad. He knows that they're watching him and that they've probably been following him for ages already.

It's a good job he hasn't scored yet.

It's ridiculous how obvious it is, the leather jackets and the casual chat and he can't believe they're being so blatant about it.

He wonders if this is down to her as well.

Easier to grass me up, he thinks, to get me tugged, than look me in the eye.

He's sweating anyway, but suddenly it's like he's dripping with it. He knows he has to get away fast and the instant the lights change he's across the road and taking a sharp right into Lansdowne Crescent. He is trying not to run, to attract any attention, and every few feet he checks to see that the coppers aren't following.

When he's sure he's lost them, he stops and ducks into a driveway, and he doesn't start moving again until his heart has stopped hammering. Instantly he's thrilled that he's outsmarted the Feds, and, when he clocks the number of the house, he's absurdly delighted that he's only a few doors away from the hotel where Jimi Hendrix died.

That he gets how ironic it is.

Chris starts walking again, heading on a roundabout route towards Shepherd's Bush now, though he doesn't know it, or care. He makes the effort to keep his head up, because now he knows they're on to him he needs to be careful. It's never a good thing to be pulled in by the police, but today it's really the last thing he needs.

Not when tomorrow's his chance to tell Little Miss Pain-Isn't-Shameful exactly what he thinks. When he gets to show her what she's done and what she's responsible for.

When Lucky Heather's going to get everything she deserves.

. . . THEN

'You fancy going in?' Caroline asks.

'For real?'

They're standing in the courtyard outside St Paul's church in Covent Garden. Someone on their way inside has told them it's called the actors' church, but having hung around for ten minutes they have yet to see anybody they recognise.

'Yeah, we could. It *is* Sunday.'

'Still . . .'

'Come on,' Caroline says. 'For all we know Benedict Cumberbatch is on his knees in there.' She giggles and Heather does likewise, until finally she shakes her head.

'It's not really my thing.'

'OK.'

'Sorry.' Heather hunches her shoulders, a little embarrassed. 'I did try once, but I just thought it was all a bit creepy.' She stares up at the large clock above the portico. 'Plus, I prefer getting help from someone I can actually see, you know?'

'Makes sense.'

'I didn't even know you were religious.'

'I'm not really,' Caroline says. 'Robin was telling me about it, that's all. He goes now and again, I think. Well, it's a bit of a thing with a lot of them in NA, apparently. A higher power and all that. I don't think he's a proper God-botherer or anything, but he says it helps him. So . . . '

'I'll wait,' Heather says. 'If you want to go in.'

Caroline looks as though she's thinking about it. Then she says, 'No, sod it.' She tosses her hair back. 'Benedict's prayers are not getting answered today.'

Heather laughs.

'Be just my luck though, wouldn't it? If he *was* in there and it turns out he's actually a chubby-chaser.'

'You sure?'

'Yeah.' Caroline puts an arm through Heather's. 'Come on, let's go back to the piazza, take the piss out of a few mime artists.'

They walk back up towards the tube, the street crowded with tourists, gathering in large groups ahead of them around the station entrance. They hear accents which sound eastern European, others which are probably Scandinavian. There are a good many jester's hats and backpacks on display and, judging by the way the sky is rapidly darkening, it seems as if the umbrellas being held aloft by tour guides might soon come in handy.

'Here we go,' Caroline says.

They stop at the edge of a small crowd enjoying the sporadic antics of an elaborately made-up 'robot'. It squawks whenever someone poses for a selfie, and each time someone drops a coin into the small box at its feet it moves a little.

They watch the routine for a few minutes, then, a little too loudly, Caroline says, 'Do you think if we stuck a fiver in his box he might piss off and get himself a proper job?'

Heather grins, shushing, then starts to laugh at the look of fierce disapproval from a woman standing next to them. The woman shakes her head and leads her two entranced toddlers away.

'Seriously,' Caroline says.

The robot emits a squawk of disappointment when the first, fat drops of rain begin to discolour the ground around him. Umbrellas go up quickly and the crowd starts to disperse.

'Shall we get something to eat?' Caroline asks, as they begin to move.

'I'm a bit skint,' Heather says.

'It's on me.'

'That's not fair.'

'Not a problem,' Caroline says. 'It's amazing how much you can save when you live on raw carrots and lettuce leaves all week.'

They pick up speed as the rain gets heavier, Heather moving ahead, then slowing to wait for Caroline to catch her up.

'I could murder a Big Mac.'

'Me too, but I thought—'

'That's the whole point.' Caroline waves the concern away. She's walking as fast as she can, but other pedestrians are going past as though she's standing still. 'If I eat like a rabbit all week, I can treat myself at the weekend.'

When the real downpour begins, they follow others into the station to wait it out. Caroline pushes through the soaking crowd and manages to find them a space against the wall.

'Bollocks.' Her shirt, patterned with flowers, is plastered to her arms and chest and she starts to pick at the sopping material. Heather is trying not to stare at the black bra that is clearly visible beneath; the sturdy cups she could fit her head inside.

'Doesn't matter.' Heather smiles and drags fingers through her hair. 'It's only water.'

Caroline stares at her. 'What's the matter with you today?'

'How d'you mean?'

'You sure you haven't taken a few too many happy pills?'

Heather shrugs. 'Just in a good mood, that's all. Any reason I shouldn't be?'

'No, but your mood's not usually *this* good.' Caroline leans back against the wall. 'And, you know, the way the last session ended.'

'A lot can happen in a week,' Heather says.

Caroline turns to look at her.

'I met up with Tony.'

'What does that mean? "Met up."'

'He reckons I'd make a good therapist, so we had lunch and he talked to me about it, that's all.'

Caroline waits and watches Heather's eyes dart away from her own. 'That's *so* not all.'

'We had lunch, then we just walked about for a while.'

'Did something happen?' It's clear that Caroline has forgotten all about being drenched and uncomfortable.

'Yeah, if you like.' Heather wraps arms around herself, clutches her wet suede sleeves, unable to keep the smile from her face. 'Something.'

'What?'

Pedestrians are still crowding into the station to avoid the rain and, as the crowd shoves and thickens, a man is pushed against Caroline. She swears at him and pushes back, hard. Ignoring the muttered apology, she turns to look at Heather again, waiting to be told.

. . . THEN

There is still an empty chair in the circle, but Tony insists they begin. Heather asks again if they can wait a while longer, but Tony refuses, reminding her that group members need to arrive on time.

'It's not fair though,' she says. 'It's my turn this week . . . you know, to talk about shame, and I really wanted him to be here. I made such a big deal about him doing it.'

'You didn't pressure him,' Tony says. 'It looked like support to me.'

'That's right,' Diana says. 'And remember what you got for your trouble.'

'Outside the group, I mean. I nagged him.'

'Rules are rules,' Robin says.

Tony nods and says, 'I'm sorry.' The truth is that he has been half expecting this after the way Chris had left at the end of the last session. The rage and the blame. That slammed door had felt fairly permanent.

'I think you're the only one who's bothered,' Caroline says. 'That he's not here.'

'Yeah, because it's my fault.'

'That's stupid.'

'Has anyone spoken to him since last week?' Tony asks.

Heads are shaken, but it's only Heather's gesture that seems sorrowful.

'OK. Well, I'll call him again tomorrow,' Tony says. 'But for now, we need to crack on. Heather?'

'I'm not sure I want to do it now.'

Robin sighs, loudly.

'Well, it's up to you, of course.'

'You're being stupid,' Caroline says.

'Shut up,' Heather says.

'Nobody else made a fuss.'

'You haven't even done it yet.'

'Why don't you tell him in private, if it's so bloody important?'

'Caroline's right,' Diana says.

Tony raises a finger and waits until they are all looking at him. 'Look, it's Heather's call, ultimately, but whatever happens, I don't want this session to be all about the one member who isn't here. We're—'

All heads turn when the doorbell rings and all eyes follow Tony as he gets up and hurries from the room. Walking through the kitchen towards the front door, he can hear Robin grumbling loudly behind him.

'Somebody wants to make an entrance . . . '

The bell rings again just as Tony opens the door and it only takes him a second to see what's happening. Before he can say anything, Chris is already past him, moving quickly, and by the time Tony gets back to the conservatory, he is sitting on his chair. Arms folded. Good as gold.

Tony remains standing. He takes a breath, then steps across until he is standing next to Chris. He says, 'You can't stay, you know that.'

Chris lifts his head slowly, says, 'This is my chair.'

Tony looks down at him, well aware there's little point in asking the usual question. Chris has clearly not had a good week, a good day, a good hour.

357

Eyes like glass beads and the smack-sweat stink.

'Has she done her bit, yet?' Chris waves a hand in Heather's direction. His words are slow, if not quite slurred, but the effort involved in preventing it is apparent. 'I didn't want to miss her *amazing* story, whatever the hell it is.'

'Jesus, Chris,' Heather says.

Chris suddenly leans so far forward that it looks as if he might tumble off his chair. He says, '*Jesus*, Heather.'

'You need to go,' Tony says.

Chris puts a hand on the floor to steady himself, then uses it to push himself back upright. 'This is my chair, though,' he says.

Robin stands up. 'Do you want me to give you a hand, Tony?'

'Yes, for God's sake throw him out,' Diana says.

'It's fine.' Tony leans closer as Chris's head starts to drop. 'You know how this works, Chris. I can't allow you to be part of the session when you're like this. So, just leave and I'll talk to you tomorrow, OK?'

'Well, I think he should be thrown out permanently,' Diana says.

'That's not how it works,' Tony says, sharply.

'Just look at him.'

'The tendency to relapse is part and parcel of the disorder, OK? It is not a failure. Yes, I need to remove him from this session, but no, I'm certainly not going to give up on him, in the same way that I wouldn't give up on any of you.'

Diana says something else, and then Robin chips in and for a minute or two, they talk about Chris as if he isn't there, which to all intents and purposes is the situation, until finally Heather raises her voice.

'Please let him stay.'

Tony looks at her.

'Just for . . . ten minutes, all right? Just let me say what I need to say and then he can go.' She looks at the others in the group. 'I mean, as long as he doesn't open his mouth, as long as he doesn't contribute to the session in any way, then what's the harm? I just need him to be here so I can do this, that's all. Can't we just bend the rules, just a bit, you know? Ten minutes, that's all, I swear, and then I don't care if you kick him out on his stupid junkie arse.' Now she looks back to Tony. 'Please, Tony. I wouldn't ask if it wasn't important.'

Tony thinks for a few seconds, then slowly shakes his head, but it's more in disbelief than refusal. He says, 'It's up to the rest of the group.'

Heather looks across at Diana, because she knows that's where the greatest resistance is. 'I'm asking, Diana. Just ten minutes.'

Diana takes a moment and is about to speak when Caroline says, 'Oh, I couldn't care less. Let's just get on with it.'

'Only until Heather's finished her story,' Robin says. 'And as long as he keeps his mouth shut.'

Diana sits back slowly and flashes a thin smile in Heather's direction. 'It's your funeral.'

Tony says, 'All right then,' and sits down. He's by no means sure that Chris is even aware what's happening, but he repeats the ground rules to him anyway, a little louder than he might otherwise. He tells him that if he is carrying any drugs on him he must take them outside and leave them there, but Chris shakes his head. Then, just as Tony is reaching down to pick up his notebook, Chris looks up suddenly.

He stares at Heather and appears to focus.

Tony sets his notebook a little nervously on his lap. He takes a last long look at Chris, then gives Heather the nod.

. . . THEN

'It was ten years ago, maybe a bit more . . . I was in my last year at college, anyway. Trying to make up for the lack of work I'd done in the first two years, same as most people, I suppose. Trying to salvage something.' Heather aims for a smile, but it's there and gone; the blaze of headlights speeding past, then only darkness again. 'I don't think I would have, mind you, even if things hadn't turned out the way they did and I'd stuck at it . . . but there was no chance, in the end.' She shakes her head. 'Some people always manage to shoot themselves in the foot, right?

'I met this man.' She says it quickly, like it's the hardest bit; the step over the edge. 'And I'm deliberately saying "man" because back then I certainly wouldn't have thought of myself as a "woman". I was still a girl, still felt like a girl anyway, and I normally knocked about with lads. So, I met this man . . . older, but you'd probably worked that bit out already. You know, a *lot* older, twenty-odd years, but all I can tell you is that it didn't feel like it, because we clicked, simple as that and it never seemed to matter. He was married, and you'd probably worked that out as well.'

She pulls a face – *how stupid was I?* – but when she turns her head in the direction of the other group members, she is unable to look directly at anyone. She fixes instead on the spaces between Robin and Caroline, Chris and Diana. 'That did, matter, obviously, even if I told myself back then that it didn't. He said that it didn't and I believed him. Even though he always went back to his wife and kids every night, I thought that he was basically just waiting for the right time to make the move, you know? I never doubted for one second that we'd end up together, that one day I'd be the wife and we'd have kids and all the sleazy stuff was just a process we had to go through to get there. Afternoons in hotels, the back of his car, the usual.'

She searches for words. 'A necessary ... evil.

'I swear that none of that stuff *felt* sleazy though, not back then. Because I was in love with him. You really need to believe that if what happened later on is going to make any sense. It had never been like that with anyone before, never has been since. Wherever we had to meet, it was perfect, you know?

'I'd've done whatever he wanted, fucked him in shit, it didn't matter.'

She closes her eyes for a second or two; momentary regret or some remembered excitement that still shocks her, it's impossible to tell. Her fingers are wrapped around the edge of her seat by the time she opens her eyes again and says, 'Now, you're all pretty smart and at least this bit of the story is fairly predictable, so you won't exactly be gobsmacked to discover that he didn't leave his wife and we didn't ride off into the sunset. He didn't love me as much I loved him, simple as that.' She hesitates. 'Well ... maybe he did, who knows, but he certainly wasn't brave enough to be with me long term. At the time it just felt like he'd had his bit of fun then ended it and settled for an easy life.'

Her eyes narrow. 'The path of least resistance.

'And I was ... destroyed.' She shrugs, helpless. 'I know that sounds stupidly melodramatic, like maybe I was just immature and maybe I was, but God's honest truth, there isn't another word for how it made me feel. What he'd done to me.' She winces as she swallows. 'I didn't eat, I didn't wash, I didn't ... get out of bed for Christ knows how long. I thought about doing all sorts of stupid things, you know? I emptied pills into my hand and stared at them. I froze my tits off standing on bridges. I looked at all those freaky websites that tell you exactly how to make a noose and what to do so you won't be found in time ... and then one day something inside just shut down.' She clicks her fingers, studies the chewed-down nails. 'Like a switch had been turned off ... or on, maybe.

'So, I went another way.'

She leans forward slightly and begins to talk a little faster. 'There was someone else,' she says. Another big step and now she has momentum and it can't be stopped. 'And this one *was* a lad ...

'He wasn't at college, he already had a job, but he was the same age as me and we'd been seeing each other quite a bit before all this. He was great, you know, sweet and all that ... but the truth is I always knew he liked me more than I liked him. All the same, I was happy to let him take me out, buy me stuff, you know? Happy enough to shag him when I felt like being generous, and let him take me on holiday ... and then, when I met my married man, I dropped him like a hot brick. I was a selfish cow and I chucked him, and I know he felt every bit as awful then as I did when the bloke I dumped him for finally dumped me.

'So ... when that switch was thrown, I called him. I called my lovely, dependable ex-boyfriend, and he told me to come round and I knew straight away that he still felt exactly the same. He was just so happy I was there, that it was his shoulder I wanted to cry on.'

Heather takes a breath and holds it, and it looks as if she would welcome that shoulder, *any* shoulder now, but she keeps pushing forward.

'I cried, because it was easy enough ...

'... and when I'd finished I told him the man I'd been seeing had raped me. I told him that I'd been trying to leave and he'd raped me ...

and I couldn't go to the police, *please don't make me go to the police*, because I didn't want everyone to know, and I felt dirty, and there was nobody else I *could* tell except him. I told him every sick detail, and I made it as nasty as I could, to where I could see it was like punches landing, and he was pretty much in bits by the time I'd finished.

'By then, it was almost like I believed it myself.

'I pressed the button, then I sat there and watched him get angrier, working himself up until he was kicking at the walls and smashing stuff in his flat. Telling me he'd sort everything, that he was going to make the bastard pay for it, and I'm going, *No, you can't, don't be stupid*, but only because I knew that's what I was supposed to say. I knew he wasn't really listening and that he'd already made his mind up to teach the bloke a lesson.

'Which of course is exactly what he did.

'He beat him to death two nights later outside a pub.' She gnaws her bottom lip for a few seconds. She slides her feet forward until her training shoes are perfectly parallel. 'He had an iron bar or something in his coat pocket, and the man I'd falsely accused of rape, because he'd had the nerve to go back to his family, had an abnormally thin skull. Shitty luck for all concerned, as it turned out.

'Well, everyone except me.

'He never mentioned my name, not once. Never told anyone why he'd done it. Never said a word, even after they'd sent him to prison.' Now she looks at Tony, the first member of the circle with whom she's made eye contact since she began. When she speaks again, her voice is steady and low; drained of colour. 'He's still in prison, while I sit here every Monday night feeling sorry for myself, because my benefit money's a day late, or I want a better flat, or I didn't have any real friends to come to my stupid birthday party.'

There is one more half-hearted attempt at a smile, but it's not even close. She straightens in her chair and one hand flutters up at her knee, just for a second or two.

She says, 'That's it.'

*

363

Tony leans to lay down his notebook. He takes a long swig from his water bottle, then sits up and looks around. Nobody seems keen to speak, but the circle is crackling with energy and none of it is positive.

Shock, condemnation, fury.

Even Tony is struggling to formulate the simple and standard *thank you*, to acknowledge the courage necessary to say ... what Heather had said, but he is saved the trouble when Chris lurches from his chair.

The others watch as Chris moves slowly across the circle towards Heather; casual, deliberate. He looks a lot steadier than he did when he first came in, though the aimless smile is nowhere to be seen.

Tony stands up, says Chris's name.

Heather shakes her head and lifts a hand to let Tony and everyone else know there's no need to step in. That she's been expecting whatever is coming and is fine with it. It's only when Chris is standing over her, his legs pressed against hers, that she turns her face away just a little and closes her eyes. Flinches.

The circle holds its breath.

There seems no real effort involved, no obvious movement of the head or neck, and it's only when Robin emits a groan of disgust that Tony sees the thin string of brown spittle dropping from Chris's mouth on to the sleeve of Heather's jacket. Now he moves across, but Chris is on his way out before Tony can get there; walking towards the door as though he's simply noticed he's in the wrong room. Raising a hand to waggle his fingers *goodbye*, without turning round.

Tony fetches a tissue from the box beneath his chair. He hands it to Heather, then sits down again and looks at his watch, pretending to ignore the sound of the front door closing. Nice and gently, this time.

'I wouldn't normally do this,' he says. 'But maybe it wouldn't hurt to have a short break. Just a few minutes.'

Diana says, 'No,' as she gets to her feet. 'I think I've had quite enough for one night.'

'You're not the only one.' Robin stands too.

'Well, it's up to you,' Tony says, though he is not particularly happy at the group's choosing to cut the session short.

Caroline is reaching for her bag and umbrella, the coat on the back of her chair. She looks across at Heather who is still trying to remove Chris's spittle from her jacket; wiping and wiping. 'You're full of surprises, aren't you?'

'We should definitely carry on with this though.' Tony stands up. 'Next week, OK?' He watches Diana and Robin as they move together towards the kitchen, Caroline as she hurries to follow them. 'Plenty to talk about, I think ... '

When Heather finally looks up, she doesn't seem surprised or disappointed to see that the others have gone. She hugs her jacket to her chest.

'That went well,' she says.

Tony says, 'I need to talk to you.'

. . . NOW

Tanner could see that Tony De Silva was enjoying his morning; engrossed in the Saturday *Guardian* at a table outside the Crocodile café, a cigarette on the go, an espresso in front of him. He didn't see her until she was close enough to smell the coffee, pulling a chair across from an adjacent table, and it was clear from his expression that he wasn't enjoying himself any longer.

'I only need five minutes,' she said.

He folded his paper and laid it down. He reached for his coffee cup.

'Do a lot of you smoke?' Tanner asked. 'Ex-addicts?' She nodded towards the ashtray which contained three or four butts. 'I always thought you had to give up any kind of drug.'

'I don't really,' De Silva said. 'It's just a treat. A ritual, that's all.'

'Harder to give up than heroin, I heard.'

'Like I said, I don't really smoke.'

A waitress stopped at the table to ask Tanner if she wanted anything. Tanner asked for a glass of tap water. 'I tried cigarettes once,' she said. 'Didn't like them. Not much of a drinker either. I suppose some people just aren't wired that way.'

'You're close to someone who is though, right?'

'Excuse me?'

'The last time we spoke. I got the impression you were asking certain questions on someone else's behalf.' De Silva laid his cup down and leaned forward a little. 'Your partner, maybe? Wife? Girlfriend?'

Tanner smiled, though something had begun to jump in her gut. She guessed that De Silva was not in the habit of dispensing therapy free of charge outside cafés on a Saturday morning. It was an assertion of a certain sort of power, she understood that; an attempt to gain control of his situation.

She wondered if she'd make a decent therapist herself . . .

'I wanted you to know that we're almost there,' Tanner said. 'With the Heather Finlay case.'

'That's good to hear.'

'I gather you're starting the group up again.'

'Yeah, I thought it was about time, and my other clients are keen to carry on.'

Tanner nodded. 'Good. Well, I'd like you to do me a favour and imagine that group sitting there in a circle again. The five of you, next week or whenever it is. Chris Clemence, Robin Joffe, Diana Knight, Caroline Armitage and yourself. All of you sitting around in that lovely conservatory of yours, sharing and caring and supporting one another . . . and I want you to think about Heather Finlay rotting in her flat. I want you to think about her father laying what's left of her to rest. Will you do that?'

De Silva shook his head. 'Do you seriously think we won't remember Heather? That we won't talk about her . . . honour her memory and the place she had in the group?'

'That sounds very nice. Very . . . spiritual.'

'You don't think we care?'

'Up to a point, yes.'

'I'm not sure why you're being so sarcastic.'

'I just want you to know that when I picture that group, it's because I'm certain that somebody in that circle is responsible for Heather's

367

death. One of those people who'll be sitting there "honouring her memory".'

'Sorry, but I must have missed something,' De Silva said.

'It was all here in your notes.' Tanner removed the sheaf of papers from her bag. 'When we eventually got them.'

'What was?'

'Well, I should start by saying that they were a bit vague, but perhaps you were in a hurry, or distracted.' De Silva started to say something. 'Never mind.' She flicked through the pages. 'Funny that you hadn't mentioned anything about asking Heather to look for another therapist.'

'Sorry?'

'That's in your notes, too,' Tanner said. 'But you never said anything about it when we first talked about her.'

'I was rather more concerned with the fact that she was dead.'

'Why was that? I mean, why did you not want her to come to the sessions any more?'

De Silva pointed. 'As you said, it's all in there. I felt that by the end of that final session there were certain . . . tensions within the group that could only be eliminated if she wasn't part of it any more. That's all.'

Tanner nodded. 'Never needed to in the end though, did you?'

'Never needed to what?'

'Ask her to leave.'

De Silva hesitated. Then: 'Sadly, no,' he said. 'I didn't.'

Tanner went back to looking at the notes. 'So, as I understand it, in that last session Heather confessed to being responsible for one person's death and for somebody else being sent to prison.' She put the papers down and looked at him. 'That's two lots of brothers, sons, fathers, husbands. That's a lot of people who might have wanted Heather to pay for what she did, even after all this time.'

'And it just so happens one of them is in my Monday night recovery group. Is that what you're saying? It's a bit of a stretch, isn't it?'

'Don't think we haven't been looking elsewhere,' Tanner said. 'She wasn't killed by a stranger.'

'Maybe I could start the next session by just asking everyone.' The therapist stubbed out his cigarette and immediately drew a new one from the packet. '"Nice to see you all again. Now, as we're all being honest with one another, hands up if any of you killed Heather." Would that be helpful?'

'Now who's being sarcastic?'

De Silva sat back in his chair, hard. 'Well . . .'

Tanner took her water and thanked the waitress. She took a drink. 'It's funny, you getting so irate at the idea that you might not care. The fact is that up to now you've had a strange way of showing it.'

De Silva broke off lighting his cigarette. 'For God's sake, do you mean my reluctance to divulge information?'

'It certainly wasn't helpful.'

'Do we really need to go over this again?'

Tanner shook her head. 'Listen, obviously you care about Heather, I know that. I mean how could you not?'

'Thank you.' He threw up his arms and lit his cigarette, relieved at finally getting blood from a stone.

'All that stuff you told me about empathy,' Tanner said. 'Listening to your clients, *guiding* them. I'd say it would be almost impossible not to get close to some of them. Or for them to get close to you.'

'There are boundaries, obviously.'

'Of course, but there must be . . . infatuations. Flirtation, I should imagine.'

'I suppose.'

She looked at him. 'More than that, sometimes?'

De Silva turned away, used the moment to catch the eye of the waitress and signal that he was ready for the bill. He said, 'Look, I'm really not sure where you're going with this, but I know it's got nothing to do with your investigation.' He smiled and licked his lips as he leaned across the table. 'Maybe you're borderline voyeuristic. I should imagine a lot of police officers are.'

Tanner smiled back, said he was probably right, then waved the notes. 'All right, let's get back to these.'

De Silva sat back; bored, or pretending to be. 'If we must.'

'Well, as I said, they're a bit vague, unfortunately. So, bearing in mind where we are with the case, it would be enormously helpful if you could tell me anything that Heather said that night that isn't in these notes. I'm sure there are things that weren't particularly relevant from a therapeutic point of view, that you never even thought of putting in your notes, but which would really help me a lot.' She waited. 'Look, I think we're way past the whole confidentiality thing, considering everything I've been told by members of the group already.'

'Well, I don't know what you've been told—'

'On top of which, look how easy it was for me to get these. Now, bearing in mind my genuine suspicions, I don't think I'd have any trouble persuading a judge that you telling me what you know was in the interests of public safety. *Making* you tell me, see what I mean? I'm sure you'd rather we had that information quickly, Mr De Silva.' Tanner reached into her bag for her notebook. 'Considering how close you were to Heather.'

De Silva waited until the waitress had handed him the bill and left. Enough time to look as though he was considering it.

Then he told her.

'That's as much as I can remember, anyway. It was a while ago.'

Putting her notebook away, Tanner thanked him and said she'd let him know if she needed anything else. He hadn't given her all that much in the end, but she felt like it might be enough. A name, a time frame. A detail or two that gave her somewhere to start.

When Tanner stood up, she said, 'Just so you know . . . the someone else, those questions I was asking.' She waited until he was looking at her. 'I'm dealing with it.'

... THEN

Heather follows Tony into the kitchen, stands and watches him make his fancy coffee. She waits to see if he's going to offer her one, but right now he doesn't seem keen to say anything. Like he's building up to something. He's making her nervous and she guesses that now might not be a good time to move up behind him, wrap her arms around his waist.

Anyway, is his wife not around somewhere?

She's still trying to process what happened, the reactions to her story and why the session ended so early. She knows perfectly well that what she said in the circle was shocking: how could it not be? She had not been expecting that silence though, the weight of it and such desperation to get away. Like they might catch something. What Chris did afterwards was hideous, no ... *humiliating*, but at least there's a simple enough explanation. People that high are capable of anything and how can she, of all people, not forgive a junkie?

The others, though? And now, Tony's being weird and when he finally turns round to look at her, it's obvious the one person she was hoping to get some support from isn't in a very supportive mood.

'That wasn't very . . . cool,' he says. 'In the session.'

'Cool?'

'What you said.'

Heather steps towards him and doesn't miss the fact that he takes half a step back. She feels like she's back at school, being told off for something that wasn't her fault. The unfairness of it starts to burn and bubble up. She says, 'Have you got any idea what it took for me to tell everyone that? I'm still shaking—'

'Not your story.'

She blinks. 'What, then?'

'Before, when you asked me to let Chris stay.'

'I don't understand.'

'Which was a huge mistake. For him as much as anyone.'

'I wanted him there to hear it,' Heather says. 'It must have been obvious how important that was to me.'

'It was the way you asked.' He looks at her, as though she should know exactly what he means. He sighs when she fails to respond. 'It wasn't just you asking me as a therapist, you know? You were appealing to something else, to . . . whatever's between us. It was like you were trying to twist my arm because of what happened the other night, like that should be a reason for me to let you get what you wanted. Like you expected it.'

'I needed Chris to be there.' Heather is trying to sound calm, rational; someone who would never dream of using the emotional blackmail Tony seems to be accusing her of. 'I mean yeah, I hoped you'd care enough to see that.'

'You persuaded me to act against my professional judgement.'

'I'm sorry,' she says, and now she knows that touching him, trying to, is probably not a good idea. 'I didn't mean to.'

He nods, and just for a second or two Heather thinks that's the end of it. That the teacher's just going to let her off with a warning.

'We can't see each other again,' he says. 'And it's probably a good idea if you find another therapist.'

She stares at him.

'I can help with that ... recommend someone.'

'Because I asked you for something?'

He looks away, then half turns to reach for his coffee. He picks it up, puts it down. 'Because I love my wife.'

She can't do anything about the laugh that bursts from her like a cough, or the taste it leaves in her mouth. 'Oh ... right. Yeah. That was pretty obvious the other night when you had your fingers in my knickers.'

'Don't—'

'It was just what I was thinking, when I was on my knees and you were moaning and groaning. Christ, this bloke really loves his wife, I thought. Only reason I didn't say anything at the time was because I had my mouth full.'

'It was a mistake, all right?'

'No,' she says. '*This* is a mistake.'

'Please, Heather ...'

She steps back then starts to walk slowly round the island, stabbing a finger against the granite. 'You really think you can do what you did and just trot back to your missus? I mean, for real? You think that now you've got into my pants you can just stand there and talk about your shitting wife and tell me to find another therapist? Like we're not quite ... hitting it off or something?'

'It's the best thing for both of us, I really think that.'

'Because you're the therapist and I'm just the stupid ex-junkie who let you pull her into that alley?'

'You didn't need pulling anywhere.'

'Well, sorry, but you don't get to do that. I think you need to seriously reconsider, because the last thing you want is me telling your wife about what happened. A quick phone call, maybe, or an email. Actually, it would be far better in person ... is she here now? No, course she isn't, or you wouldn't be brave enough to do any of this.'

'Have you finished?'

'Maybe I'll take her there.' Heather nods, pleased, like it's a stroke of genius. 'You know, show her the scene of the crime. Maybe I'll tell her how much you pestered me and pawed at me and how eventually, when I told you to leave me alone, you got rough and did what you wanted anyway.'

'Hold on—'

Heather isn't listening. 'Maybe I'll show her that nice metal door you pushed me against, *forced* me against while you were trying to rip my knickers off, even when I was telling you to stop. Begging you to. Even when you were really hurting me.' She stops pacing and sits down on one of the leather barstools. She reaches for the lever to adjust the height, then waves at him, like someone spotting an old friend across a room. 'How's that sound?'

Tony nods, as though weighing it up, and the nod becomes more confident. The assessment of someone who prides himself on his ability to read people; to empathise when it really matters. He says, 'I don't believe you.'

Heather jumps to her feet and jabs a finger towards the conservatory. 'Were you not *listening* in there? I wasn't making that up for anyone's fucking amusement.'

Tony pales, reaches behind to wrap fingers around the edge of the worktop. 'You'd seriously do that? You'd make something up to destroy my marriage? You'd ruin my career?'

'You do not get to do this to me.'

'You're not that person,' Tony says.

'I *deal* with shit like this.'

'I don't . . . believe you're that person any more.'

Heather says, 'Fair enough,' and starts walking towards the kitchen door. Tony can't see the smile when she hears him sigh with what sounds like relief, so she glances back over her shoulder to give him a good look. Then she closes the kitchen door and leans back against it. She takes off her jacket and lays it across a table near the door.

Tony takes a few small steps towards her. He holds out his arms. He says, 'For God's sake, Heather. My wife will be back at some point. My daughter.'

'Obviously,' she says. 'They live here.'

'Please . . .'

Heather doesn't move.

...THEN

It's busy in the pub and their usual table is taken, but they've managed to snag a spot in a corner near the toilets. They're pushed a little closer together than they would otherwise have been, but the huddle suits them; the conspiratorial air of it. Though all three seemed lost for words only fifteen minutes before, they suddenly have plenty to say.

Now, they are fighting one another to be heard.

'Well, that changes everything, I'd say.' Caroline looks meaningfully at Robin. 'In terms of what she clearly is and isn't capable of, if you see what I'm saying.'

'I know,' Robin says.

Diana looks from one to the other. 'What?'

'Looks like Heather's now clear favourite on the blackmail front.'

Diana looks shocked, but not for very long. 'I never thought of that.' She sips her mineral water. 'Makes perfect sense.'

'She's gambling again,' Caroline says.

'Ah . . .'

'Back on the scratch cards.'

'I got a second letter,' Robin says.

They look at him.

'A couple of days ago.' He nods, slowly. 'The price has gone up.'

'You've got to do something.' Diana puts a hand on his arm. 'You need to confront her.'

'I will,' Robin says, but it looks as though he is still thinking about the story they have all so recently heard. 'It's the false accusation I can't get over though,' he says. 'What happened afterwards sounds almost like a horrible accident, as though it couldn't be helped ... but to say a man has raped you just to get some sort of stupid revenge ...'

'It's unforgivable,' Diana says.

'You can call it an accident all you like,' Caroline says.

'It's not what I would call it.'

'It still wouldn't have happened if she hadn't made the story up.'

'She *wanted* it to happen.'

'That was the plan.'

'I mean why tell him otherwise?' Diana looks at the others as though it's obvious. 'She said it herself, didn't she? She "pressed the button".'

'I've done some bad things myself.' Robin is swirling orange juice around in his glass, staring into it. 'We all have ... but nothing like *that*.'

'God, no,' Caroline says.

Diana puts a hand on Robin's arm. 'You did the things you're talking about *after* you started taking drugs.'

'Right,' Caroline says.

'Absolutely,' Diana says. 'She had no excuse.'

'To be that ... vindictive, though?' Robin's voice is low; that angry rolled 'r' coming out. 'To ruin lives like that.'

'You thought I was being harsh, didn't you?' Diana looks at Caroline. 'Talking about women with those sorts of morals. Women who target married men and their families.'

'Maybe a bit,' Caroline says.

'Yes, well. Now you see the damage they can do.'

377

Caroline nods.

Diana says, 'Vile,' and when she reaches for her water again, it's as though she needs it to take away the taste of something foul.

'Oh, here we go.' Caroline raises a hand, as if to hide behind it, and the others turn to see Chris coming across to the table.

Robin stands up.

'No, it's fine,' Diana says. 'He's got every right to be here. Tony's not turning his back on him, so we shouldn't either.'

Robin sits down again.

'Besides, back there, when she'd finished ... he only did what I'd wished I was brave enough to do.' Diana waves at Chris. 'I'd have spat in her face though.'

When Chris gets close, he grabs an empty chair from an adjoining table, pulls it across even when a man at the table tells him the chair is taken. Squeezing it in, Chris sits down next to Robin, and when the man comes over to remonstrate, Robin says, 'I'm sorry, but my friend's not feeling well.'

The man says, 'What?'

'This is my chair,' Chris says.

Robin raises a hand. 'Look, I'm a doctor and I promise you he needs to sit down.'

When the man has gone back to his table, Chris turns to Robin. 'Am I really your friend?' he asks.

'I hope so,' Robin says.

Caroline leans towards Chris. 'It's going to be all right.'

'You start again,' Diana says. 'Right?' She looks at the others who nod their support. 'You come back to the group next week and we'll all be there to help.'

'Not her though.' Chris jabs a finger, as though an invisible Heather is sitting among them.

Diana looks at Robin, who shrugs. 'Well, maybe we can talk to Tony about that.'

'It's all her fault.'

'It doesn't matter,' Caroline says.

'I was doing really well, you know? Sorting myself out. I was going to get a flat and everything.' Chris makes a fist and hits himself on the side of the head. 'She's so good at *persuading* people ... making them do things to keep her happy, and then they do them and everything falls apart.'

'It's OK,' Caroline says.

'She made me talk about my dad and then after I called Woody she set the police on me.'

Caroline says, 'I know,' though she really doesn't.

'You've got no idea what she's like.'

'Oh, I think we do,' Diana says.

'I was doing really well.' Chris is trying to look at each of them, struggling to focus. 'You know?' He seems pleased with their reactions, then confused when Diana, Robin and Caroline suddenly lean away from him at the same time. He's still struggling to formulate his next sentence when he feels the hand on his shoulder and hears Heather's voice.

'Chris ... I'm really glad you're here,' she says. 'Can we go somewhere and talk?'

It's like a surge of voltage shooting through him, and he's pushing back his chair and shouting almost immediately; glasses clattering and those around the table moving quickly to avoid the spillage.

'What, so you can tell me what a great thing I did again ... telling my bedtime story? Some more crap about how my pain isn't shameful? What about *this* pain?'

'Chris—'

'No, shut up.' He lurches again and another glass falls and rolls off the table. 'I hope tomorrow you wake up feeling like I did ... when you think about what you said tonight. Your stupid ... non-existent rape or whatever. I hope you feel empty and shit-scared and go scrounging around for some gear again. Come and talk to me then, OK? Because I'll happily jack you up myself ...'

By this time, one of the bar staff has come hurrying across. He has hands on Chris, trying to pull him away from the table as Diana and Robin apologise and gather bar towels to wipe away the mess.

'You need to get on your way, mate.'

'She put you up to this, did she?' Chris struggles to lunge at Heather. 'You grass me up again?'

'Come on, mate—'

'I'm *going* . . .'

They all watch Chris stagger away and out through the door, his phone already in his hand. Before he leaves, the barman asks if everyone is OK, but it's clearly as much of a warning as anything, and, when those at nearby tables have stopped gawping, Heather is left staring down at the empty chair. She moves to take it, then hesitates when she clocks the faces of the other three. Instead, she lifts an arm and uses her sleeve to wipe away the tears.

'Happy?' Diana asks.

Heather stares at her. Her mouth falls open.

'What kept you?' Caroline shakes her head, disgusted. 'Like I can't guess.'

Heather closes her eyes for a few seconds and her features tense as she struggles to contain what might be a scream or a sob. When she opens her eyes again, she manages to say, 'Any reason why I shouldn't sit down?'

'It depends,' Diana says. 'If you're looking for support, it's probably not a good idea. You know, if you're waiting for us all to tell you how brave you were this evening. How . . . *inspirational*.'

'I don't understand.'

'Oh, for pity's sake.'

'You and I do need to talk though,' Robin says. 'I really didn't want to think it was you, but now I feel rather stupid for ever thinking it wasn't.'

'Wasn't what?'

'It's a bit late to play the innocent,' Diana says. 'Don't you think?'

When Heather looks from one to the other, the hostility on their faces is evident enough to force her away from the table. She pulls her bag up on to her shoulder and clutches it. When she says,

'Sorry,' a second or two before turning for the door, it's cracked and whispery.

Robin, Diana and Caroline watch her leave and Diana says, 'It's not us she should be saying sorry to,' and they don't bother to acknowledge the man from the adjacent table, when he steps across to take his chair back.

'Fucking junkies,' he says.

. . . THEN

Group Session: March 22nd

An unfortunate start to the session when Chris arrived, clearly under the influence of drugs. Asked him to leave but was persuaded to let him stay by Heather on condition that he did not speak. Rest of the group agreed, though this was certainly against my better judgement.

Heather told her shame story and I can't recall a reaction as profound from the others in the group. A truly shocking confession involving a false accusation of rape which unfortunately led to the murder of a man with whom she'd been involved and the subsequent imprisonment of his killer.

The session ended prematurely after Chris exhibited what could easily be interpreted as threatening behaviour towards Heather. Diana, Robin and Caroline seemed happy to leave early.

In light of events at the session, I must consider whether I should now advise Heather to seek out a different therapist. Her story seems to have alienated others in the group and I will definitely need to focus on Chris in forthcoming weeks if his relapse is not to be long term. Heather has been an important member of the group, but her continued presence may be counter-productive from this point on.

A shame, but I believe that such action is justified and would be in the best interests of the group as a whole.

Tony closes the file on his computer then sits and thinks for a few minutes. He looks at his watch, then checks his phone to see if Nina has sent a message.

Nothing.

He walks slowly downstairs, stopping at the bottom to glance towards the kitchen – as though he's afraid that Heather might still be there – before trudging into the empty sitting room. He drops on to one of the deep cushions and lies back.

There's an open fashion magazine on the coffee table in front of him, an empty cup and a pair of Nina's glasses. He reaches for the glasses and starts cleaning them with the bottom of his T-shirt.

You think . . . you can just stand there and talk about your shitting wife . . .

Heather had stood there for no more than ten minutes in the end. Staring at him from the kitchen door and saying nothing, like some silent, bunny-boiling . . . harbinger. Like she was just happy to watch him suffer and let it sink in.

The threat, the solemn promise to tear his life apart.

It wasn't until several minutes after that, when Tony had closed the office door behind him and begun writing his notes, that he had finally stopped shaking.

He puts the glasses back on the table, wondering how difficult it would be to pull out of the tour he has lined up in a few months' time. Yes, the rock star will probably throw his toys out of the pram and sulk for a while, but he'll get over it and all Tony can think about is how good it would be to take Nina away somewhere instead. Maybe Nina *and* Emma, if his daughter wants to come of course and if the dates work with school. They need to spend some time together as a family, they need to reconnect.

On second thoughts, it might be better if it was just the two of them. He wants to show Nina that she's far more important to him than any of his clients. He wants to do something which will signal a fresh start, usher in a new chapter, whatever.

He wants . . . her. He knows now that, above all else, he wants his wife and his daughter. He wants his house and his car and his job.

Assuming Heather Finlay lets him keep them.

He'd told her that he didn't believe she'd go through with it. He'd faced her down and told her she wasn't the same person any more, the person who'd done such terrible things all those years ago. He knows he'd been trying to convince himself as much as her that she'd abandoned that rage a long time ago.

Now, he's not quite so confident.

Could the feelings she once clearly had for him turn into something else that quickly? His own had, after all; on a sixpence. It was only a few nights since he'd been lying in bed with Nina, surreptitiously bringing his hand up from beneath the sheets to sniff his fingers.

Christ . . .

What had she said when she'd been telling her story? *Like a switch had been turned off.*

He stretches his legs out in front of him then kicks the empty cup from the table. He shouts in frustration as it rolls, unbroken, across the floor. He had wanted it to smash, but now he can't quite bring himself to pick it up and throw it.

I went another way, she had said.

Tony knows that, as things stand, Heather can do anything she wants and that short of telling Nina himself, he's completely helpless.

He's rigid with fear and with fury. His hands are balled tight into fists at his side.

He reaches for his phone and sends Nina a text message.

Asks her if she knows what time she'll be home.

. . . THEN

Heather paces her flat.

She moves from bedroom to living room and back, smacking her hand against the walls, talking to herself. She walks to the window and lays her forehead against the cool pane, but the headache continues to build; the pressure. She turns and grabs a chair, stands on it and reaches up to tear down the HAPPY BIRTHDAY banner that has been there since the party.

The party she threw for *them*.

It's such a strange feeling, being so angry and so sad at the same time. Being this confused . . .

She's upset that Chris blames her for relapsing, for the state he's got himself in, but she understands it, at least. She knows that he's just lashing out and that when he's sorted himself out he'll realise that none of it is her fault. The Chris who spat on her, who flew at her in the pub, is not the Chris she knows. The pearly queen she loves.

The others, though?

Diana doesn't need much excuse to get on her high horse. Heather had half expected it, had seen the reaction – the pursed lips and the icy stare – as soon as she'd mentioned the married man. Caroline is just tagging along because she doesn't want to feel left out and because she's clearly pissed off because of what had happened with Tony. The business with Robin is still a mystery, though. She's been racking her brains since she walked out of the pub and it's driving her mad.

What the hell is she supposed to have done?

She can't get the picture out of her head, the way the three of them had looked up at her, back there in the pub. Judging and passing sentence. Wiping their hands of her, like all those things they'd shared and been through together were worth nothing.

Like she was worth nothing.

She's as furious with herself, of course, as she is with any of them. Tony had only done what she'd known he would do, even while she was with him in that alley. She's been stupid, simple as that, and though she knows she had every right to react angrily, she's horrified and ashamed at the things she said to him after the session. That stuff about his wife, for heaven's sake.

She's not that person any more, Tony was bang on about that, at least.

She'll call him, she decides, when she's calmed down a little. She'll call and tell him she's sorry, that she didn't mean any of it.

She's standing in her kitchen and the screwed-up mess of kitchen towel in her hand is getting soggier by the minute. She's not even sure why she's crying any more, or who for.

She walks across to where the three clip-frames are fixed on the wall near the door. All those stars and smiley faces. She looks at them, then reaches up and takes down the middle one.

You are not alone.

It's ridiculous, she decides, thinking something like that – writing the words out, nice and neat and putting it on the wall so she can look at it – can help. It's just childish, when the people who really should be helping can be so cruel.

She's never felt so alone.

She carries the frame across to the bin, but can't quite bring herself to drop it in, and she has just hung it back on its wonky nail when the doorbell rings. She reaches up to straighten it, but the bell rings again, so she hurries towards the door instead, pressing the kitchen towel to her eyes.

Making the effort.

The tears come again when she sees who it is; as she says, 'I'm really glad you've come.'

Before she can open it fully, the door is pushed into her and she struggles to stay on her feet as Chris rushes past her.

Raging, roaring, out of it.

... NOW

'Having looked through everything you've put together, Nic, on balance I think you're probably right. It could well be down to one of the Monday night lot.'

Tanner had worked with Martin Ditchburn long enough to know there was a major 'but' coming. She'd known from the moment he'd called her into his office having reviewed the case file. It wasn't as if she'd been expecting him to uncork a bottle, but like most coppers – even the ones occupying the senior ranks – he normally allowed himself a moment or two to relish a good result.

When they had one.

The 'probably' didn't sound good for a start.

'Here's the thing though . . . ' Ditchburn said.

So, not a 'but'. A 'here's the thing'. At least he was doling out the disappointment in fresh and interesting ways.

'If it *is* someone in that therapy group, and I'm including the therapist in this, I really wouldn't have the faintest idea where to start.' He opened the file in front of him. 'No shortage of possible motives, I'll grant you that.'

Tanner said, 'Sir.'

'Clemence seemed to blame Heather Finlay for falling off the wagon . . . Joffe thought she was blackmailing him and De Silva was giving her one.' He shook his head and turned a page. 'Then there's the possibility that we're looking at a revenge killing.'

'A strong possibility, I'd say.'

'OK, let's assume you're right, and we go down that road. It's really not going to be as simple as looking at each member of the group, finding out if they had a relative or a close friend who was killed or sent to prison ten years ago, is it?' He didn't wait for an answer. 'Someone who's spent ten years waiting to do this will have put the work in and they won't have made it easy. I'm guessing new life, completely new identity. They'll have made sure there's nothing for us to find.'

'Agreed,' Tanner said. 'That's why I think we'd have more luck trying to identify that original offence. Find out who Heather accused of raping her and who got sent down for killing him.'

'Sounds fine, but what have we actually got?' Once again, Tanner answered his own question. 'We've got a murder committed ten years ago. Maybe ten years, could be more, could be less. We've got a possible first name—'

'John.' Tanner nodded towards the file. 'Joanne Simmit, the college friend of Heather's, thought the ex-boyfriend was called John.'

'Like I said, a *possible* first name.'

'We only need to trace one of them,' Tanner said. 'That's all. Once we get one name we get the other. I'm convinced that whoever murdered Heather Finlay is connected to the man who died or the man who was sent to prison for killing him.'

'That's *all*?' Ditchburn closed the file again. 'This is exactly what I'm talking about. How many people were murdered approximately ten years ago, do you reckon?'

Tanner did not bother hazarding a guess.

'How many people called John, *if* he was called John, went to prison? And most importantly of all, where are we meant to be looking?'

'Well, Heather was at college in London.'

'Right, but there's no guarantee that's where it happened. This older bloke she was seeing might have worked in London, but he could have lived anywhere, and if he was killed near his home we've no idea where to even start.'

'It shouldn't be that hard.'

'Not if I had dozens of officers with nothing to do but sit in front of computers all day.' He sat back, held up his hands. 'I just don't have the resources for it, Nic. Nobody does.'

Tanner nodded.

'I know you think I just trot this stuff out, but seriously, it's a bloody nightmare. We've got to lose another three thousand officers in the next two years and that's just so we can keep standing still. In some places they're sending Neighbourhood Patrol cars out on serious response calls. Panda cars, for crying out loud, without bloody sirens.'

Tanner nodded again. 'So, I'm guessing there's no point asking if we can just put surveillance on everyone in the therapy group. For a couple of weeks?'

'Not even for a couple of hours.' Ditchburn closed the file and sat back. 'How many other cases are you currently working?'

'Three open, two coming to court in the next few weeks and that domestic that came in overnight.'

'So . . .'

Tanner reached down and lifted her bag on to her lap. 'That it, then?' She was not going to argue, because it was evident there was little point and because she was not that kind of officer. She simply wanted to confirm the situation. 'One for the cold case lot to have a crack at in eighteen months' time?'

'Well, that's it for you, certainly,' Ditchburn said.

'Sir?'

'We're not just letting this go, Nic. I really hope you didn't think that.' He looked at her. 'Doesn't matter to me if Heather Finlay was an ex-junkie or a bloody nun.'

'I know,' Tanner said. She'd worked with more than a few officers who prioritised victims according to social status and Ditchburn wasn't one of them.

'We're just moving it sideways, that's all … coming at it from a different angle.'

'What angle would that be?'

'Would you say that our killer is likely to carry on going to the therapy sessions?'

'Absolutely,' Tanner said. 'As you said, they're clearly not daft, so they know that suddenly leaving is only going to look suspicious.'

Ditchburn said, 'That's what I thought. Which is why we're putting someone in there with them.'

'In there as part of the group?'

'Well, not *us* … someone from one of the Northwest MITs.'

'Right.' Tanner was already running through the names of the officers she knew on Murder Investigation Teams in that part of the city.

'I've never come across this bloke and he's not an undercover officer as such, but apparently he's done something similar before. Lived on the streets a few years back, after three rough sleepers were killed.'

Tanner remembered the case, but could not recall the officer's name, if she ever knew it.

'So that's the plan,' Ditchburn said. 'Obviously De Silva won't be in on it as he's one of the people we'll be looking at. Our man goes in and gets his feet under the table, tells a few stories about his made-up addiction, and we wait and see if our killer slips up.'

'You never know,' Tanner said. She could see that Ditchburn was relieved when she stood up and stepped towards the door. 'The other things, though. Those days and nights in front of the computer. Any objection if I do some of that in my own time?'

Ditchburn was already studying an unrelated file. 'If it's in your own time I couldn't give a stuff, though personally I'd go for a good book, myself. Round of golf now and again.' He watched Tanner open the door. Said, 'I know this hasn't quite panned out for you, but you did everything you could.' He reached across to slap a hand across the Finlay file. 'This is great stuff.'

He looked like he meant it, but the praise didn't mean much to Nicola Tanner one way or another.

She knew she'd done a good job.

. . . THEN

'Oh,' Heather says, 'it's you,' and she's crying tears of relief as much as anything as she turns and walks back into the flat.

'You OK?' Heather's second visitor of the evening closes the front door, checks to make sure that it is firmly shut, and follows her into the kitchen.

'I've been better.'

'Is it Chris?'

Heather turns and nods, reaches to tear off a fresh sheet of kitchen towel from the roll near the sink.

'I saw him leave.'

Heather says, 'I thought you were him . . . thought he'd come back to have another go. He burst in here, shouting the odds, you know? Screaming at me. Telling me it's all my fault that he's using again.'

'That's ridiculous.'

'It's not just Chris.' Heather leans back against the sink. She's beginning to calm down. 'It's men in general. They let you down. Well . . . you heard.'

'The older man in your story.'

Heather nods. 'They make you promises. They make you feel stupid.'

'You're talking about Tony now, right?'

'I'm such an idiot. I mean, what did I expect was going to happen?'

'I've no idea.'

'I just tried to call him,' Heather says. 'I left a message ...'

'Maybe you should steer clear of married men. Maybe Diana's got a point.'

'Maybe.'

'Stop screwing Daddy.'

Heather blinks, looks at her visitor.

'I'm no expert ... I'm not Tony or anything, but I presume that's what's going on, some father-figure thing. Not that you're thinking about that when you're actually doing it, because you're too busy enjoying yourself.' A smile, a slow move sideways to stand directly opposite Heather. 'Come to think of it, now's probably a good time to ask what you *were* thinking? Ten years ago, I mean. When you were screwing *my* daddy.'

In the few seconds that crawl by before anyone speaks again, the colour drains from Heather's face, while her visitor's flushes with pleasure at seeing it. Heather's hands creep across the edge of the worktop as she tries to steady herself

'How can you be ...?' Heather is talking to herself as much as anyone and she begins to shake her head violently. 'No, that doesn't make sense.'

'What, because we've got different names? I've been Caroline Armitage for quite a while now.' She nodded, smiled. 'I swear, sometimes even I struggle to remember who I used to be. Come on – it would have been a bit obvious otherwise. You might have remembered the name of your lover's sixteen year-old daughter ... did he ever mention it?'

Heather says nothing.

'And I could hardly have used my real surname when I started writing to your ex-boyfriend in prison, could I? I don't think he'd have been mad keen to see me, do you?'

'I didn't mean that,' Heather says. 'Not the name.'

'Oh, you mean because my father was a slim good-looking bloke and I look like this? You think I was always this big? You don't think maybe I started shovelling chocolate and chips into my mouth after somebody murdered my dad?' Caroline narrows her eyes. 'You don't think something like that might screw you up just a bit?'

Something has begun to flutter behind Heather's ribs and she struggles to swallow or draw spit into her mouth. Aside from the tremor that is starting to build in one of her legs, she is perfectly still. She says, 'You went to see John?'

'Oh yeah,' Caroline says. 'A few times, actually ... we got quite matey. I started going just because I wanted to know why. I never believed it was just some random thing outside a bar, so I wanted to find out what really happened.' She smiles. 'That was all. Then I found out he'd killed my father for somebody else.'

'He mentioned my name?'

Caroline laughs. 'Oh God, no. He'd never do that, bless him. He's still madly in love with you, poor bastard. You do know he's out very soon, don't you?'

Heather shakes her head.

'Pound to a pinch of salt he thinks you're going to be there waiting for him. Arms wide open and legs spread. I mean, least you can do considering what he did for you. The time he's spent inside, without telling anyone who put him up to it.'

'That's not how it was.'

'Isn't it?'

'I didn't want John to kill him ... I loved him. I didn't think—'

'You knew exactly how John would react, you said so. You used him as a weapon, because my father chose his family over you. Because he chose *us*.'

Heather's hands move across her chest. The flutter of confusion has gained strength and grown quickly into something crazed; fear that's stronger than any drug she's ever known, any withdrawal, flapping madly inside her. She struggles to get her words out. 'I can't get my head around it . . . you being in the group. It's completely mental.'

'You don't get it, do you?'

Heather is breathing quickly. She finds the strength to shake her head.

'What, you think it was just a coincidence? A chance in a million?' Now Caroline shakes her head; sighs at Heather's idiocy. 'I don't care about the way I look, the way I am. I'm not trying to give up painkillers, I bloody love them. I wasn't in that group because I've got a problem, I was there because you were.'

'How . . . did you know I was there?'

'I've been looking a long time.' Caroline's handbag is on the worktop next to her. She pulls it a little closer. 'Once I began to think John had killed my father because of someone else, I started digging around. I talked to his family and as many of his friends as I could find and guess whose name eventually came up. The girl he'd been obsessed with, the one who broke his heart. The "crazy ex" one of them said. It was a piece of piss after that. I called your dad and told him I was an old mate of yours and he told me you were in London, that you'd had a few "problems". When I'd stopped laughing about that, I found you on Facebook . . . I friended you, actually, started poking about in some of those groups you were in. You and all those other whining ex-junkies. You even mentioned Tony by name in one of them, so you actually made it rather easy for me in the end.' She reaches for her bag and unzips it. 'Been quite fun, actually. Sitting there and listening to you all every week, winding everyone up and watching the sparks fly. Oh . . . in case you were wondering what Robin was banging on about in the pub, he thinks you've been trying to blackmail him.' Her face contorts into a mask of theatrical contrition. 'Oh, I think I might have had something to do with that. Sorry.' She leans closer, as though examining Heather's face for tell-tale clues. 'It wasn't you, was it? No, thought not. Far too squeaky clean now for that kind of thing.' She looks into her bag then reaches inside. 'He was probably right the first time, thinking it was Chris.'

Heather can't look at her any more. The expression on Caroline's face that ratchets up the terror; the urge to scream or rush for the door. 'What do you want?'

'I've got what I want,' Caroline says. 'Took a while, but I wanted to hear you say it, to own up to what you did. You were very brave, by the way, confessing everything like that.'

'So you heard how sorry I am.' Heather's whisper is ragged, desperate; the voice that had once begged for money or gear on credit, for one last hit.

'Oh yes, and it was lovely to hear.'

'I don't know what else I can do.'

'You don't need to do anything,' Caroline says. 'I'm happy as Larry. Well, almost.'

Then, Heather glances up and sees the look on Caroline's face, a sheen of sweat and the thick fingers curling around the black handle of a small knife.

She runs for the door.

Caroline moves far more quickly than Heather could have expected and, when she reaches Heather, clutches at her hair and begins to drag her back, she is far stronger.

She grunts with the effort of pushing the knife into Heather's back and again when she spins her round. For a few seconds, Heather struggles and flails, sending a plant pot and glasses crashing to the floor. She opens her mouth to speak, to beg, but there are only gasps and delicate sprays of spittle each time the blade is punched in, then finally, a murmuring of blood before Caroline lets go and Heather drops like a bundle of wet rags.

Drops and looks up, then closes her eyes as the warmth starts to thicken and spread.

The darkness, the terrible high.

Caroline steps away and takes a few deep breaths. She rips off another piece of kitchen towel to wrap around the blade of the knife, before dropping it back into her bag. Then she moves forward and slowly leans down, her hands on her knees to take the weight.

'*This* is what I was addicted to, see that? The need for this. To find out what really happened to my dad, then to find you and do whatever it took to make me feel this good. To take *my* pain away.' Caroline laughs, easy and light. 'Tell you the truth, I can see what you lot were all on about now, what a rush it is.' Heather can no longer hear her, that's obvious enough, but she carries on talking anyway, like they're drinking tea somewhere or walking in the park.

Like they're sharing secrets in a circle.

'Now I can start my recovery, but something tells me it's going to be a damn sight quicker than yours was.'

PART FOUR

A SAFE PLACE

. . . NOW

'It's not going to be the same,' Robin said.

'Well duh!'

Robin looked at Chris, but there was no anger apparent in his voice. 'You know what I mean.'

'Yeah,' Caroline says. 'Because we were a group.'

'That's right.'

'Like family, sort of thing.'

It was the first time they had gathered in the pub *before* a meeting, but all had agreed it was a good idea. It would almost certainly be an emotional session, Tony had told them, and Robin's suggestion that they meet up half an hour beforehand had been eagerly accepted. 'I'm not sure you can actually get Dutch courage from water and Diet Coke,' he had said. 'But, you know . . .'

Now, Diana was nodding. 'The group is a family and the family is a group,' she said. The smile was tinged with just the right amount of sadness and she looked as though she might be about to invite everyone to join hands. 'Remember what Tony always says.'

'Really?' Chris smirked. 'That's what you think? Seriously messed up kind of family, you ask me.'

'No more messed up than the ones most of us have got. You as much as anyone, if I remember.'

Chris looked momentarily furious, but took a few seconds; closed his eyes, until his own smile slowly appeared.

The group fell silent for a while.

The pub was relatively quiet, but each of them was well aware that they were being studied by a group of teenagers at an adjacent table, that with a couple of hours until the football was due to start on TV, they were something of a spectacle. The disparity between their ages, the way they were dressed surely meant that nobody could have mistaken them for a group of close friends. Even work colleagues would be a stretch. Perhaps their conversation had been overheard or maybe it was just the fact that they were sitting in a pub and none of them was drinking alcohol. Caroline raised her glass of sparkling water to the audience in an ironic salute and the teenagers turned away.

She looked at her watch and said, 'We don't want to be late.'

Chris's mouth dropped open in mock-horror. 'God forbid.'

'Think about it, though. Do we all want to be sitting there when the new bloke walks in?'

Robin nodded. 'Like a weird welcoming committee.'

'Might be a bit intimidating or whatever.'

'Were you intimidated?' Chris asked. 'First time you came?'

'Not remotely,' Caroline said.

'There you are then.'

'We're all different though, aren't we?'

'Yeah, bloody good job an' all.'

'You think he knows, the new bloke?' Caroline looked from face to face. 'Why there's an empty chair.'

Chris shrugged. 'Most of us have known someone who's snuffed it. Some of us have come pretty close to it ourselves. Part and parcel, isn't it?'

'Not like this, though.'

Nobody spoke for a while after that. They ate crisps or tapped the table in time to the landlord's appalling choice of music. Chris and

Diana looked at their phones and Caroline sat tearing a beer mat into tiny pieces.

Then, Robin said, 'Does anyone else feel guilty?'

The others looked at him.

'The way we were with her, I mean. In here, that last night.'

'She was blackmailing you,' Diana said. 'I don't think you should feel bad about being angry.'

'Well I do,' Robin said.

Chris said, 'I don't feel guilty exactly, because I was out of it. If I was going to beat myself up about every horrible thing I've said or done when I was like that, I might as well top myself.' For a few seconds he studied his finger as it rubbed at an old stain on the tabletop. 'I know it wasn't her fault that I got like that, though. Nobody's stupid fault but mine.'

There was another silence. Diana looked across and saw the barman who had thrown Chris out weeks before, cleaning glasses, watching them. She turned back to the table and said, 'I was probably a bit harsh, too, that night. It was that dreadful story, the way it chimed with what was happening to me. Stupid, of course, thinking back.' She took a sip of water and shook her head. 'Unforgivable, bearing in mind what . . . well, you know.'

Caroline was sitting next to her. 'I've been starting to think that she made all that stuff up about her and Tony.'

Diana turned to look at her.

'That's the reason I was so pissed off with her, but the more I think about it, the more it feels like . . . something that was probably all in her mind. Just something she wanted to happen.'

'That makes sense,' Diana said.

'Apart from anything else, I can't believe Tony would ever do that.'

'Absolutely.'

'He just . . . wouldn't.'

'Bang on,' Robin said. 'I think you're bang on.'

Diana turned to face front again and sat up straight. 'We should have a toast.'

'To what?' Chris asked.

'To *who*, you idiot.' Diana smiled and shook her head. 'Who do you think? Just to raise a glass together and say goodbye.'

'We can do that at the funeral, can't we?'

'Whenever that is,' Caroline said.

Robin leaned forward and lowered his voice. 'Sometimes they don't release the body for ages. If they make an arrest and there's a trial, the defence sometimes demands a second post-mortem.'

'Not any time soon then,' Caroline said.

Diana held up her glass and cleared her throat. 'Damn, I've finished my drink now.'

Chris laughed.

'What?'

'It's sort of appropriate, when you think about it, that's all.' He looked to the others at the table for support, then leaned forward, enthused by the idea. 'A dry toast. Come on . . . '

After exchanged glances and nods of agreement, they all finished their drinks, some taking longer than others.

They held their empty glasses out, touched them together.

They said Heather's name.

As coats and bags were quickly gathered to cover the embarrassment, Diana saw that the teenagers at the next table were staring again.

She turned, slowly and deliberately, to look at them.

Said, 'Would you please mind your own fucking business?'

. . . NOW

On a street in Muswell Hill, fifty yards or so away from Tony De Silva's house, the police officer sat in his BMW and decided that psychotherapy must pay a lot better than he thought. A lot better than his job did, anyway. Maybe he would pick up enough over the next few Monday evenings to have a crack at it himself.

On the other end of the phone, his best friend said, 'So, what are you wearing?'

'Not sure this is really the time for dirty talk.'

'Seriously. What look is today's fashionable junkie-about-town rocking?'

'I don't think there's a uniform, as such.'

'Actually, thinking about it, I'd've thought most of your wardrobe would be fine.'

The police officer laughed sarcastically, even though his friend had a point. A woman walking a golden retriever stared in at him through the window as she passed. He smiled and wondered what he looked like to her. An estate agent? A second-hand car salesman? An undercover copper? He knew very well that, save for those desperate few on the streets or prowling the stages of arenas with electric guitars and dead eyes, a junkie was no easier to spot than a serial killer. He'd encountered more than his fair share of *them* and had no desire to meet another, but if anything he was even more nervous about what this particular job might entail.

About the people he'd be spending his Monday nights with for the foreseeable future.

According to the report he'd been given a week earlier to study, they were a ... volatile bunch, and if the officer who'd put the case together was right, one of them was someone he would need to be very careful with.

'What's she like, then?' he asked. 'This Tanner?'

Phil Hendricks laughed.

'What?'

'I don't think you'd get on.'

'Well, she's certainly thorough.' Her report had been well thought out and perfectly put together. 'I's and 'T's suitably dotted and crossed.

'She's got a stick up her arse.'

'Are you suggesting I'm not good with authority or something?'

Another laugh. 'I think she's got a problem with the likes of me,' Hendricks said. 'A bit homophobic, you know? Old school. Should have heard her at the post-mortem, going on about the piercings.'

'Well, you do look like you've had an accident in an ironmonger's stockroom.' Somebody said something in the background. Hendricks's boyfriend Liam, he guessed.

'So, what's your story, anyway?'

'What?'

'What are you telling them you're hooked on? Your drugs of choice. How about cowboy music and a third-rate football team?'

'Not sure that's treatable. I thought I'd just go with coke and booze.'

'Fair enough.'

It would be easy enough to fake, he reckoned. Almost impossible in his job to avoid an intimate acquaintance with addictions of all kinds

406

and of every degree. He didn't think he'd have much problem with the stories he might be expected to tell either: the damage and the dark secrets. It was hard to deny a certain . . . propensity; an urge to move towards those things, those people, that belonged in the shadows.

He wondered if that was why they'd thought he was the best man for the job.

'I should probably make a move.'

'Call me afterwards,' Hendricks said. 'Oh, and if anyone asks what the root cause of your addiction is, tell them it's homosexual panic.'

... NOW

Nicola Tanner did not believe that small electrical items had any place in a bathroom, so she had turned up the radio in the bedroom and left the door open. Having washed herself quickly, she lay listening to Radio 2, humming along with Michael Bublé and Mumford & Sons, letting the assorted frustrations and niggles of the day drift away as the water cooled.

Emails that had gone unanswered, bolshie lawyers with something to prove, a DC who didn't know her arse from her elbow.

Nothing Tanner wasn't used to.

There was an arrangement of candles at one end of the bath, short, smelly ones, but they were there for decoration as much as anything and Tanner never lit them. She could never be bothered with oils, either, or scented salts, any of that stuff people always thought you'd just love to be given for Christmas. It was all far too fancy and self-indulgent.

Just soap and water, as hot as it could be without actually taking the skin off.

The domestic that Tanner had picked up a couple of weeks earlier had proved to be fairly run of the mill and the pre-trial stuff on two other cases was moving forward smoothly enough. Nothing too demanding and all leaving her far too much time to think about Heather Finlay and whoever had killed her. The strange new 'family' she had been part of. Tanner would wake up convinced she knew which one of them it was, but by lunchtime she had usually changed her mind. She could only hope this new approach might yield something positive, though she seriously doubted that the person they were after would slip up any time soon.

Let Malcolm Finlay get those photographs out again.

She sat up when she heard the front door open and close above the aimless babble of the DJ. She heard Susan shout up to her and she shouted back, told her where she was.

Then she waited.

No more than a minute into the next song, she heard Susan shout again and climbed out of the bath. She pulled out the plug and wiped around the edge with a cloth from beneath the basin. She lifted her dressing gown from the back of the door, turned off the radio and went downstairs.

Susan was in the kitchen, opening and closing cupboards. Tanner watched her from the doorway, water running from her hair down the neck of her dressing gown.

'Where's the wine?' Now Susan was on her knees, reaching deep into one of the low cupboards near the fridge. 'We had loads.'

'I threw it away,' Tanner said.

Susan stood up, stared at her.

'And I've made an appointment for you to see someone.'

It was the way it had to be, simple as that, because that's how Nicola Tanner did things. A problem meant chaos and her first instinct when it came to solving that problem was to restore order. Always. It was how she did her job and it was the same way at home, and she didn't much care if others saw it as odd. If they thought she was a nutter or a neat-freak because she did her paperwork on time and the books on her shelves were arranged according to the colour of their spines.

That's who she was.

She was the straightener of pictures, the filler-in of forms, the nudger into line.

'How dare you?' Susan said.

'I'll come with you—'

'How fucking *dare* you . . . ?'

Tanner could only stand and watch as Susan raced around the kitchen, throwing open more cupboard doors, becoming increasingly agitated, and she felt the tears pricking at the corners of her eyes.

Not because Susan was shouting at her, but because Susan was unhappy.

Tanner said, 'It'll be OK, I promise. I'm getting things organised.'

. . . NOW

Emma had heard the doorbell ring twice in quick succession, so she knew that the freaks were starting to congregate downstairs, that the circus was back open for business. She'd missed it in a messed-up kind of way, but now Monday nights would be something to look forward to again.

It had always given her plenty to tell her mates about.

She took a long slow hit of her skinny joint, let the smoke out slowly, then reached for the remote and turned the music up. She giggled, then turned it up a little further. Her mum was out, same as she usually was when that lot were cluttering her lovely house up, and now her dad had his ringmaster's hat back on, so there'd be nobody coming up to tell her to turn the volume down for at least a couple of hours.

Lying back on the bed, she decided that once she'd got the letter done, she would wander downstairs and sit not playing the piano for a while.

Sneak down to the kitchen and have a listen . . .

She picked up her pen and waved it lazily back and forth above the blank page in the notebook. Waiting for the right words to come, the

411

ones that would really make the old bastard think. The money was going up again, too bloody right it was, and that was nobody's fault but his. Fifteen hundred now, and that would buy her enough weed to see her through to the holidays, maybe further, so she wouldn't need to dig into her living allowance once she was at university.

Even if it didn't stretch quite that far, she guessed it would be easy enough to get more. If she scared him enough to pay up once, why couldn't she do it again? If he was going to cough up at all though, she needed him to know right now that she was deadly serious; that if he ignored this one, he was going to regret it.

She would do it, too.

One anonymous phone call to the police and another to whatever the organisation that kept doctors in line was called. She could always Google the name, though she guessed her dad had all that kind of information on his computer. Just as easy to get it off there, same as it had been to get Dr Robin's address or anything else she fancied looking at.

Piece of piss when her own birthday was the password.

How lame was that?

Emma closed her eyes, and it might have been a minute or it might have been ten, but when she opened them again, the joint had burned down in the saucer by the side of her bed and she knew exactly what to say. She scribbled the few lines down quickly before she forgot them and began hunting in the folds of her duvet for a lighter.

She would write it out properly later.

. . . NOW

Once seats had been taken and the circle was complete, Tony made the necessary speech, describing the group and its aims. He made the introductions, then waited for the newcomer.

'I'm Tom,' the man said. 'I've been clean and sober for four and a half months.' He waited, smiled nervously. 'Isn't this when I get a round of applause or something?'

Chris laughed and said, 'This isn't America, mate.'

'Fair enough. Sorry.'

'No need to be,' Robin said.

Caroline said, 'Well done though,' and her congratulations were quickly endorsed with smiles and nods around the circle.

Tony handed the laminated sheet to Diana and she happily read out the statement. 'This circle is a safe place. It cannot be broken or violated and that which is discussed within it should never be taken outside . . . '

When she had finished, Tony replaced the sheet beneath his chair and shook his head sadly. 'This is where I would normally ask if everyone has had a good week, but for obvious reasons, it's been rather longer than that since we were all together.' He looked around the circle. 'I think, if Tom will bear with us, that we should take a few moments to remember Heather.'

'Absolutely,' Robin said.

Tony lowered his head.

Caroline leaned towards the newcomer. 'We lost someone.'

Tony glanced up. 'I explained everything to Tom on the phone.' He looked down again and, for half a minute or so, everyone else did the same, hands clasped together or arms folded, ignoring the sound of the piano that had begun to drift down from the floor above.

'So, how has everyone been?' Tony asked afterwards. It was the same coded question, if asked a little differently.

Chris was quick to speak up. 'Well, I'm a hundred per cent better than I was,' he said. 'Wouldn't be difficult, mind you, considering the state I was in last time we were here. I think it gave me the incentive to clean myself up again, you know? What happened to Heather.'

'That's good,' Tony said.

'Something like that puts everything else in perspective, doesn't it?' Diana looked at Caroline who nodded enthusiastically.

Chris agreed and announced that he'd started to sort out a lot of the other stuff in his life that he'd been ignoring. He'd been to see his brother, he told them, who had spent the last few years in hospital with serious mental health issues and he was trying to pluck up the courage to tell the truth to his mother about who he was and how he'd been living. 'I'm trying, you know? Bloody hard, though.'

'These things are always difficult,' Tony said. 'But being honest is usually the right way to go.'

Robin cleared his throat and sat forward. 'Yes. It's why I've decided to talk about what happened to Peter.'

He told them that his son had been killed in a car accident and that he had been driving. That although he had passed a breathalyser test at the scene, he had been drinking earlier that evening and still believed that his son's death had been his fault. 'I took drugs for the first time the day after we buried him,' he said, looking around.

'Should have told you all a long time ago, instead of stupid stories about lying to my parents when I was a child.'

'You've told us now,' Diana said. 'That's the main thing.'

Tony seized the opportunity to reiterate his theories about shame and its links to addiction. He focused on the newcomer and explained the project the group had been engaged in before the enforced and tragic hiatus.

'Now I wouldn't expect you to do this at your first session,' he said. 'Not unless you want to, of course . . . but it would rather be throwing you in at the deep end.'

'Yeah, a bit,' Tom said.

'Plenty of time,' Diana said.

Tony said, 'Of course,' and turned his attention to the woman sitting next to Tom. 'What about you, Caroline? I know that a few weeks ago you said you didn't feel you had anything to contribute.'

'Still don't,' Caroline said, laughing. 'Sorry.' She sat back and held out her arms; helpless, apologetic. 'I've done nothing to be ashamed of.'

'Really?' the man next to her asked. 'Everyone's done something, surely.'

Caroline turned to the newcomer and smiled. 'No, not that I can think of.'

Tom Thorne smiled back.

Acknowledgements

This one being a standalone, dealing largely with a subject which is thankfully outside my personal experience, I needed even more help than usual to get to this point. Mike Gunn, to whom this book is dedicated with much love, pointed me in the right direction, and I am immensely grateful to the two gifted practitioners whose insight and advice were invaluable and without whom this novel could never have been written. David Charkham (actor and recovery coach) was enormously generous with his time and expertise, as was Rob Green, MBAC, (Accred) Psychotherapist. I am particularly grateful to Rob for recommending the following books, which were all extremely helpful: *Group Psychotherapy With Addicted Populations* by Philip J. Flores, PhD; *The Theory and Practice of Group Psychotherapy* and *Love's Executioner* by Irvin D. Yalom. This last was where I found the Thomas Hardy quote which provides the epigraph for *Die of Shame*.

The Little, Brown team remain an unbridled joy to work with and thanks, as always, are due to David Shelley, Tamsin Kitson, Robert Manser, Sean Garrehy, Emma Williams, Sarah Shrubb and Thalia Proctor. My editor Ed Wood improved the book immeasurably, as did Allison Malecha at Grove Atlantic and I can only apologise to her and to those US readers unfamiliar with cockney rhyming slang for leaving in the one joke I couldn't bear to part with.

The two people to whom I *always* owe a debt of thanks are Wendy 'span/spun' Lee and my wonderful agent, Sarah Lutyens. Both are eagle-eyed and peerless when it comes to furniture.

And, of course, the biggest thank you of all to Claire, Katie and Jack.

My only addiction and my best support group.